How Not to Succeed in Hollywood

Marissa Thomas

Published by KINDLE Direct Publishing

ISBN: 9780692924426

Chapter 1

Why don't I want to be a veterinarian? I like animals. I grew up with a dog and a few adorable cats here and there. In first grade, there was Fluffy, our cat. Not the friendliest of pets. But aside from the typically cold nature of cats, the contribution of a six- and-seven-year-old dressing you up and insisting on holding you all the time can bring out the bitch in anything. When I was in third grade, we got Peaches, the poodle, whose main job was to prevent my fear of strange people breaking into our house. Instead, her protective skills consisted of hiding behind the nearest person and barking in a high-pitched, yelping manner, thereby annoying anyone within hearing range from approaching the house. Then, as an adult, there was Punkins, the first feline lesson in the concept of caring for any form of dependent, a competitive task alongside my ex-idiot, Aaron. Punkins was also the final compromise after we broke up, with me receiving full custody and officially ending our relationship. Eventually he got sick; and the vet, not being able to figure out the cause or even general diagnosis, forced me to make the decision to sign him up for the same permanent vacation Fluffy and Peaches had unwillingly left for a number of years earlier. Wait, the responsibility and snuggles that go along with owning a pet have always been great but plotting the dates for my fur babies to "buy their farms" was a devastating and intentionally avoidable experience. Devoting myself to added time and tuition to acquire a PhD so that I could draw up these calendars for numerous pet owners might not be the best career goal. All right, one mystery solved.

It's not odd to ponder random questions like this, leading you off into mental tangents while waiting for your assigned time slot at an audition. You have time to create excuses that by some small, even microscopic, chance might justify standing up and walking out in an attempt to avoid the welcomed stress that automatically goes along with this process. The weight of influences of the desire to stay or go will depend on how badly you want that part. Is this a small part that will serve as a time filler, something fun to keep you entertained and fill your free time, or is that character you've been working toward since you made the decision to pursue a career in acting? This being the role that could show your range, skill, even your ability to become the character and fulfill the vision of the director and writer, doing it all within three minutes so you can create the perfect reel, or simply lock down your first paid gig, regardless of the significance of the paycheck. Is this the part that will allow you to pause the movie and tell friends to squint and look a little off to the right and they'll definitely see you, or are you the main figure on the movie poster?

Looking around the room, it can be difficult to plot out the competition and guess who will get the part. Attempting to figure out which one is trying to conquer her nerves and which one is simply reviewing the small chunk of script in order to calmly get an idea of what type of project she'll be working on. Utilizing facial cues to get some sort of indication of whether this one is desperately trying to appear as if she is on top of things or an expert in her craft who cannot be intimidated by any cold read. Or was she the attractive one who woke up confident, knowing she could land any role regardless of her lack of skill. All she had to do was utilize her talent for improvisation by dropping the script throughout the audition and giggle as she bent over at the waist to pick it up.

Do other people take this process very seriously, or did they just get up this morning and have an accidental opening in their afternoon schedules? Analyzing other people can be difficult when you're supposed to be reading a script and creating your own take on the character. During most auditions, while awaiting your turn to perform, you'll be sitting in a cold room on some hard chair, trying to sit up straight to appear fit and confident. You'll also test your ability to turn your eyes, instead of your neck, to the absolute limit of every possible corner to scope out the room.

On my left, there is the brunette looking down at the script and mouthing the lines, then looking up at the ceiling and trying to recall what she just read. On my right is a bleached blonde obnoxiously chewing her gum with her mouth open, twirling her hair with one hand and texting with the other, as opposed to reading the script. Investigation time is constantly interrupted when the casting director pokes her head out from behind the large black door of fate to call in the next person to read for her. This is the improvisational experience we all have in common: whipping our heads up from whatever task or position it was devoted to less than two seconds ago and appearing incredibly interested and attentive to the name being announced, ready to jump up as soon as they call the magic one.

This door, painted a simple solid black, has every person on the outside of it intrigued and wondering what could possibly be waiting on the other side, just as it has many casting directors' assistants wondering how many times they'll have to poke their heads outside, jealous of those who get to step outside and light up. Is that a heavenly white light glowing around the edges or did the janitor accidently put in a slightly stronger bulb? Could that walk down the hallway, the one that turns five steps to the second door on the left into a seemingly endless journey, be the last one I ever have to take, the final destination securing me a solid reputation as a popular actress, guaranteeing that I won't have to endure some cattle call audition like this again! Promising me that my goals will be achieved, proving to myself and the rest of the world that this wasn't simply a childish fantasy or a frivolous waste of time, but instead that my efforts have led to a justified cause! It almost seems too cruel to allow myself to imagine such things, but it also seems impossible to keep the optimism from sneaking into the building blocks of possible results. Now, in the real world, I'll probably just go home and make a peanut butter sandwich and veg out on the couch, avoiding texts and friends, waiting for a phone call that won't ever come.

The vision ends; and after realizing I've been staring at the door for at least two minutes, my jaw not locked and my lips on the verge of just falling open all together, I come back down to the real world, looking around the room to see who may have noticed, pretending to resituate on the hard chair and scratching a nonexistent itch on my right arm, sucking in my stomach just a little tighter, trying to look a little more desirable than those around me. While rehearsing this seemingly useless tactic, I'm coming to the conclusion that I might be thinking too much. My philosophical thoughts are turning a short wait time into an eternity, and I begin to wonder where this all started. My first car was a brown Chevy Celebrity, but that would be too obvious. Wait. Yes, that's it. It all started with the talent show.

?

Chapter 2

The adults coordinating the first ever elementary school talent show thought it would be the perfect way to open. And students were talking about how excited they were to participate. Lucky for me, one of those adults was my best friend's mother. She asked my mom if it would be okay if I did it, and my mother jumped on board. She was so excited. The month leading up to the big performance was filled with bonding sessions consisting of picking out the hairstyle I would wear, the outfit we would sew together, whether we wanted ruffles, what color fabric we would use, and whether I would wear matching sandals or matching tennis shoes. The fun of wardrobe and makeup was consistent with rehearsals occurring twice a week, inadvertently teaching everyone involved just how much work goes into the glamour of any performance. Finally, background was cast, costumes were sewn, and the scene was staged.

The curtain opens to a large but typical-looking school stage. Homemade props of cardboard green bushes, tall trees, and pseudo playground toys decorate the stage. It's crowded with fourth graders cautiously pretending to play with jump ropes and baseball gloves and drowning in theater lights, attempting to make it appear like a sunny afternoon at the park. Cheesy background music is a timer, cueing the children of when to pretend to play the sports and counting down the time to when they get to leave the stage, all the while improving looks out into the audience to spot their parents and see if they get a smile to recognize their talents. One and a half minutes of swinging one end of a larger jump rope almost feels like an eternity to the one little girl who gets to introduce the first line.

I skipped over to the bench where Tom was sitting with his baseball and glove and let it rip.

"Tom? Tom, what's wrong?" I asked, making more of a statement than inquiring and waiting for him to respond as we had practiced.

"The talent show," he said, turning away from me and tossing his ball repeatedly into his glove.

"What did you say?"

"The talent show!" he exploded at me. "You said I had to do it. I talked myself into it. Then everyone else in the group quit!"

"That doesn't mean we can't still be in the show. You'll have—ooops, I mean, we'll have to come up with something on our own!"

Improvisation was not one of my strong points in the beginning. It took years to figure out that even if you biffed a line, you had to keep going with a live performance. I was still proud of the fact that I corrected the line and assumed my mom would be proud of me too. Though the rest of the performance was a blur, I remember smiling and turning to the audience to try and find her, assuming I'd find that obvious look of pride on

9

her face. However, I found that the bright lights flooding the stage made it almost impossible to see any member of the audience.

A few more unknowingly monotone lines were delivered, and our big debut drew to a close after a slightly awkward, randomly placed line of fourth graders took our place on the stage to take a bow. A few of the children left after the first round, but about three of us couldn't get enough of the courtesy applause.

After the show was over, things only got better. There was a meet and greet in the cafeteria afterwards where cookies and fruit punch waited. Mom met me with a big hug and congratulated me on a job well done. I was happy to receive the compliment but was more concerned about the cookies waiting on the table just out of arm's reach. Other mothers were mingling; some were passively-aggressively leading their children from station to station, bragging about good grades excellent art skills and other achievements and providing onlookers a glimpse at what their own children should look like. It was almost like a scene from a dog show, minus the dog collars, with owners biding for a gold medal, which in this case was equivalent to having the unsaid satisfaction of knowing that your own child was better than the one standing next to him. And like the excitable, carefree animals at the shows, the children being shown off could've cared less about the competition but instead about the treat waiting at the end of the runway show.

While the mothers were randomly conversing about the show and claiming their talented children, I was excited to see my friends. Obviously, those that were attending the mixer afterwards had either attended the show or been in it. All of us who had been in the show agreed that although we had fun doing it, we were relieved that it was done. We no longer had to worry about remembering lines, having to sit still at rehearsals, and, most importantly, not being able to wear our cool outfits and uniforms to school before the unveiling of the talent show.

Not only was I greeted kindly by other kids from my school I'd never met, but other kids in my class, the ones I wasn't sure even knew I existed, were telling me it was cool. Regardless whether their mothers forced the civil greeting or the compliment was legitimate, I loved it! The reviews were in, and I seemed to be a hit! I was on top of the world. All it took was the rush of a short stage performance and I knew I'd be the most popular kid in the fourth grade. Soon the entire Minneapolis area would know my name. Cloud nine was great. Surrounded by all the positive reviews, I was pretty sure that no one could rain on my parade now. That is, until I found my sister picking out a cookie at the treat table.

She was picking up each cookie and studying it, making sure to avoid raisins. She found one with no spots and decided try a bite. Less than impressed with the taste test, she put the cookie back and kept looking for the one with the chocolate chips. I ran up next to her, hoping to get a chocolate chip one too and giving her a chance to offer her praise about my performance before inquiring as to whether or not she liked the show. A moment passed, and except for the fact that she had to walk around me to get to the lemon bars, she barely acknowledged I was there.

I was too impatient to wait for her to finish her snack before complimenting me.

"Michelle! Michelle, did you see the show?" I asked her with a smile.

"Yeah, I sat by Mom," she responded, more interested in the sweets.

"Well, did you like it?" I asked, offering a gateway for her compliments.

"Nah, it was boring. Everyone in it kind of sucked," she answered, not even looking in my direction.

I could feel the happy expression melting off my face. She didn't like me. Everyone else had been so encouraging, telling me how good I was in the show. Mom was bragging about me, even more than she usually did when I'd paint her a picture or get an A on my weekly spelling test. I had no idea how to respond. All I could do was stand there and stare at her. Being on stage was wonderful, how could my own sister not appreciate my talent? I solemnly carried my paper plate to the nearest chair, carefully balancing my chocolate chip cookie so I wouldn't lose it along with my hope of performing in another show in the near future. I could cope with not getting presents of my own on someone else's birthday, the far-fetched idea that Santa had always been a fictional character, even the off chance that our cat Fluffy somehow got out of the van on the way home from a ride to the vet with Mom and ran away, never to return. But now I had experienced real heartache. I had experienced my first critic.

⏴

Chapter 3

My guaranteed part in the grade school production became my first experience in theater. Even though I'd had a great time throughout the process, I don't remember giving it much thought throughout the rest of my school days. I was always more fascinated by the people on TV. No matter what went wrong, everything always found a way to come together in the end. Little did I know how fictional it was to fit all that drama, turmoil, and reconciliation into one half hour. Life still had a lot to teach me, but it was important to start with the basics. So I pursued one of those radio ads for "auditions" to open the door to a fabulous career in an upcoming industry.

At Edwardo's School for the Fine Art of Acting, the talent could be immersed in the culture of the entertainment industry in general: terminology used for theater and film, different methods relied on by successful actors to portray realistic scenes, and one-on-one tutoring, along with the other eleven students in your class. Otherwise, for the savvy clientele of the Minneapolis area, all of the above would be crammed into a one-hour session on Tuesday nights at 5:00 p.m. for a twelve-week stretch for the bargain price of $399.99 if you purchased them all at once.

Since I was seventeen, and didn't have the entire down payment, I had to twist my mother's arm for an entire month. I had to convince her that even though he had acquired many of his students through some scam acting agency, insisting that their talent pay up front for the training that would later produce successful careers, that he was a talented instructor who could offer me a lot of insight.

That first Tuesday was filled with mixed emotions: anticipation for the education about the world of film and television and a touch of nerves over the fact that I might be the least knowledgeable about the topic at hand. These random thoughts weren't derailed by the fact that his studio was located in an older building along the freeway in Bloomington or the fact that I walked in to bare walls, a small desk with an average-looking receptionist doodling on one of those large yellow notepads, and the aroma of every structural update that had been performed on this particular office since 1973. There were only six folding chairs in the small reception area, so I was happy to have gotten there early enough to tag one after checking in with the seemingly uninterested, underpaid attendant. I filled out a generic questionnaire consisting of all our personal contact information, no doubt to be used as a tool of future reference as we graduated level to level, ever striving to reach our full potential. While usually an inconvenience, this was a good opportunity to scope out my new classmates.

I could only imagine the beautiful people that would be pushing that heavy, squeaky door open at any moment. The thought of meeting other teenagers my age who were interested in acting was both exciting and intimidating. The teenage girls would have endless suggestions about makeup and resume-building experiences in the seemingly growing film industry in Minneapolis. The teenage guys would simply be hot! And wanting to embrace my education, I'd have an instant icebreaker cleverly hidden under the veil of rehearsing, performing required scenes for our teacher.

As the knob turned, I sat up a little straighter, readjusting a little to flatter my nonexistent figure as best I could. The first person that walked in the door was a little less then I had hoped for. A young man, probably late teens or even early twenties, with long, shaggy hair that looked like it hadn't been washed in a week. His wardrobe, consisting of oversized jeans and a green T-shirt with the picture of the latest rock musician seemed to portray the character of an introverted young man, constantly pondering how to complete the next level of his favorite video game while inadvertently figuring out a way to rebel against his mother's nagging to get off the couch. He took the clipboard and turned to the first chair available, pushing his bangs off to the side but avoiding eye contact with anyone in the room. I wasn't sure his look was desirable but tried to imagine that there was an audience for almost every venue.

The next person that walked in was somewhat older than a teenager. Due to her feathered bangs, scrunchie, and bright-pink lipstick, I guessed her to be in her early to mid-thirties. She walked in, proudly adorned in a white silky button-up blouse with obvious shoulder pads and black pants, which I swore I had seen in my mother's closet at some point but could be differentiated by one of the highest waistlines I had ever seen. Smiling from ear to ear, she looked at the young man and politely stepped toward one of the open chairs by me. Assuming she was filling out the paperwork for her son or daughter, I politely smiled back and went back to completing my paperwork. After determining that there was no younger family member lagging behind to utilize the bathroom, I realized that it was possible that she too could be one of my classmates.

The students I anticipated never arrived. With a variety of different people, some of them having to stand, it seemed pretty obvious that I was looking at one of the graduating classes for February. We didn't have to wait long before we were herded by the receptionist into one of the larger back rooms containing lights, a backdrop, and sufficient seating for all twelve of us to be audience to the focus of the room, a pseudo stage. After only a few minutes of settling into our folding chairs, the random conversation began.

"Oh, excuse me, I was just going to sneak into that chair on the other side of you," said the grinning older woman I had seen in the reception area with the flare for early-nineties trends.

"Oh yeah, no problem," I responded with a polite smile.

"Hi, my name's Sharon. Have you taken these kinds of classes before?" Sharon asked, bundling her purse and her jacket under one arm and extending her open hand.

"Ah, Lisa. No, I haven't taken classes before," I responded with a short handshake.

"I think you'll like them. I know I enjoyed the first round," she informed me as she set her things on the floor.

"Wait, you've been through this process before? Have you booked any real acting jobs from them?" I asked, optimistic.

Sharon's answer was less than reassuring. "Actually, I thought I was doing very well. But when I had my consultation with my agent, you know, where we discuss advancements in my career and I pay my yearly membership fees, he told me he just couldn't see the emotion in my headshot. I'd already redone them a couple of times, so he suggested I take advantage of the sale price and really get in touch with my art. It's like, I need to rediscover myself. Again. He really is a great guy, gets me all the deals so I don't spend too much while I'm getting started."

Hoping I hadn't been delivering the blank stare that comes when looking at someone you want to smack some sense into, I simply replied with a forced giggle. "Oh, that's good. No surprises for you."

"Well, let's see, I think I have his card in my purse here somewhere," she said, reaching for her purse. "You should really check him out. He's had me on a great track for about three years. And he gives referral discounts!"

"Oh, super," I replied, accepting the card and immediately placing it in my pocket so I could throw it away later when she wasn't looking. Luckily, we didn't have to wait much longer for our instructor to arrive. A shorter man entered the room wearing a brightly patterned silk shirt and tinted glasses.

"D'accord. Classe Bon. Pius-je attention sil vous plait?" he yelled, even though he walked into a mostly silent room full of students waiting to get started.

Seemingly impressed by the idea of a bilingual instructor, we all stared as he made his way to the front of the room.

"Welcome, class. I am Edwardo," he said calmly with a Midwest accent, shattering the first impression. "I know you're all anxious to learn. To release the actor inside you, to express all of your inner emotions, even your demons. We have much to cover. But one must always remember - Un voyage de mille miles commence par une seule étape."

A few heads rocked along with these words of wisdom, before turning to their random neighbors to silently inquire as to whether they understood what he was saying.

"Come, come. Now I would like to go around the room and everyone introduce yourself. Your name and why you wanted to take this class," Edwardo ordered.

I just sat there, not really paying attention to the nine people announcing themselves before me but rather dreading what I was going to say. I figured it would be tacky to say that I was simply hoping to get my mother's money's worth. But I knew I could do better than the shaggy kid who was utilizing his turn at introduction.

"I'm John. I get to borrow my mom's car on Tuesdays," he said, brushing his dirty hair out of his eyes, yet again.

A couple more people and it would soon be my turn. I'd heard people offer the generalization that they were interested in how the acting techniques they would learn could assist them in their own daily lives and that they'd always been fascinated by the world of entertainment and wanted to learn more. One man, probably mid-twenties, had even announced that he was simply taking the class for fun. Finally, it was my turn.

"I'm Lisa, and I want to be an actress." It was the simplest, most obvious explanation I could think of. It almost seemed as if my classmates were surprised to hear someone get straight to the point. After a brief blank stare, it was Sharon's turn.

"Hello, everyone! I'm Sharon. I've taken this class before, and I promise you are all going to get so much from it. I've been in the industry for a while, and my agent suggested that I take this class again because there is always something new to learn!" she proudly announced, wearing the grin to match.

"Yes, wonderful. Well, let's jump right in. I have scenes for all of you. I'm going to partner you up, and I want you to take a few minutes and prepare to cold read for the class," he said, passing out sheets of paper. "And on the last day of the class, we'll read the same scenes with the same partners and see if we can utilize the skills we will be learning up until then."

The sheets had numbers on the bottom, and we just had to locate our partners. I was hoping for almost anyone besides John. The number at the bottom of my scene was 4. It's never been a lucky number for me, but there was at least a chance that I could work with one of the students who had acquired a sense of hygiene before enlisting in an acting course. The other students were pairing up, and things were looking grim.

It was almost as if I was watching the process of him heading toward me in slow motion. With yet another flick of his hair, he found the script with the matching number. And it was mine. I was hoping not to portray the sour look of a deer caught in headlights, so I tried to crack a smile.

"I guess we're partners," I managed to say with an awkward laugh. "We should probably start reading through it."

"Yeah, cool, whatever," John replied, once again fighting the greasy mass of hair that seemed to be glued to his forehead.

"Great," I replied, practicing my expressions with a polite smile. And with that, we began to read through it on our own. My one last hope was that it wouldn't be a romantic scene. I was wrong about that too. But at least it was about a break up and there was no touching involved. After a few minutes of a read through, I would've been happy to improvise slapping him in the face, if I hadn't been afraid my hand would stick or be smeared with oil that hadn't been approached by any kind of grooming in what looked like months. I figured his appearance and lack of sincere talent was an obvious motive for my character.

(Female character) "How could you do this to me?" I asked, trying to portray anger.

(Male character) "Do what?" he responded in a forced attempt to try and read his line.

(Female character) "You know what you did!" I was on a roll, showing the passion of a woman scorned.

(Male character) "You don't know what you're talking about," he stated.

I suspected his delivery was similar to the way he'd respond to his mother when she told him to bathe.

(Female character) "I know exactly what I'm talking about. And I have nothing more to say to you," I said with finality, starting to appreciate the concept of method acting, utilizing the fact that my acting partner was annoying me with his lack of effort throughout our five-minute scene.

(Male character) "Then there's nothing more to say," he said, laughing awkwardly as he said it.

(Female character) "You just said a mouthful. It's over," I barked as I turned to walk off the stage area.

The scene was painful, extremely, but we had gotten through it. I could only pray that the scene following ours would contain bad content or bad actors so everyone in the room could be sidetracked from what they had just witnessed. It was a relief to be done. Then I remembered Edwardo had to critique the scene.

"Brilliant. I could almost feel your pain. You were tormented by the loss of your one true love. I have a couple of corrections though. I think we need to work on portraying a connection with the other character. We need to sense the relationship between the two of you. I don't think either of you were making yourselves emotionally available. These are things we'll have to work on before performing the scene at the class graduation," Edwardo preached, randomly glancing at the two of us over his reading glasses while writing notes on the note pad in his big black leather folder.

Once again, I was experiencing the humbling effect of a critic's opinion. I had anticipated the corrections after he warned us they would follow each scene, so it was a little more palatable than the insulting manners of delivery in the past. However, something irritated me about it. I wasn't sure if it was the determination of similarities in John and my acting abilities that bothered me or the simple fact that he called John's character my true love.

Although I was trying to build a passionate scenario out of a one-sided conversation with a complete idiot, I was told that my abilities were lacking and that I had to offer my partner a little more. I knew this class wouldn't necessarily be easy, but I had no idea what more I could do. He gave me so little to work with. He wasn't attractive, or even hygienic! How could I interact with his method portrayal of a dyslexic loser? As I watched him pick his nose, wipe it on the underside of his jeans, and then turn the page to read about the next step in the process of learning to act, which was solo acting, I started to feel the urge to actually follow the cue of the male lead. I was more than ready to move on to the exciting world of monologues.

With our new direction of study, the new few weeks presented a thicker line between who was there with a serious interest in acting and who was there to get their mothers off their backs. As intimidating as it seemed, having to carry an entire scene on my own, I only had to remind myself that I had already been doing that with my previous partner. The only difference would be that I'd be the one talking the entire time so I'd have to memorize a few more lines. My confidence restored, I was focused on my performance. However, after receiving Edwardo's harsh criticism, I had to wonder if I was kidding myself. He was just as hard on me as he was on those I felt had the talent of a porn star trying to perform Shakespeare. Perhaps I had been lying to myself about my own talent, or lack thereof, and had to know if I was wasting my time and money.

I asked to speak to Edwardo after our class, and he agreed to meet me in the hallway after class. I wasn't sure how to ask him to cut the crap and tell me if I was actually doing anything right, so instead I started by telling him how much I had enjoyed the class up to this point. I also informed him that I had learned many new things I didn't know before by making a verbal list. When I couldn't think of more than two things right off the bat, I quickly changed the subject to the topic I was curious about.

Somewhat afraid of his response, I wanted to tread lightly. "So, I guess what I wanted to ask you, is how I'm doing."

The look on his face was blank, even somewhat annoyed. "I've given feedback as we've been transcending to more complicated scenes. And at the end of the series of classes, I'll provide the information you need to graduate to the next series of classes."

"Great. Great." I had to think of how else to word it. "I think what I meant to ask was, do you think I'm any good.

Do I have a future in this? Whether I take your next series of classes or not, do I stand any chance of trying to pursue this industry?"

He looked at me seriously and suddenly dropped his accent. "The truth?"

I was very surprised. "The truth."

"I think you're brilliant." He smiled, turned on his accent again, and bid me a good evening.

I was a little disturbed by him dropping his accent when he asked me if I wanted to know what he really thought, but it was outweighed by the flattery and excitement from the approval of my acting instructor.

I carried Edwardo's compliment with me over the next few years, though I didn't pursue any opportunities to display my talent. I also discovered that his classes were less than desirable to list as acting experience on a resume. Regardless, I always carried his advice with me when it came time to expand my horizons, and when a family friend suggested entering myself in a pageant the summer after I graduated high school, I decided to try it.

I received packet upon packet in the mail, explaining what to bring, what to expect, what I stood to gain from the pageant, and what it would cost to enter. I was more excited about the cash awards than about the emotional connections with the other girls, but I had to admit that every picture showed a happy, smiling young woman. I had heard horror stories about pageant moms, so I knew this was either a matter of amazing photo selections or the pageant was being held in Wisconsin.

My mother agreed to support me and helped me prepare outfits and monologues and all the other crap they told me to bring. We arrived to a large event space where a stage had been built to accommodate the room. There were dozens of young girls with their mothers exploring the room and schmoozing with people they assumed were judges. Naïve to the process, we found it to be a very energetic and inviting scene.

While I can't remember much about the contest itself, the behind the scenes antics have always stuck with me since they were my first taste of competition in an industry based on good looks, with a hint of some kind of talent. I had always been a social person and decided to extend a courteous greeting to one of the girls and her mother on the way to the dressing room. She simply looked at me as if she didn't speak English and looked at her mother to translate. The girl's mother shook her head at her, put her hands on her shoulders, and guided her away from me, muttering under her breath that she shouldn't become chummy with the competition.

I was disappointed to see that pageant stereotypes were there for a reason. It wasn't I wanted to continue with the contest, but my own mother put her hands on my shoulders and reminded me of the time and money we had invested in this project. She insisted that it would be a good opportunity to practice what I had learned in my classes with Edwardo and act like I liked these bitches. She also hinted that if I were to ever move to Hollywood, the women would be just as welcoming.

Her aggressive encouragement paid off. After performing our assigned monologues, I was named Teen Actress of the Year. This included a trophy with a gold plate and a white sash bearing the title in blue writing. Standing up on that stage, hearing the applause, I felt that same rush of endorphins. Standing up there smiling, I felt the same rush of confidence that had come with Edwardo's feedback. However, I decided never to participate in another pageant, unless I came with a box of mixed donuts. Hopefully that would satisfy the animalistic behavior that apparently came from bouts of anorexia provoked by psychotic guardians trying to live vicariously through their unsuspecting offspring.

Chapter 4

College is an exciting new world for any teenager. It's a chance to spread our wings, expand our horizons, and get away from the structured life created by our parents. We can only imagine all the new experiences awaiting us. And aside from the seemingly small, often passive-aggressive, influence of our financial aids, also known as Mom and Dad, we get to decide what we want to do. We can stay close to the security of our families and friends, or we can move to pursue a career that gives us the opportunity to explore a new location as far away from them as possible. We can attend our classes and get involved in extracurricular activities, or we can skip our homework and hang out at frat parties every night. We can rely on our parents' money or student loans to avoid having to work and get straight As in order to obtain scholarships, or we can work our way through to avoid not only debt but also any hope of having a social life. It's a new opportunity to pursue the temptations of our limited teenage freedom and avoid the risk of gaining the freshman fifteen.

We imagine the door to our new world opening as we send our parents away from our dorm rooms so we can meet our new roommates and dive in to the social scene. However, in my case, I spent three years after graduating high school opening doors to nonprofit buildings for local auditions during the week and scooping ice cream on the weekends. After embracing the fact that I wouldn't be discovered while cleaning out bottles of chocolate syrup, the journey to my new world took a new turn with my mother politely holding open the door labeled "Enter" to the local community college and pushing me inside. Taking the lead, she scrambled through the maze of students, announcing each turn as we followed signs to the financial office. She then cosigned my student loan two days before classes started. As appreciative as I was for her help, I could have lived without the animation she portrayed as she held my arm while sharing her school stories as we made our way back to the car.

Even after a three-year delay, this new and exciting environment consisted of a lot of familiar faces I would've been happy to leave back in high school. Sending my mother away wasn't an emotional scene since the social event of the month was the math team bake sale. She simply waved good-bye, warning me not to try the lactose-free brownies, and confirming that she'd see me later at home for dinner. So here I was—at the beginning.

After a couple of classes consisting of the typical first-day syllabus reading and confirmation of books and materials needed, it was time to take a break and explore the cafeteria. It was a little further away than I had been used to in high school but somewhat easy to find considering the signs on the walls everywhere would guide you through the maze.

Once I got there, I saw that I pretty much had my choice of meals, from vending machines to the salad bar to the daily special and almost everything in between. Aside from the lack of variety of ethnic foods, the area almost reminded me of a food court in a small mall. I decided to get a fruit cup and a bottle of pop and find a place to sit. It was easier to study the tables in the cafeteria without looking like the new girl if I pretended to study the bulletin board just beyond the cash register. It was covered with random flyers for summer and part-time jobs for college students. There were small posters for upcoming art shows and different programs and clubs to join within the college. After looking over all the papers I wasn't interested in, I found one that caught my attention.

The headline said "AUDITION" in large capitalized letters. I didn't even look at the name of the play they were auditioning for. But still, when I thought no one was looking, I quietly ripped the paper off the pin that was holding it up. It served two purposes that day. I was interested in the auditions themselves and it was the perfect cover to balance, along with my food, over to the corner seat I had spotted out of the corner of my eye. I sat down and opened my drink and continued reading the details. It was a play being produced by the theater department, and the auditions were coming up within a week. Since I hadn't participated in theater in high school, this was my college adventure. Excited and nervous at the same time, I had to dig out my class schedule to see if I could make it. While turning around to get my backpack off of the back of the chair I was sitting on, I looked up to see one of the hottest guys I thought I had ever seen looking in my direction.

Caught off guard, I paused for a moment, looking back with what was probably a blank stare and then snapped myself out of it, tucking my hair behind my ear and looking around to see if anyone else had seen my moment of weakness. I also wanted to check and see if he was looking past me at someone or something else. It was then that I reminded myself that I was sitting at the end of a table, pretty much in a corner. So he was either looking at me or a brick wall. And since he wasn't covered in dust, dirt, or the obvious pattern of a farmer's tan line that comes along with working in construction, I assumed I won by default. I was flattered and a little bit curious but pretended to be busy reading my flyer.

It seemed to work. While finishing my fruit cup and gathering my garbage and paperwork, I planned it all out. I could go to the auditions right after I finished my last class. Trying to motivate myself for the next two hours of syllabus reading and filing my notebook back into my bag, I was caught off guard again when I looked up to see that the same eye candy I had enjoyed along with my fruit was standing right next to my chair and looking down at me.

"I think they wanted that flyer to stay posted," he said to me with one of the most gorgeous smiles I think I've ever seen.

"Oh yeah," I responded, stalling with a nervous laugh to buy a little more time so I could try to choose my words very carefully. "I was about to put it back, I just had to write down the details." I tried to continue packing up my things and looking busy. But there are only so many times you can rearrange plastic wrap in a plastic cup.

"So are you going?" he asked.

"Ah, yeah. I think so," I answered.

"Cool, me too." He extended his hand. "I'm Aaron." His smile never faded as he was talking to me.

"Hey, I'm Lisa." I shook his hand and smiled back with what I hoped wasn't a goofy smile or one lined with the food I'd just eaten. I was afraid I was holding his hand a little too long, so I stopped, looked at my nonexistent watch, and stood up to pick up my things. "Well, I have to get to class, but I'll see you at the auditions. Do you need the flyer? You know what, I'll hang it back up, and you can check it out there. In fact, whoever wants to look at it will see it and get the details. It was nice meeting you."

I didn't give him a chance to respond. I rushed over to the bulletin board, pinned up the flyer, and rushed out of the cafeteria. With a few awkward statements, I was pretty sure I had said too much. Suddenly, focusing on a teacher's expectations and impending homework for an entire semester didn't sound so bad.

I found my classroom and sat outside of the door, waiting for it to start and recapping the conversation in my head. I wasn't the smoothest character in the conversation. I could only hope I wouldn't see him at the audition. Although, I thought, it might not be the worst thing in the world. Would it really be that bad if I made a new friend? A new friend who was interested in acting just like I was? A new friend with a great smile. A hot new friend with a great smile who might share an interest in acting. This could be bad. This could be really bad.

After sitting through the boredom of fighting to stay awake while watching my math professor try and get the class hyped up about the fun of logic, I was back on track worrying about classes instead of extracurricular activities.

A week later I had almost forgotten about the audition, until I saw it on my pocket calendar. After painstakingly making it through my last class, I started to make my way to the auditorium. I wasn't sure what to expect. I hadn't done a lot of acting, and I certainly didn't have to try for the few roles I had landed. They had either fallen into my lap by default, or I bought them by signing a check over to the instructor of the classes. Would there be a lot of competition? Would there be people with more experience than me? Questions circled my mind as I found the entrance to the auditorium. There was a table outside of the door, and a homemade sign taped to the wall above it informing actors to sign in once they arrived. There were a few people lining the hallway outside, some sitting on the floor and a couple standing. The one thing they all had in common was that they were all quietly studying a piece of paper. I wasn't sure I recognized any random faces from any of my classes, but a sense of relief still came over me when I realized we wouldn't all be auditioning in front of each other. This was it. It was time to sign in for the next allotted time on the list, take a copy, and start preparing for a cold read.

The next slot to sign up for was still about twenty minutes away. This was a decent amount of time to be able to read through the scene and picture it a few different ways. Since I wasn't very familiar with the play itself, I wasn't sure what they would ask of me. The best plan of attack, I decided, would be to find my own spot in the hallway to sit down and unload my school luggage. There was a spot about ten feet away from the sign-in desk. This would also be a good opportunity to scope out the competition.

It didn't seem like much. The other students' ages seemed to range from late teens to maybe even early thirties. The majority of them were facing down, noses buried in the two pages of script they would soon be announcing. None of them really stood out to me. Then as I was making my way to the open spot, I saw him yet again. He looked even better sitting on the floor, relaxed with his legs extended out in front of him, crossed. He had his backpack with him and was studying a few papers of his own. It was good to see him, but at the same time, I didn't want it to seem like I was finding the open spot on the floor because it was next to him.

I tried to see if there was another place to take advantage of and was happy to keep walking past him when fortunately, or unfortunately, he looked up. He was even hotter with that tough look of concentration on his face. And the final straw, when, during his double take at me, his serious look melted into a smile.

"Hey, Lisa, you made it," he welcomed me. "I was starting to wonder if you were going to."

"Oh yeah, I just got done with my last class." I had such a flare for offering unimportant details. "It was my logic class."

He just smiled and nodded.

"Yup. Pretty boring," I shared, trying to think of some other way to direct the conversation. "Is anyone sitting there?" I pointed at the empty floor, glad I had spotted it before I saw the scenery around it.

"You are. I saved it," Aaron replied. "Here. Have a seat."

I sat down and put my backpack on the floor next to me as casually as I could. Of course, since I had forgotten to zip my bag when I was quickly loading it to leave class, my pop bottle fell out and started rolling away. Aaron and I both went to reach for it, and our hands touched. Not having much experience in the "cheesy romantic moments" department, I pulled my hand back and let him hand it to me.

"Thanks, I hate when that happens." I smiled. "Have you been waiting here long?"

"Nah, maybe ten minutes," he replied.

"Cool, that's not bad." The questions seemed to help the conversation more than the statements. "How does the script look?" I asked, looking down at the lines.

"Eh, it could be a little tough," he answered.

"Yeah, Shakespeare can be hard, but when you break it down, it all comes together and makes sense," I stated, figuring I should portray confidence. "I'm not sure why so many people get frustrated with him."

"Yeah, I guess. But I hate Hamlet," Aaron said, looking down at his packet.

"Really? Then what are you doing here? What part are you auditioning for?" It was a legit question with a hint of sarcasm. Why would someone audition to study and memorize a character for weeks on end and then perform that character for what the production hopes will be a full auditorium?

"No, I mean the play is called I Hate Hamlet," he answered calmly. "I'm actually not auditioning."

"Oh, just hanging out?" I was actually confused at this point.

"No, I have to submit some of my work to see if they'll let me make the posters and programs for my graphics project," he told me. "I guess everyone has to work on some major project, something like that. I know there are a few other people from my class here. They'll probably let us work together."

"Good. Cool. That makes sense. For a minute there I thought you were here to see me." I knew I shouldn't have said it before I even finished saying it. It was almost slow motion when I tried to laugh off what I had just said. And it seemed like an eternity before he responded.

His response was accompanied by that gorgeous smile. "Well, that wouldn't be so bad, would it?"

All I could do was smile and pray for an interruption. And thankfully I got one.

"Lisa? Is there a Lisa?" The student running the desk was less than thrilled to search for the person matching the next name on the list.

"That's me. I'm Lisa." I got my things together and stood up. And before I walked away, I figured, what the hell. "No, that wouldn't be bad at all."

"Break a leg!" he told me, winking as I turned around to walk away.

It was a very nice way to transition from one obstacle to the next. Being on cloud nine, I can barely remember how the audition went. Just that twenty minutes after entering, we were told on the way out of the auditorium that there would be a callbacks list and that the second audition would take place Friday evening. When I walked out of the auditorium, there he was again with a small group of students, all of them with folders comparing creations from previous semesters. I didn't want to interrupt, so I looked over, hoping to catch his attention for one brief moment to wave good-bye. He seemed very interested in what he was doing, so I figured I would see him around school at some point. Hopefully. Maybe figuring out his schedule and randomly appearing outside of a class or two. The thought made me laugh, and I turned to head home.

"Hey, Lisa, wait!" Aaron yelled, jogging toward me. "You forgot this." He handed me the notebook I had left on the floor when I was packing up for the audition.

"Oh, thanks." I grabbed the notebook, but was suddenly suspicious. "You waited just to give me back my notebook?"

"Well, I figured you'd need the paper"—he looked down and grabbed a pen out of his pocket—"so you could write your number down for me."

I smiled and flipped to the first available blank page. I wrote down my information and tore it out to hand to him along with his pen.

"Cool, talk to you later," he said.

I had always daydreamed about working in film or television, but God help me, I love theater!

And, few days later, I got one of the calls I was hoping for. I was sitting at the desk in my room, a source of convenience and torture all in one, suffering through homework, when my phone rang. I noticed it was a random number I didn't already have in my phone, and suddenly became intrigued, I let it ring a couple of times so I wouldn't seem too anxious.

"Hello?" I was trying to seem unattached, not interested in who might be on the other end.

"Hello, Lisa?" It was a man's voice, trying to see if he had the right number.

"This is her." It was the perfect excuse to take a break from the tedious paperwork ahead of me. I set my pen down and spun my chair away from my desk and faced the window.

"Hey Lisa, this is Adam. I'm the assistant director of the play you auditioned for on Monday, and I was just following up to let you know that we'd like to see you again at callbacks on Friday. Are you available around seven o'clock?"

It was a man, his name started with an A, and he was inviting me out on Friday night. It just wasn't the exact situation I was anticipating.

"Yeah, that definitely works for me." I was still excited. This was great news too.

"Great, we'll see you then. We'll have the scenes available when you get there, and it should take about an hour."

"Sounds good. I'll be there," I said, hanging up my phone and setting it back on my desk so I could pretend to want to get back to work.

Barely five minutes later, my phone rang again. And again, I didn't know the number. I assumed I just hadn't been paying very close attention and it was just Adam again having forgotten to give me some important detail about the callbacks. I was even more surprised when I answered the phone.

"What did you forget?" I laughed, thinking it was pretty funny that I was ahead of the game.

"Well, I usually start by saying hello. But I guess I forgot to ask you if you wanted to hang out Friday night." The voice on the other end was a man, but sounded different from Adam.

"Wait, who is this?" I was confused.

"This is Aaron. So, what do you say?"

"Oh! I'm sorry, I just got a call about the second round of auditions for Friday night, I thought it was Adam, the assistant director, calling to remind me of the time or something. Whatever. So, what were you saying?" I babbled.

Chapter 5

After that, Aaron and I saw a lot of each other. Not only were we both working on two different aspects of the same production, but it was also fun to catch a movie after rehearsals or just going over to his apartment, letting him try to cook, and sitting and doing homework together with the TV on in the background.

Everything seemed to be falling into place. Whenever my phone rang and I saw that it was Aaron, I couldn't help but smile. It was fun to get text messages from him in the middle of class and reply with updates as to what I was learning. Meeting him in the cafeteria for five minutes between our differing schedules was sometimes the highlight of my day. It seemed like some cheesy, teen-heartthrob crush, but I didn't care. I felt good being around him, and the feeling seemed to be mutual.

The production was coming along well too. I had fewer scenes than the rest of the cast, so I wasn't required to be at rehearsals every night, and it would be an easier script to memorize. On the flip side, I had to deliver it all with a Russian accent, which seemed to fade away the more I utilized it. I knew it was coming, but that fateful Thursday evening, it happened. We were told that we had to be off script by the following week. It seemed simple enough, obviously scripts aren't utilized as stage props to read from during the actual performances. But the part that worried me was being off script with an accent. All my lines were scribbled all over with little hints I'd written down about how to stretch the sounds and pronounce the words differently so that I could somehow convince an audience that I was Russian. The part about looking as if I'm in my sixties was wardrobe and makeup's problems.

I knew I needed a somewhat neutral audience to work on lines with me. And since I was heading over to Aaron's apartment to watch a movie, I figured he was close enough. I headed over with popcorn, candy, ice cream, and script in hand. His end of the deal was to supply the movies and the beverages, as long as they didn't consist of rum. The benefit of letting him pick out the movie we would watch was that I'd probably have no interest in watching it anyway, so it could be easier to focus on the task at hand.

I knocked on his door, juggling a paper bag of munchies in one hand and my backpack over my other shoulder.

"Be right there!" he yelled from the other side.

He opened the door and offered to take the paper bag. As I handed it to him, I leaned in for a quick kiss hello.

"Hey, how was your day?" I asked him.

He set the paper bag on his kitchen counter and started unloading it. I decided to help him, and in his tiny apartment, that made it easy to stand right up next to him. He pulled the first box out of the bag.

"Better now. How was rehearsal? Oh, extra butter, great choice!" He was digging through the bag as if he was looking for treasure. "And chocolate of all different sorts for dessert! I love it. You know what goes great with this well-balanced meal?" He turned and opened the refrigerator door. "Beer." He twisted the top off and handed me an ice-cold bottle.

"You read my mind." I smiled and took a drink. "Well, rehearsal went well. We need to be off script by next week. I don't suppose you know any hot guys that might want to help me memorize my lines and practice my accent, do you?" I did my best to make a puppy-dog face.

He smiled and gave me a kiss. I figured I could take that as a confirmation. We made the popcorn and moved all the munchies to the coffee table in front of his couch. We had front row seats to sit back, relax, watch a movie, and pig out. I snuggled up to him with the flannel blanket he kept on his couch. I figured I wouldn't like the movie but could still give it the first twenty minutes to pretend like I gave it a chance.

After the self-promised amount of time, I sat up and grabbed the script off the table.

"Okay, let's get to work!" I said.

"Hey, the movie just started," he responded, taking a sip of his drink.

"Well, we can leave it on. Here, just run a few lines with me. See what I already have memorized." I handed him the script. "It's really the accent I'm worried about."

He took the script but kept watching the movie.

"Come on, you said you'd help me." I tried a guilt trip on him.

"Yeah, after the movie. Come on, just sit back and watch it. You'll do fine." He was less than interested in helping me study.

I started focusing on the picnic spread on the table. As I popped a piece of extra-buttery popcorn into my mouth, I knew I'd have to bust out the big guns. I moved closer to him.

"You know, they say it's really not that hard to speak with an accent, you just have to utilize different muscles in of your mouth." I smiled and kissed him.

"All right, all right. You're not gonna play fair. I give up. Let's work on it. At least let me grab another beer." He surrendered as he stood up and headed back to the kitchen to replace his empty bottle.

A couple of hours later, the movie was over and had gone back to the home screen. Not wanting to hear the theme repeat itself nonstop, we simply muted it and kept eating and talking, randomly working on saying different lines from my script. I thought just sitting with him, laughing, and trying to decide which one of us had the worse accent would be the highlight of the night; but I had no idea what was in store.

"You swine!" I said it with the evilest Russian accent I could muster while working on my fourth beer and trying not to laugh.

"No, it's svine," he said, holding up his hand to enunciate where the accent played in.

"Swine. Swine. Swine." I tried to repeat it and see if it could fall into place.

"Not swine. Svine. Svine. Svine," he repeated it and pointed to his lip this time.

"All right, I give up. Why doesn't the director impose some creative power and just make her a Canadian or something. That's pretty close to a Minnesota accent, right? Should be easy enough." I set the script back on his coffee table and leaned back on the couch to relax and take a break. I checked my cell phone and saw what time it was.

"Whoa, I should get home. I have to be up early, and you have classes tomorrow morning too, don't you?" I started gathering up the empty wrappers and lost pieces of popcorn off the floor.

"Why don't you just stay here?" he asked.

"Oh, that's sweet. I'd love to, but I don't have my toothbrush or any clothes for tomorrow." It was cute of him to invite me, but I figured he knew by now that I wasn't fond of going to class with a fuzzy smile.

"Well, maybe you should start keeping one here," he said, taking another sip of his beer. "I mean, you're over here often enough. It might be easier to keep some clothes here."

With the bottle in the way, I couldn't really see his expression to get an idea of what he meant by that.

"What?" I asked, with a short laugh. "Wouldn't that get in your way?"

"Get in the way of what?" he asked, almost amused that I wasn't sure what to think.

"I don't know, um, what if you accidentally use my toothbrush?" I wasn't even sure what I meant but I tried to be logical yet again. "Wouldn't other people notice if you had a woman's pair underwear sitting around your room?"

He laughed. "What other people?"

"Well, I don't know, roommates, family members, other women?" I wasn't sure I should have said that last one and looked away to keep cleaning up.

"Well," he mocked me, "I don't have roommates. I let family members enjoy the courtesy of my couch, and there are no other women looking in my room right now."

Joking had always been a defense mechanism when I wasn't sure what to say.

"Oh, I won by default, huh?" I laughed nervously at my own attempted joke. "Besides, you could probably fit a bunk bed in there."

"No, not by default, I'm just not letting the other women in there right now." He winked at me.

"What are you saying?" All I could do was smile and hope for the right answer.

"I'm saying you should move in here. I have plenty of space, and I don't want to see anyone else. Besides, it'd be nice to have someone else wash my laundry again," he joked.

I threw a pillow from the couch at him.

"Seriously, though. I love snuggling up to you and falling asleep and waking up next to you. So you might want to have a toothbrush so we can make that a more pleasurable daily occurrence."

"Well, that's a lot to think about. I mean, I love hanging out with you too. But I'm sure I'm not rainbows and sunshine to be around all the time. And makeup, you don't know how much makeup it takes to look this natural. I don't wake up looking like this." It was a legitimate warning.

I'd have to take up space in his closet for my clothes, his bathroom for all my grooming products, and his cupboard for my PMS meds, which would be a whole other complicated issue on its own. In the short time that we had known each other, he had only seen my happy, easygoing, all put together layer. He had never seen me tear my room apart trying to find my keys, wearing no makeup and the most unflattering workout gear to the gym, and he certainly hadn't caught any whiffs of my dirty laundry. He hadn't even met my mother or my sister. Oh God, my mother and sister, what would they think? What would they say? They'd probably only frighten the poor guy away. He had the unfair advantage of having family five states away.

On the other hand, he understood my interest in acting and wanted to help me find real, local agencies and see what it required to get started and also who the best recommended photographers were and where to find legitimate auditions. He seemed supportive of my goals and what I wanted to do, instead of just brushing it off as if it was some kind of childish dream or waste of time.

But we would be sharing one bathroom. One bathroom. You can't hide anything when you're sharing one bathroom—and with someone you're dating. Everything you don't want your significant other to see would be readily available for his viewing displeasure. Nothing would be off limits.

"And what if you get sick of me? Sick of having me around all the time? What do we do then? I'm not pleasant 24-7." My warning seemed to fall on deaf ears.

"We all have our mood swings," he responded.

"Well, some worse than others." I maintained my skepticism.

"No, for real, men have cycles too. Besides, I don't think I could get sick of you." He smiled.

"Because you drink?" I thought maybe sarcasm might make him understand.

He moved closer, put his hand on my cheek, kissed me, then looked me right in the eyes. "Because. I love you."

I didn't even know what to say. So I just kissed him. It was the sweetest thing anyone had ever said to me. Yes, my mother would say I love you before she hung up the phone or left for work, but she was obligated to. He seemed to say it because he wanted to. I wasn't sure what I had done to make him feel this way, but moving forward, I'd have to try damn hard to remember.

What if living with him changed everything? What if he really did expect me to do his laundry, to clean, to cook? Would it make him less attractive to see his dirty underwear or to have to wait a half hour to use the bathroom after his morning rituals?

After debating both sides in my head, I decided to do it. Screw what my mother would say, screw all the negative possible outcomes, and screw his dirty underwear. All the overanalyzing running through my brain since he had brought up the idea had actually paid off. Resolutions unknown, all the petty bases I could think of off the top of my head had been addressed. Even the smallest reasons not to had been covered. There was only one more thing I would think of to say.

"I love you too. Let's do it."

Chapter 6

"Absolutely not!" my mother roared at me. "It's ridiculous! You've only known each other for about a month! And bills, what will the two of you do about paying the bills? You barely work twelve hours a week! And what about school, are you just going to forget all about that?" Her logic seemed never ending and a little more legitimate than my cosmetic surface concerns.

I even ran the idea by a few friends, who naively assured me that all we needed was love and the rest would fall into place. I assured them that they had heard too many happy-ending fairy tales growing up. While it was a cute little notion, I had to admit Mom was right. First thing was first. I'd have to find a job to pay the bills. I'd had a side job serving ice cream to kids in the mall since I was fifteen. But I was pretty sure this wasn't going to cover rent or the other sprinkles on the financial sundae.

With everything going on—the play, the end of the semester, the lack of a sufficient job—I had told Aaron that we should wait at least a month before I moved in with him. This should give me enough time to get everything together. I was filling out applications left and right but had still not heard anything back. Meanwhile, I was still working with the ice cream, and even tried to ask for a raise. My manager told me I could receive a dollar raise if I agreed to open up my availability. I agreed but knew it would be tricky to balance with school and acting.

The whole idea had me stressed. Even sitting in my classes all day, I was secretly taking a list down the side of my homework notes titled "other places to apply for a job." Oddly enough this didn't exactly come in handy during my math class. We were partnered with students sitting around us to work through different math problems we had been assigned for homework. Though my partner looked pretty normal, showed up to class wearing jeans and T-shirts, hair thrown up into a simple bun, and limited makeup, I wasn't sure this would classify her as a math genius.

We stayed in our seats and cracked open our books. Since we had been sitting next to each other for a few months now, it didn't seem that introductions were in order. Besides, it wasn't a major project, just practicing a few math problems to which we'd get the answers to by the end of class, anyway.

"Okay, I think we're supposed to start with number five," she said, flipping a few pages and getting her notebook ready to write down answers.

"Um, yeah, I think it was number five." I tried to side glance at her book and see what page she was on.

"All right, I figured this one out. If we start here, then work this part out, that should give us the answer to this part. Then we take that answer, move it over her and..." She looked up, noticing that I was scribbling down the side of my notebook instead of writing down what she was telling me. "Do you already have the answer. I'm not even sure mine's right."

"I don't know if mine's right either. I actually started here," I said, showing her my notes for the problem. "I think we got the same thing."

"Not really in the mood to work on math, huh?" she randomly asked.

"Oh, sorry. I'm just stressed. I have to find a new job." I was pretty sure she didn't care, but I felt like telling her anyway. "See, I need to make more money because I'm about to move into a new apartment, well, my boyfriend's apartment. And I don't want us to fight about money because I've heard people do that. And there are so many other things we can fight about instead. Not that we want to fight. I mean, we hardly ever fight. I don't think we've ever fought. I don't know, I'm just so stressed about it."

Before I could keep rambling about working out any problem not involving math, she cut me off. "Whoa, whoa. I get it. Not sure if it helps, but I'm a server. It's pretty flexible, and you can make some really good money," she informed me. "You should apply at my restaurant. I'm sure you've heard of it. Pommes? Just put down Kristen Adams as a referral."

"Yeah, I know it. That's cool, thanks." With that piece of advice, I could concentrate on math again.

I planned to apply as soon as possible. I knew I had some time the next day, between my last class and rehearsal. It was a national chain of restaurants, so I figured it wouldn't be too hard to pick one to apply at. I drove into the parking lot of the strip mall and parked almost right in front of the door. As I walked in, the teenaged hostess greeted me, almost right away, after sending her text and putting her phone back on the shelf of the host stand.

"Hello! Welcome to Pommes! Were you wanting a table or a seat in the bar?", she asked me with an almost forced cheerful tone.

"Ah, no. No, thank you. Actually, I was hoping to fill out an application?" I said.

"Oh, yeah. Here's one. You can sit at one of the high top tables in the bar. Just let me know when you're done, I'll give it to the manager." Her cheery demeanor faded to a somewhat neutral tone. While most people would find this less welcoming, even rude, but I was actually more excited to fill out the application. She was proof that this could be an obvious place to inadvertently rehearse my improvisation skills.

"Great, thanks. Any table?" I asked, holding the application and pointing to the nearest table at the same time.

She seemed even less interested after the eight-foot trip to the bar area. "Yeah, that's fine," she said as she was already turned around and heading back to the host's stand.

I settled into the seat and started filling out the application. The first thing I wanted to do was put my classmate's name down so I wouldn't forget to include her as my referral. With my short work history, it didn't take long to complete the paperwork. I noticed as I was filling it out that another guy had walked into a similar situation to what I had just done. He was sitting at a table behind me and filling out what seemed to be the same application.

Once I was done with mine, I walked my application back up to the front to give it to the hostess.

"Okay, great. I'll bring it to the manager. Are you able to wait and see if he has time to talk to you?" There was that cheerful attitude again.

"Yeah, that's cool." It was somewhat promising to think I could get an interview right away.

"Great, have a seat. I'll bring it back to him," she said, once again as she was walking away to the direction of what I assumed was "the back."

I sat back down in the same spot where I had filled out the application. I wasn't sure how long I would have to wait, but it gave me a chance to absorb my surroundings. It seemed like a basic bar and restaurant. There were a couple of televisions in the bar showing games I couldn't even pretend to be interested in. And against a neutrally painted wall were the pictures of local sports teams. The floors and tables seemed pretty clean. The servers coming and going from "the back" were wearing black pants and polo shirts bearing the logo of the restaurant. The few full tables in the restaurant after the lunch rush seemed to be filled with people who were neatly dressed, usually a good sign for the restaurant industry. There were a couple of patrons at the bar. Both had half empty glasses of beer sitting in front of them, and they were talking to what I assumed was the game playing on the televisions. After their teams had scored or lost, they would sip their beers and debate about whether it was a missed call or a botched effort. The place seemed decent enough. Suddenly I heard someone talking to me.

"Hey, sorry to bug you. Was she coming back?" he asked.

I turned around to face the table behind me to see if he was actually talking to me or the bartender. He was looking right at me.

"Oh, I think so. She said she was just bringing him my application," I informed him.

"Cool, now she'll get to make two trips." He laughed.

"I'm sure she won't mind." I figured friendly was the key to getting this job.

"Do you know if they're hiring, or is this just for 'funsies'?" he asked me.

"I'm not sure. I'm just hoping they're hiring for a few day and weekend shifts," I informed him.

"Awesome, I'm hoping for night shifts. I'm Mike, by the way," he said, standing up to come over and shake my hand.

"I'm Lisa," I said, meeting him halfway. "Have you worked at a place like this before?"

"As a server? No, but I'm in college, and I heard it was a fast way to make easy money," he replied.

Before we had a chance to get to know more about one another, the hostess came back to fill me in on the latest details.

"Okay, he said he should be out in about five minutes. He just wants to look over your app," she informed me. "Did you want something to drink? A pop, a water?"

"Um, sure. Can I please have a water with a lemon—oh, wait, sorry. Can I change that to a coffee?" I knew this had to be my final answer. I figured a little caffeine buzz would help me insure that outgoing attitude I'd run into when the hostess first greeted me.

"This ain't a buffet, Kit!" I heard Mike's voice coming from behind me. He was holding up his completed application and laughed at his own joke as he attempted to hurry the process of also getting an interview within the next half hour.

"Okay, okay, sorry. Yeah, just the coffee, please." I couldn't help but laugh at his joke too. "And apparently decaf for my friend here."

"No, that's cool. Water will be fine," he told her, handing her the completed application. "Do you think he'll be able to squeeze me in too?" He smiled at her, almost using charm to assure an interview. He was attractive, and it seemed to work.

The hostess left to drop off his application and fetch our drinks. She returned with his water, and my less than hot, obviously-brewed-earlier-in-the-afternoon coffee. His was delivered first. He smiled and winked at her as she set it down. I said a generic thank you and started reaching for the sugar packets. He was obviously using his boyish charm to score a few points in the referral department. After one quick sip of almost burnt coffee, I was met with introductions from the manger.

"Hello! Welcome to Pommes! I'm Kurt. I'm one of the managers here," he said, sitting down across from me. "So you're looking to join the orchard, huh?"

Not being fluent in the language on the planet Pommes and having the taste of over-simmered coffee in the back of my mouth, I simply smiled and nodded. "Yup, that's right."

"Great. Well, let me give you a rundown of how we run things around here," he said, following the statement with random facts about how the restaurant got started and what they expect from their employees in order to deliver the finest quality experience to the customer. He went over the training process and asked about my availability. I barely got a chance to answer his random questions, but apparently, my short, sweet responses were exactly what he was looking for. After what seemed to be a half hour of him talking, but I later realized was ten minutes, he was still looking down at my application. I wasn't sure what was left to read but figured it was a good sign when he said he was going to pass it on to the hiring manager. I would've though he was a hiring manager but thought it best not to question the hierarchy. Suddenly he stopped reading.

"Oh, you have a referral. That's interesting. I know who that is," he said it with a somber tone and a serious look on his face as his eyes focused on that line.

Suddenly, I wasn't sure if I should have relied on her generosity or just tried applying on my own. The only thing left to try was the disclaimer.

"Yeah, she's one of my classmates at the community college. She's in my math class. We've worked on a few projects together." I had absolutely no idea if sharing this information would be remotely helpful to my case.

Then he responded, "Yeah, she's great. Very easy to work with."

It was a huge relief. From there, we just set up the second interview. He stood up, smiled, shook my hand, and said he had to go back into the office and file my application. He walked away still looking down at my papers and rubbing his chin as if he was deep in thought. I wasn't sure what he could possibly be analyzing at this point but figured maybe it was just a relief to him to think about new hires instead of ketchup bottles.

He disappeared into the mysterious "back," where I assumed the office was, and I stood up to gather my things and choke down the last of the liquid sludge the hostess had brought me in an attempt to maintain a good pending work relationship. I turned around, waved at Mike, and was ready to head for the door.

"Got the second interview, huh?" he asked.

"Yeah, here's hoping it all goes well," I responded. "Maybe we'll be coworkers. Break a leg."

"See you soon!" Mike finished as Kurt was making his way to the table where he was sitting.

I left feeling pretty good about the interview. Now I could concentrate on the play.

I met Aaron later that night at his apartment for dinner. It was my turn to cook, and after debating what he was in the mood for, we settled with pepperoni. We sat down on the couch and started grabbing at slices and placing them on our paper plates. After settling in for our romantic meal together, I told him about my day.

"So I applied for another job today," I told him, mouth semi-full.

"Cool, where at?" he asked, studying his pizza.

"At Pommes, you know, that family restaurant, bar and grill place," I answered. "I applied for a serving position."

He looked up at me with a mixed look of shock and disgust. "Why would you want to be a server? They only make minimum wage, don't they?"

"Plus tips and benefits." I was almost defensive about it. "I think this could be a good thing, having cash, flexible schedule, and health insurance. That's not something I can get serving ice cream or working in retail."

"Okay, fair enough. Are you gonna have to carry one of those huge trays or something?" he joked. "Cause I know for a fact that you can barely even carry multiple bags of groceries up the stairs all at once."

"That's because you always make me carry the heavy stuff so that you can reach your keys and open the door!" I stuck my tongue out at him. "Besides, I don't know about the trays. But if I get the job, they'll train me. And who knows, maybe I'll be good at it. Don't be so skeptical."

"Ah, yes, you will, sweetie," he sarcastically consoled me. "In fact, you can practice now and get me another slice."

"Yeah, I'll even practice what I'm going to do to people's food when they annoy me!" I made a spit sound over his slice and handed it to him and smiled. "Here, it'll even taste better."

And maybe it would work out. I told myself not to worry about it until I was called back for a second interview. A few days later I was called back. The second interview went smoothly, and before I knew it, I was being set up for orientation and training.

Orientation consisted of learning about the history of the restaurant itself, being paired with another experienced server to follow around and observe, filling out the paperwork and availability, including the play. I wasn't sure what they would say about the fact that the play took up a lot of my spare time, but it seemed to be okay as it was only a temporary schedule. I was glad I didn't have to endure the first day alone. There were a few of us sitting at the table and filling out our paperwork in silence including Mike.

"So are you working day or evening shifts?" he asked me when the manager left us to fill everything out.

"Days, except Tuesdays and Thursdays. I have classes. But I'll work a double shift on Wednesdays," I told him.

"Cool. I'm gonna be working the night shifts. I have classes every day," he informed me.

"If we make it, passed training this week, who knows, we might even work together on Wednesday nights. Could be fun!" I replied. "If not, they'll just get rid of us."

"I'm not that lucky." He laughed at his own joke.

He had such a confident, inviting personality, I couldn't help but laugh along with him.

"Amen to that!" I confirmed.

It was a relief to feel like I sort of knew someone at my new job. I wouldn't be learning everything on my own. There was one more girl in the class who seemed content keeping to herself. While filling out her paperwork, she would give the occasional strained glance upward when we laughed but made no obvious attempt to lift her head, or even compose similar expressions of amusement. I found it odd that someone about to start work as an employee requiring somewhat massive social skills seemed so introverted but figured it was her loss if she didn't want to meet a few allies.

We were then assigned to experienced employees who we were expected to follow around like long-lost puppies. Luckily, I was assigned to Kristen. Since she "had referred" me, the managers assumed that she and I knew each other and would get along well for training purposes. While we could merely point each other out in our math class and now at work, it was still a relief to have some kind of connection with a trainer teaching me the ropes.

It was almost a tap dance. I had to follow closely enough to hear what she was saying to tables and how she was communicating with other employees but had to stay far enough back so that it didn't seem like we were snuggling. Walking behind someone can become tricky during the lunch rush, with tables hustling in and out of the restaurant. You have to dodge not only customers but be ready to jump out of the way at the drop of a hat when your trainer turned around and tried to rush to the kitchen to retrieve refills or plates piled with food. You almost have to be psychic. You're only supposed to observe, but when you get "the look" from your trainer, you know it's time to silently step in and do your share, regardless of what it might be. You can also learn how many personalities a person has just by working with them. It's by studying these people that one can find out what triggers these personas to surface.

"Excuse me. Excuse me. I think we're ready to order," the customer said with a courtesy smile on her face. "We're in somewhat of a hurry. We're on a lunch break and have to go back to work."

The customer had interrupted Kristen midsentence as she was just beginning her table-greeting monologue of welcomes and specials. "Great, I'll be with you in just a moment," Kristen replied with a large, fake smile.

All I could do was watch the train wreck. Glancing back at the table, the women sighed and went back to her conversation about her hairstylist. Kristen finished getting the drink orders from the new table and turned around to help the impatient customers.

"All right, thanks for waiting. What can I get for you?" Kristen asked, pen and paper in hand, not glancing up at the table for fear they would see the annoyance in her expression.

After two of the women placed their orders, the third, and seemingly most impatient of them, who had been trying to flag Kristen down after her unacceptably long five-minute wait, was debating her choice. "Well, I can't decide if I should have the soup and house salad lunch special or the Asian chicken salad."

"Well, it is a tough decision. They're both excellent choices," Kristen said with a big cheesy laugh, pretending to care.

"Well, I am on a diet, so I suppose I should just have the salad," the woman shared, her concerns falling on deaf ears.

"Sounds good, I'll get that ordered for you." Kristen's smile never faded. I wasn't sure how she wasn't twitching by now, having to consciously force her smiling muscles to function.

"Oh, and can I get extra dressing on the side. I just love that dressing. It's so sweet and creamy!" She seemed excited by the idea of her extra dressing.

"Yes, and that'll be $1.99 extra?" Kristen looked at the customer with a questioning look.

"What, I thought extra dressing was free. When did you start charging for it?" she asked, almost angry that Kristen had suggested it.

"Just kidding! Of course, it's free! Just a little serving humor!" She winked. "Just wanted to make sure you were paying attention!"

It was almost difficult to be the useless appendage, simply watching the tension build on both sides. I could only stare at the table until my owner made her getaway from eccentric bunch around the corner and toward safety behind the walls of the kitchen.

We stopped at the expo counter, and Kristen filled me in. "Stupid bitch. Whatever amount of fat or calories she's allowed to eat in a day is in this dressing. It can take years to get rid of cellulite. Did she really have to interrupt me to get a fix five minutes sooner than I was planning? People are assholes."

"I guess so." It was all I could think of to say and backed it up with an awkward smile. I wasn't sure if anything else would set her off against me.

I followed her right back out to the table. She had a big cheesy grin when she set the dressing next to the fussy customer. "There you are," she said. "Is there anything else I can get for you right away?"

The women, shaking their heads without looking up, already had mouths full of food and were scooping up the next loads onto their forks. The scene almost reminded me of my grandfather's farm. During the messy feeding rounds, it was every animal for itself.

"Great, enjoy." She turned and looked at me. Her smile faded instantly, and she rolled her eyes. We headed back to the kitchen and pursued the next round of orders to be delivered.

I learned that day that the lunch rush was just that—a rush. It was a relief to sit down and talk to Kristen after the crowd died down. There was a packet we were supposed to be filling out after every shift.

"So what did you learn today?" Kristen asked, staring down at the packet, adjusting her pen to get ready to write down the answer.

"Um, just smile and nod." I laughed.

She gave a courtesy smile. "How about be patient with the customer and don't take orders and frustrations personally?"

"Sounds like a plan," I responded.

"Basically, yeah, when it's really busy like that and someone is bugging you between every bite. The best advice I can give you is not to get flustered. It's going to take as long as it's going to take, and you just have to get through it. Stay focused, don't get flustered, and multitask. It'll be your best friend!"

Don't get flustered? Easier said than done. I had a script, stage blocking, a menu, and chapter upon chapter of logic methods to memorize before my midterms. All of this was to be accomplished while packing my things on the side in order to take up residence with my gorgeous boyfriend. Who knew if I could accomplish a focused multitasking when I was grasping at straws just to maintain my sanity.

Our meeting was short and sweet, and I was happy to clock out and head back over to Aaron's and wait for him to get home from work. Even though I hadn't moved into his apartment yet, he gave me a key to get in since he worked at the sports store and had a random schedule. However, I assumed it was less stressful being that he was so familiar with the job. I wasn't sure exactly what he did, but I knew he looked really cute in his khakis and blue sports store polo.

I decided to have dinner waiting for him when he got home a few hours later. I figured it would be the perfect way to relax after my crazy day of training and a sweet surprise for him when he got home. A few hours later, he still wasn't home. I assumed he had to stay late at work, which had been happening more and more often lately since one of the managers had left.

"Hey, what's going on?" He sounded tired.

"Oh, nothing. I made dinner. It's cold now, but I could throw some in the microwave for you, if you want," I offered.

"Nah, that's cool. I got off early and met a few friends for happy hour. We had some wings," he informed me. "Actually, I need to take a shower."

"Oh, need some help getting those hard to reach spots?" I asked, wrapping my arms around his waist and giving him a short kiss. I could taste the beer on his lips.

"I wish. I'm exhausted, and I have to be back at work at 7:00 a.m. for the shipment," he declined.

I let go of him so he could head to his closet and get a towel. "I thought the managers always did that," I inquired with a statement.

"Yeah, that's the fun part. I went out with the guys to celebrate. They offered me the management position," he announced.

I was only somewhat surprised. "Well, that's cool. Does it come with a raise? Are you gonna get a set schedule?"

"Salary. So, yes and no. I'll probably just work a few days a week," he yelled from the bedroom.

"Well, that's a good thing. We'll have time to spend together, and you'll still have time for classes. You only have, what, a year left anyway?" I was content in pointing out all the positive aspects of this promotion.

"Actually, no. I'll probably have to take some time off from school. I'll have three-day weekends, but that means I'll probably be working open to close on the others. Probably just thirteen-hour days. Not exactly sure yet," he said it as if it was no big deal. I figured it had to be the beer.

"Well, that's exciting." I tried to utilize the fake, yet seemingly realistic, grin I had learned at training earlier. "You should have called me. I could've gone out to celebrate with you guys." I was yelling from the kitchen as I started putting the leftover food in containers to pile in the fridge.

"I figured you had rehearsal after work," he responded while walking into the bathroom. "Besides, it was just a few of the guys from work and a couple of friends. You probably wouldn't have had much fun."

"Well, I would've been hanging out with you—that's fun. Besides, if we're going to be roommates, I should probably meet at least a few of your friends." I was pretty sure he couldn't see me sticking my tongue out at him, but it made me feel better anyway. He had been working on the posters and pamphlets for the performance, I thought he would have a general idea of what the schedule was.

He came out of the bathroom wrapped in a towel and smelling great. With any kind of male- scented body wash, I was pretty sure it was impossible for him not to.

"I'm sorry. I'll definitely call you for the next outing." This time he wrapped his arms around my waste and gave me a real kiss.

Even though I wasn't really all that upset, I was sure that he couldn't honestly think that this would make me forgive and forget, even though he did smell amazing and was a very good kisser and was standing half-naked with his arms around me.

"All right, I suppose I can forgive you, just this once." I tried to sound firm in my disclaimer.

He paused after a short kiss, and the moment of magic was over. "So how was training?"

"Oh, you know. Just observing, learning how to use the computers. Nothing too exciting. What's more exciting is that next week is opening night for the play! You didn't forget, did you?" I didn't want to get into the gory details. I wanted to keep making out with him so I didn't give him much of a chance to answer but was relieve when I got a smothered "mmm-hhmmm" from him.

I believed this to be our first fight, and I was so proud of the way we both overcame it. Nothing petty, nothing drawn out, just straight to resolving the issue. It made me look forward to living with him even more. Regardless of the obstacles that I thought lay ahead, I knew that it would all be worth it, as long as we were together. I had to succumb to all the fairy tales I'd been subject to as a child. The fables you know aren't real but secretly hope to be based on true stories. Yes, I was struck.

"I love you," I told him. Short and sweet.

"I love you too." He smiled and kissed me again.

[?]

Chapter 7

After five shifts of following Kristen around, it was time to turn the tables. She had to follow me for a couple of shifts. I wasn't looking forward to it, except for the fact that after these, I would be free to work on my own, and good or bad, actually get to keep the tips.

It wasn't easy to justify my tagalong to the customers, but I utilized my improvisational skills and simply introduced her as my babysitter. It was a great way to break the ice and start the experience off on the right foot. As the afternoon went on, I found that starting off on the right foot was a very good idea, especially when you're a new employee and it appears to be "opposite day."

Almost every customer that ordered a half-salad got the full sized. This was a pretty easy fix as it just required a price override on the tickets concerning customers that weren't willing to compromise in favor of the higher-priced meals. The bigger challenge were the burgers that came out overcooked or underdone and the broccoli that came out looking suspiciously similar to the fries that were originally supposed to come with the meal in the first place. There was a lot of compromise and menu educating that came along with that shift, mostly on the part of the customer. I was thrilled when Kristen gave in and wanted to call it a day before she lost any more money on my training.

We were in the kitchen when Kristen told me, "Okay, I think that's good for the day. We have a decent list of things for you to concentrate on for tomorrow." I could tell that she was stretching her patience as far as she could without breaking down and telling me that I was too stupid to work at a restaurant. I took her direction and was relieved to be leaving.

Oddly enough, the familiarity of rehearsal was a nice stress reducer, even though we were in the final countdown to opening night. I headed back to Aaron's afterwards to wait for him to get home. Since he had accepted the management position, I knew it wouldn't be until about 10:00 p.m. I finished my homework and stretched out on the couch for an evening of reruns. Not exactly my first choice for an exciting night, but I wanted to keep my mind off the events of the day. It actually made me miss Aaron. I had seen him that morning, but I wanted to see him again. He would take my mind off my less than perfect day at work. I must have bored myself to sleep on the couch when I was woken up by Aaron.

"Hey, how was work?" I asked him.

"Oh, you know, the usual. One guy didn't show up for his shift so that'll be fun to deal with tomorrow," he informed me. "Ready for bed?" He was already heading back to his bedroom to get his towel and his jogging pants to start his evening ritual of showering and heading to bed.

"Oh, yeah." I stood up and stretched and started to slowly follow him while trying to keep up on the conversation.

"How was your first day of waiting on tables? Did you make lots of money?" He sounded hopeful. Then suddenly his tone changed. "Wait, I thought you were going to do laundry today." He sounded irritated.

I got into the bedroom and sat on the bed just in time to deliver the bad news.

"Sorry, I didn't get to it. I had rehearsal and still had to finish my homework for tomorrow. You know Friday night is opening night. You're still going to be able to come, aren't you?" I asked, thinking this was the end of the previous issue with the laundry.

"Great, so now there are no clean towels for tomorrow." He seemed to be more annoyed and turned to look at me. "I can't come Friday. I told you I was going to try and come Saturday or Sunday."

"Wait, what? I thought you said Friday. Don't you want to be there opening night? You've been working on this thing too." Now I was getting annoyed.

He turned back toward his dresser and started digging though his drawers. "I made a few posters. I had a much smaller part. I was done about a month ago. Besides, I already got my grade for the project," he said. "Can you at least put the laundry in the dryer if I start it tomorrow morning before work? I'd like to at least have a clean towel so I can take a shower when I get home."

His mood had changed from annoyed to outright crabby. His laundry and his towels seemed to be the most important thing on his mind, and he seemed to be forgetting the fact that he should be coming on opening night in order to support his girlfriend in her debut as a supporting character.

"Gee, yeah, why would you want to come on opening night like you promised me you would." I emphasized the word me in the hopes that he would pull his head out of his ass and realize that it was important to me.

"Look, it's been a long day. I'm not going to argue. I told you that my schedule was going to change. I won't be able to make it Friday. We can just go out afterwards—or something." Again, he was preoccupied. "Great. Do I even have a pair of clean socks for tomorrow?"

"Calm down. There's no harm in wearing them two days in a row. Your feet aren't that nasty." I laughed, but my attempt at humor fell on deaf ears.

"You're hilarious," he said with a straight face.

I jumped after he slammed the dresser drawer and headed out of the room.

My smile quickly faded. Why was he getting so mad? His attempt to become the wicked stepfather over a plastic basket of dirty socks was less than appealing. I certainly didn't want to be treated worse at home than I was at work when I didn't follow customers' orders.

"Wow, okay. Well, on that wonderful note. I think I'm going to head home," I said as I walked the opposite way than he had and headed toward the couch to collect my books.

"Come on. You don't have to leave. It's almost midnight. Let's just go to bed," he said, drinking from the bottle of orange juice that was in the fridge.

"No, that's okay. I don't think I want to reenact this scene when you see that I didn't make your bed. No worries though. Feel free to dock my pay or take it out of my tips," I responded. I didn't even bother to look from the task at hand. I couldn't believe that he was blowing up at me this way. There was no reason for it.

I stood up and was heading for the door. He stepped in front of me from the kitchen door.

"Hey, come on. You don't have to get so mad. Just stay," he said, almost trying to sound innocent of his earlier persona.

"Seriously? You're telling me not to get so mad? Do you not remember five minutes ago?" Now I was mad. "I'm sorry if you had a shitty day at work. If you want to come home and bitch to me about it, great. But if you're going to bitch at me, you better make damn sure I deserve it. And last time I checked, I'm not your mother nor am I on your payroll. Therefore, you can wash your own nasty socks because frankly, my dear, I don't give a shit right now. Have a great night."

I walked out before he had a chance to answer. I was so irritated, replaying the situation in my mind over and over again, trying to figure what exactly I could've done to set him off that way. I was so lost in my thoughts that I barely remembered driving home that night.

I arrived to a dark, silent house. No one was expecting me to come home. I tried to sneak in to my room, but I was less that quiet when I stubbed my toe on the coffee table. Suddenly my mother came running around the corner in her bathrobe, turning on the hall light and squinting, waiting for her eyes to adjust to the shock.

"What the hell are you doing? You scared me to death!" She started walking toward the couch.

"Ouch. Sorry. I didn't anticipate breaking my toe on the way to my room," I said. "Whose idea was it to get this stupid thing again?" I hobbled over to the couch to sit by her and show her my injury.

She was less than sympathetic. "Why would you sneak in at midnight anyway? I have to work in the morning. I thought you were going to stay at Aaron's. Let me see."

I lifted my foot to show her my injury. "It's my baby toe. Pretty sure it's broken. Just like my relationship. Aaron and I had a fight."

She wanted to hold my foot as she examined my toe.

"Stop! Ow, that tickles." I squealed as I was trying to pull my foot away.

She rolled her eyes at me and attempted again to grab my foot. "Don't be such a baby, let me see." She examined it and made me wiggle it to prove that it wasn't actually broken.

"It's bleeding. Where's the blood coming from?" I asked desperately, almost sounding like a young child. Something about having your mother in front of you, nursing your wounds makes almost anyone feel like a small child, regardless of the severity of any injury.

"Well, you didn't break it, but you did rip off half of your toenail. Good thing sandal season ended last week," she joked, trying to relieve the stress. "Now what did you two fight about?"

"Oh, he got mad at me because I told him I'd clean his laundry and I forgot about it. He made a really big deal, and I told him I was too tired to fight." As I filled her in on the details, even I could see that it was a stupid, meaningless quarrel and neither one of us should have gotten as irritated as we did.

"Wow, honey, if you're fighting this badly about laundry before you even move in, what the hell are you gonna do about vacuuming and bills after your stuff is unpacked?" she asked me, dropping my foot back to the floor.

I cringed. Both my toe and her question hurt. But being too tired to confess that she was right, I resorted to humor.

"Well, you'll have to have a sleeping bag ready for me," I said sarcastically. She gave me a mocking cackle, and I echoed it back, both of us making faces at the other. It was the mother-daughter unspoken body language that I really did understand what she was saying, but I just didn't want to talk about it anymore.

"Now go get some ice, shut up, and go to bed," she said. She was less than interested in nurturing my injury and my ego and just headed back to her own room.

I got up and hobbled toward the kitchen. Unfortunately, my physical pain was a great escape from the emotional stress of everything going on. I got the ice I needed and made my way across the living room to get back to my bedroom very careful to avoid the legs of the chairs and table in my way. I was relieved just to be able to go to sleep with my sound machine instead of a homemade remix of nagging and bickering. I turned off my phone and just focused on what I had to get done tomorrow.

I woke up the next morning and turned on my phone, hoping to receive at least a text message containing the apology I knew I deserved. Unfortunately, I didn't see one. However, I did see a voicemail waiting. I saw that it was one from Aaron. Since I had to go to an early class and then to my final day of serving with a babysitter, I decided to wait to listen to it. It was probably him calling to yell at me about something else I did wrong, and that's not how I wanted to start my morning.

I went about my day. I attended class, got my homework, and headed to my last day of training. I was guilty of looking at the voicemail log on my phone a few times. Just making sure the symbol showing me that there was a new message was still there. But I still didn't want to deal with it. Luckily, I was preoccupied with my final "test" at work, so I didn't have time to think about anything else. It was a relief to see that I wasn't the only trainee on my final day of being babysat. Mike was also there, and his babysitter looked less than thrilled. As we were all gathering for our usual morning meeting before we opened, I made it a point to find Mike and see how things were going.

"Hey! How are you? I thought you were only going to be working nights?" I asked him.

"Good. Yeah, actually I am. I had the day off at school, so I wanted to come in and get this crap over with," he answered.

It was good to hear that it wasn't very enjoyable for him either. "You're having fun too? Kristen seemed pretty irritated with me yesterday. I'm almost surprised she didn't try to hit me with her car while I was walking into the building."

"No, you're not that lucky."

We both laughed.

"Seriously, though, during the dinner rush, this job is tough. People get so pissy about refills."

"No kidding. And that whole trying to keep up on the dishes while taking care of our tables thing? That's going to be interesting," I mentioned.

"Excuse me? I'm not here to do dishes. I'm glad I'll be working the night shift. We have someone who does that for us," he replied as he was tying his apron on. "The only people I'll be a bitch for are the ones sitting at my tables, and that's because they're paying me."

The lists of flaws probably could have gone on and on, but we had to pretend to pay attention to what was being discussed in our pre-shift meeting. It lightened the mood and was a little more relaxing to start the shift off on a humorous note. While the manager was preaching about welcoming us new people, Mike was smiling. While the manager was looking in our direction, he had a serious, focused look on his face, as if he was listening. Once the manager turned around in an attempt to make eye contact with every employee, Mike was mocking him and shaking his head to every word. I tried not to laugh out loud and kept it refined to a large smile. If nothing else, it made me look cheerful and positive about starting the lunch shift. It wouldn't hurt to score the points.

Watching Mike's different expressions made me realize that I shouldn't worry too much about venturing off to my own section without my babysitter. It would simply be a way to practice and master my improvisation and acting skills. All I had to do was pretend to care, and my day just might go a little more smoothly. This seemed like such an obvious revelation. How I hadn't come to it sooner, I have no idea. I made a mental note to ask Mike if he had ever done any acting.

Maybe it was a coincidence, but my shift did go a little smoother. Starting it off with a good laugh and knowing that I wasn't the only rookie on the floor made me feel a little more relaxed, and oddly enough, in a fast-paced job like a restaurant, the more relaxed you are, the more you can focus and efficiently multitask. I was even able to smile at a few tables as they were leaving. Kristen rarely had to jump in and correct me. She even complimented me at the end of the shift.

"That was actually pretty good. You seemed confident and like you knew what you were doing. I'm signing off that you're ready to take our own sections," she said, less than thrilled, but seemingly okay with that fact that she wouldn't have to spend her next shift with a shadow.

"Sounds great. Someone will have to show me how to use that sanitizer spraying machine in the dish area, but other than that, I think all of my questions were answered. I'm ready to make some money!" I was excited about actually getting to keep the tips that were left on the table.

"Whoa, don't tell the manager that. We're here to 'give the guest the experience they want to pick.' Remember the slogan? Just tell them that if they ask." She was less than enthusiastic about the restaurant slogan. I understood why. It was painted across the wall by the host stand. It was written across all the menus, and it was just plain cheesy as hell! But she was right. It couldn't hurt to repeat it back to a manager here and there, to make sure it seemed like I was onboard with their whole system.

"Great, see you tomorrow," I said. I was relieved that I had conquered one obstacle for the day. Now I knew I had to face the one I had been avoiding since earlier in the morning. Just as I was about to break down and finally listen to the message, I was greeted by a welcome interruption.

"So how did it go?" Mike said, sitting across the table from me. "I think my trainer liked me." He laughed at his own joke, and it was hard not to laugh along with him.

"How can you tell? They all seem to walk around with that fake smile all day, every day." I laughed, putting my phone down.

"Oh, I know he did. He's just shy," Mike said, waving to his trainer, not sure whether he was looking in our direction or not.

"I'm pretty sure mine just tolerated me. But it's all good. I'm done with training! I survived!" I said, adding my own sarcastic, dramatic effect. I figured with his outgoing personality he would be amused by my attempt. But since he seemed more interested in wrapping up his apron and checking his phone, it seemed like a good time to change the subject. "Now I can focus on my play."

"Oh, are you a writer?" he asked, taking a break from his phone and looking at me.

"No, an actress. This job is probably the closest I come to creating a script," I told him.

"Do you do a lot of acting?" he asked. "I used to do a lot with the drama club in high school. I've been thinking about getting back into it in Minneapolis, once I'm done with school."

"I've been looking into it more and more. You can actually find tons of auditions for theater productions around here. I just need to get some new headshots. That's the fun part, getting a decent picture without having to sell a kidney for the shoot." I hated to sound skeptical, but it was true.

"Yeah, I suppose that can be a pain. Is theater what you really want to do or are you more into film?" It was a legitimate question until he asked. I hadn't really considered it. I wasn't even sure I had met anyone else around my age pondering film opportunities in Minneapolis.

"Honestly, I love acting in general, but I'd really love to work in films. There are so many independent films being made here, but it's tough to figure out exactly how to get started. There are a lot of 'agencies' that are happy to sell you class after class, but it'd be great to find the one that'll get you audition after audition. It can be frustrating to try and figure it all out. So where did you go to high school? Are you from Minnesota?"

"No, Wisconsin, actually. I moved here about nine months ago for school. Mine doesn't really have a theater program though." He made a sad face. "But it is something I'd like to pursue."

"That's cool. What are you going to school for?" I was curious.

"Some IT crap. I go to a business college. It's a tough schedule, but I'll be done a lot sooner," he told me. "And it's the perfect excuse to not have to go home for every holiday without getting nagged at." He really could find the silver lining of just about any situation.

"I know what you mean. Speaking of being nagged at, I'm pretty sure my boyfriend left me voicemail earlier. I should probably break down and listen to it. If I'm lucky, it'll be him admitting he's wrong. Then I can just replay it again and again." I tried to laugh it off, but I really wasn't looking forward to hearing what he had to say.

"My boyfriend knows better. We don't get to see a lot of each other during the week. So he knows if he irritates me, I can stretch out the time between our visits." He laughed. "I just had to teach him that I don't need him to be happy. I'm happy being single, but I make myself available to him because I choose to." He shrugged, making it all seem so simple, and I admired him for that.

"True. Very true." I knew I had to face reality. "Well, I have to go see what my 'complication' requires of me. Are you going to be working Wednesday nights too?"

"Of course. I'll be here!" He sounded so excited about it. Now I knew he was an actor.

"Cool, well, I'll see you around then. I'm going to work double shifts on Wednesdays." I got up to walk out to my car and realized I had to decide whether to go home or to Aaron's. No one was home either way, but I wasn't looking forward to either place. I figured I'd listen to his message to help break the tie.

I got into my car and got settled and finally listened to what Aaron had to say about the previous evening. I was anticipating an apology but found the message to be somewhat lacking.

"Hey, it's me. Call me back," he said. He sounded somewhat monotone, so it was a little difficult to hear how sorry he was.

I figured this had to end sooner or later, so I would have to be the better person. It was hard to dial his number, but I knew it had to be done. The phone rang a few times, and as I was about to hang up, he finally answered.

"Hey." He sounded out of breath.

"Hey, are you at work?" I asked, trying to sound casual.

"Yeah, that's why it took me a minute to answer. I had to run back to the office. So what are you doing?" he asked, even though I'm sure he knew what I was doing since I had a pretty tight schedule.

"You know, the usual. I just got done with work and have to head to dress rehearsal for Friday," I said, reminding him again of the importance of that evening.

"Well, I have a surprise for you. I reworked my schedule so I could make it to opening night," he said.

I was starting to recognize that he had a habit of doing something nice when he knew he was wrong. He would never admit it, of course, but luckily his actions could speak louder than his words. I couldn't help but smile. "That'd be great. And we can go out afterwards for the cast party."

"Sounds good. So, are you coming over tonight, you know, so we can work out the details?" He was so cute when he was avoiding the subject.

I, on the other hand, wanted to cut to the chase. "Okay. But just to give you a heads up, your dirty clothes are right where you left them after freaking out on me last night."

"All right, all right, I get it. I'm sorry. I'm just under a lot of stress with the new job. There, I said it. Besides, I got up early and got it done," he confessed.

"Good. Because last time I checked, I'm not your mother," I reminded him.

"No, you're not. She cooks better." He was trying to be funny.

"Really? Well, no worries then. I'll let you show me one of her recipes when you get home from your long, stressful day," I replied.

"Ha-ha. All right, well, I have to get back to work. I'll see you when I get home. Love you." He sounded rushed.

"Love you too, bye." I finished and hung up. Hopefully the day would stay on this track, making it easier to concentrate on the finishing touches for the play.

I walked in to the crew making final adjustments to the set. I was a little early, so I wasn't expecting to run into any other cast members. I ran into the woman in charge of wardrobe, and she decided it would be the perfect time to try on the dress I would be wearing in the second scene.

It was a floor-length purple formal, long sleeved with sparkles embedded in the fabric. Apparently, it still needed to be hemmed, but it was still a little more flattering than the two-piece business suit with the silk blouse that had two flowing pieces connected to the collar so that I could tie one of those large bows that looked like it came from straight out of the eighties.

I didn't have to worry about styling my hair since I would be utilizing a wig to make my hair look like that of a sixty-year-old woman. My costumes were pretty much set, and I felt good about the script since I had spent almost every night either at rehearsal or just going over it on my own.

Rehearsal took a little longer since everyone had their final wardrobe checks before we started. Other than having to check each costume before each scene, things went very smoothly. Before I knew it, we were through the timely session and our director had already delivered final instructions for the final rehearsal that would occur the following evening.

I was finished with my long, tedious day and was heading over to Aaron's. With the longer rehearsal, I hadn't had a chance to have dinner. Aaron beat me home with some takeout food for us. Now I could tell he really was sorry. I was met at the door with a kiss and an offer to fetch me a beverage to go with our late dinner.

"Oh, orange chicken. Smells good." I started digging into one of the takeout boxes. "Are there egg rolls too?"

"And cream cheese puffs." He pointed out.

"I'm starting to think you're spoiling me." I winked. "Maybe you should be a prick more often. Wait, scratch that." I didn't bother getting my own plate. I just wanted to dig into everything.

"Well, nothing's too good for my baby. And again, I'm sorry about that. It's going to be a compromise for both of us, but I'm really looking forward to it," he said, leaning in to give me a kiss.

I was more focused on my food, but I tried to give him a side kiss without turning my head or letting any food fall out of my mouth. It was somewhat less than romantic, but I was pretty sure he got the point.

He got the point that I was starving, and it wouldn't be a good time to get any action, so he started trying to get into some of the food before it was gone and changed the subject.

"So is everyone ready for the show on Friday?" he asked between bites.

"Yeah, I think we're good to go," I responded. "I'm glad you're coming to opening night." I took a break from eating and looked up to make eye contact so that he would know I was serious.

"I know. I'm glad I get to come. It seems pretty important to you," he replied.

"It is. We've all been working on it for months," I reminded him.

"Well, is it because you've been spending all this time on it, or is it because it's something you really want to do?" he asked.

It seemed like a very obvious question. I hadn't thought about it that way. Why do we put all the time and effort into projects like this? Projects that don't provide a paycheck, cause us to rearrange our schedules, and even add stress due to the unwritten requirement to provide a quality performance. He really made me think. It wasn't even a conscious decision on my part. I welcomed the chaos of the production into my life. The answer to his question was as obvious as the soy sauce on the egg rolls.

My mind started to wander. I almost felt like I was becoming a part of an actors' anonymous group and professing my addiction. My name is Lisa, and I'm an actress. I could picture the scene: Beautiful people sitting in a circle, each of them with a monologue in hand. And everyone waiting his or her turn to speak about the repercussions, good and bad, that the industry has had their lives. It was like a support group, to help each other through the bad auditions, drop hints about where to find the legit ones, and tips on how to nail them. Who knew how true that statement was? After a brief moment of fantasy, I was back to reality.

"I do. I really want to do it." I turned back to my food and continued eating. "It's something I want to pursue." It felt good to say it out loud, to admit it to myself.

A couple of days and a juggling act of school, work, and rehearsal later, it was opening night. I had a smaller part and wasn't incredibly worried. I was actually looking forward to it. This is what we had prepared for. I had a mix of nerves and endorphins, an addicting feeling provided only by certain experiences throughout our lives. Experiences that anyone else might avoid, mock, or even be intimidated by. Only actors can truly appreciate it. And it added to the excitement to think that not only were my mother and my sister in the audience to support me but so was Aaron. And I loved him even more for it.

This was a much larger stage and audience than that of grade school, but I felt I had a lot more to offer this time. I waited behind the curtains offstage, listening carefully to the lines to wait for my cue. I finally felt that I had somewhat conquered the difficulty of my character's accent. And if not, what the hell, it was a comedic play anyway.

There it was, the preparation for my entrance. I felt good about my lines, my delivery, and my costume, now all I had to do was not trip over the props on the set. It seemed simple enough, and the time had come.

I entered the stage, the lights were incredibly bright, and I couldn't see any audience members, except for those sitting in the end seats and out of the direct glare on the stage.

"Well, hello," I delivered my first line, and from there, I knew the entire play would be smooth sailing.

The costume changes went smoothly, everyone remembered his lines and blocking, and we ended with an incredible applause from the audience. It sounded even better, considering it wasn't a sympathy appreciation from doting parents, unable to see their own children's flaws. These were strangers, who were showing us their appreciation for our performances.

Our family members and friends and random audience members found us after the show to congratulate us on jobs well done. One of the other drama professors, who had seemed indifferent to this production, had even gone down the line of actors and congratulated us each individually.

He leaned in to talk over the loudness of the crowd exiting the theater. "Great job. If I were you, I would buy that purple dress from them." I was flattered. I hadn't thought there was any physical appeal to my character, and I was flattered to be recognized.

All the hard work and long days had paid off. It was time to relax and party. You can really get to know other actors in your production, but on stage it can be under false pretenses. Good or bad, you're actually getting to know their characters. It was fun to get to know the real people without the pressure of performing. It was almost like making first impressions all over again. I might not get to know them as well as their characters, but one thing I knew for sure, it had felt really good to stand on the stage after that show, next to the other actors, and take a bow.

[?]

Chapter 8

Being finished with the play was both a blessing and a curse. On the positive side, my schedule was more open and the only things I had to focus on were school, work, and Aaron. On the flip side, I had plenty of time to pursue headshots and local auditions for independent films. As it turned out, one of the girls in the production had the perfect photographer to capture the perfect headshot I would need to manipulate the opinion of any casting director in my favor. I was skeptical but agreed to check out the website and a few weeks later decided to make the appointment.

Headshots, as I was to find out, were not going to be one of my strong points. Photo shoots involving productions were pretty easy since everyone in front of the camera only had to play a character. With headshots, I had to bring my own character to the mix. While simple, even insignificant for most actors, this felt like a lot of pressure for me. How could one smile portray every kind of character? Would recipients notice all the same flaws I saw? How could I capture onlookers' attention with one picture?

I knew I was overthinking it, but I couldn't help it. After checking out the reviews online, I decided to trust the photographer and the makeup artist/hairstylist. A little on edge, it was almost a relief to think that someone else had to worry about making my hair and makeup look good and capturing every flattering angle. My shoot was a week away, and I was trying not to worry about it, but even in the short time they may have known me, the people around me could tell that something important was on my mind. It was at my next shift with Mike that someone actually called me out on it.

I approached my first table of the evening with a positive, can-do attitude. Lucky for me, all I had to do was follow a protocol and everything would go well. I put on my work smile and greeted the table. "Hello! I'm Lisa. I'll be taking care of you this evening. Can I start you off with a beverage or an appetizer?"

I did the usual and made eye contact with the first of four customers on my left, who ordered a soda. The trend continued until I got to guest number three, who ordered an Arnie Palmer.

"Sounds great!" I said, jotting down the name I had never heard of. "Can I see your ID?"

It was a logical question, and I was proud of myself to remember to card anyone ordering a drink who appeared to be under the age of thirty. The customer still seemed confused by my question and gave me a strange look as he fished out his wallet. "Um, okay, but I don't think you need it."

"Well, the law is the law. And I'm afraid we all have to abide by it." I smiled, remaining the calm voice of reason.

He handed me his ID, and by this point the entire table shared in his confused expression, communicating the mutual feeling of amusement through eye contact as I motioned for him to hand me his ID. I looked it over and made sure not only that he was of legal drinking age but that there were also no alcohol restrictions. I winked and handed the card back and finished with the final drink order and an assurance that I'd be right back with the drinks.

I wasn't sure how to ring up the third drink. I thought I had paid pretty close attention, but I couldn't remember if it was rum or vodka. Then I realized, I should have utilized the opportunity to up sell the liquor. But first thing was first, I had to figure out how to ring this thing up. I didn't want to seem stupid to my former trainer or as if I wasn't paying attention to the wisdom she had imposed upon me, so I went to a familiar source.

And lucky for me, he was already standing right by the computer.

"Hey Mike, how do I ring up an Arnie Palmer?"

I tried to say it quietly, but apparently Mike didn't realize the extent of my naiveté. "Um, I think you just ring up the lemonade and then go fill it the rest of the way with iced tea. Hey, that's the second time table number 18 has stopped me to get a refill. Isn't that your section?" Mike asked, refilling glasses for his own tables.

"Yeah, I'm sorry. I'm on it. I just have to run this food out to number 19 first," I replied, starting to dread the fact that I had to face this table again, trying to figure out how I would play this off as a joke and somehow recapture my efficiency.

"What's up? Is something wrong?" he asked. I could tell it was a legitimate question. Genuine concern just takes a different tone when you're in the middle of a dinner rush. This will generally consist of bitchy tables who need something every time you walk by; tables with small children where the parents haven't established enough authority through deal making to order their children out of your path, essentially preventing them and the server from tripping and being harmed by heavy glass plates; and the silent tables who communicate nothing and basically leave you the same equivalent in tips after they leave. To the random onlooker, it may seem very simple, but oddly enough, it can all be very time and energy consuming. This was the joy of multitasking.

"Oh, it's stupid. No big deal. I'll get the refill. They shouldn't be bothering you anymore," I lied.

"No biggie, just don't want them to be bitches to you," he warned. "You can tell they're one of those tables who's looking for any excuse not to spend money on the tip."

He was right. Anyone who has worked in any type of service industry that includes tips can always tell who is and who isn't going to tip. While I loved to be wrong about my first impressions of customers, it usually turned out that I was right. And the needy table was no exception.

I dropped off the drinks and made an attempt at the best stand-up impression I could perform. "I'm so deaf. I thought you said, um, Long Island Tea." Even I knew it was a failed attempt, so I hurried to finish taking their food orders and prayed for a way to walk away from the table gracefully.

"Excuse me. Excuse me, can I get my refill please." Her voice was like nails on a blackboard, but it shook me out of my self-induced stressed state. "Oh, and can I get change for this five-dollar bill?" This was never a good combination of questions, especially when the change represented less than 10 percent of the overall total of the bill. However, my shitty, cheap, demanding table couldn't have called me at a better time.

After the three-dollar lesson I learned from that table, I tried to spend the rest of my shift focusing on the task at hand and trying not to be stupid about my job and petty about the upcoming shoot. After a night of ups and downs, I retreated to a night of safety. Since I had worked a double shift, Aaron was actually done with work before I got home.

It was nice to go home to someone being there and welcoming me back. He greeted me with a short kiss and a generic "How was your day?" I told him it was good, but fortunately, or unfortunately, he knew me better than that.

"Come on, what's on your mind? Midterms are pretty much over. The play's done. You're out of training and making real money?" His last statement turned into more of a question.

"Yeah, I know. I'm just a little nervous about that shoot for my headshots," I told him.

"Why, you said you checked the woman out, and she was legit," he reminded me. "What's the big deal?"

"I'm just nervous. I mean, I'm not a model. How am I going to get a decent shot that doesn't look like I'm posing for a high school yearbook?" I asked him.

"Well, you know, just don't do that over your shoulder, staring off at the sky thing," he joked and then struck a pose. "You know, if you're nice to me, I might be willing to give you a few pointers."

I couldn't help but laugh at him. He had one finger pointing up to the side of his chin, and he struck several different poses, attempting to look shy. I appreciated his attempts. Stupid as it may seem, I had been stressing about the shoot since I made the appointment and needed a good laugh.

"Yuck. I'll get over it. I just want to get it over with!" I stated, playfully pushing him so he fell over on the couch and would stop modeling for me.

"Yuck? I'm insulted. I thought I was catalog ready. You have no idea how hard it is to strut like that," he said, making a playful sad face.

"What, and maintain your dignity?" I stuck my tongue out at him.

"I'm secure. Come on, quit overthinking everything so much. It'll work out."

Finally, the morning had arrived. I gathered the plain outfits I was told to bring. The drive to the photographer's studio seemed to take forever. It was in one of the further suburbs, in a business district, so I had a lot of time to think. It probably was a really stupid thing to stress about, but I had never posed for headshots before. Acting was the seemingly easy part. You could justify your character through lines and blocking. But when it came to headshots, you wanted casting directors to justify a character with the expression from your one photo. No wonder models always looked so serious, even crabby. Any other expression would have made the rest of their bodies being in the shot obsolete, which would have made the pic a headshot. This picture thing was way too complicated. The silent debate almost turned the somewhat short drive into a long trip. But I was there.

I noticed right away that the studio I was looking for was located in a more casual strip of office spaces. I walked in the front door to a hallway leading straight back to elevators, and long hallways to the left and right, both lined with doorways every ten feet. Luckily, there was a sign on the wall to direct the random onlooker, such as me, to the right suite. Off to the right I went.

I found the right door, suite 110. The door was plain, obviously designed to match the other doors in the hallway. Expecting a reception area, I opened the door to find that I was stepping immediately onto the set. There were extremely high ceilings and, on one side of the room, a desk with makeup scattered all over it and a mirror on the wall just above it. There were a couple of flat irons and hair products, but I didn't see anyone standing around the desk to utilize any of these things.

Looking over on the opposite side of the space, closer to the windows and natural light, was a large, white backdrop with lights right above it and on both corners. With colored tape, there was a small X centered with the sheet and located about ten feet in front of a large camera on a tripod. Along the wall there were other props, other equipment, and what looked like other backdrops, neatly rolled up, available for use at some point. There was a smaller table next to these props with a laptop, speakers, and other office supplies.

I wasn't sure exactly how to get started, but luckily, there were two women standing at the desk, looking over a few papers and quietly discussing its content. Having never met her in person, I assumed this was the photographer and, most likely, the makeup artist.

"Hello. Are you Lisa?" the woman asked, setting down her clipboard and walking toward me with her hand extended.

"Yeah, I'm here for my headshots." I did have a flare for the obvious.

"Great. I'm going to be taking them. Go ahead and set your things down over by the makeup station. You can set out the shirts you brought, and we'll decide which one is best for your photos." She looked at the other woman and asked her to go get Aspen. Assuming then that she was an assistant to the photographer, I wasn't sure if I was more relaxed in knowing that there were multiple people working on making my shoot a quality project or if I was dreading the audience.

"Great." I smiled. It was all I could think of to say. I walked over to the makeup station and found a clear spot on the table. I started unzipping my bag, and suddenly another woman was coming to greet me.

"Hey, I'm Aspen. I'll be doing your hair and makeup today. Let's see what you brought for outfits." She sounded ready to get to work. She smelled, however, like she was coming back from her fifth smoke break of the day. Seemingly serious about her craft, she looked very interesting. It was as if she was passionate about her artistic expression or had just come back from band practice. She had a green hombre; eyebrow, lip, and nose rings; and trendy black glasses with thicker frames. She had on thick black eyeliner and bright red lipstick, somewhat like a pinup ad from the forties. Her black apron covered up her brightly colored shirt and jeans, but her nails were neatly painted with black polish.

"I brought three different shirts. All solid colors." I told her, pulling the shirts out of my bag one by one.

"Okay," she said, popping a piece of gum in her mouth and then grabbing each shirt to hold up in front of me. She seemed to be quietly studying each piece. And having one in each hand, after about five minutes of trading them out, she suggested we go with the light-blue shirt. She told me that we would be doing hair and makeup first.

It was incredibly relaxing having someone else do my hair and makeup. I figured she would know what type of look the photographer was wanting to see. After about a half hour of being face- to-face with Aspen and with her making strange faces as she was studying mine, we were finally finished. She handed me a mirror to check out the finished product. I was excited to see what she had done. I held up the mirror and was somewhat surprised. After all her huffing and puffing and recreating the expression of the tortured artist, I looked very plain.

"Oh, okay." It was all I could think of to say.

"We want you to look natural," Aspen responded, focusing on rearranging her makeup brushes.

Adding my courtesy smile to my signature look, I set the mirror down and waited to be told what to do next.

"Go ahead and put the blue shirt on," she said, still too busy to make eye contact as she delivered the instructions. "Then you can walk over and stand in front of the backdrop."

"Sounds good," I responded. I wasn't sure it looked good, but she made it sound simple enough.

I made my way across the room to the backdrop and waited for the photographer to come and instruct me. I felt out of place just standing around, but it was sort of cool to see all the lighting and equipment it took to put together a decent photo.

After working on her laptop while she was waiting for me to get ready, the photographer stood up from the stool she had been sitting on and turned around to head toward her camera, which was just a few feet right on front of me. The wall had large windows, and the curtains were open to reveal the almost blinding sunlight. She turned on the lights, and they added a lot to the blind factor. It was hard to look at the camera with my eyes wide open. But as she instructed, that's what I had to do.

I turned my head and adjusted my stance and facial expressions per her ongoing instructions. It seemed to be going a lot more smoothly than I had originally anticipated, and I hoped this would help me to relax and get a good shot. I figured she would take charge and tell me if I had a hair out of place, an unflattering roll bulging over the waistline of my pants, or just a booger hanging out of my nose. And in exchange I would try to keep my eyes wide open and stare across the light-soaked platform and into the lens of the camera.

We got through it, and it was time to see what we had gathered. I've never been fond of staring at pictures of myself and welcomed her input as to which pictures would be sufficient to represent what I had to offer in the finicky world of auditioning. I didn't see any I really liked. I didn't think any of them even looked that good. I thought the shots of me staring into the sun made me look like I was in pain. And, on the flip side, the pictures of me smiling instead of being blinded made me look like I was posing for a yearbook or a graduation picture. Hopefully she would direct me toward some sort of middle man that would work in my favor.

She picked out a few that she said looked very promising. Drawn to my own flaws, I didn't see the appeal but figured she was the expert. So I picked out the lesser of the evils and agreed to make 150 copies. Wrapping the session up with the payment, I gathered my things and headed for my car. I was relieved to have it over and done with. But I also hoped that in the mad rush to get it done, I hadn't sacrificed any quality I could possibly contribute to my own picture. I had definitely learned something new about myself. I had always been pretty outgoing and was comfortable, even loved, to perform on stage. But in front of a simple photo camera, I felt very shy.

I had to be back in a week to pick up the shots. I figured it would be pretty easy to remember how to get there since it was just a few blocks off the freeway. Now all I had to do was concentrate on anything else.

I was hoping Aaron would be home when I got there so I could tell him all about my exciting afternoon. I liked hearing his opinions on certain situations. He always made things sound better, especially when he knew I was being ridiculous and overthinking them. I stopped to check on the mail, and when the box was full, I knew he wasn't home yet. I cleaned it out and carried my bag into the apartment. I set it on the table and walked over to the couch to sit down and dig through the letters. They were mostly bills. I laid them out and figured out what my share was. I was discovering the benefits of having cash at the end of my shifts made it easier to deposit my part of the bills into Aaron's account. With the slow process of transitioning my life into his apartment, one of the first things Aaron wanted to do was to add my name to his bank account. I could see the logic for paying bills, but I wanted to keep everything else separate until I was finished with school.

I was relaxing and watching television when Aaron got home. I could tell by the look on his face that he hadn't had the best day and simply smiled at him and waited for him to make the first sound. Unfortunately, it wasn't the friendliest of greetings.

"Wow, you really have to leave your bag on the table like that?" he asked, setting his keys next to it on the table.

"Oh, sorry, I was gonna move it before you got home. I got tied up in the mail. Lots of fun stuff," I informed him.

"Great. Bills? I don't even get paid until next Friday," he informed me. "Did you already put your check in the account?" he asked me while he was looking over the amounts due.

"Well, no, I have my half right here. Do you want me to put that in the account tomorrow?"I asked him, treading lightly since I knew money was one of the least favorite topics around the apartment.

"Why don't you just use the joint account?" He was starting to get annoyed.

"I told you, with school payments and everything, it's just easier to put my half of the bills into your account. Once I'm done with school, my money can be our money. But until then I think we should keep separate finances." I hated having to explain myself to him yet again. I was pretty sure I had figured out why couples fought over money.

"So, basically, you don't trust me." He looked me right in the eye as he said it.

"I never said that! Believe it or not, this is my contribution to peace and sanity about money. We just have to be sure and communicate about the bills. It's not the most fun topic, but we have to show the bills to one another. Right?" I was trying to justify my side of the argument. I really didn't think things had to be this difficult. "Now quit being crabby. Let's go out for dinner and celebrate my new pics."

He was still being a jerk. "Why is that a reason to celebrate?"

"Because I was really nervous about getting a good headshot. I think I got one," I told him.

"Well, let me see it. Why were you nervous? It's just a picture," he said, expecting me to show him what I had worked on all day.

"I don't have them yet. I have to pick them up next week. I know it seems stupid, but I don't know how models do it. How is one picture worth a thousand words?" I joked. But he was right, it was probably stupid to get myself so worked up about the process. I stuck my tongue out at him.

"Well, if it's a picture of you, I'm sure it's hot," he replied.

"You charmer." I gave him a kiss. "You're just trying to suck up for coming home and being such a jerk." I had to forgive him though. I wasn't sure what it was exactly, but he had some sort of power over me, and I couldn't stay mad at him. I guess this is what they called love. And as long as we both felt this strongly, I hoped these little kinks would work themselves out and occur less and less as we learned and accepted each other's habits. "Besides, we need to go shopping. I need to pick out a costume for work."

"I thought they gave you guys uniforms." He sounded less than thrilled to have to go shopping.

"They do, but I guess we get to dress up for Halloween," I told him. "So what do you say, you wanna help me pick something out?"

"I've been on my feet all day, dealing with rude people trying to use expired coupons on expensive tennis shoes.

There's nothing else I'd rather do," he said with a fake smile.

"And I love you for it." I smiled back.

"I must love you too," he said, standing up and walking toward his keys.

We took his car, and as we were pulling out of the parking garage, we were trying to decide what type of food we wanted. Dinner would fuel the shopping fun that would follow, so we narrowed our choices to restaurants around the nearest mall.

We hit a red light right outside of the parking lot of the apartment building. In spite of his mood swings, Aaron was a very affectionate boyfriend and he liked to hold hands when we drove anywhere.

Sitting at the red light, Aaron looked at me and smiled. "Let's go elope," he said.

"What?" I was genuinely surprised by the statement.

"Come on. I love you. You love me. We should just get married," he argued.

"Well, I want a huge wedding, so we'll have to wait until I'm done with school," I argued back.

He wasn't deferred by my answer. "Nah, let's just go to Vegas. We can save that money for our honeymoon."

"But, sweetie, every day with you is like a honeymoon." I tried to end the conversation with a joke.

"Whatever. I think we should do it." He seemed less than amused but was willing to take the hint and change the subject.

Dinner went well, as I just let Aaron vent about his day at work—the good, the bad, and the ugly of customer service. It seemed to do him well to get it out of his system. Besides, I'd rather have him bitching to me instead of at me.

We finished dinner and headed out into the mall. I wasn't sure what I wanted to wear to work. It was a family restaurant, but I still wanted something fun, maybe even flattering. Larger tips would never hurt anyone.

We studied the map of the mall and found a Halloween store on the other side of the mall. We started our journey, and I figured this would be a good time to text Mike and find out what kind of costume he was planning to wear. I started typing and falling behind, and Aaron became curious.

"Who are you texting?" he asked. The question came out as if it was a substitute for simply telling me to hurry up.

"It's Mike from work. I want to know what kind of costume he's getting," I answered, still walking slowly and typing.

"You guys exchanged phone numbers?" He seemed more curious about the message.

"Yeah, I was going to trade a shift with him. I'm glad I have it though," I told him.

"Should I be worried about this?" he asked in a passive-aggressive way. "Is he single?"

"That is so cute. You're jealous." I stop walking and texting and looked at him. "Well, no, but if he were, he'd be more interested in you. And you're taken, so why are you asking about him. Should I be worried?"

"Shut up. I'm not jealous. You just haven't really told me much about your new job or any of your coworkers." He made a motion for me to start walking again. "Now, come on."

"Well, I've only been there a few weeks. Mike was hired at the same time I was." I went back to finishing my text. "It's cool that there are other new people. Then if something goes wrong, I'm not the only suspect. And he's interested in acting too."

"Oh, good. Has he told you about his costume yet?" He sounded less than interested.

"Yeah, I guess he's going to be a zombie. He said it's a pretty simple costume," I answered.

Mike didn't strike me as the kind of guy that would do anything in a "simple" way. But I figured he was probably doing it since he would be wearing it while serving food. This made the think the best way to go was to just get one of those costumes that came in a bag with all the accessories.

We walked into the Halloween store, and the teenager working to stock the racks hollered out a generic, "Can I help you find anything?"

"No. No, thanks." I looked around. There wasn't much left to choose from, for women's costumes anyway.

"I like this one." Aaron had picked up a bag with a picture of a go-go dancer in a skimpy tube top, mini skirt, and platform heels on.

"Yeah, I bet you do." I hung the bag back on the rack. "I do have to wear this at work."

We both started shuffling through bag after bag. They all seemed to have common themes: professional skank and just plain skanky. There was the naughty nurse, an all spandex devil, a sexy cop, and a French maid.

I appreciated the fact that none of my coworkers had ever seen me naked and believed that the devil costume would accentuate the lack of mystery about my body parts, so I could count that one out. The police uniform was incredibly short, low cut, and skintight. Serving can get a little crazy during the height of a meal rush. One deep breath in that costume and I'd probably pop a button and be able to arrest myself for public nudity, so I could count that one out too. While it was a risk to wear bright white while working with food, I thought the nurse costume looked respectable enough to wear. However, I knew I wouldn't be able to squeeze into a dress that was two sizes too small and had to cross that one off the list.

The French maid won by default. It seemed loose enough that I wouldn't be showing off my "daily specials." The neck and shoulders had elastic, so I was pretty sure I could wear the neckline high enough to keep the customers from avoiding eye contact. And it seemed long enough that I could pick up dropped silverware without blushing.

"That one's hot too," Aaron informed me.

"Well, it's not my first choice, but it'll work. And I won't be put out of work for wearing it, I don't think." I wasn't sold but didn't have any other option at the moment. "I probably shouldn't have waited until the last minute. All right, French maid it is."

After waiting at the counter for a few minutes, the teenager finally noticed us and slowly walked over to check us out. She went through the tedious process of going through the clear costume bag to make sure that everything listed on the side was actually in there. I appreciated the reason behind her effort, but the process of buying it painfully slower than finding it in the first place. Finally, we got to pay and leave.

"See, that wasn't so bad," I told him.

"Nah, it wasn't so bad. Want to try it on for me when we get home?" he asked.

His joking around told me that he was in a good mood, so I played along. "Maybe, is there some cleaning to do?"

"I'm sure there's something to do. My girlfriend tends to leave little messes here and there," he said.

"If she's really that bad, I could just let you borrow the costume and clean it up yourself?" I asked, giving him the "be careful or you'll be sleeping alone" look.

"Point taken." He quickly changed the subject. "Are we heading home now?"

"Yeah, I got everything I need," I answered.

A few days later, it was time to put my costume on. I had bought fishnet stockings to go with the costume and had an old pair of black two-inch heels. I figured since they were shorter, they wouldn't kill my feet by the end of the night. I put on my makeup, including bright red lipstick, and pinned my hair up and put the headband on. I had planned on wearing short biker short underneath the dress, just to be on the safe side. I figured that even though I would have to tie on my black apron for work, it still made sense to tie on the little apron because if nothing else, it would at least appear to look like a little white belt. I put on the dress and looked in the mirror.

It wasn't what I expected at all. I thought I had made the right choice, picking out the more respectable of the skanky costumes. I probably should have tried it on. It wasn't as long as it seemed in the picture and trying to get the shoulders and neckline to stay up at a respectable level was going to be interesting. I contemplated just wearing my work uniform and telling my tables that my uniform was actually my costume, but I knew that was lame, and we had all agreed to dress up. I didn't have any other options. I was a little nervous about wearing it all night, but figured there would probably be another female somewhere in the restaurant, employee or customer, modeling something far more revealing.

Even after the self-pep talk, I was a little unsure with how my costume would be received. So I put my uniform in a bag to take it with me, just in case. Luckily, the weather had taken a cooler turn, and it seemed logical that I should wear a jacket. It would also give me a little wiggle room to scope out the other costumes when I got to work and see if mine would pass.

I pulled into the parking lot and tried to find a spot somewhat close to the front door, just in case I would have to rush out and make a costume change before I punched in. I walked up to the door and slowly opened it and walked in, hoping to spot other employees who had dressed up for the shift. I made my way back toward the kitchen, and suddenly, something caught my attention. I was stopped in my tracks when I saw him, and I'm pretty sure I performed a double take, to be sure of what I was actually seeing. It was Mike. He was sitting in a booth, finishing a pre-shift meal, and he was dressed up like a zombie.

When he had told me that he was going to dress as a zombie for Halloween, I expected torn clothes, maybe some pale makeup on his skin with darker circles around his eyes. I could see that he had put a lot more effort into it than just some eye shadow.

"Holy shit! You look awesome!" I told him as walked over to the booth to sit down with him.

"Hah! Thanks! What are you wearing?" he asked, taking another bite.

"Oh, just something from the Halloween store. How did you put this all together?" I inquired.

Between uncontrollable laughing fits, he described how he had put the whole thing together.

"The clothes were easy, just rip up the sleeves and the bottoms of the pants, and splatter them with cheap red dye. The veins are just rolled up toilet paper dipped in homemade plaster with red food coloring, you know with the flour and water. Then you just stick them on your face or wherever. And then you just dribble the red dye so it looks like dripping blood. It's all actually really easy. You just make a big mess," he explained. "Hopefully customers aren't too grossed out."

I couldn't help but laugh at his costume. It was gory and great. And as long as nothing dripped onto some vegetarian customer's salad, it would be a big hit for the occasion. Sitting and chatting with Mike, I had found out early on, usually consisted of each of us getting in a story or two here and there and then spending the next five minutes fighting to catch our breaths from laughing so hard. I was very grateful to have him as a coworker. No matter how stressful things got, he always had an amazing attitude and was able to lighten any tension.

"Now spill it. What are you wearing under your coat? Or are you keeping it on until they tip you enough to convince you to show them what's underneath?" he said it while rubbing his hands together as if I had put together some evil plot. It was hard to humor his attempt to sound evil when he looked so ridiculous.

"No, no strippers here. Besides, I can barely give that away to Aaron," I informed him. "I'm a respectable employee. Somewhat like a janitor, if you will." I was pretty sure he was wondering what the hell I was talking about, but I was clutching at straws.

He had a confused look on his face and looked at me with one eyebrow raised. "A kinky janitor?"

"Can janitors be kinky?"

We both had a good long laugh at the question.

Another one of our coworkers came to sit down with us. She tried to get in on the conversation but seemed to be thrown that we were laughing so hard and she couldn't see any reason why. She was also wearing a costume, a skimpy cop costume.

It made me feel like I had made a little more of a conservative choice, so I knew I'd be safe from getting into any unforeseen trouble with my manager. So I decided to take off my coat and show Mike my costume. When I removed my coat, I noticed that the neckline and shoulders had slid down, revealing my bra straps, and accentuated my somewhat limited cleavage. I adjusted the top of the dress to cover everything up. While this look would make me a lot of money working in a sports bar, it seemed less than appropriate for the family restaurant.

"Oh, you look good. If my boyfriend wouldn't kick my ass for it, I'd be tempted to ask if you and the girls there want to hang out after work," he joked.

"You're hilarious. Let's see if me and the girls can make some decent tips tonight." I matched his humor. "Do we even know what sections we're going to be in tonight? Hopefully I'm just working the bar area."

"You're probably in section five!" He could barely get it out without laughing and almost choking on his last few bites.

"Hell, no." I gave him a skeptical look. But if I was, some good could come out of it. This section typically housed larger parties, including families. When several people were getting together to have dinner, it was usually to celebrate a positive occasion. When families consisting of more than two children came to sit in the section, it was usually to take advantage of a coupon. If the men were paying, they'd most likely leave me good tips in exchange for the visual appetizer. If the women were paying, they'd most likely try and punish me, through lack of a decent tip, for giving their men the visual dessert they wanted to provide. Either way, I was hopeful things would just balance out and we could all have a fun night.

Once we were finished trading beauty secrets, we had to join the pre-shift meeting in the kitchen. The range of costumes wasn't as amusing as I thought it would be. Our manager had simply worn scrubs. I wondered why I hadn't thought of something so simple and comfortable. She looked at the ten of us, and it was hard to read her expression. But her words summed it up.

She stuck to the scripted topics of projected sales and announced the servers who would be checking us out at the end of our shifts. As we were all scattering to our sections, I heard her talking to Mike and asking him how he put his costume together. But while listening to his answer, she was looking at me and the police officer. "Yeah, I don't know if we're going to be able to do this again next year."

"No kidding. Three people showing up with the same costume, how embarrassing!" He laughed.

"What? Who showed up in the same costumes?" She was literally confused.

"You saw the three that dressed up like Pommes servers. Looks like they should've discussed their outfits. Aren't servers supposed to communicate? Yuck! How awkward," he said, walking towards the exit to the dining area.

It took her a minute, but she finally understood, and even laughed at what he had told her. She didn't say anything about anyone having to change out of his or her costume, so it seemed logical to just look good and be confident with what I was wearing. As long as I didn't drop anything and have to bend over or crouch down into a yoga position to pick it up, it could be a smooth night.

The dinner rush started early, and people were pouring in. Some were wearing costumes, and some had children with them who were wearing costumes. People seemed amused by our outfits, and I was pretty sure I'd heard a few tables teasing the three servers who had decided not to participate.

About halfway through the shift, I was starting to realize why I had never worn heels to work before. My feet were already killing me, and larger parties naturally came with a lot more refills. On one of my many trips to the soda machine, I passed by Mike and he told me that one of his tables had complimented me on how I looked in my costume. Even though my feet were literally throbbing, I couldn't help but smile. It was flattering to be noticed, even in this costume and even though I was wearing it to celebrate Halloween. It was almost like performing for an audience and getting a positive review. The compliment also made me feel a little better about the whole headshot thing. It's amazing how far a few positive words can go.

"Maybe it's because I look better standing next to you. People aren't afraid that I'll ooze all over their buffalo wings," I told him.

"No, they laugh at my costume. It's because that outfit is incredibly flattering on you," he corrected me.

"Oh, stop, you'll make me blush." I laughed again. "Can you imagine the following I'd have if I had a feather duster?"

"No, actually, I think people would prefer me oozing on their food as opposed to you getting dust all over their fries from some nasty-looking duster. Besides, how would you carry that and four plates?" he asked. "And seriously, would it match your shoes? Just stick with the outfit."

"Trust me, I'm ready to ditch the shoes. Seriously," I told him.

The rest of the night was filled with interested looks from men and side glares from women. I was incredibly grateful when the manager told me I was cut for the night. My feet were ready to explode. My closing side work seemed to take forever, and I couldn't wait to sit down, even if it was just for the few minutes it took to check out with the manager.

All the receipts were accounted for, and my larger-than-usual tips were collected. I was ready to leave, but as I looked at the unusual bunch sitting in one of the booths after their shifts, I was amused by the after party of washed up characters and couldn't resist asking, "So do you think we can do this again next year?"

She just looked at me, laughed, and rolled her eyes, the answer left to interpretation. But regardless whether we would be celebrating next year, we had a hell of a time this year.

After spending an hour or so sharing stories of our evenings in costume and getting one final laugh at each other, it was time for all of us to go home and take off our costumes. I was happy to wash off my makeup. My coworkers were almost breaking the customer's record for lack of eye contact. I wanted to go home and share the fun with Aaron.

I said good night and wrapped up in my jacket to head out to my car. When I got home, the apartment was quiet and Aaron had left the hall light on for me. I was hoping to sneak in and find him awake so I could show him the costume he had helped me pick out. I did sneak in, but he wasn't awake. I crawled into bed next to him, still wearing the costume. This woke him up enough to have a short chat.

"Hey, babe. How was work?" he asked, eyes still closed.

"It was good, lots of people dressed up." I figured I knew what would wake him up. "Speaking of which, did someone order maid service?" I tried to strike a sexy pose lying next to him.

"Hah, right. I think I scheduled that for tomorrow. I'm the opening manager tomorrow morning." He rolled over to go back to sleep.

"Well, there was a mix up in the schedule, and the maid is here tonight. She even provides bed service." I was running my finger up and down his arm. "She can turn down your sheets, lay out your jammies, or—"

"Seriously. Stop. I need to get some sleep!" he barked, still not looking at me.

I just sighed. It was disappointing. He didn't seem to care about my sexy costume as much as my coworkers and customers. "Fine. I smell like cheeseburgers anyway."

I was a little relieved to take the costume off and put on a comfy pair of pajama pants. I quietly crawled into bed next to him and turned off the light. I was treading lightly since I didn't want to risk waking him up again and unleashing the mayhem. When he moved to roll over, I was bracing for impact. Luckily, he was still asleep but rolled over to spoon and put his arm around my waist. I figured I should relax and appreciate it since it was all the action I was going to get for the night.

A few days later, it was time to go pick up my headshots. I wasn't as nervous about seeing the photographer I had helped pick out the picture that would be used. The only thing that was weighing on my mind was that I hoped they hadn't misspelled my name.

Finding my way back was pretty simple as I had expected, but I still double checked my directions to make sure I was getting off at the right exit. Everything was going smoothly, and the building was just a few blocks away. Like any good driver, I was focusing on the road ahead. There was no way I could get lost now. I could pick up the shots and even get home with a little extra time to relax before my lunch shift. I was relieved not to be in a rush, to actually be ahead of the game. Suddenly, I was proven wrong when my agenda came to a crashing halt.

Chapter 9

There was a loud noise coming from the extreme crashing of the metal and the shattering of the glass. Time stood still for a moment. I didn't remember the initial impact. The first thing I remember was time moving in what seemed to be slow motion. It took me a minute to grasp what had happened. I felt something warm on my lip. I raised my hand to touch it and see what it was. I looked at my fingers. It was blood, and there seemed to be more and more running down my face and onto my shirt. I looked up, and all I could see was the driver's side of a large black van. The driver seemed to be slumped off toward the passenger seat, and the passenger was facing the driver. She seemed frantic, crying and screaming, trying to wake him up.

After only a second of staring at them, I could feel that there was more and more blood rolling down my lip and I tried to grab the closest thing to me to try and catch it. Unfortunately, I was to find envelopes aren't that absorbent.

I wiped away what I could, grabbed my phone, unbuckled my seat belt and tried to get a grasp on what had just happened. I was in shock and couldn't take it all in. I got out of my car to see exactly what I was dealing with. It was like a real-life nightmare. The car I had learned to drive— the one I had to beg my mother for, the one that proved that 1989 was, in fact, a decent year—it was totaled. Knowing it was a used car from the very beginning, that it was functional, but not necessarily visually appealing had never concerned me. The spots of rust and bubbled paint would've redefined the term mint condition in comparison to the fact that the front end was now folded up like an accordion.

And the van that caused it was sitting in a T-bone position, the area all around the driver's side door completely dented in. I was in shock. I noticed the disaster more than any pain or injuries I may have sustained. How could this have happened?

In this short amount of time, the police and multiple ambulances had been called. Their lights were flashing, and their sirens blaring. They parked a few feet back since the scene was framed with broken glass and car parts.

I was bombarded with questions about what had happened. Was I dizzy? Was I able to move all my limbs? I was already out of my car, which I would've thought was a good sign, but they tried to bring me back to the ambulance, insisting that I might have broken limbs but just not feel the pain of the fractures yet due to the initial shock. I could hear them, but it was if I had stepped outside of my body and was just watching them frantically talking to a victim. Not sure what else to do, I walked to the back of the ambulance with the EMTs. I sat on the stretcher while they checked all my vital signs. Everything around me seemed to be moving so quickly, and the police weren't far behind.

With the EMTs poking and prodding me and trying to clean up enough blood to see my face, in particular my nose, where all the blood seemed to be coming from, they were taking notes the entire time. With this process already in motion, I saw that there were policemen already surrounding the other vehicle, still allowing the other ambulance team to remove the driver and passenger. One made his way to the ambulance I was located in and started asking questions about what had happened.

But I couldn't focus, and there was something I had to ask him.

"What happened to the other driver? Please tell me he's not dead! Please tell me I didn't kill anyone!" I could feel the tears running down my cheek, and I was shaking at the thought of anyone having been seriously hurt or even killed in the accident.

"Calm down. Calm down," the EMT was telling me before he turned to speak to the police officer. "Her blood pressure's going up. She needs to relax. We have to get her to the hospital. You can follow us there."

The policeman agreed and had one last question to ask before we left. "Is there anyone we need to contact for you?"

"I need to call my mother and my boyfriend." I still had my phone in my blood-soaked hands. I tried to dial my mother, but the policeman stopped me and told me he would contact her and tell her to meet us at the emergency room. Somehow I was able to give him her information, and he walked back to his car to contact her. I wanted to call Aaron too, though.

I waited until everyone seemed busy filling out paperwork or grabbing more supplies. I dialed, and one of the employees answered the phone with the usual greeting. I asked to speak to Aaron, and the employee cheerfully put me on hold. It seemed like forever, and I hung up and called back.

The same employee answered, and I was past being casual. "Please, I need to speak to Aaron. It's an emergency. Please don't put me on hold."

There was no response, but it sounded like the employee had instead just set the phone down and was talking to someone in the background. I couldn't make out exactly what they were saying, but once they went quiet, I could hear the phone being picked up. His voice never sounded so comforting.

"This is Aaron," he said, sounding casual and ignorant of the urgency of the call.

"Aaron, it's me. It wasn't my fault. I don't know what happened," I was crying frantically.

"Wait. Whoa. Calm down. What happened?" he asked.

"I'm sorry. There's been an accident. I was in an accident. I'm in the ambulance, and we're going to the emergency room. Please meet me there. Please." I knew I was rambling, and they'd see that I was on my phone, so I had to keep it short. "Please, I have to go, just meet me there."

"Of course. I'll see you soon. I love you," he answered.

"I love you too." And with that, I hung up the phone and submitted to the care of the EMTs.

Before I knew it, we were already at the hospital. Once again they asked me if I needed to call anyone, but I had already contacted the most important people, and I knew they'd be there soon. But first I was handed off to the first available doctor to be checked out for unseen injuries. With the help of an IV and a little medication to calm my nerves, the initial shock and raised blood pressure had subsided.

I was asked again if I could feel any extreme pain anywhere else on my body. While changing into the hospital gown, I noticed dark bruises that covered both kneecaps. There was a red line across my stomach where the seat belt had attempted to hold me back. But the most apparent I noticed after I accidentally looked in the mirror when I was trying to load my bloody clothing into the plastic bag they had given me. It stopped me in my tracks. Even with the calming medication, I was appalled by my own reflection. My nose was swollen to almost twice its normal size, and I already had black eyes on both sides as the bruising spread. I tried to use a damp paper towel to blot off the blood that was left along my upper lip, even though having it gone didn't improve my look. I knew I couldn't dwell on the fact that I could use my current look to frighten all the small children within a five-foot radius, so I finished packing my clothes into the bag and went back to the bed in an attempt to get as far away from the mirror as I could.

I had barely gotten back into the bed when one of the nurses opened the door to let Aaron in. I figured the policeman had taken his sweet time to call my mother but assumed she'd be there shortly too. Aaron rushed over to the bed, and I sat up to give him a hug.

"What the hell happened?" he asked, trying to be gentle and cupping my face in his hands.

I was glad he was there but was still embarrassed for him to see me looking like a Neanderthal. "I don't know. I was driving to get my pictures…my pictures! I didn't get my pictures. Oh shit, I have to call her! She's going to think I just ditched my appointment!"

"Whoa, not important right now. We'll call her tomorrow," he stated firmly. "So what happened, did you run a red light or something?"

"No, of course not! I was driving along, and all of a sudden, it was like the van came out of nowhere. It happened so fast. I couldn't stop in time," I answered him. With the light-headed feeling that came along with the medication the doctor had given me, I was struggling to remember the specific details. I just kept picturing the aftermath.

"Well, the important thing is that you're okay," he said.

"The other driver was unconscious. I asked if he was dead, but no one would tell me anything. Oh God, what if I killed him?" I asked, for some reason thinking Aaron could give me the answer the police wouldn't. "I mean, he's not my best friend right now, but I just want to know that he's at least alive. You know what I mean?"

"Yeah, I know what you mean. I'm sure the police would've told you if you had killed someone. They would've at least arrested you." His attempt at humor wasn't completely wasted.

"Very funny! Why would you even say that?" I responded.

Before our conversation could go any further, there was a knock on the door. It was the same nurse, but before she got a chance to say anything to me, my mother pushed her way through and rushed over to the bed to give me a hug.

"Oh my God! Are you okay? The police called me, and I left work as soon as I could! What happened?" She was very worked up, and before I got a chance to tell her the details, she changed the subject on her own. "Never mind. Never mind, the important thing is that you're alive. Now how much longer do you have to stay here?"

"I don't know. They said they have to get some X-rays of my nose and my knees," I said, feeling more relaxed having my mother with me.

Five hours, three nurses, and two X-ray sessions later, the doctor sent me home with a prescription for pain medication and a referral to an ear, nose, and throat specialist. I was ready to agree to just about anything. I was extremely drowsy and just wanted to go home and go to bed.

My mother offered to come and spend the night and take care of me since Aaron had to go back to work the following day. But I ensured her that I would be fine and that I would call her if I needed anything. We came to a mutual agreement that she would come over after work and make dinner, so we were free to head home, and I could just pass out for the night and worry about everything tomorrow.

The ride home went very quickly and smoothly, most likely because of my buzz. It was an amusing path through the hallways to get to the apartment. But finally we made it, and as Aaron was helping me peel back the covers, he asked if I needed a glass of water. I told him I was okay but couldn't resist asking him one more question. He was leaning over me, and I grabbed his arms and looked him straight in the eyes. "Aaron, tell me the truth. Do you think I'm pretty?"

He seemed very amused by the question. He was cracking up until he saw that I was trying to ask him a legitimate question.

"I'm serious. I'm too ugly to live. I'm going to have to move out of here and go live under a bridge." Expressing my fears only made him laugh harder. That seemed to be my answer. I couldn't look at him anymore, and I pushed him away so I could turn over and go to sleep.

Once he caught his breath after laughing too hard, Aaron gave me as serious of an answer as he could. "Baby, you're as hot as you ever were."

I was pretty sure that was the end of our conversation, at least, that was the last thing I remember before passing out.

The next morning, I woke up with what felt like a horrible hangover. I decided to set up shop on the couch so I could relax, call work and let them know I wouldn't be in for the next week, and take another round of pain meds before passing out in front of the TV. Standing up out of bed brought on the sensation of having knives shoved through my kneecaps. Bending them to sit down was just as bad.

I couldn't remember the exact diagnoses I had left the hospital with, but I was pretty sure that all my aches and pains included a concussion. My head was pounding, and I was desperate to get some relief. I knew I should have been contacting my insurance company, figuring out what the next steps would be, trying to find a new car, and get back to some normalcy. I also needed to call the ear, nose, and throat specialist that the emergency room doctor had referred me to. But with the pain of my injuries, I just wanted to curl up on the couch and pass out.

That must have been exactly what I did. Shortly after 4:00 p.m., my phone started ringing. Halfway between sleeping and awake, I cracked one eye open enough to see that it was my mother.

"Hello?" I answered the phone, still sounding half-asleep, and used my other hand to massage my temples.

"Hey, it's Mom. I'm about to leave work and head over. I just have to stop at the grocery store first. What do you want for dinner?" she asked. She sounded rushed.

"I have no idea. I'm not all that hungry," I replied, wanting to end the conversation as soon as possible.

"Oh, come on. You're supposed to take your meds with food. Don't make Mommy force-feed you!" she joked.

I wasn't amused. "Seriously, Mom. My head hurts, just get whatever you want."

"All right, I'll see you soon. Leave the door unlocked for me," she finished.

"See you soon, bye." I dreaded having to get up to unlock the door.

As I stood up, the rush proved I needed to take things slowly. I inched toward the door, grabbing on to almost anything in my path to keep me from stumbling. It was tough to see straight enough to flip the knob to unlock the door. Feeling somewhat accomplished, I turned back toward the living room area to prepare for my journey back to the couch. I stretched and tried to gently rub my eyes. I could feel the swelling on my face, but it felt good. I must have gotten a little too lost in the moment, and I bumped my nose. The pain brought me back to reality, and I had that same warm feeling of blood running down my face.

"Oh, shit." I turned to walk into the bathroom and grab the nearest towel. I looked in the mirror to see that the bruising and swelling had gotten a lot worse overnight. I looked like I had just gotten out of a boxing match. I looked like a purple troll. Luckily, it didn't take long for the bleeding to stop, and I was able to get away from my reflection and head back to the couch. I wanted to be ahead of the game and keep the towel with me, just in case my nose decided to remind me how irritated it was again.

After my round trip to the door and the bathroom, I almost felt winded, and it felt great to just lie back down on the couch. Having the low volume noise of the television in the background was incredibly calming, and I was just about to fall asleep when the sound of the door opening jerked me awake.

"Hello! It's Mom! Anyone home?" she yelled, carrying a bag of groceries in each arm.

"Mom, damn, I'm right here on the couch. You don't have to yell." It was painful to sit up.

"Sorry, sweetie. How are you feeling?" she asked.

"Look at me. How do you think I'm feeling?" I answered her question with another question.

She peeked her head around the corner while she unloaded one of the bags. "Oh, I'm sorry. Look, I brought apple juice. Did you want me to bring you some?"

"No, I have water here. I got a nosebleed after you called. It sucked," I informed her.

"That's too bad, but the doctor said it would probably happen a few times," she said. "He also said you should be icing that to keep the swelling down."

"I will, eventually. Right now I just want to lie here and die. Speaking of which, wasn't Michelle coming with you?" I asked.

"No, she had to work late. Are you supposed to sleep when you have a concussion?" she asked.

"Probably not, but I'll risk it. My head is killing me. I think the doctor's specific instructions were to rest," I answered.

"See? Rest, not sleep," she corrected me. "Here, drink this." She brought me a glass of apple juice and a Ziploc bag of ice.

"Mom, I said I was fine," I reminded her.

"Well, this used to make you feel better when you were little." She smiled.

"Yeah, when I had a sore throat or a cold, not when my face was bashed in by a steering wheel at forty-five miles an hour." I took a sip anyway. It did taste pretty good. I took another gulp and slumped down the rest my head on the arm of the couch and iced my face.

"Did they tell you when they were going to call you about the police report?" she asked.

"I don't even want to think about that. But yeah, they said it would take a few days, and then they'd call me when it was written up," I told her. "I'm guessing I need to get a hold of the insurance company. And I know I have to make appointments with the nose doctor and the orthopedic doctor."

"Yeah, but not today. Sit back, relax. I figured I'd make meatloaf for dinner." She smiled. "Then you and Aaron can have leftovers."

"If I make it that long." I was skeptical. But Mom, with her eternal optimism, started finding her way around the kitchen and cooking up a storm. It was odd, but as excruciating as my head pain was, the familiar clanking of pots and pans and the smell of her cooking was a comfort.

I must have dozed off, and the next thing I remember, Aaron was waking me up and asking how I was doing. I told him everything was fine and tried to go back to sleep to the humming of him and my mother bonding over her cooking. I heard him ask my mother why I had used the towel from the bathroom when my nose started bleeding, but I was in no mood to argue and pretended to sleep through it.

The next morning I woke up to Aaron's alarm and rolled over to make sure he was up too. He rolled over to face me and was about to give me a good morning kiss. Since my head wasn't throbbing, I'd almost forgotten about my injuries, until Aaron almost jumped back, leaving me hanging mid-kiss, and gave me a small peck on the forehead instead. It reminded me of everything I had to get done regarding the accident.

I sent Aaron off to work and went to take a shower before making appointments with the doctors. I knew it was a long shot, but I was hoping my nose would shrink somewhat overnight. But the swelling and the bruising were still there. I knew I didn't want to face anyone, and I would have to contact my professors too. Luckily I had some time before finals, so all I had to worry about was finishing homework and minor tests. One less thing on my mind.

The next few weeks brought on the scheduling of appointments to follow up on my injuries and several phone calls to fight with my insurance company about the replacement of my car. I was told I would only get $400.00, as it was the value of my car. For some reason, I had to remind them that my car might not have been worth much but it was a functioning vehicle and I'd never be able to replace it for $400.00. After agreeing to compromise and finding another used vehicle for a reasonable price, I submitted the receipt to my insurance company, holding my breath to see if they'd cover a car only two years newer than my seventeen-year-old scrap metal.

The peanut on the shit sundae was that along with the shrinking of the swelling of my nose came breathing problems from the fracture. The dark bruising around my nose and eyes slowly faded out to a rotted green, then jaundice-yellow color. My face looked like I had surpassed its expiration date.

Aaron seemed supportive, even though I was pretty sure that he was extremely irritated about having to babysit me. He had to pick me up and drop me off for work and physical therapy and doctors' appointments. Trying to lighten the mood, I reminded him a few times that he'd forgotten to tell me how pretty I look in purple and green.

Our schedules had always differed, but in an attempt to try and ease up on my reliance on him, I reached out to friends who would be able to swing by and pick me up on the way to school or work. While it let him off the hook several times, it usually meant that I would get to my destinations a lot earlier than I needed to and end up spending more quality time with my coworkers or classmates.

The conversations between Aaron and me were sometimes limited to text messages from him, wanting to make sure that I had a ride to or from work. Thinking it was sweet of him to worry about me, I would soon recognize his effort as a clearance to go out with his coworkers or friends and tell me all about it when he got home after bar close. We spent a lot of time together since I was homebound without a car, so I usually wasn't invited to the outings or informed about them until after they ended. I thought it was incredibly rude, and it really bothered me, but I knew I had to pick my battles since he was my main means of support.

I finally got my new-used vehicle, and it took a tremendous weight off Aaron. I was able to drive myself to and from work, school, and my twice-a-week physical therapy appointment. Apparently when your knees have been smashed into a dashboard at forty-five miles per hour and come out looking like rotten heads of cabbage, there is the possibility of long-term effects. I didn't want to admit it, but even after the bruises disappeared, my knees were still very sore and the machines they used to massage them helped a lot with the pain. When the swelling and the bruising cleared up from my face, I thought those troubles were over. But the doctor delivered the bad news after a routine checkup.

He asked if I was having trouble breathing. I did notice I was waking up with my mouth hanging open a lot more often but assumed that would end once my nose healed. He had checked inside one nostril and then moved right on to the next. When there's a man right up in your face with a tool inserted into your nostril propping it open, the term uh-oh is the last thing you want to hear after he's been studying it for about five minutes.

I was pretty sure he hadn't found the marble my sister convinced me to stick up there when I was four. The one that got stuck that she insisted would sink down into my stomach, sprout, and grow a marble tree. When I told her I liked the idea of having a new collection of marbles, she told me I wouldn't get to enjoy it because I would explode when the marbles bloomed. Quite reassuring to have such a knowledgeable sibling. But sticking to the topic at hand, I cut right to the chase.

"What? What's 'uh-oh?'" I asked, hoping he was just concerned over the color of my snot.

"Well, the swelling has gone down, and the fracture seems to have healed," he said, putting away his tools and reaching for his clipboard. "But the injury seems to have caused a deviated septum."

"Okay, so is that going to take longer to heal then?" I was trying to stay optimistic.

"It can, but it's not going to fix itself. We're looking at surgery," he said, calmly writing more notes on the clipboard.

"Surgery? Why would I need surgery?" I was pretty sure I knew the answer. I just wanted him to justify it one more time.

"A deviated septum can make breathing very hard and in extreme cases prevent oxygen from getting to your brain. I think we should schedule this procedure within the next few months."

"What exactly has to be done? Will this change the way it looks? I mean, breathing is more important, but I like the way it looks. Don't you think?" I knew I was babbling.

"Well, we can discuss the specifics after we schedule the surgery. You might want to consider adding an implant to match your chin. Just a few things to think about. Call the office when you figure out the best time to schedule, you'll want at least two weeks off, probably three," he finished. He shook my hand before telling me to have a good day and leaving the room.

It took me a minute to take it all in. I walked out to my car and pondered and pondered the repercussions on my way to work. I'd never been put out for any kind of procedure. I'd never had a major procedure. I'd never even had stitches. And Aaron wouldn't want to take care of me, having to take time off from work to drive me to have surgery, wait for it to be over, and then drive me home to play doctor for at least a week. I'd have to check my mother's schedule and stay with her, hoping my sister would be somewhat willing to help without irritating me by giving me a guilt trip for her efforts.

I wasn't just concerned about the procedure being an inconvenience to everyone's schedule, but also about how much pain I was bringing on myself. This was major surgery, and the doctor had given me a pamphlet to give me a little more of an idea what I was in for. It looked awful, having to break and reshape my nose. It looked like too much to handle, why would anyone do this on purpose?

I walked into work with a heavy load on my mind. My favorite coworker was there, so I knew he'd clear my head, and I could decide later. I hadn't expected to see Mike during the lunch rush, but that was the beauty of the restaurant business, we had very flexible schedules and could trade shifts whenever we needed or wanted to.

I clocked in and started setting up the condiments. He could tell I was worried about something, and he was never one to beat around the bush.

"What's up? Are you a closer today?" he asked while he was stocking glass racks by the pop machine.

I didn't hear him right way. I had a lot on my mind.

"Hello? Did you hear me?" He stopped stocking and looked at me, waiting to get my attention.

I was setting up ketchup bottles and did a double take when I noticed him staring at me.

"What? Sorry, I didn't hear you. Yeah, I'm good. How are you?" I asked, looking back down at the bottles.

"I'm good. Glad you're good also. But that wasn't what I asked you." He could see right through me. "All right, spill it. What's going on? Did you catch Aaron cheating on you?"

The question broke me out of my coma.

"Ha, yeah, right. I'm not that lucky." I rolled my eyes at him. "Besides, he barely has enough time for me, how the hell would he be able to balance two of us?"

"Eh, don't be so sure," he continued. "We make time for what we want to make time for. And I saw the way he looked at me when he had to pick you up from work." He winked at me and picked up the empty glass racks to bring back to the dish area.

"You're hilarious. But you can't go by me. I was told my brain isn't getting enough oxygen." I gave him the short version of what the doctor had told me earlier. "Be sure to check with me after I have surgery. Maybe I'll be able to work out a courtesy laugh or two."

"Surgery? To get a sense of humor? Does that involve stick removal?" He laughed at his own joke.

I couldn't help but laugh along with him. "I wish. I'd just get a towel to bite on and make Aaron pull it out for me. I'd save a lot of time and money, and who knows, Aaron would probably think it was some kind of foreplay. Get back my sense of humor and spice up my relationship." I stuck my tongue out at him.

"Well, I'm out of ideas then. What's going on?" he asked, opening a package of napkins.

"I have to have surgery on my nose," I confessed.

"A nose job? Be careful, it can become an addition. Just look at Michael. If they try and talk you into multiple procedures, just beat it!" He started singing along with his joke.

"Well, it is a nose job, but it's for function, not looks. Wait, actually, the doctor did suggest that I let them put an implant in to match my chin. Who the hell wants to match this chin?" I said, pointing at my face.

"It seems to work for Jay Leno," he consoled me.

"Thanks. That thought will make my day so much brighter." I rolled my eyes at him again and finished stocking the napkins.

"Seriously, though. Not sure if you've heard, but breathing is pretty important. If you want to do that other cosmetic crap, that's up to you. If it were me, I'd do it," he told me.

And he was right. I wasn't concerned with the cosmetic aspect, unless there was a risk of my nose falling off. Since the doctor hadn't brought it up and the pamphlet didn't list it as a side effect, I assumed I was safe from that consequence. The only conclusion was that I had to do it. Now how would I explain to Aaron that I needed his help.

Mike's advice played over and over again in my head throughout my shift. And I knew he was right, so I explained things to my boss, and she was actually very supportive. I was surprised that she only requested as much advanced notice as I could provide—as opposed to my resignation for having to take so much time off—between the accident and having surgery. I walked out of the office to find Mike hanging out and having a meal after work.

I sat down in the booth across from him. "Well, I broke the news to the boss. Now I just have to break it to Aaron. Want to come over and watch the train wreck?"

"Come on. He's your boyfriend. He loves you. He'll just want to make sure you don't suffer," he said, pouring the dressing over his salad.

"Here's hoping. Want to come over and hang out for a while?" I asked.

"Do you have whiskey?" he replied.

"Beer?" I offered.

"Well, I'll have to make a stop then. But yeah, sounds fun. I just have to call and let the man know that I have something better to do tonight." He laughed and finished prepping his meal to eat.

I pulled into the parking lot and gathered my things to go into the building, making sure I had the procedure pamphlet right on top of the pile. I walked in and set my things on the kitchen counter, grabbing a beer and heading to the bedroom to get out of my work clothes. After changing into my casual gear, I grabbed the pamphlet and sat down on the couch to reread the information and wait for Mike to call and let me know he had arrived.

I didn't have to wait long. I walked down to the lobby and let Mike in, offering the grand tour along the way. We walked into the apartment, and I gave him the rundown on our location of luxury.

"Looks like a bachelor pad," he joked.

"That's because it was," I replied, taking a larger gulp of my beer.

"Ah, I can see that we need shots!" he declared.

"Fantastic idea," I agreed, thinking the liquid courage might do me some good when I had to confess the news to Aaron later.

A couple of hours and a few beers later, after half of a bottle of whiskey and a pizza, Mike noticed Aaron still wasn't home. I explained that he had to close the store and would probably be home in a little over an hour. But in reality I was having so much fun, I hadn't noticed how late it was getting.

"So have you thought about contacting a lawyer?" Mike asked me, taking the conversation to a serious direction.

"Why would I need a lawyer? I read the police report. I didn't do anything wrong. The other guy thought it was a three-way stop. He was wrong, and I had the right of way. As long as he survived, it's over." His question started to kill my buzz, so I poured us two more shots.

"No, I'm serious. It's not because you did anything wrong, but look at everything going on. You have emergency medical bills and lost wages. You have permanent injuries that are going to require ongoing care, even surgery. What if you come out looking like Michael Jackson? Don't you want reimbursement for that?" he pointed out.

"I hadn't thought about that. But you're right. I barely got my insurance company to replace my car." I had a realization. "I suppose it couldn't hurt to talk to someone."

I didn't have much time to think about it right at that second. Suddenly, I could hear the key in the lock, and in came Aaron with the usual look on his face.

"Hey, babe! Welcome home! Look, we have company!" I hollered with a slightly drunk accent.

"Yeah, I see that. I'm Aaron, Lisa's boyfriend," he stated, forcing a half smile.

"Oh, the Aaron. I've heard so much about you. I'm Mike, Lisa's coworker." His smile was legitimate. Even though I wasn't sure if it was the meeting or the liquor that was causing it.

"This is the Mike I was telling you about. Sit down, he was just telling me about his family in Wisconsin. It's hilarious. Do you want me to get you a beer?" I asked. I thought things were going well. He finally had a chance to meet Mike, and if we all had fun, it would be a good way to break the news to him about the impending inconvenience of assisting me during and after my surgery.

"No. Thanks. I'm going out with the guys," he declined, heading to the bedroom to change.

"Oh. Well, give us a minute. We can go with you," I offered, standing to pick up the empty bottles and garbage.

"Oh, actually, I can't. It's getting late, and I have to be up early," Mike said, making a stressed out face and pointing at the direction of the bedroom.

I pushed his hand down and silently shushed him.

"I'm just going with the guys. You probably wouldn't have any fun," he hollered from the bedroom.

I sat back down, disappointed.

"Yeah, that's my cue. I'm running late...on getting out of here," he said quietly. "Good luck. I'll see you at work."

I walked him to the door and gave him instructions on how to get back to the freeway. Once I shut the door, I turned around to face the doorway to the bedroom and paused for a moment to think about what I should say.

I walked in and sat on the bed and just looked at Aaron. He was finishing looping his belt, then looked up and saw that I was staring at him.

"What? You don't even like my friends," he pointed out. "It's not a big deal. I'll be home in a couple of hours." He moved in to give me a kiss.

I pulled back and looked at the floor. "I have something important to talk to you about."

"Okay, you can tell me later if you're still awake." He saw the frustrated look on my face as he was putting on his shoes. "Well, it couldn't have been that important. You were sitting there having drinks with a guy from work. If anyone should be pissed, it's me!"

He finished putting on his shoes and started making his way out of the bedroom. I followed him, stumbling a little from the remnants of my buzz.

"It is important. I invited you to hang out with Mike and me. You said no. I really need to talk to you. Your friends have gotten to see more of you in the past week than I have," I reminded him.

"Maybe because they don't nag me," he fired back.

"Whoa. Let's not even go there." I tried to hold back, but I wanted to go there. "You're out with them almost every night, sometimes not even giving me a courtesy heads-up. So I get the pleasure of finding out when you come in at 3:00 a.m. and try to crawl on top of me and get a piece. You're the one that twisted my arm to move in here. And nagging, I can tell you about nagging. Nagging about laundry, nagging about dishes, nagging about the bathroom towel because I had an emergency. Now my coworker can't even come over and hang out? I feel like I'm sleeping with the enemy!"

"Seriously, I nag you?" He actually seemed surprised. "I work fifty to sixty hours a week. You really think it's wrong of me to ask for a little help cleaning up around here? And coming in and crawling on top of you? That should be reassuring. It tells you I'm not cheating."

"What are you saying?" I asked.

"Well, you and Mike were having a pretty good time," he reminded me.

"Aaron, he's in a relationship! With another man! And I look like a gym teacher! Pull your head out of your ass!" I had to walk away and sit on the couch. "I feel like you're making excuses. It's like you don't even want me here. Is that what's going on?" I wasn't sure I wanted to hear his answer.

"Come on, you're drunk. You don't know what you're talking about," he spoke quietly. "I'm not discussing this with you when you're drunk."

"I'm not drunk. And what do you mean 'discuss it'? Is this something you've been meaning to bring up?" I pushed.

"I'm leaving." He walked over to the table to grab his keys and then started making his way to the door.

I stepped in front of it and made him look at me. "I tried to warn you that wouldn't be some kind of fairy tale. You insisted you were willing to communicate with me to make things work. Do you want me to move out?"

He had nowhere to go. "Fine. Yes! I want you to move out."

I was stunned. He pushed past me and walked out the door. After he slammed it shut, I locked it and headed back over to the couch. Luckily, Mike had left the bottle of whiskey. Whether it worked or not, I appreciated the shots. I tried to utilize to make sense of what had just happened. We had only been living together for a few months. This was still supposed to be the honeymoon period. The time when you're happy to take in everything you can learn about the other person, and your only concern is what type of air freshener to keep in the bathroom for when the kids need to go for a swim.

I had a few more beers and passed out on the couch. I was woken up when I heard Aaron sneak in around 3:00 a.m. but pretended I was asleep when I heard him walk into the bedroom and shuffle around, then come out and peek around the corner. I assumed he was checking to see if I was sleeping on the couch. I heard him sigh, and he went back in the bedroom and went to bed, leaving the door open.

Courtesy of my several nightcaps, I didn't get the pleasure of waking up before Aaron. I heard him getting ready for work and, again, pretended to sleep through everything. I wouldn't even know what to say to him at this point.

I had one class, just reviewing for finals, which I could do on my own. And then I would have the rest of the day off. I decided to start my attention span off on the right foot and go stalk up on some caffeine. I texted my sister to see if she wanted to meet me, but I figured she would have to work. So I even went as far as to try my mother. She sent the same response. So I went out on a whim to see if Mike was up for the sequel to last night's cliffhanger. And lucky for me, he was up and anxious for his usual morning buzz.

The weather was nice enough, and my hangover appreciated the breeze. So when Mike got there, I was already sitting at a table outside the door and sipping on my latte.

"Oh, good, you got a table. Sorry I'm late. I just had to get cleaned up. I'll be back in a minute." He rushed inside to get his coffee.

I was somewhat jealous. I woke up, feeling like crap, seeing no reason to change out of my pajamas. Cleaning up for me meant running a brush through my hair to get it back into a ponytail, washing off my mascara-induced baggage, and covering up at least one-third of my face from my brows to my cheekbones with conveniently large-lensed sunglasses. No wonder Aaron found my housekeeping skills to be lacking.

A few minutes later Mike rushed back out, sipping on his hot coffee. "Okay, I'm ready. Tell me what happened!"

"I didn't get to tell him anything," I told Mike. "We had another fight, and he said he wants me to move out."

"What? Where the hell did that come from?" He seemed shocked by the news. "I thought you guys were so happy together!"

"I thought we were too. I guess with everything going on, with school and the play and the accident, we were just too busy to see that we aren't." It hurt to say it out loud.

"In all fairness, I had warned him ahead of time. I told him it probably wouldn't always be fun to live with me. Although I can't say the blame is all on me."

"Oh God, what did he do?" he asked, waiting for details.

"Nothing. Nothing at all. He just seems to shut down whenever something is bothering him. Whether it's me or work or his family. He doesn't tell me anything. He literally just shuts down or goes out with his friends. I'm sure they know more than I do," I said. "We've only been living together for a few months. He was the one that wanted to get married. This should be a happy time. I have no idea what crawled up his ass and died, but apparently it has thorns."

"Well, what do you want to do?" he asked me.

"What do you mean? I want to finish school and pursue some acting," I answered. "Who knows, maybe I'll move to Hollywood." I figured he'd laugh at me, but he seemed to get it.

"Would you be able to move to Hollywood if you stay with Aaron?" he pointed out.

"Well, it never hurts to have support. I'm pretty sure I won't be signing a four-picture deal the second I were to pull into town. It'd be nice not to go alone." I was laying down the disclaimer for Mike and for myself.

"It sounds like he hasn't been that supportive. I'd want to be there for the person I love. You know, support them through career choices, daily struggles, a car accident." He accentuated the point I had been trying to avoid. "How is he not curious about what's going to happen with whole thing. Does he realize how serious your injuries were?"

"Yeah, he does. He was sitting there in the emergency room when the doctor broke everything down," I told Mike.

"Well, what about the follow-up appointments, the ones he didn't have to drive you to but could have attended to get an update?" he pointed out. "Has he been to any of those? You know, to be involved in your life and show his support?"

I couldn't argue with his logic. "No, he hasn't. He gets annoyed if I ask him to take work off to go with me or if I try to tell him what they tell me at the appointments."

"So?" he asked.

"I guess I'm single. Time to move on." It sounded so simple.

"Would you really want to move out to Los Angeles?" he challenged me.

I had to stop and think about it for a moment. Then I answered, "Yes. Yes, I would." It felt good to say it.

"You realize it's expensive, overcrowded…it's polluted. And it's going to take a while to get through this crap with the accident." The glass was definitely half empty. "But I've thought about it too."

Maybe the glass was only half full. So I took another sip of my coffee. "Well, a journey of a thousand miles does begin with a single step."

Chapter 10

I left coffee with Mike to head back to my mother's house and scope out my room before she got home. It was tough to be back as more than a guest. I just had to decide where I wanted everything to go now. I decided to rearrange the room and hopefully give myself some motivation to get everything back into it and call it home.

Since it was mostly empty, except for the bed and dresser, it only took a little huffing and puffing to move the furniture to opposite walls in the room. I wasn't sure my doctors would approve of me lifting heavier furniture, so I broke each piece down as far as I could. Just as I was plugging the last drawer back into the dresser, I heard the noise I was trying to avoid.

"Hello? Lisa! I'm home!" my mother yelled from the front door. "Lisa! Are you here?"

I just wanted to finish putting the dresser together and get back to Aaron's to repack my things. "Yes, Mother! I'm here!" I responded, checking my phone to see if he had tried to call or text me. There were no missed calls and no messages waiting to be viewed. It was time to break down and tell my mother that she was right.

Not that I needed more reassurance, but she walked into the room as I was setting my empty phone back down on the top of the dresser.

"Hey, what are you doing here?" she asked.

I didn't want to look at her. "Just cleaning up."

I could just picture the look of suspicion on her face as she was slowly walking away from the door to sit on the bed. "Oh, okay. Rearranging the furniture for me, huh?"

"Yeah, I figured the room needed a new look." I knew I'd have to tell her sooner rather than later. "Because I'm probably going to be moving back in." I turned to face her.

She stayed calm but had a look of surprise on her face.

"Really? Why is that?" she asked, even though I was pretty sure that she already knew the answer.

"Well, I had my doctor's appointment for my nose. He says I'm going to need surgery to fix everything. I could be out of commission for a few weeks," I told her.

"Oh, and Aaron's too busy to help take care of you?" She was fishing for the real answer.

I was caught. "I don't know. We didn't get that far. We had a huge fight, one of our huge fights, and he said he didn't want me to live there anymore."

"Well, I'm sorry to hear that. You know you're welcome here any time. But I think you two should sit down and discuss this instead of making a decision in the heat of the moment."

I didn't want to face things, but she was right again.

"Yeah, I have to go pack up my stuff anyway," I said, justifying the act of going back to his apartment. "Good thing I've only been there a few months and didn't completely unpack." My attempt at humor fell on deaf ears.

"Come on. I'll make you some dinner," she offered.

"I'm not really hungry," I declined. "Besides, I have to go pack up my crap."

I had done just about everything I could do not to go back and face Aaron. He hadn't tried to call or text or anything. I figured he was still pissed, probably at work, busy with anything else, and already making his plans for after work. Maybe it was a good time to collect my things.

I parked, making sure I didn't see his car anywhere, and slowly walked down the hallway to face the apartment door. I was almost afraid to put my key in the hole to unlock the door. I slowly pushed the door open, treading like a stranger over the threshold. I knew there were a few boxes in the living room, so I decided to start a pile to-go there.

"Hey." The greeting made me jump. It was Aaron.

"Hey, what are you doing home? I thought you had to work," I replied, trying not to show any emotion.

"I was just the opener. I got off about an hour ago," he informed me.

The conversation was borderline awkward. That still didn't stop me from giving it a shove in the wrong direction. "Oh? I figured you'd have plans after work. I just came to pack up my things."

"Just wait, I want to talk to you." He stopped me as I tried to move past him.

"Really? Had some extra time at work to figure out what to add to the list of everything I do wrong?" I asked, flexing my sarcasm.

"Of course not. Look, I don't want to fight," he said. "Come sit on the couch."

I was skeptical but followed him to the couch anyway. "All right then, what do you want?"

"I need you to know that I don't want to end this." He was actually opening up.

I was glad he was finally talking to me, but I was still confused. "Then why did you tell me you wanted me to leave?"

"I didn't tell you to leave, and I didn't tell you that I wanted to break up. I just think that we rushed into this. I've had roommates before, and that's all we were, roommates. We were lucky if we saw each other once a day, more than twice a week, and everyone always did his share to keep the place clean and livable," he told me.

"And you didn't think you'd be seeing me that often when I moved in? Didn't I warn you about the definition of this whole coinciding arrangement? Where did you think I was going to be?" I had no idea what he would say to that.

"I just figured we would both be so busy with everything going on, we would actually have to schedule dates. Then with your accident and having to be on bed rest and me being surrounded by idiotic teenagers all day, it just got to be too much. But I don't want to break up with you. I think we should work on this." He was so sweet and yet so ridiculous at the same time.

"Well, I don't know what to tell you. I have to have surgery, and I'm going to need someone to suffer through all those extra hours with me," I fired back. "That's what I was trying to tell you last night. I'm scared to death, but the doctor says it's a common procedure, and I need to have it so that I can breathe and get enough oxygen to my brain. I'll be out of commission for a few weeks."

"I'm sorry. I should've listened to you. I want to be there for your surgery though. Have you already scheduled it?" He really did seem to care.

"No. I'm waiting to find out when it'd be best for my mother to take a little time off of work. I'm just gonna move back in with her." I broke the news to him.

"But I love you," he said.

I didn't want to admit, but I was backed into a corner. "I love you too."

"How are we going to work on our relationship if you're living with your mother?" he asked. He really did sound serious about mending things between us.

"I wasn't thinking about that," I confessed. "What, do you think I should look for my own place?"

"Well, stay here, and we can check out a few places." He leaned in to kiss me.

It was crazy how things had turned around in the past few minutes. I was so confused. I didn't even want to kiss him, but he kept leaning in until I had come to the end of the cushion and was blocked in by the armrest. So finally I gave in—and ended up spending the night.

A few weeks later I had survived finals and finished my first semester of college. This included the extra credit portion, which consisted of my mother grilling me for answers about what exactly was going on between Aaron and me and where I was going to end up.

Adding to my juggling act, my sister worked a second job, cleaning offices a few nights a week; and she referred me to one of the office building's tenants, a law firm with a husband and wife pair of lawyers that worked on an "only pay if you win" basis. It sounded perfect, and I thought it would be worth it to hear what they had to say. It was a tedious process to get them all of my information and doctors records, and we ended up speaking on the phone at least twice a week.

After reviewing the police report and the follow-up care for all my injuries, they were sure we had a case. They told me to stick to the doctor's plan of continuing care and schedule my surgery. I figured they were right since my health was at stake. I scheduled my surgery in the spring, so I could get it over with and actually enjoy my summer instead of living it like a countdown to my impending torture. And if for no other reason, since they wouldn't get paid if they didn't win my case, I left the hard work to them and focused on the difficulty of my own case. I had to find an apartment before my surgery.

I was torn between just moving home and saving my money to pay for school. Having more money meant that I wouldn't be "apartment poor" and I could afford to work a less strenuous schedule, allowing me more time for auditions and acting. However, I couldn't deny that Aaron was important to me, and I wanted to make sure I was trying to do everything on my part to make things work.

I hadn't seen anything that really caught my eye. I wasn't sure if it was because they weren't up to my standards or if I just wanted to stay with Aaron. I had been calling around to check prices, hoping to find a happy balance between something affordable and something I'd be happy to live in for at least a year. I'd learned by now that the best way to find a deal was to simply ask them right away if there were any move in specials going on. Finally, someone had an answer I was interested in.

"Oh, really? That is a good deal. When can I stop by and look at it?" I asked, scribbling a list while watching Aaron make a sandwich. "Great, I'll see you guys at 1:00 p.m."

"What's the deal on that one?" Aaron asked, looking back down and putting his sandwich together, then digging in the cupboard for some chips.

"Well, this one actually sounds really good. It's a newer complex. The apartment is on the third floor and has vaulted ceilings." I read the list out loud, repeating what the woman had told me. "And there is a washer and dryer in the unit, a pool, and a gym."

"Sounds pretty sweet. But which one of your kidneys do they want in exchange?" He laughed and took a bite of his creation.

"Actually, it's not too bad. If I sign a year lease, I'll only have to pay $699.00 per month," I informed him.

"Oh, that is a good deal," he said with a mouthful of sandwich and chips. "Want me to go with you to check it out?"

"Sure, I'm going over at 1:00," I told him. I was sure he was open but didn't want to come off as a forceful nag. I was also pretty sure that his curiosity would get the best of him, and he would insist on coming along to see the apartment.

We pulled into the parking lot, and I have to admit, the complex looked great from the outside. Four buildings with a large parking lot in the middle and a pool right in the center. So far, so good. We located the office and parked outside to go in and find the employee I had been talking to over the phone.

We were greeted by a few different people in the lobby, all seemingly hoping to sell a lease. We finally tracked down the property manager I had spoken to, and she offered to give us a tour of the unit. We walked across the parking lot, checking out the pool area. It was huge, and there was actually a difference in depth between the shallow and the deep end. Things were looking good so far.

We walked into the building, and she directed us to look off to our left sides and see the gym area. I was excited to see that it was located in the same building I'd be living in and grabbed Aaron's hand to lead him to come check it out with me. The property manager held her card up to the scanner, proudly explaining how secure everything in the complex was and opened the door for us to walk in.

We both stopped once we were in the door. The gym was somewhat lacking. One wall consisted of mirrors with a short rack of random weights in the corner. There were two treadmills, one stair machine, and one cross trainer along the opposite wall but facing the mirrors. Closest to us was a machine with some sort of bar that looked like it was supposed to work a person's arms. Other than that, there were a few exercise balls rolling around on top of two carefully placed mats and a bench. Since there wasn't much of an area to look at, we quickly took it all in and moved on to the actual apartment.

The property manager unlocked the door and, in a courteous manner, motioned us to go in first. The layout of the apartment was very similar to Aaron's with one major difference—it was a lot bigger. The ceilings were a lot taller too. There was a deck instead of a set of windows, and above the sliding doors was a large fan-shaped window that welcomed even more natural light into the room. The kitchen included a breakfast counter, which provided an open concept feel through the opening connecting it to the kitchen. The bedroom was larger with huge windows and a walk-in closet. This was certainly more spacious than the cardboard boxes I was relying on in Aaron's apartment. Between the doors of the bedroom and the larger, modern bathroom was a skinnier door that opened up to an attached washer and dryer, vertically stacked.

I could picture myself living here. I could already picture how I would set everything up in here. I smiled at Aaron and looked for a little encouragement.

"Isn't this great? And you could come over here and swim. And if you're nice, I'll even let you bring your laundry." I winked at him.

He didn't look that happy for me. "Are you sure you want to move in here?"

"What? Yeah, this place looks great! And it's almost half of what yours cost per month! I could actually afford this!" I smiled and swiped my hand over the kitchen counter. "And look, I can still see you!" I looked at him through the opening from the kitchen to the living room area and laughed.

He was still less than amused. "This would really make you happy?"

"Well, yeah." I was extremely confused. "What's going on? You wanted me to move out, but you don't want me to move in with my mother because we won't have any privacy to work on our relationship. I find an amazing place, for an unbelievable price, and now you're acting like an abused puppy dog?"

"I just didn't think you'd be this excited to get away from me," he said.

"I'm not excited to get away from you. I'm excited for you to pick one personality and stick with it," I said, walking back over and standing in front of him. "It's not the ideal situation, but shouldn't we both stay positive?"

"Yeah, I guess." It was like pulling teeth, trying to get him to say it.

"Did you want me to be miserable? That might not be the most ideal foundation upon which to build a positive relationship." I was trying to stay positive enough for both of us.

"I guess you're right." It was big of him to admit it, even though he was still acting like a pouty eight-year-old who didn't get chocolate frosting on his birthday cake.

I decided I had better things to worry about right now. I asked the manager, "So what's the next step?"

"Well, we'll start the paperwork for your credit check, and when that's done, we'll just need the first and last month's rent, and we can sign the lease," she explained.

"Sounds good." I looked at Aaron and grabbed his hand. I squeezed his hand until I forced a smile out of him. Then we followed the manager back down to the office.

The next week I was pretty much glued to my phone. I even considered upping the number of minutes available on my monthly plan. Not only did I have to account for the usual calls from my lawyers, but I also had to plan for calls from the manager of the complex and family and friends who volunteered to help me move in. I was pretty sure they were trying to earn an invite to relax around the pool, but I was still happy to take advantage of their offers.

Aaron didn't seem thrilled but acted like he was trying to stay positive. After all, it was his idea for me to move out but to still stay together and try to make things work. The next checkup with the neurologist should have been scheduled for him, to see which medications would be best for his bipolar disorder. But in an attempt to avoid fighting, I didn't bring up his PMS or offer to help him find his testicles again.

The furniture and the boxes were moved into my new apartment, and Aaron offered to stay the first night and help me unpack. We didn't get much work done, but it was still nice to be with him. It proved that there was a chance for us to still make our relationship work, especially since there was no lack of physical attraction between us. Aaron had to leave somewhat early in the morning, and I was looking forward to the break that working the lunch shift would provide.

I was looking forward to seeing my coworkers. And becoming accustomed to the position, I was actually looking forward to rude customers and overrated recipes. A few of my regular customers knew I had gotten a new apartment, and a couple of them gave me a generic congratulations. Throughout the course of my shift, I invited a select few coworkers to come over for a housewarming party.

Near the end of my shift, Mike was on his way in early to get some dinner before he started. I checked on the few tables I had and made my way over to share the good news.

"So you gonna come over and see the new place on Saturday? I'm having a few people over to check it out," I told him.

"Yeah, I think we'll be able to make it. Is everything moved in?" he asked.

I'm guessing because he didn't want to be suckered into helping me carry boxes or furniture.

"Yes, everything is moved in. Not necessarily unpacked, but definitely in the apartment. I already had a private unpacking party last night. We didn't get much done, but we really broke a sweat." I grinned at him.

"Gross. And he's cool with you celebrating your new place? Wasn't he the one that told you that you had to move out and find it? That could be awkward," he said.

"No. We're cool. Keep in mind, he insisted I find the apartment so that he and I could stay together and work on our relationship," I responded. "It'll work out. He'll be there on Saturday too."

"Well, just warn me what time. I don't want to get into trouble again," he said.

"I'll text him and find out," I said, already sending him the message since he never responded right away, especially from work.

I checked out my last table and finished my side work. Mike was tying on his apron and getting ready to start his, so I just gave him a quick wave good-bye and walked out of the building. I got to my car and checked my phone to see if Aaron had responded to my message. But there was nothing. I figured he was probably just busy at work and headed back to my new apartment to try and get everything looking somewhat decent.

I walked into the apartment, and it suddenly hit me. I was living alone. It didn't matter if I unloaded and cleaned everything up right away. Who would get mad at me? I just looked around. I could leave the dishes on the kitchen counter, the towels on the bathroom sink, and blankets on the couch. I could wait an extra day or two to do laundry. As long as I had clean under, it didn't matter. That was the beauty of having the washer and dryer in my unit, I wouldn't need extra quarters to wash multiple loads.

On the flip side, I had total freedom. No one would make me do anything. No one would make me clean up or go to my classes or even to work. I was an adult, so I was aware of what I had to get done on a daily basis. But I wasn't used to the silence. There wasn't always going to be someone with me to share the news of my good and bad days. And there wouldn't always be anyone there to help create good and bad days. It's not like I didn't have a friend or family member who was just a phone call away, but there would be a lot of nights that I would be home alone and sleeping alone. It was almost frightening to think that I had committed to this lifestyle for at least the next year.

I decided to pour a glass of wine and turn on the television for some motivation and background noise while I started to go through the boxes. Almost two hours later, with half of a bottle of wine and two boxes down, I decided to check my phone and make sure I wasn't ignoring anyone. Fortunately, no one's feelings would be hurt since my messages were empty and there were no missed calls. This freedom thing was going to be very tricky if I had to stay desperately chained to my electric leash.

I wondered why Aaron hadn't gotten back to me yet but again chalked it up to him having a busy day. And if his day was that crazy, he most likely wasn't going to be that much fun to talk to anyway.

The place was very slowly, but very surely, looking better and better. And shortly after ten o'clock, I felt like I deserved a break. Since I didn't have cable hooked up yet and had uncovered my box of DVDs, I decided to pour another glass and snuggle up under a blanket on the couch to watch one. I fell asleep before the movie was half over and woke up in the same spot to my alarm, informing me it was time to get up and go to work. I noticed as I turned the alarm off that there were still no responses. However, I had to get ready for my day, so I didn't give it much thought.

Looking around my apartment on the way out, I could see there was a lot left to do before I would be ready for company. But again, I was relieved to leave for another day of serving bliss. Luckily, the lunch rush was busy and didn't give me much time to think about anything but extra napkins and refills. I finished my side work just in time to sit down and have something to eat before leaving work. Servers, including Mike, were heading in for the dinner shift.

"Hey, what's going on? Just getting done?" he asked, stealing a fry.

"Yup," I answered, taking another bite of my food.

"Was it busy?" he asked.

"Yeah, it was decent," I answered, not really paying attention.

"Decent people, decent tips? What?" he wanted to know.

"It was fine. Just the usual assholes, no one freaked out or anything," I informed him.

"Hello? Are you even listening to me?" he asked, waving his hand in front of my face. "What's wrong with you?"

"Stop it." I laughed and waved his hand away. "Nothing's wrong. I was up late unpacking so that everyone can come over tomorrow after work. I have another exciting night ahead of me too."

"Wow, sounds like fun. Did Sunshine tell you when he's heading over?" He helped himself to more fries.

I looked at my phone. Again, there was no response to the message I had sent him. "Um, no. He's been pretty busy with work, so I haven't heard anything back yet."

"He hasn't said anything? Did you guys have a fight or something?" He was looking at his own phone.

"No, not at all." I looked up at him, annoyed that he asked. However, I wasn't sure if I was annoyed at him for asking or at myself for not being able to figure out what Aaron was pissed about.

"Oh, okay, my bad. Sorry I asked," he responded, seeing that I was a little uneasy about the situation. "So, is everyone bringing food tomorrow or just beverages?"

"Whatever they want to bring. I figure I'll just get some snacks. Speaking of which, I should get going so I can get to the store and go unpack." I passed my plate to him. "Here, you can have the rest. I'm not as hungry as I thought I was."

I gathered up my things and stood up to put on my jacket. I adjusted my hair over the collar, said good-bye, and turned around to start walking toward the door.

"Wait. Aren't you missing something?" Mike said, holding up my cell phone.

I stopped in my tracks and turned around. "What? I said good—" I walked back toward the table, having a slight realization. "Yes. Yes, I am." I grabbed my phone, smiled, and said good-bye again.

I got to my car and set the phone on the seat. I was just being stupid. It had only been about a day and a half. I should be happy not to have to walk on eggshells. When he had time to calm down from his schedule, he would get a hold of me. He knew I was having a little get-together and that I wanted him there.

I went back to my apartment to pick up where I had left off the night before. I turned on the television and started digging into another box. Randomly shuffling through the contents, I could already tell that it was one of the boxes that would do just fine in the back of my closet. Just as I was about to close it, I noticed an envelope of pictures. I picked it up to go through them and saw that it was a roll of pictures that Aaron and I had taken just a few weeks ago before I moved out. We used a real camera and got double prints so that we would each have some pictures to frame and put around our apartments. The idea was his, and I knew he had the same set of pictures.

Even with everything going on around us, we looked so happy. No one would ever guess the useless drama we were participating in. Even with his "hot and cold" bipolar attitude, I still thought he was damn cute. I knew I still loved him. Flipping through the pictures, I found one where he was smiling and I was giving him a kiss on the cheek. I knew this one would be perfect for a shelf in the living room, to remind me that things could work out between us.

After I picked a few out, I put the pictures back in the envelope and put it back in the box. Then I noticed a large black folder. I opened it to find my acting resume. It listed my training and experience. I'll admit it was a short list, but it reminded me that I should spend my time adding to it. It was a welcome task. I loved my new apartment, but I wasn't sure I wanted to spend all that time alone. I left the black folder out of the box and put it in the back of my closet.

Before I knew it, I had the place looking presentable enough to have my little gathering. I worked in the morning, so midnight was a pretty logical time to give up for the evening and get some sleep. I woke up and actually was excited about going to work. Saturdays are pretty busy work days, and before I knew it, I'd be home relaxing and hanging out with friends.

I took a little longer than usual to get ready since I wanted to look like less of a hot mess when I got off work. My efforts put me a little behind, and I had to rush in to work and get started. All my tables were pretty easygoing. I did have one little brat whose parents weren't watching him as he pulled all the sugar packets out of the container and practiced how hard he could squeeze the ketchup bottle before it would explode all over the table, but I didn't get as irritated as I normally would.

Mike and I were planning what kind of drinks we wanted to start the evening off with. Filling salad dressings, folding silverware, and stocking glasses seemed much more worth it when there was light radiating off a very strong margarita at the end of the tunnel. I said good-bye to everyone, reminded those that I wanted to see later of what time to arrive, and rushed out of work to get ready to party.

I got home, changed, and set up the area that would be used for the bar. I adjusted my hair and makeup and decided to make a margarita for quality control purposes. I wanted everything to go down smoothly, as smoothly as my margarita was going down. I knew I had to keep my phone in sight, just in case anyone got lost or was at the front door. I checked to see if anyone had tried to get a hold of me, but there was nothing yet.

About an hour and two high-quality drinks later, people started to arrive. I welcomed them and gave multiple tours of my new place, convinced I was getting better each time, almost as good as the property manager who had sold me on it. Finishing up one of my rounds, I noticed my phone ringing on the counter and saw that it was Mike. I answered it and told him I'd be right down to let him in.

He greeted me warmly even though we had just seen each other earlier at work. "Hey! How's it goin'?"

"Good! How are you, guys?" I asked, giving him a hug.

"We're great. Lisa, this is Joe. Joe, Lisa," he introduced us.

"Hi, I've heard a lot about you," he said, extending his hand.

"All good, I'm sure! Oh, come on, we're all friends here!" I pushed his hand away and gave him a hug as well. It was probably inspired by the liquid encouragement I'd been utilizing, but I gave him the same welcoming I had given Mike. He seemed a little taken by surprise but gave me a courtesy hug back.

"So, is everyone here? Having fun?" he asked as we made our way to the elevator.

"Yeah, pretty much everyone I invited. People have brought different beverages to share. So far, so good." I informed him.

"Is he here?" he asked, giving me a cautious side glare.

"Who, Aaron? No, he has to work until at least ten," I told him, making it sound like nothing.

"Good. Then we can have some fun before Daddy comes and shuts everything down." He laughed at his own joke. Joe smiled, not fully aware of what Mike was talking about.

I laughed too, not wanting to bring down any high spirits. "Shut up!" I gave him a playful backhand to his arm.

We got back to my apartment, and Mike was greeted by the coworkers who recognized him. He jumped right in and started introducing himself to those he didn't know. Joe seemed a lot quieter than Mike but was somehow managed to keep up with his social skills.

He had reminded me that yet again I had heard nothing from Aaron today. He knew that I was having people over. But I knew that he had to work. I decided to try once more to get a hold of him. On the other end it rang twice and went to voicemail. There weren't enough rings for him to have missed it, but the fact that it rang at all told me that his phone was on. So there was just one undeniable question left: why was Aaron ignoring my call? I tried to think back a few days, to the last time we had talked. We hadn't fought, and even ended the conversation with "I love you." I wasn't sure what was going on, but I was running out of excuses to make for him. So I sent one last text: "What's going on?"

I had to face the facts, but I wasn't going to do it tonight. Not wanting to be a bad hostess or spend the night bitching like a drama queen, I turned the sound on my phone off and set it on the counter, where it would remain for the rest of the night.

Later, as most of the people were leaving, Mike and Joe stuck around to chat a little longer. Sitting on the couch, each with a beer in hand, and keeping the lighting low since it was too cold to sit out on the deck and stare at the stars, we just sat and recapped on the evening, hoping to catch a glimpse of the night sky through the limited windows.

"Well, it looks like everything went well," Mike told me, staying positive.

"Yeah, it was fun. I'm glad almost everyone stopped by," I said, thinking about Aaron again.

"Anyone happen to call and say they couldn't make it?" he asked, one eyebrow raised as if he was speaking in code.

But, unfortunately, I knew what he meant. "Nope. No one at all."

"What happened?" He was asking a legitimate question.

"I have no idea," I said, studying my beer for a moment, then chugging the rest. "I think we need a few shots."

It was a good excuse to walk away for a minute. I figured it would be a good way to bring on a new topic.

"None for me, thanks," Joe said.

"I'll have his!" Mike yelled as I made my way into the kitchen.

I brought the three whiskey shots back and went through the usual ritual of "Cheers." Then a quick clink on the table and down it went.

It burned all the way down. But I was right, the direction of the conversation changed. "So have you really thought about it? About getting out of here and trying something different?" I twisted my shot glass in my hand, fidgeting yet patiently waiting for an answer.

"Yeah. Of course, I have. Have you?" He looked me straight in the eye.

"I have," I answered.

"Actually, Joe and I are planning on moving out there in a few months when my lease is done and I'm finished with school," he boasted.

It took me by surprise. Moving away, especially toward what seemed like the magic of Hollywood always seemed like a far-off dream. It was the kind of impossible mission the heroin in any movie of the weeks pursues before coming out on top and stealing the hearts of anyone within listening distance.

"What?" I asked, simply as a reflex.

"Yeah, we're saving now and want to move out there pretty soon. You didn't think I was picking up all those random shifts to see the a.m. bartender, did you?" He laughed and looked at Joe. I assumed Joe had been told some of the horror stories from the restaurant, and he just smiled back, mostly as a courtesy.

"Wow, yeah. No, I mean, that's great!" I tried to recover and break down the timeline in my head. After a few shots and beer chasers, it was a little tougher to put together. He could see the look on my face and automatically tried to console me.

"That's a good thing! Don't you want to come with us?" he asked.

"Wow. I hadn't even thought that far ahead. I want to. I have to be here until the lawsuit's over, and I just signed a year lease." They sounded like shitty excuses to me too.

"That's a bunch of crap. All you talk about is acting and different auditions around here. Hell, you even sacrificed your face getting your headshots. You need to just wrap all that shit up and get on it. If you want it, it's never gonna be easier to jump in than now. With us. We could get a two-bedroom apartment or something. Split the rent, you know, however we need to do it. It's financially smart. And then you're not out there all alone. Think about it," he told me.

"Yeah, you're right. You're right. This really would be the best way. I had no idea you were thinking about going so soon. Why didn't you bring it up earlier?" I asked.

"You seemed so wrapped up with your boy toy. Every time we talked, it was about that crap. I don't mind listening, but I never got the chance to bring it up. And the way he acts, I didn't know what he would say or do to try and talk you out of it." His words seemed to paint a picture for me, themed "Obvious."

"I can't go yet. Seriously, I just signed the lease. They would keep my deposit and everything. I wish you would have told me. I would have moved back in with Mom," I defended myself, but the portrait he had created was becoming more clear. "I've been so stupid."

"Why?" Mike asked, genuinely puzzled.

"I let him take over my life, and I've been focusing on the stupidest things. He never wanted me to actually be successful as an actress. He talked about supporting me, then whined whenever he had to. Now I'm stuck here for another year." I was upset. I was pissed that Aaron wasn't calling me back. I was pissed that he played this game even after I had proven my devotion to him and our relationship by moving into and paying rent for an apartment I didn't technically need. I was pissed that neither my mother, nor my sister, tried to stop me from getting the place. I was pissed that some jackass couldn't read the print near the stop sign stating that cross traffic does not stop. I was pissed that the photographer never returned my phone calls, treating me as if I simply blew off the appointment to get my pictures. I was pissed that now

I would be stuck here without my best friend. And, most of all, I was pissed at myself for letting it all happen.

"Wait." I could feel my eyes bouncing around the room as an idea was providing a cherry for the top of the shit sundae. And I didn't mind verbalizing my thought process, just in case anyone listening could impart his wisdom. "Maybe I can talk to the landlord. I mean, I haven't finished school, but technically, I could do that anywhere. And headshots, I should get headshots there. They know what they're looking for anyway! I have to have surgery but as long as the doc—"

"Yeah, exactly." Mike laughed. He could tell I was simply rambling with a buzz.

"Yeah, you know what I mean. You know what, I have a meeting with my lawyer on Monday. Are you working any days this week?" I asked.

"Yeah, I think Tuesday or Wednesday. Who knows, I have to look," he said, taking another drink of his beer.

"Well, I might have some really good news for you next time I see you." I winked and offered a toast. He leaned over and gave my glass a quick "cheers," and we both took a drink.

⁉

Chapter 11

After the party on Saturday and a slight hangover on Sunday, the weekend zoomed by and it was time to be serious and focus on my meeting with the lawyer. I tried to schedule the meetings or phone calls in the morning, but it was a double-edged blade. I could get the unpleasant conversations out of the way but then be caught involuntarily contemplating the news for the rest of the day. Even though the pressure was technically on him, I dreaded the meetings we had to discuss my progress in physical therapy and the impending torture of surgery to repair my injuries.

We'd always open with him asking how I was doing. If I told him I was doing well, he would shake his head and tell me that that shouldn't be my answer because there would appear to be no permanent injury. If I told him I was in pain, he would tell me not to milk the injury but instead insist that I had good and bad days as far as pain was concerned.

Since the day I had hired him, he would call to inform me of the daily topic of debate between him and the insurance company. The updates were stressful. The silver lining was that I didn't really feel like I was stuck in the middle, that it was only between my lawyer and my insurance company and all I had to do was pay each of their fees.

I parked my car in the usual spot and made my way toward the door to the lobby of the building. Counting on a short meeting not dragged out by sentiments, I made my way through the lobby to the elevators. The first thing I always noticed when I walked into the building was the smell. It seemed to be a mix between the trendy cologne worn by middle-aged businessmen and the almost antique smell of anyplace built before 1960.

I stepped to the elevator and pushed the button for the third floor of the six-story building. As I watched the numbers rise, I couldn't help but wonder why was he located on the third floor. He was only halfway to the top. Was that an unsaid metaphor, indicative of him only winning half of his cases?

My thoughts were interrupted by the ding of the elevator, letting me know that I had reached my destination. I walked out to my right and headed for the second door on the left. I opened it to find Mrs. Valcourt, my lawyer's wife and business partner, on the phone at the front desk. She looked up and saw me and gave me a motion to tell me she would just be a minute, then went back to frantically writing down what the caller was telling her. After just a few minutes, she ended the call and greeted me.

"Hello. Sorry about that. I was just on the phone with another insurance company. Frank and I are all set up for you in the office." Then she offered, "Did you want a coffee or anything?"

"No, thank you," I replied and followed her back to the office.

Frank stood up to greet me with a handshake. "Hey there. How are you doing?"

"Good. Good. How are you, Mr. Valcourt?" I returned the courtesy.

"Oh, you know, another day. Please call me Frank," he said, sitting down, motioning me to sit on the chair facing his desk, putting on his reading glasses, and starting to shuffle through the papers in front of him. "Did you get a chance to look over the updates and get copies of the medical bills I asked you about?"

He barely looked up at me as he was speaking. It was almost as if I was sitting in the principal's office. Even though he was working for me and we were seeking the same outcome, the desk was representative of the fact that we were motivated by different definitions of the word win.

"Yeah, I have all of it here." I handed him the papers he'd requested.

"Okay, one minute here." He started looking over the papers. "Okay, so you have surgery scheduled in a couple of weeks. You've been seeing the physical therapist at least once a week. The cost of the car. Lost wages." He was verbalizing the list as he was writing it down. He made a few scribbles on his paperwork, took off his glasses, and looked up at me with an unsure expression.

"So, I've never been involved in anything this severe. How long does it usually take to settle these cases?" I knew it was a naïve, random question to be asking at this point, but I really did want to know if he would have any kind of answer for me.

"I don't know," he sighed. "It's close. We're a 'no fault' state. So to prove permanent injury, they generally require a certain amount in medical bills. We'll keep going. I'm sure they'll want to avoid court, but it doesn't sound like the other insurance company is willing to pay."

"What does that mean? They won't cover my medical bills or the cost of having to get a new car? The costs I acquired because their client wasn't paying attention to the road signs?" I was trying to ask calmly but was pretty sure he could tell I was irritated.

"Well, right now, that doesn't matter," he said, continuing to write as he flipped through the paperwork.

"What do you mean 'that doesn't matter'?" Now I was very irritated.

"Well, insurance companies will do anything to save money. Until your bills add up, it's just your word against theirs that you're even hurt. When it comes down to it, they don't even know who's responsible."

"Well, I know who's responsible. I know that I didn't have any of these problems before he decided to make up his own driving laws," I told him.

He took off his reading glasses and looked up at me. "Unfortunately, that doesn't matter to anyone. It all comes down to the money."

Even though I appreciated his blunt honesty, I still had the urge to spit in his face. I had to remind myself that he was actually on my side, with that hope that he would be bringing in a significant amount of money for both of us. I had no idea how this all worked, so I had to put my faith in his knowledge and greed and trust that he would at least see it through for selfish purposes.

"Well, I think that was all I needed. Do you have any more questions for me?" he asked as his wife was bringing in more folders to add to the stack located on the desktop set up in a perpendicular manner to the one Frank and I were sitting at.

Since I was pretty sure I already knew what he would tell me, I wasn't excited to have an accidental witness to the conversation. "Well, actually, I did have one more question."

"Yes?" He looked over his reading glasses right at me. His wife looked up and gave me a courtesy smile, proving she was paying attention, then going back to organizing the folders.

"Well, I might be moving out of state. Will I have to postpone that until this is settled?" I asked calmly.

"Yeah, you will have to postpone that. Otherwise, we might as well just drop this now. If you're well enough to pack up and move out of the state, then your permanent injuries can't be that bad. Do you see what I'm saying?" he asked, annoyed that I would even insinuate such a thing.

"I know what you're saying. It's not anything set in stone." I tried to make it sound like moving wasn't a priority.

"All right. Good. Just get that thought out of your head. Focus on upcoming surgery, and I'll be in touch." He said the words mechanically, once again looking back down at his work, seemingly too busy to even say good-bye.

Frank's wife walked me out. Though it was a cooler farewell, essentially walking me to the door to make sure the door didn't literally hit me on my way out, it was still warmer etiquette than her husband had showed me.

As I walked to my car, all I could think about was him acting like my case didn't matter. Him telling me essentially, none of my suffering mattered. Even though the span of my insurance company's knowledge of me consisted the cleared payment made to them every month and even though they wouldn't have been able to put a face with the name on the checks received until now, they'd be willing to drop me like a bad habit if the extent of my injuries should cost too much. Regardless of the fact that even though I was living in a "no fault" state, the accident was found to be the fault of the other driver.

It didn't make sense, but I was unraveling one of life's great lessons. No one will stand up for me, except for me. The only person I could truly count on was myself. I might be screwed.

Clinging to the idea that there would be a way to redeem the day, I decided to stop into the apartment office and see if anyone had more promising answers to my questions. I pretty much knew there was no hope, but figured I had to try.

The secretaries greeting was a lot warmer than what I had just experienced, even though she was only being paid a very small percentage of what I would be paying my lawyer if we won our case. She led my back to the property manager's office and left with a smile.

"What can I do for you?" the manager asked with a smile.

"Well, I had a question about my lease," I said cautiously.

"Oh, is something wrong? Should I pull it out here?" She started to spin her chair toward the filing cabinet.

"Oh, no. No, that's okay. It's a random question." I didn't know how to say it. "I was wondering what would happen if I was to move out before my lease was up. I might have a job opportunity coming up out of state. I just needed to know what kind of timeline I should give them."

I was pretty sure that she could tell I was lying since she had seen my paystubs and knew I was simply a waitress. It sounded just as ridiculous to me, even as I was saying it. But it was the best excuse I could come up with.

"Well, you wouldn't get your deposit back. You'd have to reimburse the discounted cost of the rent per month and pay the full amount of the monthly rent until another tenant moves in." She was straight to the point. However, she was so friendly, you couldn't be mad at her.

It sucked, but I knew the answer wouldn't be pretty. I nodded and replied, "Yeah, I figured it would be something like that. Just wanted to check out all my options." I tried to laugh it off, but the conversation had become somewhat awkward.

"Were you wanting to move forward with the process?" she asked with a more serious tone.

"Oh no. No. Like I said, I just needed to know what time frame I should give them." I tried to smile and hide my disappointment.

"Good. Was there anything else I could do for you?" she asked.

"No. That was it. Thanks for your time." I took the hint and stood up to leave the room.

It was a very disappointing morning. Everything around me seemed to be holding me back from going with Mike and Joe. I got into my apartment and opened the shades in front of the deck door, hoping to absorb some sun. It seemed appropriate that the clouds had gotten thicker, and it was starting to rain.

I sat on the couch and turned on the television, hoping to find something to keep my mind off the impending downward slope of my day. But with everything that was going wrong, it was hard to stop my mind from spinning and just sit back, relax, and find something cheerful to watch.

Clutching at straws of positivity, I tried to concentrate on what I could accomplish while I was essentially stuck here. I was having surgery in about a week and a half, and a couple of weeks after that, school would start again.

I was going insane thinking through reasoning of staying or going, and I knew I had to get out of my apartment and find something to keep myself busy. Since I had taken the day off from work for the meeting with my lawyer, I had the rest of the day to stew over every decision. I decided instead to do something constructive. I put on my work uniform and started heading down to my car. It was out of the ordinary to head into work on my day off, but I figured I could start doing what Mike said he had done: save money to move.

I arrived at work shortly before the p.m. servers were supposed to arrive, and my manager seemed surprised to see me.

"What are you doing here?" she asked. "You're not on the schedule, are you?" She started looking over the list of employees and assigned sections on her clipboard.

"No, no. I was just coming in to see if anyone wanted the night off. I had to take the a.m. shift off for a meeting, just wanted to see if I could redeem myself," I told her. I was hoping my explanation didn't sound as desperate to her as it did to me.

"Oh, yeah. That's cool. Keep me posted so I can change the chart then," she said, walking back to the office.

I smiled and nodded and headed over to the usual break table. A couple of my a.m. coworkers were enjoying the beginning of their free evenings with a burger, and there didn't appear to be any p.m. servers working on a pregame snack.

I sat down at the next table over, hoping to avoid my daily coworkers possible questioning of my shift change. Luckily, I was pretty sure that they had better things to worry about than my schedule. I started playing random games on my phone, keeping an eye out for anyone I could propose the gift of a night off to.

"Hey! What's up? I thought you didn't work today." Mike's greeting scared me since I must have gotten too involved in my enticing card game.

"Yeah, I wasn't going to. I had all my meetings, and I just happened to be free this evening." I tried to keep the conversation light.

"So, what all went down?" he asked, putting his things on the table so he could head over and order his usual dinner.

"That's a story for a round of shots." I hoped my answer was vague enough to be good or bad. I wanted the evening to be positive, full of humor, and good tips. For once I wanted the drama left at the door.

"Oh. Well, I'll never argue with that. So party at your place after work?" He laughed.

"Sounds like a plan to me!" I smiled. "Now help me figure out who wants to get the hell out of here!"

After a few more employees arrived, I started to ask if anyone wanted to turn around and leave again. I was surprised at how many employees said no, with the reasoning that they needed the money. I simply told them that I understood and that it was no big deal since I was determined not to take my frustration out on anyone. Finally, I randomly asked one of the servers I had never really met before, but luckily, he was wearing a uniform, so I knew he was an employee. I was relieved when he responded with a "Hell, yeah!," and we walked to the office to inform the boss.

The shift was exactly what I was hoping for. I acquired the large-party section. There was a wait time of at least twenty minutes, and all of us employees had to run around like crazy people to stay ahead of the demand. It was the perfect excuse to avoid my troubles. In fact, it was even constructive as I was making pretty decent tips. The frosting on the cupcake was working with Mike, who always put me in a good mood. It was impossible not to have fun when he was on the clock. Without him even realizing it, I saw him as a huge means of support. He was someone I admired. Regardless what was going on in his life or what shitty hoops his tables were making him jump through to collect a minimal tip, he always seemed to have a good attitude. I was amazed at how he could pull it off.

After the shift was over, Mike and I worked on finishing our side work quickly to allow us to get to our round of shots with a story-time chaser. I was done and heading home first and simply told him to call me when he got there.

"Sounds good," he answered. "Do I need to stop and get anything, or do you still have leftovers from your shindig?"

"Oh, I'm plenty stocked up. You just need to show up!" I was still trying to sound positive. Having to admit to him that there were two huge obstacles in the way of me leaving with him and Joe was also me having to admit it to myself. I had explored the what-ifs, and they had become the absolutely-nots. It sucked, but it was true.

I got home and tried to make sure everything looked somewhat hospitable. It was never a mess to begin with, but I wanted to make sure I hadn't exercised my freedom and thrown any underwear on the couch or anything.

Knowing Mike, he wouldn't have thought twice and simply brushed them aside to sit down.

I was afraid there would be a gap between when I got home and when Mike left work to come over and that I would have too much time to sink back into my bad mood. I took a quality control shot and turned on the television, looking for comedic movie or a sitcom to keep my spirits up since I didn't want to be a bad hostess.

Luckily, my phone started buzzing right after I picked up the remote to search the channels, and it was Mike telling me that he was downstairs. I was relieved to be interrupted and rushed to head down and let him in.

"Hey! Did someone say something about a round of shots?" he yelled as we rushed to the elevator. It almost sounded as if he was expecting good news, and that it was going to be a celebratory round.

"That would be me! I even tested it to make sure it was, you know, acceptable for the guest." I wanted to keep the positive vibe going as long as possible.

"You are so generous!" He laughed. "Is it just me, or is this elevator going really slow?"

"It's just you," I informed him, providing the introduction to less than desirable revelations.

We walked in, and Mike sat his keys on the kitchen counter as I was setting a second shot glass next to my own.

"Whiskey?"

"Have we met?" he asked, watching me since I was already pouring from the bottle I had grabbed when I asked.

With a quick clink and a tap on the counter, we drank the shots, grabbed the shot glasses and the bottle, and headed for the couch.

"Okay, that was fun. So what happened?" he asked, getting straight to the point.

I looked at him. His eyes were huge, and he was waiting for a positive answer. I knew his decision to move out to Los Angeles didn't depend on me in any way, but it would've made it easier on both of us, emotionally and financially. And, for some reason, I really felt like I was letting him down. But I needed to be completely honest.

"Well, the decision was unanimous!" I told him. "Between my lease and the lawsuit, there is no way I'll be able to move within a few months. Ready for another shot?"

I was already pouring the drinks since I didn't want to see his response.

"Bummer. I figured it'd be a lot easier if we all drove out together. Then we could take driving shifts or split the travel costs." His response was more positive than I had expected, even though he could tell how upset it made me.

We took another shot and set our glasses down. "It just sucks. Everything I did—getting this apartment, trying to work things out with Aaron, school, acting—it's useless. I'm stuck. I thought I was doing all the mature, responsible things. Turns out I was just being a naïve idiot. Now I can't get away from any of it."

"Oh, please. Stop being such a drama queen. What, are you working on your dramatic monologue?" He rolled his eyes at me.

"Wait, what?" His words took me by surprise. "Drama queen?"

"Yeah. Just because you won't get to spend all that quality time traveling out there with Joe and me, doesn't mean you won't move out there later," he informed me.

"Yeah, you're absolutely right. So I suffer through another winter and save a little more money. That could be a good thing." I was trying to convince myself.

"Exactly. So you'll spend a few more months in the cold weather while we're sitting under palm trees and lying on the beach," he informed me as I rolled my eyes at him. "So you'll keep serving the coupon-clutching Minnesota-nice people, and I'll be waiting on Hollywood royalty with tons of cash to throw around. No big deal."

"All right. I think I have a grasp on this," I said, cutting him off as I threw a couch cushion at him.

Everything he said was true. Looking at the situation as if it was the end of the world would be another stupid waste of my time. I would get out there. I just had to wait it out and tie up a few loose ends. The rest of his logic was about to throw me back into my funk, so we changed the subject and let him tell me the horror stories of his past few shifts. We spent the rest of the evening laughing and talking shit about stupid customers.

Right up until my surgery, I found that picking up extra shifts was not only good for my finances but very good for my sanity. I hadn't heard from Aaron at all. Part of me hoped that there was some small part of him that had a conscience and that he would at least fulfill his promise of being there for me during or after surgery. However, the other part of me was afraid I'd try to scratch his eyes out if he ever had the nerve to try and talk to me again. I tried not to think about him at all since it made me feel stupid to be so vulnerable to another person.

I had my final doctor appointment a couple of days before my surgery. The appointment was spent going over the doctor's instructions about preparing for the procedure, what exactly he would be doing during the surgery, and timelines for aftercare and recovery.

Regardless of the importance of such a significant event, I studied the pictures in the packet he had provided me more than I listened to his instructions. As long as I didn't eat anything the night before, I figured I was doing my part. I was in the middle of learning the anatomy of my nose when the doctor wrapped up the session with the usual commentary.

"Do you have any other questions for me?" He was looking at me when I peeked up from my lesson.

"No, nothing I can think of now," I answered. It was an honest answer. There was nothing I could think of that he had left out of our consultation.

The next day I decided I only needed to work one shift. Since I couldn't eat anything twenty-four hours before surgery, I figured I wouldn't impress anyone by serving food to my tables with low blood sugar. Instead I utilized the opportunity to move my mother in so that she could babysit me throughout the surgery.

After dropping off the five suitcases she would need to spend the week with me after surgery, my mother sat down on the couch and started looking over the information about the procedure and aftercare.

"Wow, so they're pretty much going to break your nose and reset it?" she asked while reading through the information like it was a simple grocery list.

"Fracture, Mother. Fracture," I corrected her to keep myself somewhat calm. "Saying that I'm paying someone to break my nose makes it sound like I owe money to someone in the mob."

"Doesn't sound like it's going to be fun. They're at least gonna give you some decent pain meds afterwards, right?" She looked up at me, genuinely concerned. "Coz this looks like it's going to hurt. A lot."

"Yes. Thank you, Mother. Thank you for emphasizing that I'm going to want to die when they're done." I wasn't sure why she was trying to torture me when it sounded like the doctor was going to do a fine job all on his own.

"And the bruising. It says here that you're probably going to get two black eyes. You might look like you just had a boxing match." She seemed very neutral about the information, like she was reading random statistics, not something that was about to be done to her own daughter.

"Yes, Mother. I'm going to be in pain—and ugly. Thank you for pointing that out. I was waiting for you to add insult to injury," I said as I grabbed her reading material: a gossip magazine she'd brought with her to read while I clung to life in the operating room.

"Oh, it won't be that bad. And you'll have your pain meds," she said, finally realizing what her flare for the obvious was doing to me.

I kept nervously flipping through the pages of her magazine. "That's easy for you to say, you're not the one whose nose they're going to hammer into."

"Wow, they're going to use a hammer? What page is that on?" She sounded excited and started flipping through the pages to find a picture.

"Mom! Really? You're killing me. I'm two seconds from taking a cab to the doctor's office!" I snapped at her.

"You will not. Calm down, why are you so crabby?" She sounded surprised.

"Well, I'm not really thrilled about the idea of having my face operated on. I'm not really thrilled about having anything operated on," I confided. "I'm scared. This sucks. I can barely breath out of my nose, so I know I have to do it, but I'm really scared."

"Everything will go just fine. You're worried for nothing. According to this packet, they do hundreds of these surgeries every year," she consoled me.

"Yuck. I hope you're right. I just want to get it over with!" I whined.

Moms are usually very comforting. Which is why when we're ill from a paper cut to a broken limb, we seem to feel better with our moms around. However, my mother saw this process as some documentary where she could learn about nose jobs. She seemed more interested in the entertaining aspects of the gory process than in the sympathizing with my fears. Still, I knew she would probably be the best one to take care of me when it was all over. Assuming I would survive the procedure.

"Worrying about it won't get it over with any sooner. Try not to worry. Get some sleep." She stood up to go put on her pajamas. "Am I taking the couch or the bed tonight?"

"I'll be setting up camp here for the week, so I'm gonna try and break it in tonight," I said, reaching for the remote.

"Sounds good. I'm going to bed so I can get my beauty rest. Maybe I can keep up with you tomorrow." She winked at me as she said it.

"You're hilarious." I rolled my eyes at her.

I didn't get much sleep that night. Usually I can find something on television to fall asleep to. However, documentaries on horror stories from emergency room disasters and realty shows about messed-up cosmetic surgeries kept me wide awake. The last time I checked the time, courtesy of the guide on my television, I had about two hours before I had to be up and moving to get to the doctor's office. I must have finally passed out after that because the next thing I knew, I was waking up to my mother's cheerful impression of an alarm clock.

"Lisa, wake up! It's your big day!" she said loudly as she headed into the kitchen.

"Ugh, Mom." I could barely open my eyes, and when I realized I wasn't dreaming, I flopped my head back down on the couch and pulled my blanket over my head.

"No, no, sleepyhead! You need to get up and get moving. We have to be there in about an hour." She made it sound like a field trip.

"Really? A big day is something you look forward to, something you want to happen. I feel like I'm about to willingly submit to my own demise," I said, slowly getting myself into a sitting position.

"Or something significant that will allow you to look forward to the future and leave the drama in the past," she said, pouring herself a cup of coffee.

"Super." I swung my feet to the floor and stopped to rub my eyes.

"Now get moving! If the doctor can wake up this early to slice into you, the least you can do is be on time to be sliced." She took another sip and smiled.

"Great. Just so you don't think I'm oblivious to your humor, let me tell you, you suck." I walked into my room to grab my clothes for my shower.

My half-asleep brain was racing throughout the process, and I wasn't sure I had everything I needed. But I just wanted to get it over with. I made my mother drive and just tried to focus on not having a panic attack.

It wasn't necessarily the idea of pain that scared me, it was the process of being knocked out. I'd never been put out for surgery and the only point of reference I could imagine was smoking pot. I was never into that. It always made me paranoid. Not the kind of paranoia that instills the fear of being discovered and grounded by one of my parents, but the kind that makes me feel like I can't breathe. The kind that makes my pulse feels like its racing and makes me dizzy. I had no idea if the two feelings were actually similar, but I was scared anyway and stewed over it all the way to the parking garage, where we stopped in the entrance to get our parking ticket.

We found our parking spot, and my mother stopped to study the rates on the ticket. "Wow, I hope they validate."

"I'm sure they will." It was the least of my concerns.

"Seriously, do you see these rates? I hope the doctor works quickly," she said, gathering her purse and magazines. "Wait, what if he has some deal going with the hospital and milks out all the surgeries to make the patients pay more for parking?"

She made a funny face when she said it, but her attempts to cheer me up were falling on deaf, somewhat annoyed, ears.

"Yes, Mom. I bet that's it. You solved the mystery."

We headed for the front doors of the hospital, and as we got closer and closer, I could feel myself starting to shake. I was pretty sure it was a mix of the cold weather and my nerves. I don't remember the walk to the doctor's office, but once I walked up to the front desk to check in, I was snapped out of my trance by the receptionist handing me a clipboard with consent forms to be filled out.

I could only imagine what I was excusing the doctor's from: over anesthetizing me, causing me horrible pain and suffering, or even making my nose fall off. I forced myself to finish the paperwork and give it back to the receptionist. She smiled and said the doctor would be with me in a few minutes. I simply smiled back and headed back to sit and wait.

I couldn't sit still. My legs were shaking and bouncing, and I hoped that if I kept shifting my position in my chair that my mother wouldn't notice. My thoughts were racing yet again. What would I do without a nose. I would look like a zombie. The only acting roles I'd be able to audition for would be for horror films or one those documentary films about procedures gone wrong. Not exactly the type of film I'd want to star in.

And how would I breathe? Would they have to sacrifice my pseudo nostrils so that I wouldn't inhale bad things like dust? Or would they leave them completely open so that I could breathe, and then I'd just have to wear one of those surgical masks everywhere? I was pretty sure I didn't want one of those prosthetic noses that celebrities wear when they didn't want to admit they'd had multiple surgeries. My eyes started to water at the thought that it would take me twice as long to get ready in the morning!

I knew I was just being stupid again and was relieved when the nurse called my name to go back to see the doctor. Before I left my things with my mother, I took the time to check my phone and see if there were any new messages. There was one from Mike telling me to break a leg. That was sweet, but the fact that there weren't any from Aaron made my eyes water. It was all I could do to choke back the tears. Yet again, it was painfully obvious that it was all over.

The march through the lobby door and back to the curtained area where I would be changing into one of those hospital gowns seemed to make my pulse race even more than it had been when I sat in the lobby in anticipation. The nurse gave me the gown and told me to open the curtain once I had taken off my top and put the gown on. Aside from the fact that I was freezing after removing my long-sleeved sweatshirt, I was still pretty comfortable, maintaining my sports bra and yoga pants under the short-sleeved gown.

Not long after I pulled the curtain back, the doctor and one of his nurses came into the room. He once again confirmed the procedure I was there for and asked if I had any last-minute questions. I knew I had no logical questions, so I declined the offer to vent. I figured that was it, and we would get started, but he said that he had one last question for me.

"So did you think any more about the implant we discussed?" he asked, looking me right in the eye. "I think we need to do it. Our objective here is to make sure you can breathe, but in the long run, we also want to make sure things look good and natural. So if we match your chin, no one will ever know you had surgery."

I was confused since I was under the impression that he already knew I didn't want any kind of implant, especially if it put me at a higher risk for having to have more procedures. "No. I don't want an implant. I just want to be able to breathe. I have no desire to match this chin!"

My attempt at a joke made me feel like my mother when it wasn't received and even seemed to annoy the doctor.

"Are you sure? I think you're making a mistake. You probably won't like the way it looks afterwards." He almost seemed upset with me.

"Well, are you planning on chiseling it off?" I laughed at my own joke but knew I was being passive-aggressive about his intentions with the surgery.

"No. No, of course not. I'm trying to consider long-term goals. The decision is ultimately yours. But I think you'll regret it." He shook his head and looked back down at his clipboard. "All right then. We just need to check your blood pressure and other vitals. Once those are cleared, the anesthesiologist will get started."

I just nodded and watched him leave the area, drawing the curtain behind him. I couldn't believe it. He actually seemed mad at me for not wanting to get an implant in my nose. Wasn't it my face, after all? Now I felt really shitty. I trusted the doctor throughout the process of planning the surgery since he always seemed confident that this was the best plan of attack. The fact that he now doubted the end result just stressed me out even worse. Since he and I had different visions, was he going to do his best to fulfill my expectations? I wondered if I should have consulted another doctor before scheduling anything.

Now I was here, and we were about to begin. I could only sit on the bed and wait for the nurse to come in and test everything, hoping the doctor could achieve my goal, basically getting it right so I would never have to see him again. Looking around the curtained area, I was searching for signs of blood or death of previous patients. I couldn't see anything in particular so that was a good sign. Regardless whether it meant that surgeries were always successful or that they simply had an amazing janitor, it was still a good sign.

The nurse came in and started with my blood pressure. She wrote everything down, and then it was time for the IV. I've never been afraid of needles and figured this would be the smoothest part of the morning. The needle went into my arm very smoothly, and she informed me that it was in preparation for the doctors to utilize. She finished with my temperature and hooking up a heart monitor to my finger. She finished her notes and left the area.

I expected that the next time the curtain swung open, it would be the anesthesiologist. I was right, but he came in with another purpose. He explained to me that my blood pressure was too high put me out. Although his choice of words made me feel like the family cat, I understood what he meant. He said that this was common, and that with the stress that comes along with having a major procedure, it wouldn't be logical to simply wait for me to calm down. He said they would give me something to relax and then check my blood pressure again in ten minutes. I wasn't thrilled with the idea but agreed to it. I lay back on the bed and watched him empty the syringe into my IV. I thought I would dread the feeling of it spreading through my body, but that didn't seem to be the case.

Slowly, but surely, I could tell there was a difference. I wasn't freaking out, and I didn't feel paranoid. I couldn't really concentrate. I suddenly thought of a question or two I should ask the doctor before we began.

"Did I already sign everything I needed to?" I asked, clinging to what was left of my sobriety.

"Yes, you sure did," the doctor said, going about his work of disposing of the syringe and throwing out his rubber gloves.

"Good. That's good. Coz right now, I might not be in the right frame of mind," I admitted.

"All right, sounds like the medication has taken effect. We'll just test your blood pressure again," he said, wrapping my other arm.

"Oh, and please, please make sure my nose doesn't fall off. I know they say that good pictures are a matter of angles, but I don't know if I can tilt my head the right way to pull that off. You know, for my headshots. And I don't know if I can pull off a prosthetic," I informed him, but he seemed to be ignoring me. "I just wanted to, you know, tell you that."

After that, everything else seemed blurry, like a dream. It was an incredible annoyance when I woke up to an audience.

"Lisa. Lisa, wake up. You're all done," my mother said, leaning over me and smiling. "The doctor said that everything went perfectly!"

I felt as if I was looking at her through a tiny hole in a fence, but I couldn't really focus enough to respond to her. I really just wanted to go back to sleep.

"When are they going to start?" I managed to mutter, then wanted to go back to sleep.

"Yeah, she'll be loopy for a while." The nurse smiled and continued changing tubes and pads and staring at her clipboard.

"No, sweetie. You don't understand. They're all done." Mom was consoling me.

"Good. When do we get to go home?" It felt like my nose was stuffed, making it harder to say the words and be a mouth breather at the same time. "Can I blow my nose?"

"No. Nope, none of that until the doctor says so." The nurse looked directly at my mother and me when she said it. "How are you feeling? Are you in pain?"

"I'm sleepy. I want to go to sleep," I told her.

I really couldn't feel any pain. I couldn't even feel my legs. I just wanted to cuddle up under a warm blanket and pass out for the next week. We were told that we needed the doctor's orders before we could leave, and I was somewhat relieved. The walk to the car in the chilly weather sounded awful. So for the time being I was thrilled to stay under the warm blanket and try to sleep, although it would have been a lot easier without the audience.

"I'll let the doctor know you're awake." The nurse smiled and disappeared behind the curtain.

Just as I was about to drift off to sleep again, the doctor came in to wake me up and look at my wounds.

"Well, how's our patient doing?" he asked, rolling up his stool to sit closer to the bed.

I turned to face him, although between the pain killers and the swelling, he was a big blur. "I'm good."

"Brave too! That's what we want to hear." He made a few markings on his clipboard, then looked up to explain what all happened with my deviated septum during the procedure.

I was somewhere between sleepy and high, and all I could really see was him making shadow puppets. But, seeing Mom off in the distance, smiling and nodding along with his report made me feel confident that I would get to go home and sleep on my own couch soon. Now I just had to let him touch my face while I was awake.

Luckily my eyes were almost swollen shut, so the light from his headband wasn't blinding me at this point. It felt very weird to have him even lightly touching my nose. I couldn't decide if it hurt or if it tickled or if I just wanted to go to sleep. Luckily, it was a quick exam. He said I only had to wait a couple more hours, and he would come back when it was time for me to go home.

I wasn't sure how time was passing since I was in and out of consciousness, but soon I heard the doctor's voice announcing himself and reaching for the curtain to make his entrance.

⁇

Chapter 12

I was ripped from yet another dream by the doctor getting in my face and studying his work. I was a little more sober this time, and I realized the swelling and bandages were a big part of what was blocking my view of exactly what he was doing. I wasn't in a lot of pain, so I could tell they had given me something to keep me sane until I could head home to die on my own couch. Luckily, I found out, they were about to give me another dose so I could get up and move, at least to a wheelchair.

I was cleared to leave and couldn't move fast enough to get out. I literally couldn't move fast enough since even the motion of sitting up and swinging my legs over the edge of the bed made me dizzy.

"Whoa, sweetie, your gown's gonna go up over your head if you're not careful." Mom was trying to help me get my pants on.

"I'm pretty sure it's nothing they haven't seen before." I had forgotten that I had kept my pants on. "Besides, I put on underwear today, didn't I?" I started to lift my gown so I could find the waistline of my yoga pants. I started to stretch them open so I could solve the mystery.

"What are you doing?" Mom laughed at me as she was rolling the hospital provided wheelchair to the side of the bed and setting the break.

"No. It's cool. We're good," I assured her.

"All right. That's good. Here, take my hand. Just step down and sit in the chair," she said, offering a hand behind my back to direct me.

"I'm fine. I can stand up on my own." I grabbed the side of the bed so support my while I slid off to stand up.

The rush of the physical activity made me a little dizzy, and I waivered before reaching over to grab the armrests on the wheelchair and utilize them to twist around and sit.

"See? I got this," I said, leaning back in the chair as if I had just run a marathon.

"Yes, I see that," Mom said, humoring me and gathering up her purse and magazines to set on my lap before she unset the breaks.

The attending nurse offered to walk us out and help get me in the car, but I declined. "Nah, she can do it. She's a big girl."

"Volunteering me. How generous of you," Mom said, making a face at the nurse.

"I'm a giver," I said. "Are we leaving or what?"

Being rolled down the hallway while on pain meds was like being on a ride at a theme park. If I'd had the energy, I probably would have stuck my arms in the air, like people do when they're on roller coasters. Luckily it was a short ride, and I didn't have the strength or sound mind to get them up in time.

Mom parked me by the door, and I waited for her to pull the car up. When she got out to assist me, getting up and walking seemed like a much larger chore, and because of the cotton taped to my face, I had to tilt my head down further to see where I was stepping. My legs felt like jelly.

I fell asleep on the ride home, and when we got to my apartment, it seemed to take forever to walk to the elevator and then wait for it to reach the third floor. Finally, I was home. I could lie down and die in peace, and with a couple extra blankets and a television remote, it sounded like heaven!

The next week flew by since I spent most of it asleep. The time spent awake usually consisted of having to get up to go to the bathroom, choke down some food so I could take another pain pill, or, the most dreaded, having to wake up and have my mother change my bandages.

Accidentally seeing my reflection in the mirror when I walked into the bathroom was rough, even with the influence of my medication. I wasn't really sure how my big, fat, purple face was ever going to look normal again. I was glad it was only my mother seeing me at my worst. However, after my week of drug-induced bliss was coming to an end, I had my first visitor.

"Hey! Who wants to play doctor?" Mike yelled, walking toward the couch after being let in by my mother.

He took me by surprise since I hadn't even heard my phone ring. Apparently my mother had answered and let him in. It was the first time she would meet him.

"Hey, what's up?" I responded. "Mom, this is Mike. Mike, my mom, Rhonda."

"Hello! Nice to meet you. I'm sure Lisa's told you all about me. I'm her favorite coworker!" he boasted. Then turning back toward me, his smile faded to a more serious expression. "Wow, you look so—pretty."

I was staring at him with two swollen, black-and-blue eyes and my mouth hanging open since I couldn't breathe out of my nose.

"Hard to believe I'm single, huh?" I asked. "If you're nice, I'll give you a few pointers."

"Great. I'll keep that in mind next time Joe wakes me up snoring," Mike joked "So when are you coming back to work?"

"Ick, I wasn't even thinking about that. Next week. I need to look somewhat decent before I come back," I explained.

"Not necessarily. Just pretend its Wednesday." He laughed.

Even I had to laugh at that, even if it was against me and hurt like hell to laugh. "Right. You know I'm all for sympathy tips, but I can't collect them if me going near the table frightens their children."

"Just tell them you're an actress and you're preparing for a part. Say, in a horror film or a female boxing movie. Method acting is a very deep process."

"Especially when its surrounded by so much shit." I gave as good of a smile as I could perform. "Yeah, once I can at least walk around without half a bag of cotton taped to my face, I'll be back. School starts after that too."

"Yikes. Enjoy the meds while you can." He reached into his pocket. "So a few of us got together and got you this."

He handed me an envelope. Inside was a card with a picture of a bouquet of flowers on the cover. It was a picture my grandmother would have loved. Not the type of card I would expect Mike to get for me. I opened it up and expected to see "Get well soon." Instead, there was a longer statement, reading, "We're thinking of you during this time." All around it was the signature of select coworkers.

I looked up at him. "Really? Thank you."

"Well, you know, I had gotten it for my great aunt when her husband passed away last year. But, you know, it seemed to fit," he justified.

"Why, because my relationship with Aaron died shortly before my surgery?" I confessed.

"Has he said anything? Called to find out how you're doing?" Mike asked.

"Nope, not a word. No need to mourn, he went quietly." I smiled, stating the obvious. He really had just quietly slithered away like a snake.

"What a selfish prick. You're better off without him."

"Exhibit A." I motioned around the apartment.

"Well, I have to get going. I just wanted to see how you were doing." Mike started to stand up and took one last opportunity to tease me. "I'm glad everything went well. You didn't die or end up looking like a pop star or anything."

"Thanks for stopping by." I was pretty sure I was smiling, even though my round of pain killers was making half of my face feel numb. "Talk to you later!"

My mother walked him out and said good-bye too. I wanted to lie down and pass out again, but Mom had another idea.

"What a nice boy. That's the kind of guy you should be dating," she said, starting to prepare more soup for me to chug in place of a meal.

"Yeah, too bad he's in a relationship," I said, not having the energy to explain all the details of someone else's relationship.

"Well, shoot." Mom had such a flare to wrap her passive aggression up in a sweet, charming wrapper. "Here's some soup. You have to eat with those meds.

"Thanks." I sat up to take the bowl.

Even though I wanted to drink it quickly, it was incredibly difficult since I could only breathe through my mouth. I swallowed what I could and lay back down, adjusting to the dent in the cushions I had created over the course of the past week.

The next day, with my mother's help and armed with an empty bottle of limited pain medication, it was time to face the doctor again. I don't remember much about the appointment since I was more nervous to see him this time, not wanting anyone touching my face until it was completely healed. I knew he had to check the stitches and remove the stuffing he had placed in my nose. After the usual greeting and updates of what to expect at this stage and how much pain I was or wasn't in, it was time for him to put on the headband again.

Shining it right in my face, he reached up with his plastic gloves to remove the tape holding the gauze up to my nostrils. I didn't appreciate the motion, but it wasn't as horrible as I had imagined. My nose didn't fall to the floor after he took it off, so I allowed him to continue.

He grabbed what looked like oversized tweezers and started reaching into my nose. He pulled out a long strip. It tickled and rubbed the inside of my nose the entire way out. And because of my stitches, he had to pull it out slowly to make sure it didn't get caught on anything. Not the most painful thing I had experienced thus far, but it was still torture having my nose hair stimulated with his tweezers. And what's more, I couldn't itch at it or rub my nose like I wanted to.

"Eew, that was awful," I said, breathing more heavily out of my mouth to compensate for the fact that sneezing could blow my stitches open.

"No worries. Only one more to go." The doctor smiled and started going after the other nostril.

Knowing what to expect didn't do me any favors with the second round. I couldn't only close my eyes and wait for the itch and urge to sneeze to go away.

"All right. Go ahead and take a gentle breath through your nose," the doctor told me.

I was nervous but followed his orders. "Wow, I can actually breath. That's pretty cool." I wanted to take another longer, less cautious breath. "That's great. Am I only appreciating this because my nose was stuffed like a turkey or is there actually more air getting through?"

"It's probably a mix, but you should notice that it will get easier and easier to breathe through your nose as the swelling goes down. And before you know it, you'll be running a marathon." He smiled, proud of himself for a job well done. "And you still have the packet, what to expect, the aftercare, all that?"

"Yeah, we have it," I said between practice breaths of inhaling all the air I could through my nose. I was pretty sure if I kept this up, it would make me feel dizzier than my pain meds.

My mother and I stopped to pick up takeout and arrived back at my apartment to enjoy a real dinner. It was amazing actually being able to taste my food instead of just chugging liquid constantly and calling it a meal. We both seemed to appreciate the real food, along with the fact that I didn't have to hold up my cotton mustache to consume it.

"Well, if you're doing better, I can pack up my things and go back home," my mother said, taking another bite.

"You don't have to leave tonight. You'd be caught in traffic," I told her, not wanting to be all alone after having her stuck to me like wet toilet paper for the last week.

"You're right. I suppose I could stay another night," she said, seemingly catching on to my not wanting to be all alone in the apartment.

"It's almost Friday. Maybe we could call Michelle and see if she wants to come have a girls' weekend," I suggested.

"No, she can't. She's dog sitting," she replied. "But I guess I could stay the weekend. We just need to go to the grocery store. I'm sick of food I can slurp through a straw."

We both laughed, and I noticed it wasn't as hard to laugh as it had been a few days ago. Even though I was focusing on the physical truth to that statement, I also thought there might be an emotional aspect to it. Getting through surgery, I was a significant step closer to putting the accident behind me. And in the process, I was closer to putting Aaron behind me too.

The fact that he didn't even try to call me before or after surgery showed me his true feelings for me, or his lack thereof. I had wasted my time with him. It was just some silly fantasy. He had no intention of supporting me in my goals but instead proved to be an obstacle in moving on with my life and heading out to California toward my goals.

I wasn't sure I whether I was more hurt by the fact that his words hadn't meant anything or by the fact that I was stupid enough to fall for all of it. What happened to my high school days when guys were just laying it on thick to figure out some way of kicking off their collection of notches. At least we knew they were lying pieces of crap. Whether they got their ways or not, they didn't stick around to add insults to the metaphoric injury.

There was only one thing I could convince myself of—regardless what had happened with Aaron, it was over and done with and I just had to keep myself busy enough not to wallow in what might have been. This would be easy. I had it all planned out. School would be starting in another couple of weeks, and until then, all I had to do was pick up shifts at work to fill my time. Once school started, I could start pursuing auditions again and devote myself to my performance. Yeah, this would all work out. Now all I had to do was convince my mommy to spend the weekend with me until I was cleared to go back to work. This was going to be just super.

We spent our weekend like two friends having a slumber party. We watched movies. We baked cookies, and even tried new recipes. Even though it was great having a buddy, I still didn't want to admit to her that I felt like I had messed everything up. She had warned me against it, and I had gone and done it anyway. I felt awful but convinced myself it was just aches and pains from my surgery.

When Sunday night rolled around and it was time for Mom to head home so that she could go back to work on Monday, I had mixed emotions. I was sad that I would be living in this apartment all alone yet again. I would have to return to the real world and face everything that I had avoided during my recovery time. It was for a shitty reason, but I had appreciated the break from life. On the other hand, I had a bunch of new movies and Mom had left most of the cookies we had baked.

Aside from a few short, random nosebleeds, I didn't have much pain throughout my recovery. Before I knew it, I was one week out of surgery, my bruising was minimal enough that it could be covered up with makeup, and I was cleared to go back to work.

Again, I had mixed emotions. I was looking forward to getting up and moving, but I was nervous to see all my coworkers. Even though I hadn't done anything cosmetic, I was pretty sure that most of them knew I had had something done.

I walked in to the restaurant to find everything in its usual spot. The glasses stacked along the bar, the plates piled in the kitchen, and the day shift employees crowded around the same corner booth. I walked over to say hello and get the casualties out of the way, hoping no one would even notice that I had been gone, but I was greeted warmly.

"Whoa! I'm sorry, but we're not open until 10:30. I'll have to ask you to come back then!" my manager joked, holding a hand up and walking toward me. "How are you doing?"

"I'm good. Done with everything." I smiled.

"And that's not a prosthetic, right? Because that could be a sanitary hazard if that falls into someone's salad." She laughed.

"Eew! Gross!" It was a collective groan from the other coworkers observing the conversation.

"We're clear. I tipped him extra to sew it into place." I played along.

"Okay. That's good then. How are you feeling? Done with the pain pills? Allowed to lift heavy racks and everything?" she asked, only half joking.

"Yeah, I'm good. I haven't had a nosebleed since I left the house." I shrugged off her concerns. "Besides, we can just tell people its ketchup."

We were able to start the shift off with a good laugh, and it eased a few of my inhibitions about working through the cardio of a chaotic shift without getting a bloody nose. That would be a tough act to play off for tables full of hungry guests.

While getting back to the grind reiterated the fact that I had spent the last week resting and taking it easy, aside from breaking more of a sweat, the shift went very smoothly. It was a busy lunch rush with no major issues or complaints and decent tips. Even though it was a great way to transition back into my work schedule, I was happy to see the dinner shift starting to trickle in.

"Who's bad?" Mike walked toward me, singing songs from pop stars who had overdone noses.

"Very funny. Do you take requests?" I responded while prepping my last few tickets.

We looked one another in the face and synchronized our condescending cackles. The few coworkers who were within earshot didn't quite get the joke.

"It's always a good sign if you make it through your first shift back without your nose falling off into someone's soup or salad." The serious tone of his statement was actually humorous.

"Yeah, someone tried to say there was one in her salad, but it belonged to one of the cooks." I rolled my eyes at him and finished organizing my tickets.

"So everything went well then? No headaches or nosebleeds?" he asked. "Uh-oh. You know what this means. You've healed, and you're ready to return to the real world! Welcome back! Sorry."

"Yeah, no shit," I replied. "This means I have to be responsible and get ready for school."

"When does that start again?" he asked, sitting down in the booth where we had been talking.

"Next week," I answered, not thrilled about the upcoming date. "Or a week and a half. I don't know, something like that."

"Way to take responsibility!" He laughed.

"I just wish I wasn't starting again so soon. It's cold out. I don't want to go to school. Don't we get snow days or something?" I could only hope.

"Yeah, when you're in grade school," he reminded me. "But you know where it doesn't get cold and the sun always shines? California. California would be a great place to go to school!"

"California would be an expensive place to go to school," I corrected him. "Besides, I already told you. I can't go until my lease is up, at least."

"Excuses, excuses." He shook his head at me.

I stuck my tongue out at him before walking away to finish my shift. It was perfect timing since he was due to clock in soon. I had thought long and hard about what he was telling me about moving out there with him and Joe. I knew he was right, but when it came down to it, I was stuck here for a little while longer. So the least I could do was make the most of my sentence. Even though "house arrest" didn't sound pleasant by any means, if I did something constructive, maybe the time would pass quickly. My classes, which would include homework, didn't appeal to me at all; but it would all keep me too busy to stare at a clock. A little over a week later, I rolled out of bed to begin my classes and test my theories.

I walked into that familiar smell of books, old building, and students drenched in cheap perfume. I knew the general locations of my classes but still gave myself a little extra time to pinpoint them. I made it a point to check the posts in the cafeteria and see what projects were coming up for the theater. I found an ad almost right away, listing auditions for the spring show, which was listed as a more serious production. Just what I needed, more drama.

I didn't recognize the title of the show, and even though I know it was only logical to explore different genres of plays, I was hoping for an uplifting comedy for the spring production. With the way things were going, I was expecting Aaron to walk up and interrupt me and ask me when I was going to have my nose job. Then I thought for a moment, maybe a dramatic performance would be a good thing.

Maybe I should utilize the theme to do a little method acting. There was plenty of drama in my life at this point, so I felt like I knew exactly how to portray a character whose life sucked. That was exactly what I had to do. This shouldn't be a downer; it should be a motive. Mike had told me before not to be a drama queen, and he was right. All I needed to do was devote myself to the show and people would merely think I was portraying a character. It would be a great way to turn my negative disposition into a positive. This could work out very well.

I was relieved that the auditions would be taking place on Thursday so I wouldn't have to think about them all weekend. I finished my last class before the audition and headed to the auditorium. I walked in to find a few other actors sitting outside the door to the auditorium, studying the script. I checked in with the woman sitting at the card table that was set up outside the door and grabbed a script to so that I could start reading.

As I went over the lines, I started to see that they had chosen a more dramatic scene for the auditions. I wasn't sure exactly what the play was about, but just from reading this short piece, I could tell that the female character I was auditioning for was trying to convince the male character to see things her way. She was trying to convince him that there was another point of view, that things aren't always what they seem to be. Oh yeah, I'd been preparing for this role for months.

After about twenty minutes of sitting in the hallway outside of the auditorium, reading through the scene, my name was called and I was invited in to read. I thought I would have a partner but found out that the director would be reading with me. While seemingly intimidating, this could be a very positive factor in the audition process.

The first round of auditions is open to anyone who can find his or her way to the proper location. Whether this person can act or not is another story. I had always been taught that acting was actually reacting to the situation or

216

character in a scene. Therefore, I could only hope that whoever I was reading with would give me enough emotion to react to, regardless of the genre. Since directors seem to have an idea what they are looking for in an actor, I had found that when one is even just reading from off stage, he can often hint at these expectations of character visions. So by simply playing off the reactions of my counterpart in the scene, I would have no problem portraying the character desired.

Once I got on stage, the director introduced herself to me and explained a little about the scene we were about to read. She explained that the scene took place over one hundred years ago and was about a murder. A man is murdered, and a judge has to figure out how it happened. The details of the murder are described from the points of view of the victim, the murderer, and the wife of the victim who witnessed it. The judge and a random woman are witnessing the testimonials and debating what the truth is. This was the scene I was reading. It was a very serious role, but I couldn't help thinking about how therapeutic this could be, that I wasn't the only bitch having a hard time convincing a man that he was wrong.

We started to read, and I found it very easy to tap into my own anger. The lines consisted of telling him that he had blinders on and was only considering what he wanted to, not what the actual facts were. Asking him how he couldn't see what was really going on, I could feel my own passion for the part rising. This was the climax as the last line compromises the debate and sums up the conclusion women have realized since the beginning of time.

"Very well, then. I see you've made up your mind. I can't force you to change." I delivered the last line very calmly. It was the end of the scene.

The director told me I did a great job and explained that callbacks were at the beginning of the following week. I thanked her and headed home. I kept playing the last line over and over in my head, thinking of different ways to deliver it. The words hit very close to home, except the character playing opposite of me in real life hadn't had the balls to face me and look me in the eye. So I didn't get to resolve anything, or even make a compromise.

I had convinced myself when it all started that I didn't want to wallow in it and waste my time worrying about someone that so obviously hasn't given me another thought. Besides, I knew I had cookie dough ice cream chillin' in my freezer and a marathon of my favorite sitcom begging to be watched.

In fact, over the next few days I got to reacquaint myself with a few of my favorite sitcoms. The audition was the least of my worries, although I did wonder if I had gone a little overboard with the dramatic acting. Over the next couple of days, my routine was pretty basic: go to school, work, and then home again. One of my biggest obstacles was making sure that there was never silence since it gave me too much room to think. That's where the reruns came in. A few of them were older shows, but it kept me sane, thinking that I wasn't completely alone. It was also good to be around people at school and work, especially Mike. Whether he liked it or not, he knew pretty much everything that was, or wasn't, going on in my life and he could usually make me laugh about it. Usually.

"So have they called you for the next round of auditions?" Mike asked me while we were working together the Saturday after auditions.

"Nope, nothing. Yet. But it's no big deal, right? If I don't get a callback, I'll just find a community show or something." I tried to shrug it off and convince us both that it wouldn't suck not to get cast in this show.

"Or something?" Seemingly confused, Mike stopped filling his glass and turned to me. "If this is really what you want to do, you should already have the backups lined up. There are auditions all over the Internet."

"I know, I just haven't had time," I said, avoiding eye contact and focusing on filling the glasses I was holding.

"You haven't had time? It would only take a few minutes to check one of them out," Mike reminded me.

"It's only been a couple of days. Callbacks are on Monday. I might still hear from them tomorrow. It's no big deal! In the meantime I just need to get my homework done," I told him, walking away from the soda machine with a full tray.

"You just started your classes. You don't have that much homework yet." Mike turned to watch me leave the kitchen and hollered, "You're just making excuses!"

I was trying to focus on dropping off the drinks to my tables, but I couldn't help but think about the conversation we had just had. It really irritated me. I knew what I had to do, but what would be the point of lining up other auditions if there was still a chance of getting cast? I really wanted this part, but it wasn't a big deal if I didn't get it. I kept repeating that concept in my head while jotting down the food orders my tables were barking at me. I couldn't help but think that Mike was right.

It was a scary thought to think that Mike, or anyone else, could see through my drama. Although I was doing it very calmly, I was making excuses and wasting time feeling sorry for myself about being stuck here. I was embarrassed about everything that had happened with Aaron and just wanted to be invisible. But if I wanted to maintain my relationship with acting, I had to be proactive or it would just remain another childish crush.

If I didn't get this role, I'd still want to audition for other productions. Just because I couldn't pack up and leave any time I wanted to didn't mean that I couldn't efficiently utilize my time here to build my resume. I wanted to leave the shift on a positive note, so before I left for the night, I made sure to find Mike at his usual table and say good-bye.

"What's up? Did you make any money tonight?" I asked, grabbing one of the fries from his plate.

"Oh, the usual," he answered, taking a big bite of his burger.

"Yeah, I did okay too," I informed him. "And I just wanted to tell you that you're right. I have to focus on my goals and quit making excuses."

"It's good to hear you say it," he said, looking right at me and chewing his food.

"Well, it's true. I've been moping and being lazy, and I need to stop," I confessed.

"I'm glad you came to your senses," he said with sarcasm. "Although it could have been fun to slap you."

"I had no idea you were in to all that." I played off his humor.

"Oh, gross. I'm eating here." He threw a fry at me.

"You missed my mouth." I could barely say it since I was cracking up at my own dirty joke.

"You're nasty. Go away!" He couldn't help but laugh along with me.

"All right, all right. I can take a hint." I stopped laughing. "It's obviously past your bedtime."

I was glad to leave on a better note, having faced my minor demons. I headed home to another routine evening of television and homework. I ended up passing out on the couch and woke up with my books on the floor and an infomercial about how to get younger-looking skin.

I was still coming to but realized that the models they were using were probably younger to begin with, so the product didn't have to work too hard. It was like a car accident. I couldn't stop watching the women sit and smear the cream across their faces and unlock their young potential. I started to think about the fact that these women were being paid for sitting there, smiling and smearing. I was suddenly motivated to check out these websites Mike had been telling me about.

I found a few where I was able to view auditions all over Los Angeles. It was a little depressing to think I'd have to wait to pursue any of them, but I wanted to keep searching. I found other auditions located in major cities all around the country. And there was actually a long list of auditions around the Minneapolis area. They ranged from theater productions to independent film roles. It was free to create a profile, and with a one-time-per-year payment, I could submit myself to these auditions.

It really did sound like a smart thing to do. I decided to finish up my homework that was due first thing on Monday morning. It was a slow, tedious process, and it was almost impossible to concentrate on school homework instead of the studying I should be doing on the websites. But sometime around noon, I finished and decided to take a lunch break.

I knew I needed to go to the grocery store for anything that could sufficiently pass for a meal, so I had to do a little digging to see what was left in the kitchen. Luckily, I found a frozen pizza in the freezer. It wasn't my first choice, but it would definitely get the job done. All I would have to do is wait for it to cook. I turned on the oven and unwrapped the pizza, setting in on the stove in anticipation of the little prebake beep informing me that it was time to put in the pizza.

I sat back down on the couch and started flipping through channels. Nothing really jumped out at me, so I started reading the descriptions in the guide. Even though the majority of what's showing on a Sunday afternoon are either love dramas or family movies, I found an interesting documentary about celebrity scandals. Just as one of my favorites was about to check herself into rehab, the alarm on the stove went off to let me know that it was time to put my pizza in the oven.

After setting another alarm, I sat back down just in time for her to reenter the hospital a month after leaving before her program was complete. My phone started buzzing, and I saw that it was my mother. I decided I'd call her back after the show was over. It started buzzing again. I was a little irritated that she was going to call until I answered. But after checking it, it was actually a text from Mike asking if I had heard anything yet.

He had started the message with a friendly "Just wanted to push you in the right direction." I thought it was really sweet of him to be a nag. I replied to his text, telling him that, no, I hadn't heard anything and thanked him for reminding me. I got done with the messaging just I time for the timer to go off on my lunch. I had to admit, frozen pizza had never tasted so good, especially after the hassle of getting it made.

Just as my celebrity was about to be court ordered into her third round of rehab, I was about to get up for another slice and my phone started buzzing again. I was ready to tell Mike that even though I appreciated his humor, I'd have to call him back after my girl loses her three-picture contract with one of the major studios in LA. But when I looked at my phone, I realized that it was a number I didn't recognize.

"Hello?" I answered, wondering who was calling me on a Sunday afternoon.

"Hello, can I speak with Lisa, please?" the voice on the other end asked me.

"This is," I answered.

"Hi, this is Tracy, the director of the spring production. We met at auditions?" she said in a manner that questioned whether or not I remembered her. "I was calling to invite you to callbacks. I know it's short notice. I don't have a set assistant yet. But they'll be held tomorrow evening about 7:00 p.m. Are you able to make it?"

I could feel my excitement rising. "Yeah, sounds great!"

"All right, well, we'll see you tomorrow night at seven. And we'll have all the sides for you to read from. We'll see you then. Have a good night," she finished.

"Yeah, see you then. Thanks. You too, bye." I hung up, relieved that I had been called back.

There was something about the second round of auditions. They seemed so much less stressful than the first round. The first round is some open cattle call, and the second round is invitation only. It's a confirmation of your skills. They know you have talent, and they want to use you in the production being pieced together. They just have to decide where.

I wanted to let Mike know that he could quit rubbing in the fact that I hadn't received a call because I finally had. I could've just texted the message to him, but that would have been no fun. So I dialed him up and shared the good news.

After a few rings, he answered, "Still haven't heard anything, huh?"

"Wow, you're presumptuous! As a matter of fact, I wanted to let you know that I just got off the phone with them," I informed him.

"Oh, sad. They called to tell you that you aren't invited to callbacks. You must really suck." He laughed.

"No, fart ass. They called to apologize for waiting until the last minute to call and invite me to callbacks," I corrected him. "Good thing you weren't casting this thing. You don't seem to have much faith in me."

"Oh, of course, I do." He laughed again. "I wasn't inviting you to move out to LA just so we cut split the cost of gas three ways."

"I wouldn't doubt it! But I don't want to talk about that right now. I just got my good news for the day, and I don't want to spoil it," I told him.

"You don't ever want to talk about it, but whatever. I'm glad you got called back. Break a leg! But I have to go. I'm still at work." I could hear someone in the background calling his name. "Okay, I'll talk to you later. Bye!"

"Bye." I barely got to finish the word before he hung up.

I had a sense of relief, feeling that even with all the crap going on right now, I was still going to have a chance to work on another play. Something I truly loved. Even though it would add to my work load, it still seemed to make all the stress and homework that come along with college worthwhile. It even inspired me to return my mother's phone call and see what helpful tips she would be offering me for the day.

The conversation was pretty quick and painless. She just wanted to check up on how my face was feeling. With work and school, I had forgotten to call and report my status. I was excited to tell her about the callback as well, even though I knew she didn't necessarily see the appeal. And even though she was almost always supportive of what I wanted to do, I knew she'd remind me of the extra stress I would be taking on myself. But I was happy to remind her that it was a welcome task. Our conversation lasted for quite a while, and before I knew it, I was telling her that I had to get off the phone so that I could get some sleep for Monday.

Even though I tried not to think about him much, I couldn't help but think that it would have been fun to call and tell Aaron my good news too. But for the first time since all the drama had gone down with him and I'd had to turn down the offer to move with Mike, I was feeling really good and positive about my endeavors. So I decided to remain focused on the positive news and went to bed for the night.

Chapter 13

I woke up excited for my day to start. I had a few classes to get through, then just had to kill a few hours with homework until the auditions. Even with my anticipation for the evening, my morning classes seemed to pass very quickly. I stopped in the cafeteria over lunch to grab a quick bite to eat. Suddenly, my phone started ringing, and I saw that it was my lawyer.

"Hello?" I asked, wishing that it was anyone else that would answer.

"Hello, Lisa. Frank Valcourt here. I just wanted to check in with you. We received the medical bills from your surgery. Are you still going to physical therapy for your knees?" He jumped right to the point. "If we don't reach a certain amount on the medical bills, we can't really go after the other party."

"Well, my knees have been killing me, but I haven't really had a chance to schedule more appointments since surgery," I told him.

"You need to call the doctor and find out what he has to say. If you don't get the medical care you need now, you'll be paying for it in the future. Financially and physically," he reminded me.

It figured he would list the two possibilities in that order. "Yes. I'll call his office right away."

"Good and be sure to give me a callback and let me know how the appointment goes, and we can get copies of those medical bills too. That's all I had. I'll talk to you later," he said, ending the conversation.

"Sounds good. I'll call them right away," I agreed.

It wasn't the phone call I wanted to hear. I was appreciative of my lawyer keeping me up to speed about what was going on, but with each update it became more and more apparent that he was more interested in the money instead of my health and well-being. Regardless, following his instructions could acquire both.

I called my physical therapist and scheduled an appointment. I got the usual song and dance about booking ahead since it was recommended that I come in at least once a week for sessions until I was cleared by the doctor to schedule them further apart. I agreed and made early morning appointments through the end of the month so I could get them out of the way before work since I would hopefully be attending rehearsals in the evenings.

The appointments were a blessing and a curse. After the accident, my knees had looked like rotten heads of cabbage and felt like someone had taken a baseball bat to them. The bruises went away quickly, but I had been warned not to take the recovery for granted since the injury could cause long-term dysfunction and pain. My appointments usually consisted of me lying on a table while the doctor used an ultrasound machine to massage my kneecaps. It was heaven. I hadn't noticed consistent pain since the week after the accident. But after my therapy appointments, I almost felt like I could run a marathon.

By the time I was done with everything my lawyer needed me to do, it was time to head to my last class of the day. I was like a kid in elementary school, counting down the minutes to recess. Somehow I managed to get through every painstaking moment, and even pay attention to what homework I needed to do.

Class came to an end, and I found my way to the hallway outside of the auditorium. I had a few hours to kill, so I sat down and started reading through the homework I had been assigned. I was pretty sure I had read the same page three times before I caught my mind wandering over to the script instead. I had to struggle to concentrate on what I was doing but found a way to scribble down some notes that would come in handy for future tests.

It seemed like every time I checked the time only about five minutes had passed. But looking at my phone now, I could see that the event of the day would be starting in about an hour. A few other people started to gather in the hallway, and it was a good opportunity to study the competition.

The male roles weren't what I was after, so they were of no concern. One girl walked up, looked around, and sat right down on the cold floor a few feet away from me. She looked about my age, had a curvier build, and red hair. She caught me watching her sit down and gave me a courtesy smile. The flat kind that says, "I have no idea why you're looking at me but don't want to be rude." She started digging through her bag, pulled out a book, and started flipping through the pages.

I assumed she was trying to find the page she had left off on so she could continue with the story. Before she turned another page, she looked up at the auditorium door to check for any sign of movement. There were a few more people coming to join the small group of people waiting for seven o'clock. I figured this was a good opportunity to break the ice.

"Are you here for callbacks?" I asked her.

She looked back at me as if my question took her by surprise. "Oh, yeah. It starts at seven, right?

"Yeah, that's what Tracy said," I answered her.

"Well, we have about twenty minutes to kill then." She looked back down at her book.

"I'm Lisa," I introduced myself with a little wave.

"I'm Sara." She smiled back.

We didn't have much time to introduce ourselves as Tracy came walking up and went into the door of the auditorium with a stack of scripts in hand. We both watched to see if she was going to come back out and invite us to come in as well. About five minutes later, she did just that.

"Hey, everyone," she said to the small group. "Why don't you all come inside, and we'll get started."

We all quietly entered the room, were advised to grab a copy of the script, and sign in so that Tracey knew who all had shown up. Since some of us were early, we took seats in the front couple of rows and started reading through the pages. After a few more minutes of waiting for the rest of the group to arrive, Tracey announced that we were only waiting on two people and were going to get started without them.

She explained that the second round of auditions would consist on the twelve of us mixing and matching and reading through select scenes to get an idea of who we really meshed with. Twelve was a small number of people consisting of six guys and six girls. It also seemed like I had a better chance of landing one of the three female roles.

Aside from Sara, I noticed there was a girl who looked younger than us. She was tall, skinny, and gorgeous. Not the type you would stereotype as being part of a serious, dramatic production. She looked like she was at the college for her postsecondary education program. I figured she had to be serious about the auditions, not only had she been called back from the first round but her lips didn't move as she was reading the words. I took this to mean she wasn't having any trouble understanding the sentences. This was definitely a must-have for any dramatic role not meant to be delivered monotone.

There were three other girls scattered in between the male actors. None of them stood out to me or portrayed any unique characteristics I could pick out offhand. And the guys were just as ordinary. I was very excited to be here, but I couldn't help but think that half of us were going to leave and later be disappointed. Even though that result would suck, the gamble was still exciting. And if it resulted in getting one of the parts, it would be very exciting.

Tracey sat down and started studying the names and making notes. I figured she was pairing everyone up. Had it been a love story, it would have made me think of Noah's ark. After watching her for a few minutes, I went back to flipping through the pages selected from the script. Just reading through the female roles, I was interested to see what the director had in mind for bringing them to life.

The blessing and the curse of this particular round of auditions was that we would have an audience consisting of our fellow actors. I watched a few of the scenes, paying close attention to how the younger girl and Sara performed their cold reads. I was interested to see them perform scenes of a medium conjuring up the spirit of a murdered samurai and a woman being attacked after her husband is murdered. Watching them, I couldn't say that I would have performed it any differently. They were both very good. The other three girls' scenes, even though one of them was with a guy that had already been on the stage ten minutes earlier, were less than memorable. I figured this was an example of why actors needed chemistry to create a scene.

Before I knew it, it was my turn to be on stage. I walked up the steps and took my position next to my male counterpart. He was slightly taller than me and a lot skinnier. He had glasses and was very plain to look at. I figured he was analyzing me as well when we were interrupted by our off-stage direction.

"Okay, so in this scene, you're trying to convince the judge that there's more than one side to every story. He doesn't want to listen to a random woman and thinks he knows that his ruling was the right one." Then she looked at him. "You already sentenced a man to prison, possibly death. But now you're wondering if you really took all of the details into consideration. You're trying to convince yourself that the case is closed. All right, whenever you're ready."

As we started reading, taking advantage of the one-thousandth of a second between reading the words from the paper to analyze and deliver them with as much emotion possible, I found that this person could impose a lot of passion into his character. We finished our scene, and even though I expected some stage direction so that we could start the scene over again with said instructions, Tracey simply thanked us with a "good job" and told us we could sit back down.

This was either a very good sign or a very bad one. Either she loved what she saw and knew that we were the ones to portray these dramatic characters as she had envisioned them or else she regretted having invited us to this round of auditions and was counting down the time to her next cigarette break. She didn't smell like an ash tray either of the times I had met her, so I was hoping for something at least similar to my first guess.

We both looked a little surprised, with a minor hint of impending disappointment, as we headed back to our seats. After a few more mixes and matches, Sarah took the stage and went through the same scene I had read but with a different guy. After watching her, I was a little intimidated. She seemed to know just how to create the different characters. Even in the two minutes it took to read the lines, I noticed that her face never lacked expression whether she was speaking or listening and her words never lacked tone. I could only hope that I had delivered the same quality improvisation.

Though I was hoping to at least be able to read for another character, I noticed that my partner and I weren't called to perform either of the other scenes or even matched with someone else to read the same scene. I hated to admit it to myself, but I had to consider taking the unspoken hint. I had probably gotten hyped up about nothing and wasn't sure that telling Mike about the callback audition was such a good idea after all.

When she dismissed all of us for the evening, explaining that they would have the cast list by the end of the week, I checked my phone and it was only about nine thirty. Mike had purposely sent me a text at seven thirty, telling me to break a leg. It was very nice of him to be so encouraging, but I didn't feel like giving him any updates until I knew the outcome of my efforts. So I just replied with a short, sweet "here's hoping."

 This was the beauty of text messaging. I liked seeing the symbol showing me that I had a message waiting for me, and I could wait and respond if or when I felt like it. For once Aaron had taught me a valuable attribute. If you have nothing positive to say, keep the message short and sweet or just don't respond. Although the motivation behind his strategy was significantly different, the concept seemed to apply.

I put my phone in my bag and headed toward the door of the auditorium. I returned the script and gave Tracey a courtesy smile and said good night. Sara was in front of me, returning her script as well, and said good-bye to both Tracey and me. I was a little surprised at her friendliness since it failed to appear before the readings but returned her courtesy and told her to have a good night.

I had a bad habit of replaying auditions and scripts over and over again in my head, analyzing my own performance. I was trying to pick apart my cold read from earlier and decipher when or where I went wrong and what I could have done right. I wasn't suicidal or anything, but it was disappointing to think of striking out on the project, and it was gnawing at me trying to figure out what I should have done differently. What line could I have delivered differently to make myself stand out as the perfect actress for the part.

I got home around ten and less than motivated to pick up where I had left off on my homework. I threw my unopened bag on the couch, grabbed a beer, and quickly changed into my pajamas to head to bed and watch some television to clear my head. Unfortunately, I was wide awake, and my options for viewing pleasure were becoming more and more scarce. I finally settled on an old rerun of I Love Lucy. It was crazy to think how long ago the show had been filmed. How hairstyles, clothing, furniture, and lifestyles had all changed since this was written. But it still seemed like there was at least one aspect that hadn't changed. One disposition that I seemingly had in common with Lucy: we wanted to be a main character in a show, but even though we thought we were close, there was that one person who just wouldn't cast us.

Over the next few hours, I was in and out of consciousness. During one lapse of sleep, I was somewhat awake enough to observe Lucy preparing for her trip to Hollywood. True to my drama queen nature, I couldn't help but think that even she got to get up and go to Hollywood and I had to wait. I watched, jealous of the situation, and then realized how stupid I was being, chalking it up to my lack of sleep.

The whole situation with the auditions really wasn't going to be the end of the world, yet here I was, moping like an abused puppy dog. If I was smart, I'd realize that this was a blessing in disguise. It proved that I could tap into my inner actress and make anything seem like a huge dramatic let down. Suddenly, I felt a little better. I wasn't sure if that part was the beer or if I just needed to see a neurologist to be tested for bipolar disorder. It made no sense, but either way, I felt much better about my earlier performance. My reiterated sense of confidence would be the key to unlock other auditions, hopefully in the near future.

Somehow I fell asleep. I must have stayed asleep until my alarm went off, startling and reminding me that it was time to take advantage of another day filled with my usual routine and sponsored by my schedule. It wasn't hard to stay on track, considering that as a student the variety of my week consisted of switching back and forth between school and work.

I got to sneak in a few extra minutes of sleep since my wardrobe was already chosen for me, consisting of my

Pommes polo and black pants. While I was usually a morning person, the lack of sleep made it hard to get up and moving. With the help of an energy drink or two, I somehow got moving to get ready and leave for work. It was a little more motivating that I would have access to all the coffee one could want in order to guide me through my shift.

Even though I arrived early enough to relax before clocking in and preparing for the lunch shift, I was afraid to sit down since this might inspire to me spreading out in the booth using napkins for my pillow and my thick jacket as a blanket. Instead, I decided to get myself a big glass of coffee with some ice in it so I could gulp it down quickly.

With my caffeine-induced second wind and with a few more glasses of liquid encouragement, I worked my shift on autopilot. After my shift, I started coming down from my buzz and focused on the aftereffect of my sleepless night—my tips. They seemed pretty decent, so sending a pod in to get the job done hadn't been such a bad idea. After confirming my gains, I had to take a minute to decide if I wanted to stay and get something to eat or if I wanted to get home and pass out. A familiar voice ripped me out of my daze.

"Well, hello!" It was Mike. "Do I need to roll out a red carpet to come sit down and get an autograph?"

"You're hilarious," I replied. "But you know the signing doesn't happen until opening night."

"Oh, you're right. Stupid me. What night is that? I'll have to be sure to get it off." He seemed excited about coming.

"Well, you'll have to ask the cast." It was an open-ended comment because I didn't know whether or not I had a chance of getting cast. "Besides, are you still going to be here?" This was a specific question, and I was hoping for a certain answer.

"You're right. So what's the name of this thing?" Mike sat down across the table from me.

"It's called In the Eyes of the Dragon. I don't know, something like that," I answered. "So, are you going to be here by opening night?"

He was taking off his jacket and getting settled while he thought it over. "Probably not. But you can send me pictures."

All of a sudden it seemed like there was a much more important topic on the table, and whether or not I was cast didn't seem that important for a moment.

"Have you guys set a date?" I asked.

"We've only been together for like eight months, you know. We're not even thinking about marriage!" he joked.

"I'm serious. Have you guys decided what day you're leaving?" I asked again.

"Actually, we worked it out, and we're leaving in about three weeks." The news was heartbreaking. "I already put in my notice here." It seemed like he didn't want to look at me while he was telling me.

"And you weren't going to tell me?" I asked.

"Well, of course, I was! I was just waiting for the right time. See, I knew you'd make it seem like a break-up scene." He rolled his eyes at me.

"You know that's not what I'm trying to do. I'm just going to miss you, that's all."

"Miss me? How many times to I have to remind you? You'll be moving down there too!"

"I know, but not for a good while."

"Stop turning this into such a crappy, depressing thing! This is a very good thing, and I'd think you'd be happy for me."

He was right. I'd been so stuck on my own petty problems, and I wasn't giving him the support he had been giving me over the last few months. If he could find a way to keep me positive through all my bad luck, then there was no reason I couldn't celebrate his grasping of his own destiny.

"You're right. I'm just being selfish. This is a great thing," I confessed. "We'll have to have a 'see you later' party. You know, so it's not a sad thing."

"Thank you. That sounds fun." He still had a hint of irritation in his voice. "Now go away. I want to get some food and eat in peace."

I smiled and gently punched him in the arm as I stood up to leave. I had so many things going on in my head. Good things. Bad things. Sad things. If I took a step back and generally thought about everything going on, not one of these issues could make the world stop turning. It was drama that I had created for myself in an incredibly short period of time, and I needed to just get over it and focus on the fact that it could all take a turn for the better. But it wasn't that easy. I wanted it to be, but it wasn't.

After my short drive home, I didn't feel like doing much of anything. Not even making a conscious decision to do so, I just snuggled up on the couch under a blanket and turned on the television for my usual distraction. All of this waiting for some good news was making me crabby and pessimistic. As I succumbed to my unintentional routine, I didn't bother keeping my phone next to me because I wasn't sure what one more piece of bad news would do.

I was watching an old rerun from a famous fifties sitcom. Two couples were on their way to California because one of them had a career waiting for him. It was almost like a sign that I needed to just forget all the restraints holding me in Minnesota and just head out there. I was ready to embrace the positive aspects of my revelation, when my current mood reminded me that the glass was only half full. There were two couples making the journey out to the West Coast, not one and a half. Regardless of the long drive, there were no third wheels on that trip. Maybe it was a sign that I was doing the right thing by finishing everything up before running off. The more I got into analyzing the episode rather than enjoying it, I noticed that I couldn't ignore the inner debate and had to laugh at my own bipolar-ness as I was awakened from the trance by the sound of my phone.

I shook it off and got up to go see who was trying to get a hold of me. Knowing my luck, it was probably my credit card company to tell me that I had made the check out for less than the minimum. But looking at the number, I realized it was probably something even worse and I wasn't in the mood to deal with it at the moment. It was my lawyer calling, and I assumed it was going to be him telling me that my insurance company had choreographed yet another dance to bow out of the spotlight. I was happy to let him leave me a voicemail, and I would force myself to listen to it tomorrow.

I decided to bring my phone back over to the couch and find something else to watch. Hopefully something I couldn't attach to some deeper meaning about reading the signs and trying to figure out some way to keep myself from heading out to my deck and just jumping off. Being that it was only a three-story building, it probably wouldn't accomplish anything anyway.

I found something new to watch. Something about crime in New York. Young women being murdered and police trying to follow the clues. Suddenly, my phone started buzzing again.

"Lucky bitches," I said to myself as I turned toward my phone, expecting it to be my lawyer yet again. What could be so important that he couldn't wait until Monday to talk to me.

I looked down to see it was simply a text. In a random state of optimism, I had given Sara my number at the auditions. She was about my age and seemed to be about as desperate for a role in the play as I was, not to be able to post the fact that we were cast on social media, but so that we would have positive distractions from life's real dramas.

I wasn't sure what to expect when I saw that I had received a message from her. I figured she would either be texting me to tell me that she hadn't gotten anything either or sharing her positive accomplishment. I hated to be one of those people, but I was hoping for the first option so I'd know that the director simply had flawed tastes, that it wasn't a problem with my personal talent.

I was just calling up my message options to decode the impending conclusion when my phone started buzzing again. I couldn't help but wonder, When did I get so popular? Where the hell were these people over the past week, and why were they all trying to get a hold of me at once?

I didn't recognize the number and again let my negativity get the best of me. Since my lawyer had just called, it stood to reason that this would be my insurance company trying to explain and justify everything they had discussed so that it wouldn't be left to his interpretation. I let it go to voicemail. Now I had two that I had to listen to. Knowing that neither would be a good update, I decided that I might as well just listen to the strange number first, then see what my lawyer could do with it.

I hit the button for my voicemails and found the message from the unknown number. My one solace was that it was a short message. So I grabbed my nail file, hit the Play icon, and braced for disappointment.

"Hi, Marissa. This is Tracy, the director of the play that you auditioned for last week, and I was calling to offer you the lead role of 'the woman.' Please call me back and let me know if you would like to accept, and then we can go over the schedule for rehearsals. Have a great night!"

I could feel my look of skepticism transform into a big cheesy smile, induced by the great message I had just listened to. I was even inspired to read the text Sara had sent me. It was a simple, generic. "Have you heard from them?"

I wasn't sure if I should respond with a yes or a no. If I replied yes and she hadn't been offered a part, then it could be her bad news for the week. If I replied no, then if she had been offered a part, she'd wonder why I didn't just tell her. And she would've been right. We were very different people, and it seemed to both of us that we were reading for very different parts. There really was no reason I shouldn't just be honest with her. I had earned the role, and if she was going to see the play, then she would find out eventually anyway and probably didn't act as childish about these things as I did. I had nothing to be ashamed of and should be proud of my efforts as that had definitely paid off. So that was it. I was going to be totally honest. The endorphin rush and sudden break in the clouds had made me a lot more sensitive to other's pending feelings.

Before I called back, I decided to reply to Sara, telling her that I had literally just talked to Tracy and accepted a part. When Tracy answered the phone, I apologized for missing her call, and she replied, telling me that it was no big deal and repeated the offer to take the part. I accepted and thanked her. Then reminding me that she still had a few calls to make, she informed me that the first meeting would be the following week where I could meet the rest of the cast. I told her I'd be there, and she said she would see me next week and had to go. Though she seemed short during our conversation, I was thrilled with the news so I brushed it off.

After hanging up from the call, I noticed that there was another text from Sara. She told me that was cool because she was offered a role as well and that she looked forward to working with me. The news was so great that I still had no desire to listen to the message my lawyer had left me. I didn't want any bad news to kill my buzz.

I even sent Mike a message, telling him my good news and apologizing for being such a big baby earlier. One thing I always loved about Mike, he didn't hold a grudge over any bogus behavior. He replied to me, telling me how happy he was to hear the news and congratulating me. He even added a little smiley face. I told him it was amazing news, but I wished for him to have been able to see it.

Suddenly, my phone was buzzing again with another incoming call. "Don't do that!"

"What? Do what?" I was genuinely asking.

"You're doing that drama-queen thing again," he informed me. "Just chill out and enjoy this. Don't bitch and ruin it."

I was almost surprised, but I still appreciated his complete honesty enough not to be irritated. "You're right. Once again. You just say it to make me tell you that, don't you?"

"Well, am I wrong?"

"Perhaps not," I confessed.

"Then I just have a flare for the obvious," he reiterated. "But I have to go. Joe's making me dinner."

"Lucky. I get to make me dinner," I said with a cheerful tone. "Wait, didn't you eat at work?"

"Don't tell him that. He just thinks I'm a light eater and trying to watch my figure." He laughed.

"Yeah, right, after watching you devour a pizza? I don't think you're fooling anyone. Speaking of which, it's time to get my TV dinner into the microwave. Have fun! Take a bite for me!"

"Will do. Have a good one. Congratulations! Bye!"

It was a very good not to end the conversation on. I was glad to have Mike around to keep me in check. It just made me dread not having him around on a regular basis even more. But in an attempt to be true to his influence, I snapped myself out of it and focused on preparing my gourmet dinner. After all, you had to cook it for just the right amount of time if you didn't want the broccoli to get soggy. And I felt that tonight, I deserved something a little crispy.

I spent the rest of the night feeling pretty good. Of course, I had to share this bliss with a few dozen people, including my mother and sister. But it felt good to go to sleep that night, knowing that I had better things to look forward to in the near future. Everything that had had me so down lately felt like it was a mile away, and I was actually looking forward to waking up and starting a new day. Once again, it was a reminder just how helpful the little things can be.

The next day I woke up feeling just as good. It was cold out, but the sun was shining, and I didn't have class on Mondays. It seemed cheesy, but I was more than ready to share my top-of-the-world feeling with my coworkers and customers. I'd heard it said that every emotion is contagious. And the fact that my tables would have the new lead of the spring production bringing them their extra sides of ranch had me feeling flattered for them.

I had the urge to say good morning to all my coworkers, and they seemed to notice the positive difference. I didn't have to fake my smile that morning, at least for the majority the people surrounding me, and I was thrilled to have the good feeling. I was also thrilled with the monetary compensation from the customers who recognized the good feeling. A little more method acting reflected in the providing of a "wow" experience for my tables and inspired most of them to leave a 20 percent or even higher token of appreciation for their lunch experiences.

After work, I was happy to sit, relax, and treat myself to dinner. Once I got my food to the table, I heard that familiar voice I looked forward to hearing at the end of my shift.

"Can I get your autograph!"

I turned to see Mike, unraveling his bag and taking off his jacket to sit across from me and steal a bite off my plate.

"Are you saving that for your archives so you can say you knew me when?" I played along.

"Gross. A piece of broccoli?" he asked, popping it in his mouth instead of his pocket. "Are you excited for rehearsals to begin?"

"Yes and no. I'll barely have any down time once it starts," I told him.

"Don't do it. Don't piss all over this. This is a good thing, and you know it." He looked me right in the eye and waited for my response.

"It's definitely cool. But it's just a school play." I played it down.

"And?" His glare was incredibly intimidating.

"And..." For once I was literally speechless. There wasn't any easy way that I could think of to back out of this and act like I didn't care. This opportunity had me by the balls, and it was time to grasp my vulnerability. "And I'm so excited that I got the part!" I couldn't help but follow the statement with an almost nervous laugh.

It felt good to own up to what I wanted, admitting that I put myself out on the line and risked disappointed, but came out ahead. Time was passing very slowly as we approached the beginning of rehearsals. I sat around, watching television, indulging in reruns I had seen numerous times before. Episodes I could practically recite with the characters.

Feeling my inner twelve-year-old maturity coming through, I picked my phone up to turn off the sound as I didn't feel like filling everyone in with my lack of schedule knowledge, just yet. Instead I focused on the television, and one of the scenes I had seen over one hundred times, one that I truly admired the actors for. The timing and delivery of the lines were priceless. I saw something lighting up out of the corner of my eye and was hoping to ignore it, seeing as how it was probably Mike wanting to see what was, or wasn't, going on. I finally forced myself to look down at the screen of my phone and noticed that it wasn't Mike.

I answered, assuming it was a wrong number, or even a sales person. But why would a sales person be calling me this late in the evening? In an attempt to take control of the situation, I answered the phone, assuming I could simply request that the salesperson take my phone number off any cold-call lists.

"Hello?" I answered in the usual manner, paying more attention to the show.

"Hi! Can I speak to Lisa, please?" the woman' voice on the other end requested.

"Yes, this is her."

"Hey, Lisa! This is Tracy. How are you?"

Suddenly, I was focused on the conversation. "I'm great. How are you?"

"I'm good. I'm sorry for getting back to you so late with the schedule. Everything on this production is running behind! But, you know how these things go. We're all very excited to get to work!" she explained.

I was trying to sound excited about being part of the production in the first place. However, in the back of my head, I was wondering how she was portraying a generous tone, having offered me a part that didn't even have a name. I just had to remind myself that there was nothing wrong with background. And while taking part in the little bipolar back and forth going on in my head, I missed her lowdown on the character and almost all the instructions for predicted rehearsal schedules.

Luckily, I tuned back in just in time to hear when and where the first meeting would be taking place. "Sounds great! I'll be there!"

"Great! I'll see you then." And with that, we both hung up.

Afterwards, I realized that I had mixed feelings of excitement and relief. I was excited to have gotten the part. My talent was recognized, and they believed that I would be a positive addition to the play. The relief came in that I had a positive outlet for all the free time I would've spent stewing on everything going wrong in my life. It would be amazing to focus and put my efforts into something positive and just the thought of something good happening made me smile.

It was cheesy, but as small of an accomplishment as it seemed to anyone else, I felt good and wanted to share it with someone who would appreciate it. Only one number came to mind.

I simply tapped the speed-dial button, and the phone started ringing on the other end. After a couple of rings, Mike picked up with an unexpected response.

"Ah, what happened?" he asked, seemingly waiting for the bad news that they had called to tell me that they had offered me the wrong part.

"Whoa. Wait, what is it you've been telling me about updates? Oh, that's right. Don't do that!" I was happy to imitate him. "They didn't change their minds or anything, I really got it! And the rehearsals start soon, so I'll be busy, busy, busy! So I just wanted to share a little more useless information before I'm rendered unavailable."

"Good! This whole work and school only thing was getting sad," he joked. But there was some truth to what he was saying. I had become so wrapped up in my own pity party that I was losing sight of the important things going on around me, important things that I wanted to try to be a part of and would definitely be embarrassed by reminiscing about how I had missed out on them because I was pouting.

"I know, I just needed a little shove in the right direction," I confessed.

"Or a bitch slap."

I waited for the courtesy laugh, but one didn't follow. Normally I would have been a little offended, but I couldn't argue with him. "All right. All right. Such a charmer. I'll let you go, I just wanted to keep you posted."

"Well, congratulations, again. You deserved it. I'm glad you got the part."

"Thanks. I think so too." With that, the conversation was over.

I didn't have too hard of a time going to sleep that night. It was great drifting off to a head full of positive thoughts and anticipation of things to come, as opposed to lying awake dreading the events of the following day. I couldn't remember what they were about, but I was pretty sure I had some sweet dreams that night.

The following morning I woke up with the same buzz and actually looked forward to going to work and finally sharing the good news with any coworkers who actually cared and maybe even a few customers who could fake interest. I was definitely giving off some sort of vibe and could tell that a few people had to do a double take when I greeted them with smiles and a few with coffee. I was thrilled to see that Mike was working the lunch shift, as it would make the time go faster and the pissy people seem to blend into the other tasks of the day.

"Hey! You didn't tell me you were working the day shift."

"Well, I didn't know myself until this morning," he told me. "Besides, you seem to be in the mood for surprises. And what could be better than spending a few hours with the hottest guy in the work place?"

I rolled my eyes at him but still had to laugh. "And appreciate it, I will. Now roll some silverware."

"If you're lucky, maybe I will."

"Lucky? I did get lucky. Don't jinx me, you get paid to roll!" I stuck my tongue out at him and started walking back to the kitchen to punch in and see what else needed to be done to open. Everything seemed to be almost done, so hanging up my jacket and putting my keys and phone in the pocket of my apron seemed sufficient for opening the doors. The shift seemed to pass quickly since everything went smoothly, and my head was filled with mental notes of how I would fulfill my schedule for the next day. It was going to be pretty tedious, start very early and possibly end late after the initial rehearsal, but the challenge was a welcome one.

I hung out after work and got some food with Mike and a few other coworkers. Hanging out with these guys always brought a little comic relief to my day, as well as a little physical relief for my knees. I was noticing more and more every day that they weren't happy about going to work either. But it made me realize that getting up at the crack of dawn to go to physical therapy appointments was actually worthwhile.

A quick bite turned into a few hours of sitting around and laughing, having a good time watching our p.m. counterparts suffer through the dinner shift. Before we all knew it, it was dark outside and the dinner rush was clearing out. One at a time our little post-shift party started to die out, and we all said our quick good-byes to head home.

I got home and started to get my things together for the following day since my day would start at five in the morning. Though it would be starting out with physical therapy, a few hours of learning how to break down math problems, and no doubt pages of homework, there was a light at the end of the tunnel. It came in the form of the initial rehearsal for the show. Even though this would include the receipt of a long script and hectic schedule to incorporate onto my already crazy calendar, I was looking forward to every minute of it, as well as meeting the rest of the cast.

It felt good that things were moving in a more positive direction. And with my newfound optimism surfaced a little cheese factor. I started thinking back to the first day of school. Every year, whether it was first or tenth grade, we dreaded the return to nine months of early mornings, homework, structure, and requirements of returning to school. However, we couldn't wait for the first day. For my sister and me, this excitement was capitalized by the ritual of picking out our first-day-of-school outfits.

I almost felt like I was back in high school, going through my closet and figuring out which outfit would make the best first impression. Logically, I knew that I was probably the only one who would be impressed by my appearance, but I looked forward to having fun with it anyway. After a few hours of flipping through my wardrobe, I decided on a pair of jeans and a blue V-neck T-shirt. It was subtle, but it made a statement. Perhaps the statement was that I didn't need to dig through every item of clothing I owned to find such a simple outfit, but it was worth the mess.

After picking out the perfect "red carpet" outfit, I noticed how late it was getting and decided to try and pass out for the night. When setting an alarm for the following day, it was usually accompanied by that slight feeling of dread, thinking that I'd be ripped from my blissful slumber by that noise that I'd come to resent. That noise that's supposed to sound like a magical awakening to a new day full of possibility but in reality just makes you realize that you really have to pee and can't roll over and go back to sleep. The noise that makes you want to flush your phone or slam it on the floor in an attempt to break it since just turning it off would be too polite for the alarm.

Tonight, I looked forward to the following morning and that dread was replaced with excitement. I even debated setting the alarm a little earlier in order to put some effort into my hair and makeup. Then I realized I was getting a little carried away and would appreciate the extra twenty minutes of sleep, as well as the all-natural look of mascara and a ponytail that came along with it. I knew the anticipation that came along with the following day seemed a little juvenile, but I appreciated it, and somehow, it was very easy to fall asleep to.

?

Chapter 14

My alarm went off a little earlier than usual, and I was tempted to hit the snooze button. Just as I was blindly reaching for it, I realized I had to get up and start my day. Even in my semiconscious state, I reminded myself that I was looking forward to getting everything done and heading to rehearsal.

I was excited to leave that morning, especially after putting a little effort into my looks. I would be facing the usual agenda of physical therapy and classes. And I was pretty sure none of the casual observers included in these daily events had ever seen me put much effort into my appearance. My usual style consisted of yoga pants that I had been rocking for the past week and some frumpy tank top with a sweatshirt option. As far as my makeup, I was pretty sure I could easily be confused with the local "celebrity" who would sit on the street corner and hold a handwritten cardboard sign to encourage people to throw their loose change in her direction while sometimes strumming an old guitar. While the extra income would be lovely, and most likely tax free, I was happy to provide a little differentiation from my local twin since flipping coins could cause the loss of an eye. And I was pretty sure I hadn't had a tetanus shot since junior high.

I was pretty proud of myself for remembering how to put on liquid liner, emphasizing the fact that I had used my dominant hand. One last look in the mirror, and I walked out the door to head to my physical therapy appointment.

When I arrived, I was greeted by the usual receptionist but she actually smiled at me for once. We went through the usual conversation of patient check-in, and just before I sat down to wait, she asked if I had big plans for the day. It almost caught me by surprise since she had hardly ever made an attempt to take her eyes off of her computer screen and even make eye contact, let alone notice a difference in my appearance. It was definitely encouraging. I simply smiled back and simply told her that I was heading to class after my appointment.

Even the nurses noticed that there was a difference in my appearance. Though I was flattered, it made me wonder just how nasty I looked when I was coming here before. If they truly believed that I lived under a bridge, why were they still willing to touch my flesh to perform the therapy and why did they charge me full price?

I didn't really have time to ponder these petty issues, so I decided to focus on the positive and head off to my logic class. While it wouldn't be many peoples' ideal reason for putting one's face on, but I was inspired and secretly wouldn't have minded if the hot guy that sat two rows and five seats over from me took notice.

I arrived a little early, took my usual seat, and started unpacking my books. I watched everyone randomly walk in and sit down. Some would just sit and rub their eyes, fighting the urge to pass out in their chairs. Some would start studying their phones, and others would actually unload notebooks and start looking over the class material.

I sat tapping my pencil, wide awake and anticipating the rest of my day. I randomly looked at the walls and posters about the school, acquiring no useful information whatsoever since my mind was preoccupied with everything else. I started to notice that one of the girls on the poster had some sweet highlights. I started to wonder if I would want highlights like that or if I should consider going darker all over. I was going back and forth, trying to picture myself with each look, when suddenly the beefcake of my logic class walked in.

He was wearing his usual pair of jeans and plain cotton T-shirt, which was just tight enough to see his underdeveloped pecks and decent-sized triceps. His hair looked like he just woke up, and his five o'clock shadow looked like it had snowballed to a five o'clock a.m. shadow. And somehow, he could really pull it off. As he slowly stumbled to his usual chair, he performed one last check of his phone before sliding it into his back pocket. I watched carefully, studying how the lump of his phone seemed to fit in perfectly with the curve of his ass. It was a fine collaboration, though his backside was just as pretty as the front and didn't need much help in capturing attention.

In an attempt to prevent my mouth from falling open, I came back to reality and focused on moving my eyes back up to his face. I arrived at eye level just in time to see that he was looking back at me, and it seemed like our eyes locked. I froze for a minute, but he seemed to be smiling at me. Constantly overanalyzing everything as I usually do, I couldn't be sure whether it was a polite smile, an inviting smile, or simply the wide cringe of a hangover remnant of events from the previous evening. I gave back a courtesy smile, which I was pretty sure came off as similar to the kind you give when you're busted by a person who catches wind when you fart in public and were shooting for silent and undetected results. Even though I didn't have a mirror on me to prove it, I was pretty sure it wasn't flattering to my cosmetic efforts.

I tried to look back down and adjust my books as if I was consciously making eye contact. It would've worked, but as I was flipping my hair, I knocked a book on the floor and caught the undesired attention of the students finding their Zen before class, as well as those filing in last minute to settle in for the long two hours of learning. My only solace was that they were ignorant to the fact that not only was I single but that they were catching a glimpse as to why. Good thing we were only there to immerse ourselves in mathematical logic.

Luckily, the professor walked in shortly after I recovered my book and took control of the class to dive into the lesson. I was pretty sure I hadn't been that happy to start class since grade school. The attention was on our teacher, and the focus was hopefully the math problems. Class actually went by very quickly, and before I knew it, I was packing everything back into my backpack. I tried to do it quickly so that I could do a little pseudo stalking and see if I could determine the earlier connection.

I stopped outside of the classroom and walked a few feet down the hallway and turned around to face the door of the classroom, pretending to bury my attention in my phone. He came walking out, and I noticed that he was reaching for his phone out of his back pocket. I was torn as to whether I wanted to embrace all the flattery of the earlier morning and offer to help him reach it but decided that it might be a bit soon.

My shyness turned out to be a good thing since my creeper abilities resolved any hopes I had had for starting a private study group with my classmate. The conversation he was participating in started with a "Hey, babe!" and went straight into talking about how much fun he had last night but how sick he felt this morning and how he almost threw up before class. Oddly enough, and without giving the other person a chance to respond, he followed the news with the question of when was he going to get to come over again.

I was glad his conversation had specifically addressed any interests I would've have had in making a move. I appreciated the fact that he had kept me from wasting my time and effort. I was humbled by the experience. It was too bad but also quit amusing that painting my face had caused me to count my chickens and dip my toe in to test the water. Although, it was probably a sign that I had enough on my plate and shouldn't worry about guys and dating right now since I obviously had no sixth sense about it, having confused flirtation with nausea. I laughed it off and went back to focusing on all the good things that were coming.

The day followed its usual course, consisting of a few more classes accompanied by plenty of homework. While this would usually be a giant pain, I figured the time between classes and rehearsal would be the perfect time to get it done, as well as keep me from checking my phone every five minutes in anticipation, killing the battery.

Finally, it was time to head to the auditorium. I saw a couple of familiar faces walking toward the door, and with the exchange of courtesy smiles, we headed in to take seats and wait for the fun to begin. The auditorium was huge with plenty of seats to spread out. It was one of those situations where we all knew that we should sit in the same area but didn't exactly want to snuggle up next to someone we didn't know all that well yet. There were about five of us sitting in the auditorium watching others file in. I decided that the best place would be in the second row, a few seats in from the edge, the perfect seat to remain inconspicuous and be able to observe my new partners in crime.

Finally, the director walked in, carrying a small stack of papers, which I assumed consisted of the scripts. She was followed by a girl, who appeared to be a student. My guess was that this person was her assistant director as Tracy handed her the stack of papers. The two whispered for a minute, checked their phones, and then they split up—the assistant to organize the stack on one of the chairs and Tracy leaving the auditorium with what appeared to be a water bottle.

A few minutes later it seemed like everyone was there. Sara, who I had met at the auditions, seemed to recognize me too and sat a few seats away. We exchanged courtesy smiles, and she put her backpack down on the seat in between us and settled in to her seat. We watched Tracy close the auditorium door, stop, give an instruction to the assistant, and then focused on the group of people before her. It was obvious we were officially getting started.

"Hello, everyone. Welcome. We'd like to thank you for accepting the roles for the spring production," Tracy announced. "I've met most of you already. But just in case you forgot, my name is Tracy and I'll be the director. This is Jesse. She's the director's assistant for this project. If you have any questions and I'm not available to answer them, Jesse will be able to help you. Now, before we hand out the scripts, I'd like to go around and have everyone introduce themselves and tell us what part they have in the production."

I definitely picked the right seat. I could observe a few of the people's intros and decide what to offer. After hearing a couple of people, it seemed that we simply were announcing our names and roles, nothing about majors or extracurricular hobbies. I was peacefully awaiting my turn when I felt my phone buzzing to tell me that I had a text.

I assumed it was Mike, wishing me luck and reminding me to call and tell him every boring detail when I got home. I thought it was sweet, so I figured if I held my phone low enough, I'd be able to read it before it was my turn to speak. I couldn't help but smile as I reached for it and just reminded myself to pay attention to Sara. I looked down at my phone to see what words of wisdom Mike would be offering me but saw something completely unexpected. The name on the received message was not Mike's, but instead Aaron's.

I could feel my smile melt, and the introductions around me seemed to fade to a quiet buzzing. I wasn't even sure I wanted to read it. I just stared at the name, not the message. I couldn't believe what I was seeing. Luckily I was ripped from the useless trance by Sara reminding me that it was my turn to talk.

"Lisa. Hey, Lisa, you're up," Sara informed me in a slight whisper.

"Oh, yeah. Sorry." I cleared my throat, barely thinking straight. "I'm Lisa. I'll be playing the woman."

I nodded to complete the statement, portrayed a flat smile, and sat back down to look again at my phone. I wasn't sure how to feel about it. I wasn't happy to hear from him since it reminded me of the shit show that he had put me through. I wasn't sad about it since it was at least a little flattering that he was thinking of me again. I was just very surprised by it. I had tried so hard to get a hold of him before my surgery and just wanted some sort of response to tell me that he was at least thinking of me. Finally, I got what I wanted. It was just too late to be grateful for it.

Before I knew it, the first rehearsal had come to an end. Though I made the decision to put my phone away when the student introductions were over, attempting not to let Aaron turn my banana split into a shit sundae, the rest of the announcements made by Tracy were only a blur to me. Trying not to think about it him was filling my head with memories and self-debate over what to do about it. I watched as everyone started heading over to where Jesse was sitting with the stack of papers. We all picked up the scripts and rehearsal schedules, said good-bye to our castmates, and filed out of the auditorium.

I stopped outside of the door, convincing myself that I simply had to check the time, but in reality, knew that I wanted to see what he had had the nerve to say to me. I noticed that the meeting had taken two hours and was surprised that it seemed to fly by, and I couldn't recall anything but the student intros. I started walking toward the exit to the parking lot when I heard someone calling my name.

"Lisa! Hey, wait up!" It was Sara.

I turned around to greet her. "Oh, hey. What's up?"

"I was going to ask you the same thing."

I thought it was an odd statement coming from someone I had only met a couple of times but hoped it was general conversation, not her informing me that I was acting like a fool during the meeting.

"What do you mean?" I asked.

"Well, you seemed upset. Is everything okay?" She had seemed so cold the first time I met her, but her concern appeared to be genuine.

"Yeah. Yeah, everything's cool." I figured it was the simplest response without regurgitating my life's story.

"Wait, it's a guy, isn't it?" She almost lit up, excited that she solved the mystery.

"Why would you think that?" No matter how much I didn't want to admit that it affected me, I couldn't help but wonder how she nailed it so quickly.

"You just have that look on your face."

"Look? What look?" Now I was really confused.

"Like a deer in headlights. Minding your own business until they spot you. You want to run, but you're mesmerized by the bright lights. You want to stay and see what happens, but you know you're about to get hit by a huge car, and it's going to hurt. Bad."

I couldn't believe it. She had summed it up perfectly, and it reminded me just how juvenile it was to let it affect me this much. Still, I realized it wasn't a conscious decision, and it would most likely bug the crap out of me for a while.

I laughed. I knew all I could do was confess. "You got it."

"What's his name?"

I tried to rely on humor. "Well, I call him a lying piece of shit, but I'm pretty sure Aaron is what's written on his birth certificate."

"No way."

"Yeah, that's really what I call him. Unless I've had a few, then my Tourette's comes out."

"No, I mean, that's my ex's name too."

"No way! Is yours a selfish prick too?" I laughed.

"Oh yeah, that's the short version of the story," she confessed.

"Wow. You're my Aaron twin," I announced. "Sorry for the reason but happy to meet you."

"Happy to meet you as well. You've earned a glass of wine. Want to head to my apartment and read over the script?"

"Yeah, actually that sounds cool. Thanks," I replied, having a change of heart and digging my mood out of the dumpster. I still had a lot of other things to remain positive about, and I didn't want to waste time catering to people who didn't want to support me in that goal.

I followed Sara to her apartment building. She waved me to park as she headed toward the underground garage, and I noticed the outside was a little nicer than what a person would expect of a college student. It was a lighter-colored brick with a blue trim, and you could see through the lighting of the front door that it led to a lobby instead of directly to a flight of stairs.

I got out of the car and walked to the front door. I was once again impressed that the first of two doors was unlocked so that I wouldn't have to wait out in the cold but instead in a small room with a decent temperature and a speaker with a buzzer. Something else we had in common—we weren't living like typical students in college dorms with random street parking, shared bathrooms, and pay washing machines but in comfortable, efficient apartments.

My first impressions were interrupted went Sara opened the door to let me in. I followed her up the stairs to the second floor and toward her apartment door. She provided the usual disclaimer of her apartment being a mess and welcomed me inside anyway. I walked in to find that she was wrong about the mess but revealed her true status with the décor around her apartment.

The furniture was scarce, consisting of a small round table with three mismatched chairs; a loveseat couch with an old floral pattern accented with a few mystery stains; a side table and television stand made out of two different kinds of wood laminate; and a large, flat screen TV. After she motioned me to sit down, she headed to the kitchen to pour the glass of wine she had offered and I started to notice that the few pictures lining her walls seemed to be homemade paintings. I enjoyed canvas painting in my spare time, but I couldn't make sense out of what these creations were supposed to be. Between her acting and painting, I started to make the connection of the tortured artist. I welcomed the idea of a new and creative friend but promised myself that if she asked to paint my nude portrait that I would leave and try to tell her that I had mono and wouldn't be able to hang out anymore.

She came back with two glasses, handing me one and taking a sip of the other. I thanked her and told her that I liked her artwork, following the compliment with a sip of wine.

"So how long were you two together?" she asked, getting straight to the point.

"Wow. Less than a year," I confessed, trying to study my glass instead. "Pretty sad, huh? Sad that someone I was with for less than a year, someone I technically didn't know all that well or well enough, could get to me like this." It seemed appropriate to follow the confession with another larger sip of wine.

"No, not sad. It happens, and we don't always have a say in it. Those 'first loves' will sneak up on you."

"Then spit in your face. Everything seemed to be fine until we moved in together."

"Yeah, living together is hard. I was with my Aaron for two years before we did it, and we didn't make it a year either."

Her confession was comforting. Not that I would ever wish similar suffering on another person, but it was soothing to know that I wasn't the only failure, that planning ahead for spontaneity didn't necessarily guarantee success either.

"Yikes. Note to self, next time, get a duplex." We both laughed and clinked our glasses in agreement. This led to a larger gulp of wine, followed by a few refills until the bottle was gone.

Filled with liquid encouragement, we shared our stories— where we were from, what we were in school for, and how long we had been interested in acting. Sara got up to open another bottle of wine to continue our discussion, and the moment of silence brought me right back to the issue at hand. Trying to ignore it yet again, I turned to the only logical distraction I could think of besides beverages.

"We should order a pizza!' I said loudly, even though there was an open counter to the kitchen and Sara could probably hear me perfectly.

"Cool, what kind do you like?" she asked, walking over to her phone to order online.

"I like anything with a shit load of cheese. The rest is up to you. I'm not picky."

"All right, sounds good." She started working on her phone.

I took another sip and was inspired by a new idea. "Oh, and we should get stuffed crust."

"Cool," she responded, not looking up.

"Wait, we should get it from one of those places with the garlic sauce. You know, the dip?" I acted out the motion of dipping pizza in one of those plastic ramekins.

She seemed slightly annoyed until she looked up to see the show and then started laughing. "Really? Anything else you can think of before I send the order?"

"Nope. That's it. I'm not picky." I reminded her, taking another small sip.

The pizza arrived, and we tore it up. Sitting silently with buzzes and pending food comas, I had a sudden awakening.

"You know, boys are cute. Then they talk. It just seems to ruin it all."

Sara looked over at me, a little skeptical of the statement. "Do you need a glass of water?"

"No! I'm serious! Think about it. That must be why they're cute, well, most of the time. Otherwise, the human race would just die out. They would say something stupid, show what pricks they are, and no woman would put up with them long enough to reproduce!"

"I'm gonna grab that glass of water. Don't burn your bra or anything while I'm gone. The property manager hasn't changed the battery in the smoke detector yet, and I plan on getting the deposit back from this place."

I had to admit, with each glass, I felt myself slipping further and further into that zone where nothing bugs you or upsets you, nothing can hurt you, and, aside from the spinning room, everything was wonderful. However, in some form or another, and as bitter as it probably sounded, I truly believed what I was telling her.

A few glasses of water later, we both knew it was past our bedtimes. Still feeling that bitter buzz, I decided to crash on Sara's couch. The pillows and blanket didn't make up for the fact that the couch was indeed built for parties of two, but it was nice thinking that there was someone else in the apartment. In some weird way, it was almost as if I wasn't alone.

I was hoping to pass out but couldn't resist the urge to see what exactly Aaron had to say to me. I reached to the floor for my phone, turned it on, and pulled up my messages. Was he trying to get a hold of me to tell me that I had left my socks on the floor in his bedroom? Was he trying to tell me that I had forgotten to pay him my half of some stupid bill? Or was he simply trying to text someone else whose name happened to start with the same letter as mine? I finally found his name on the list and tapped the message to open it. It was one simple line that read: "We should talk."

I could feel my eyes welling up with tears. I had wasted enough time and effort getting to know him, trying to make a relationship work, and then accepting the fact that he wasn't willing to meet me halfway. I wouldn't let him shit on me again. I turned my phone off and threw it back on the floor. I stood up and found my way to Sara's kitchen and the bottle we had been nursing on earlier. I took a gulp out of the bottle, put the top back on, walked back to the couch, and passed out.

I awoke to a nasty, wine-induced headache, which I refused to label a hangover. It sounded as if Sara wasn't up yet, but I knew I had to check the time so I could get back to my apartment and get my uniform for work. Squinting, trying to avoid as much light as possible, I tried to roll over and look for my phone to check the time. Having contorted to fit the couch, turning ignited the quiet cracking of almost every bone in my back. I couldn't help but cringe and let out a stifled groan into the couch pillow.

I found my phone and saw that I had plenty of time before work. Courtesy of the lacking sleeping arrangements, I had woken up incredibly early and might even have time to take a short nap before my shift.

Standing up wasn't much easier. Getting up, the common urge to stretch was postponed by a dizzy rush filtering through my body. I stretched anyway to make sure that my blood was still flowing. And as I did, I felt my back crack a few more times. I snuck out of her apartment and down to the first floor. Each step felt like torture, and I knew that a gallon of water was in my near future.

I finally found my car in the parking lot and turned off the radio before starting it. Though it was somewhat of a blur, the ride home wasn't as tedious as I thought it would be. I walked in and set my keys on the counter and grabbed the biggest pitcher I could find in my cupboard. A glass seemed overrated, so I headed straight for the darkest place in my apartment. I had never been so happy to see my own room. My bed was screaming my name, and I couldn't resist crawling into it and setting an alarm for the following hour.

Even though it was a small step in the right direction, waking up the second time was a little easier and I craved caffeine instead of water. I grasped at what little desire I had, managing to brush my teeth and put my hair in a ponytail. Feeling like the lovechild of death and ugly, I knew perfume wasn't an option for the day and simply put on my uniform and grabbed my things for work.

As I was setting my phone down next to my apron on the seat, I noticed that my alert was blinking at me again. Almost afraid to see who it was, I knew I had to snap out of it and be an adult. I picked it up and went back to my messages. The name I didn't want to see. This time it was a less generic message, and it seemed to be composed for me: "Come on. I know you hate me, but we should at least talk." Figuring he was half right and knowing that I felt too crappy to talk to my customers, let alone a lying piece of crap, I decided to ignore the message and focus on trying to survive my day.

I walked in to the usual greetings, although I felt like I had gotten a well-deserved double glance out of a couple of coworkers. I tried to avoid eye contact so I could try to maintain some sort of ignorance about my frightening appearance. But there was that one coworker who wasn't shy and didn't mind rubbing my nose in any type of metaphorical puddle.

"Yuck! Angry or just suicidal?" Mike joked.

"Well, I'm pretty sure it started off as a girl's night with one of my new castmates. But honestly, I slipped into that fuzzy dreamlike state after the second bottle," I confessed.

"So how did the first night of rehearsals go?" He was seriously asking as he was stocking glasses.

I was about to lay it all out. I wanted to tell him everything, but even thinking about it made me a mix of angry and sad. Mike was looking forward to his big move, and I didn't want to bug him with petty crap that probably shouldn't bug me in the first place. So as I was opening my mouth to answer, my thought process changed.

"It was cool. Pretty basic. You know, just introducing ourselves to everyone. Getting the script and schedule. Nothing too exciting," I said, casually grabbing a package of napkins so that I would have an excuse to exit the kitchen.

"Sounds pretty low key. Are you gonna be at rehearsals every night from now until then, or do you still get to have a life?" he asked me on my way out of the kitchen.

"Ha! No, we only have rehearsals a few days a week and not all of us have to be at every one." I tried again to get away from the topic of the play.

"That's cool. Then you can come to my going-away party," he said, again sounding very casual about an emotional topic.

Trying again not to be sad about something that should be a positive thing, I simply hollered back, "Yeah, of course. I wouldn't miss that for anything."

With everything going on around me, I figured that if my day kept going in this direction, my shift would produce no tips and I'd get hit by a car on my way through the parking lot. But I had to leave all of it at the door and get ready to practice my acting skills. I had myself talked into my motivation until I saw that my first table was a guy and a girl sitting in one of the booths, both on one side, snuggling. It was going to be a long day. I could only hope that when the car took me out, that I would go quickly.

I was on autopilot for the rest of my shift. My brain was filled with thoughts of Mike leaving, responding to Aaron's messages, and sides of fries. I didn't want Mike to leave. I didn't know if or what I wanted to say to Aaron. And I didn't know why someone would select steamed carrots over fries. Finally, it was time to leave for the day, and nothing sounded better than my bed.

"You've been really quiet today. That must be some hangover," Mike reminded me. "Go home and take a shower already."

"Saying I stink?" I asked, hoping he would go easy in his response.

"No, I'm saying you look like hell. Cheer up!"

"Well, as long as you're saying I don't stink," I responded with a hint of sarcasm. "A nap sounds heavenly."

"Whatever works. Find out what's going on next Thursday. That's when my party is."

"Wouldn't miss it for the world," I said, waving as I turned to leave.

I was so exhausted and thirsty for my pitcher, I couldn't concentrate on anything else. I made it home and took Mike's advice, washing the dehydration off myself as best I could. Afterwards I turned the sound off on everything I could think of and crawled into bed to pass out for the night. Clinging to what was left of my optimism, I set an alarm for class in the morning.

When I woke up again, it was six o'clock in the morning and I could tell that I felt one hundred times better than the day before. But even with my new level of comfort, I still had one nasty little buzz in the back of my mind. I didn't know if or what I should say to Aaron. I decided to concentrate on what mattered. I got up, got ready, and headed to school a little early to grab some coffee and read over my script.

Even though it was a smaller community college, I was surprised to find a decent-sized crowd already in the cafeteria that had apparently had the same idea as me. I picked out the most energy-loaded drink I could get and found an open table to set my things down. I took a sip and cringed at the mix of heat and bitterness of the coffee. I shook it off and dug my script and a highlighter out of my backpack to start flipping through to highlight my lines. I was feeling pretty constructive, drawing and sipping, when, suddenly, I heard someone call my name.

"Hey! Lisa!" Sara called, heading over to my table.

A little surprised, I looked up to see who it was. "Oh, hey."

I hadn't seen Sara for a couple of days and was a little embarrassed that I let my alcohol- provoked alter ego make the first impression.

"How you feelin'?" she joked. "Going over the script? What do you think?"

"Yeah. Actually I just started. So far so good." My answer addressed the script, but I knew I had to cover all the bases. "Listen, I hope I wasn't too obnoxious the other night. Certain people just know how to get under a person's skin. Thanks for letting my sleep on your couch."

"I get it. That's why they're cute, remember?" She took a sip of her coffee. "So have you talked to him yet?"

"No. I have no spare time with school, doctors, lawyers, the script—"

She interrupted me. "Sounds like you've thought of every excuse in the book, but you know, we aren't off script yet. Think you're going to call him any time soon?"

"Nah, who cares." I wondered why she cared so much whether I spoke to my ex or not. I figured that if I had worked this hard to put him out of my mind, it should be easy for her not to bring up someone she had never met.

"Because, you know, if you did, you might actually get some closure. Not for anyone else but for yourself. Between sips, you were telling me all the things you would've told him if you had had the chance," she reminded me. "And how getting all that crap off your chest would help you forget all about him."

I had to admit she was right. I took another sip of my coffee and told her so. "You're right."

"Now, you want to actually read through the script this time?" She smiled and held her coffee up, offering a "Cheers."

I met her halfway, and we gently tapped our hot glasses and took tiny sips so we didn't burn our lips. With open scripts, we spent the next hour gossiping about our classes, where we were from, our families, and what we wanted to be when we grew up. The positive topics were a lot more motivating.

"One of my best friends is about to move to LA, I wish I was going with him," I told her, almost bringing down my own positive attitude.

"Why don't you?" It seemed like a simple question.

I knew it would sound like the same tap dance, but I told her about the car accident and my lease and the pending lawsuit. She just shrugged. I was curious what she was thinking.

"What's that for?"

"Nothing. It's just that you're making excuses again."

"No, I'm not. I seriously have to at least stay until my contract is up and the lawsuit's over! I've talked to both my lawyer and my landlord!" I was trying to defend myself, but I could see how she saw my justifications as excuses.

"So how long are you stuck here?" she said with a sarcastic tone and a side glance, taking another sip of her coffee.

I looked back down at my script, trying to squeeze in a few more swipes with my highlighter, "Probably another year. At least ten months because of my lease."

"So what are you going to do with your classes?"

"Ah, pass them." I laughed, genuinely confused "What do you mean?"

"You're taking general classes with no idea of what your major should be, but you know what you want to do with your life. And these two specific concepts don't usually cross paths. Why don't you go to culinary school or something?"

 Now I was completely confused. "Wait. Why would I do that?"

"You said you definitely want to move, but you're stuck here for another year—no ifs, ands, or buts. That timeline would still leave you a semester short of an elite degree from this fine community college. If you're trying to have something to fall back on, why don't you go to some sort of trade school." Her plot was amazing, considering she was delivering it as she was skimming over the script.

"Trade school? Isn't that for plumbers and electricians?"

"And chefs. And hairstylists. And mechanics. They're usually, what, nine-month programs? And I'm pretty sure some sort of license or certification would guarantee some sort of work when you're finally out there." She was right again. "I'd feel more secure with a specific skill than with a two-year college degree in generals."

She was absolutely right. I had wasted so much time whining and feeling sorry for myself when I should have pulled my head out of my own ass to do something to make things better. Maybe it was worth checking out some sort of trade school. I was fascinated about an alternative route and wanted to pick Sara's brain a little longer. But before I knew it, I checked my phone and it was time to pack my things up and head to class.

I arrived a little early and had time to finish my coffee. I started thinking about what Sara had told me—getting closure. That would be a good thing. I hadn't told anyone else about what was going on, so I wasn't concerned with what my friends or family thought I should do. But I had a right to tell him what I thought about how he treated me, how things ended, and how he disappeared when I really needed him. Knowing him, ignoring him would only justify his behavior and encourage him to keep pursuing me.

Before I knew it, class had started, my professor started lecturing, assigned homework, completed the lecture, and dismissed the class for the day. At least I thought it had gone in that order. I was practicing my improvisational skills, pretending to pay attention and take notes, presenting a deep look of concentration while making a list of all the trade schools I could think of. Admittedly, I could only come up with a short list, but it was convenient that my list and the study of world economies were composed of the same body language. Maybe Sara had a point.

I spent the rest of my time before rehearsal, in and outside of class making mental lists of the risks and rewards of reconsidering my education. I made a promise to myself that my decision wouldn't be influenced by the difference in cost, lack of extracurricular activities, or the nagging of my mother. With all the time spent considering how to ditch my current comfortable schedule, I hadn't spent much time focusing on my homework or the play.

As soon as I turned the corner to walk down the hall toward the auditorium, I saw Sara and starting walking faster to catch up and tell her about the important decision I had made. Her attention was focused on the packet she was carrying. Aside from the fact that it looked familiar, I was pretty sure it was the script since I could see her lips moving and her facial expressions changing while she read.

"Sara! Wait up!" I saw her jump and turn in my direction.

"Whoa, you scared me! What's up?"

"Nothing, I just wanted to tell you that you were right." I couldn't help but smile.

"About what?" She looked a little confused, then came to her senses. "Oh, the coffee in the cafeteria? See, I told you! They recycle it every day and simmer it down until it becomes chunky so they can pass it off as something stronger! Gross! Did you get a piece in your mouth!"

"No, not at all. I didn't have to do the research to believe that!" I laughed at her assumption. "About trade school. You were absolutely right about trade school."

"Oh, great. Planning on becoming a plumber?" She looked back down at her papers.

"No, of course not. But you were right about not wasting my time getting some useless degree I'll probably never use. I narrowed down the list of trade schools, and I think I want to do hair." I looked at her, smiling with a goofy, excited look on my face, waiting for her reaction.

"Sounds dope. You're not gonna quit the play and start tomorrow, are you?"

"Of course not. I'm still paying for my classes I might as well finish them. But I was looking at schools, and there's one not too far away from here that starts less than a month after this semester ends. I'd be staying past the end of my lease, but there's no reason I couldn't get that license before I move!"

She had gone back to reading her script but looked up a minute or two after I stopped talking, offering a smile and nod in an attempt to prove she had been listening. Even though I was pretty sure she hadn't heard a word I had said, I appreciated the opportunity to say it out loud. Saying it out loud made it sound like an obtainable goal.

We walked in to the auditorium and waited for everyone to arrive to start rehearsal. I tried to concentrate on reading the script, but my mind was still spinning with this new idea. After all the actors participating in the scene arrived, the director went through her usual announcements and we walked up the steps to get to the chairs that had been set up on the stage. Once we were up there, we sat down and got to work. It was a stress-free evening since we were literally just reading through the script itself. There was no blocking assigned since we were just sitting and reading our parts. Luckily, it was enough to help me focus on the task at hand, instead of my plans for the future.

Since we just read through the pages, without any directions from Tracy, rehearsal ended early; and she had time to make a few announcements before we left. This included the fact that we would go much more in depth with each rehearsal and that we wouldn't all be expected to be present every night. This was good news since Mike's going-away party was coming up. I held my breath as she announced the changes and was able to exhale when I heard that I would have that evening off.

We all left for the night, and I headed home, having found a new source of optimism that even an ex-idiot couldn't crap on. My plan was perfect: complete the semester, take a break for a month, and go to hair school. I had always been pretty decent with hair and makeup. No one had ever told me that I looked like crap. Not that they would just walk up to me and tell me that I look like crap, but I would hope they would give me a little constructive criticism if I really needed it.

Besides, people in California like to look good. They like to look really good. This was a great option to fall back on when I moved out there. I was plotting as I walked into my apartment. I felt like I had this all figured out. I was convinced that this would be the best way to go. Sara, someone I had just met, was convinced that this would be the best way to go. Now I had one more critic to convince: my mother.

I decided to wait and just focus on enjoying Mike's company while he was still here. Seeing him at work was great since he was picking up a lot more shifts to save up his money. But it was also a nasty reminder that he wouldn't be there much longer. The day of his going away party, we worked the lunch shift together and it was probably one of the hardest shifts I've ever worked. That day, the things that would normally bug the shit out of me seemed very insignificant. I didn't care about tables yelling at me or screwing me out of tips, or even the fact that I was doing most of my coworkers' side work throughout the shift. I was only worried about the fact that I didn't want Mike to leave yet.

My coworkers must have thought of me as a lost puppy. Just watching him standing at the pop machine and filling glasses made me stop and stare. I almost felt like a mother watching my child pack up his suitcase to leave for an out of state college. What seemed like a few seconds to me must have been a lot longer. I was in the way of other servers asking me to move and trying to get to the counter, and Mike told me to just take a picture of him so I could stare at it after the lunch rush. I told him not to tempt me otherwise I would do it. And I seriously did consider doing it, until the humor helped me choke back any chance of tears.

I really tried to utilize all my improvisational skills to kill time between work and the party at Mike's. I wanted to stay positive for him, even though I could constantly feel the knots in my throat. We both closed down the afternoon shift and sat down to have a late, greasy lunch before heading to his place. This would be a little stomach preparation before the liquid antidepressant that I assumed would be the theme of the evening for me. With our meals ordered, we sat down in one of the back booths to await its arrival. We were both relieved to be able to sit down and relax.

"It feels so good to sit down. My feet are killing me," I announced, not sure what else to say.

"Tell me about it. This is the first day in a long time that I won't be working a double shift!" Mike said, sitting sideways on the seat with his legs stretched out and crossed, his head leaning against the wall, and his eyes closed.

"Yeah, definitely not fun."

He opened one eye and looked in my direction, sensing the heavy mood. "You're not going to wear that nasty thing to the party, are you?"

Relieved that he was always able to break a mood, I couldn't help but laugh. "Yes. I was totally going to wear this to your party. I wanted to remind you of the job and the friend that you're leaving behind. Not to mention the nasty smell of grease and body odor that seems to acquire on every restaurant employee's uniform. Yes, I thought that would be quite appropriate for a room full of gay male couples and possibly hot straight single men."

Amused by the sarcasm, he again leaned back and closed his eyes. "Well, at least brush your hair and put on some perfume or something."

We both laughed, and I told him the truth. Once again feeling like the mother coming to grips with reality. "No worries, I brought other clothes to make sure that I don't embarrass anyone that has to admit he knows me."

"Good. That could be embarrassing," he said, not opening his eyes.

One of our coworkers brought our plates over and sat them down in front of us, already seeming to know which one of us had ordered what. Mike swung his legs back to the floor and leaned in to start stacking his food.

"Dick." I gave him a fake evil glare. "You're just lucky to know someone like me, someone that looks like me."

With his mouth already full of food, he didn't respond so I took it a step further. Stealing a couple of fries off his plate, I chewed them with my mouth open and asked the big question. "Don't you think I'm pretty?"

Finally looking up and noticing the food practically falling out of my mouth, Mike started laughing and almost spit his out. We both tried to chew and laugh at the same time, resorting to soda to help the process along.

"Holy shit! I could've choked!" He laughed. "Don't do that to me! And FYI, I don't have to answer that."

"Uh-huh," I replied, taking another bite of my own food.

We finished our meals very quickly and quietly. It almost seemed to be a race to see who could clear his plate the fastest. Feeling full and somewhat lethargic, I looked across the table and broke the food-coma-induced silence. "Wow. In a hurry?"

"Nah, just hungry. People aren't going to start showing up at my apartment for another hour or so," he calmly informed me.

"That's cool. Just having a little time to sit back and relax," I told him, thinking it might be a good time to tell him the important stuff.

I had already decided that no matter how much I wanted to tell him that Aaron had contacted me so he could tell me what to do, I wouldn't bring it up since it had nothing to do with Mike. I knew he didn't want anything to get cheesy or sad, but I felt like I wanted him to know how I felt about him. Even though it would probably make me emotional, I knew I would feel better getting it off my chest. And the fact that it was just him and me sitting at the table, I felt like it was now or never.

"So I was going to tell you—" I started before being interrupted by his phone ringing.

"Hang on." He grabbed his phone to check and see who was calling. "Uh-oh. It's the wife. I should probably see what he wants. He's not thrilled about hosting this whole party." He rolled his eyes and answered the call with a very sweet tone. He started mocking Joe, assuring him that he would pick up the ice and the snacks and the napkins.

Intimidated by the topic at hand, I was relieved to have had the interruption. After a few minutes of repeated reassurance, Mike hung up the phone and sighed.

"I'm pretty sure my graduation party was less stressful. Good thing he's cute." He set his phone down and started checking his e-mail. "Now what were you going to tell me?"

"Nothing. It can wait. Want some help setting things up?"

"Actually, yeah, that'd be great. Want to go to the grocery store with me?"

"Sounds good. As long as you don't care if I wear this." I motioned to my uniform as if it was a new outfit.

"Well, what do you think I'm gonna wear?" he said, standing up, stretching, and picking up his phone. "Besides, I have to get ready before the party anyway."

I stood up to follow him out the door and used his own word against him. "Perfume?"

"Don't hate the player."

We walked out to the parking lot and found his car. Opening the door to sit down in the passenger's seat, I noticed that his was cleaner than mine. I usually used my front seat as a storage area for receipts, notebooks, and random papers I thought would come in handy at some point.

"That's cool. I didn't even have to move anything."

"Yeah, as long as Joe hasn't been driving my car," he informed me.

The rest of the short trip to the store was ridden in silence. He parked and immediately reached for his phone to pull up the list Joe had sent him. We went in and gathered everything on the list, plus a few items we thought looked good. After waiting in line for our turn to be rung up, we found the process itself was very quick. Before we knew it, the groceries were loaded in the back of Mike's car and we were on our way back to the parking lot so that I could get my car and follow him back to the party.

I waved him off, already knowing how to get to his apartment, and unlocked my car to get in and search for the "acceptable" party gear I had packed into my car before work. I took a deep breath and tried to remind myself that tonight was about celebrating not moping. But after knowing myself this long, I knew I wouldn't be able to sit back and party until I gave Mike the proper "see ya later."

I got to the apartment, grabbed my bag and headed toward the door. Whether it was a matter of courtesy or he just wanted help carrying in the groceries, Mike was waiting for me so I didn't have to wait. There was no talking as we walked up the stairs since we had eaten and were probably just out of shape. But once we got to his floor, three flights up, I decided to break the ice and make him proud.

"Did you bring your inhaler?" I could barely get it out since I was in rough shape too.

"Ha-ha-ha," he mocked back, but I secretly knew it was because he hadn't caught his breath yet.

We arrived at the door, and as Mike was about to turn his key, Joe opened the door with a slightly, more friendly greeting than he had provided earlier over the phone. "Thanks for picking up that stuff up! Lisa! Hey! How are you?"

His hug took me by surprise, and I was waiting for the after-smell of vodka to justify the mysterious behavior. "Hello! How are you?"

"Great, great," he answered, reaching for the bags to examine what Mike had brought home.

As he looked through the items, he started to quiz Mike about what was in the other bags and I knew this would be the perfect time to change. "Hey, guys, I'm gonna use the bathroom and change out of this shirt!" I tried to say it loudly so they would be able to hear me over the music that Joe had playing. Figuring it didn't really matter if they had heard me or not, I headed to the bathroom to change.

You could learn a lot about people from the themes in their bathrooms. After all, it's not just a room for storing your toothbrush. It's a room for hygiene. A room to utilize when you get made up for your day and a room to sit back and relax in when you got home from work. So what did Mike want to be surrounded by to motivate his day and later let it roll off his back? As soon as you walked in and looked at the framed pictures on the wall, the answer was obvious: superheroes.

It was so appropriate. Mike was a superhero. He saw challenges and risks, but instead of running away, he would face them head on. He seemed to have no fear, like Superman. And like Superman, his powers were real. They weren't the side effect of toxic chemicals or a DNA flaw but naturally who he was. I finished changing and decided to hurry out to help set up and sneak in a drink before I made myself emotional again.

I walked out to find Mike in the kitchen pouring chips into large bowls. I decided to grab a beer and noticed a bottle of tequila sitting on the counter. I grabbed two small shot glasses and decided to take advantage of the opportunity.

"Need any help?" I asked, keeping my back to him as I opened the tequila bottle and pouring the two shots.

"No, I think I got it. Joe and I decided it would be smarter to keep the food in here. Joe figured that hopefully people won't bring that much into the living room and get it all over the carpet." He moved to present the few bowls of snacks he had set up, bearing a cheesy smile of accomplishment. "Happy wife, bearable life."

I turned around, holding the glasses in my hands. "Here, but don't drink it yet."

"Oh, we're starting early." He grabbed a glass from me.

"Well, I wanted to tell you earlier. I know you said you wanted this to be a happy, positive thing." I still didn't know how to shred into the cheese factor of what I wanted to tell him.

"You're pregnant!" He laughed. "But we can't really toast to that, you shouldn't be drinking."

I knew the only way I'd get to the point was to regurgitate it. "No, of course not, nothing like that. I just wanted to say that I'm really proud of you for making this move. You're an amazing, positive person. And I'm so glad I met you. Whether you realize it or not, you have been such a huge source of support to me. You're one of my best friends, and I love you for that."

I could feel my eyes starting to well up. And whether he wanted to admit it or not, I could see the emotion on his face too.

I didn't expect it, but he responded, "You're a great person. Don't sell yourself short and settle for good enough. We all deserve the best. Or at least pretty enough to be a model and too stupid to be a dick."

I laughed and kept going. "I'm gonna miss you like hell. But I wish you all the luck in the world. And I'll see you soon. A journey of a thousand miles, right?"

"What?"

"It was a saying my old acting instructor used to say. A journey of a thousand miles begins with a single step."

"Well, here's to the single step." He held up his shot glass.

"To the single step." We clinked our glasses, then tapped them on the counter and swallowed the shots quickly, producing clenched, sour faces and a desperate hunt for chasers.

It was a good way to end the conversation with humor since all we could do was laugh at the look on one another's face. It felt good to tell him how I felt and seal it with a good laugh. Maybe it was the positive mood from my talk with Mike or the energy brought on by the guests arriving to celebrate or maybe just the buzz from the shots, but it turned out to be a great night for celebrating.

⁉

Chapter 15

Every day after the party was like a countdown to Mike's departure. I still didn't want him to go, and I must have endured my daily schedule like a zombie, brain dead but showing up anyway. I knew it was a good thing in the long run and had to remind myself not to be selfish about anything but the play. I wished that I was going with him so badly but knew it just wasn't logical at this point, considering that if I paid to drop my lease, I'd be too broke to go anyway.

My grades were solid, and the play was coming along very well. With each rehearsal, I was becoming more and more excited for opening night. Sara had become a major source of support, portraying a young, confident woman who recovered from a bad break up, simply chalking it up to another one of life's experiences. I knew she would be a great influence as an actress and a friend, and she had mentioned that she wasn't sure how she was going to keep paying her rent without her Aaron being there. Since I was at a point where my lease would be up in a few months, I saw an opportunity that would benefit us both and suggested that I move in to the second room in her apartment. I wouldn't be trapped in a lease and the location was close to the trade school I had been looking at.

Since Aaron had almost given me a complex about being a "bad" roommate, I was a little nervous about the idea. I knew it would be financially beneficial since I would be paying only half of the bills and could utilize the rest of my income for school and building up some sort of savings to move. I also reminded myself that I would be in a separate room, which was all mine, so it didn't matter where I kept my socks! Sara seemed optimistic about the idea and said that she just had to figure out a way to cover the next three months.

I felt a little more at ease about the not-so-distant future with the success of my semester at school, the play falling more and more into place, and having figured out some sort of plan of attack for what would happen next. Now I had to deal with the present. Mike was leaving when the weekend was over. I'd never been so happy to work Saturday and Sunday shifts, even offering to pick up doubles so I could hang out with him as long as possible.

Exhausted by the longer shifts, I was still happy to have had that extra time, not to mention the extra money. We were both too tired to hang out and eat after work. So we ended the night with a "have a good one" and Mike telling me that he and Joe were going to stop by in the morning for a final good-bye before heading out. He warned me that it would be early, and he would send me a text to make sure I was awake but that he would resort to calling if he had to. Even though I always woke up earlier than almost anyone else I knew, I felt reluctant to keep my ringer on overnight. But I did it anyway.

It was a cooler Monday morning, but the sun was out, and I woke up before my usual alarm. Usually this would lead to the mental planning my day. But this morning was different. Sure that I had only gotten about three hours of sleep between nightmares, I was still tired and didn't want to wake up. But I knew I had to.

I checked my phone to see if anyone had tried to call me yet and flung my legs over the side of the bed, looking forward to emptying my bladder. Morning rituals aside, I headed to the kitchen to make some coffee and then to the living room to open curtains and turn on the television for some background noise. I had the urge to keep checking my phone, anticipating and dreading the receipt of the promised message.

I sat down on the couch, holding my cup of coffee in one hand and my phone in the other. I was happy to think I wasn't going to my classes that day but sorry for the reason. I started off trying to watch the morning news but was quickly brought down by the politics and drama and decided to change the channel to find something a little lighter and, hopefully, on the humorous side. Again, I was happy to find reruns of sitcoms I had seen a hundred times. Before I knew it, working with a mix of exhaustion and caffeine, I got lost in the harmless and familiar shows. Suddenly, my attention was jerked back to reality by the buzzing of my phone, and looking at the screen, it was the name I had been dreading.

"Hey! We're on our way over! Want any coffee?" Mike asked, sounding as if he was simply going on vacation.

"No, I'm good. Thanks, though. Got an ETA?" I asked, feeling a lot more somber about the situation.

"Okay! We'll probably be there in about ten or fifteen minutes!"

I heard Joe say something in the background, and the two started discussing where they were going to stop for coffee, I decided this would be a good time to end the conversation. "Sounds good. I'll see you when you get here."

When you have to have your eyebrows waxed, they say it's the anticipation that's the worst part. But today, the event was ripping my heart out. I didn't want to dress up for the occasion, so I simply made sure that my pajamas covered everything they needed to and that they would work if I needed to walk them back out to the car.

After I finished my first cup of coffee, I finally forced myself to get up and get a refill. As I was pouring in the flavored creamer, I heard my phone buzz again. This time he was calling from the parking lot.

"Hey, you guys are here? Are you coming up?" I was hopeful.

"No, unfortunately not. The trip was plotted, and we can't stay long if we're going to stay on track."

"No worries, I'll be right down." And with that we both hung up.

I dug for any sweatshirt I could find to wear outside. Setting my cup down, I grabbed my keys and headed out the door. Out of habit, I locked it behind me. The walk down the hallway seemed to take forever as I had to force each step. I didn't want to waste time waiting for the elevator, so I took the stairs instead. Once I saw the guys outside the door, I knew I should have taken a shot to control my emotions and I allowed my brain to derail and consider what might be up in my apartment. I wasn't sure what would happen once I opened the door, but I knew I had to do it anyway.

I was greeted with big hugs and assumptions that I was still groggy. "Good morning! Hopefully we didn't wake you up!"

Mike and I laughed, and I responded, "Nope, been awake for a while. I just didn't get dressed up for you guys."

"Well, we didn't get dressed up for you either." Mike was a stickler for logic.

Trying to stay positive, I tried to think of something to say. "Are you guys excited about the trip?"

Joe replied with an eye roll, and Mike started singing "California here we come!" I wasn't sure if that was a coincidence or if Mike had been serenading Joe with the song for a while. I laughed, even though the ridiculous scene reiterated one of the many reasons I was going to miss them, and it broke my heart.

Sensing things could get awkward, Joe leaned in for a final hug. "Well, we need to get going. We have a few states to cover before sundown."

"Spoken like a true Westerner. Now you just need to work on your accent," Mike informed Joe as he was heading back to the passenger side of the car.

I leaned in and gave him a hug and couldn't help but feel the tears streaming down my cheek. "Drive carefully."

"Why are you getting so upset. You'll be out there in no time!" He returned the squeeze, and after letting go, his smile faded and he looked me right in the eye. "You should really be coming with us."

"Trust me. I feel the exact same way." I wiped my cheek off and took one more stab at humor. "Pay my way out of my stupid lease, and I could be packed up in five."

"Oh, shut up. Come here." He gave me another hug. "Love ya."

"Love you guys too. Call me when you stop for the night. I wanna know about all the exciting sights between here and Nebraska. A journey of a thousand miles has to have some interesting must-sees."

"All right. I'm off to take my first step."

"First step." We gave each other one last high five, and I watched him get into the driver's side.

Watching them drive away, I could feel the knot in my throat getting worse and the tears streaming down faster. I would've given anything to be in the backseat of that car. The thought of going to work without seeing him there sounded like torture. Who would sit and tear up a familiar meal after shifts with me? Who would I bitch about bad tips and shitty tables with? And, of course, who would I gossip about the ass of the hottest bartender with? It was too much to take in all at once, and somehow I could envision a tall shot in my near future.

Mike had given me the bottle of tequila after his party, telling me to save some for a toast when he finally got to Los Angeles. I made a promise to him and to myself to do it but figured a shot or two would be like a toast to a safe trip for him and Joe and help suffocate the feeling of abandonment so that I could focus on the positive aspects. Besides, even though it was six o'clock in the morning here, it had to be five o'clock somewhere, even if it was on the other side of the globe.

I decided to take the elevator back upstairs. Walking down the hall to find my door, I was hoping someone would be leaving his apartment to prove to me that I wasn't as alone as I felt. I knew it was stupid, but I couldn't help it. I finally got inside my door and just let the tears fall. One positive side to living alone, I didn't have to hide them from anyone.

I went straight to the kitchen and poured myself a shot. It tasted horrible. I walked over to my couch to sit down and resume the sitcoms, hoping for the day to pass quickly. I stared blankly at the screen and started thinking that if I didn't do something constructive sometime soon, I would go insane. I looked over my phone, trying to find a game or a website, something that would take my mind off what was going on, and I suddenly had an idea. Maybe it was the need for something to do or maybe it was the fact that I had taken a very large shot of tequila, but suddenly I was inspired. I dug up Aaron's text and started typing my response: "What is there to talk about?"

I was hoping this would in some way lead to closure, especially if he didn't respond. But in reality, I wasn't sure what to expect. Knowing what a diva he was, I assumed that he was still asleep and appreciated the safety of not getting a response any time soon. Proud of my attempt stand up for myself, I decided that I deserved another shot. This one tasted a little better, but not much.

I went back to my pity party and TV marathon. Out of the corner of my eye, I saw my phone light up and turned to see who it was. Incredibly surprised, and not knowing if I wanted to answer, I saw that it was Aaron. If I did answer, I just had to be sure not to get emotional. I had to make sure I didn't let him get under my skin. I had to stand up for myself. And most importantly, I had to make sure I didn't sound like I had tossed back a few this early in the morning. Fortunately, or unfortunately, seeing his name on my caller ID caused my endorphins to hinder my buzz.

I answered, trying to keep things calm and cool. "Hello?"

"Hey." His response was less than promising.

I had no idea what to say next, "What's up?"

"Not much. I just woke up and saw your text." He made it sound as if I had originally reached out to him.

"I was responding to your texts," I reminded him.

"Yeah, I know. I think we have a lot to talk about."

The floodgates were opened. "Really, and what topics did you have on the list? How you spazzed like a twelve-year-old about stupid things, ruining our relationship? How you fed me some crap about fixing it and trying to stay together and got me stuck under house arrest in my lease? Or would it be how you selfishly started ignoring me on the day of a major surgery, not even caring that I needed your support? Gee, you know, you're right. There is a lot for me to talk about and a lot for you to apologize for."

298

"Come on. Please don't do this. I'm trying to be civil."

Pissed, but trying to bite my tongue, I figured I'd have no regrets about my own actions if I at least attempted to meet him halfway. "All right, fine. So what are we talking about?"

"Not over the phone. Why don't you come over here? I want to see you, and I think we could work things out better face-to-face."

Even though I would've killed to have him say that to me a month ago, I had no idea how to respond to his request now. "Fine. I'm open tomorrow night."

"That works, I'll be home at six."

Damned if I was going to let him tell me when to show up. I made up an excuse to stay in control. "Well, I don't know when I'll be off work. I'll let you know."

"Fair enough. I'll talk to you tomorrow. Bye."

Maintaining my effort to stay in control, I simply hung up on him. I wasn't sure how to feel about the meeting but figured I could at least listen to what he had to say. The rest of the day would be devoted to mixed emotions, reruns, and the occasional glass of wine, helping to blur it all out.

The next day I woke up to a slight self-induced headache and decided to focus on the fact that the sun was shining. On my way to rehearsal, I would have to contact my professors and figure out the workload I had missed the day before. And I would have to go to work, knowing that Mike wouldn't be there today. I decided to try and improve my mood by texting him to see where they were at. Not receiving any response, I just figured that he was still the one driving and focused on getting through my day one step at a time.

I walked in to the restaurant, trying to keep a positive attitude and focus on all the little tasks that had to be completed before we opened. Aside from a few random hellos, no one really talked about anything besides food. I had never appreciated it so much.

Luckily, it was a very busy dinner rush, so I didn't have much time to think about anything else. And after sorting out the day's receipts, I thought about sitting down and having something to eat but decided that would only be self-induced torture. I had a short window before rehearsal and decided that I didn't need to sit there and stew. I could torture myself in other ways, such as inviting my mother to an early dinner and confessing the whole truth to her.

Of course, she consented, and we agreed to meet at a small deli up the road from the college. I walked in to the restaurant to find her already sitting at one of the tables. She stood up to greet me and offered me the chair across the table.

I smiled, took off my jacket, and sat down to look over the menu. "Do you already know what you want?"

"Oh, I already ordered for both of us. You still like the ham and Swiss on rye? I thought you should probably have the side of raw vegetables but the chips taste better. They won't be filming your play, right?" She winked at me and took a sip of her coffee.

"Right." I looked back down at the menu and then back up at Mom. "So I invited you to dinner because I had to tell you I've changed my mind."

She looked confused. "About what?"

"About what I want to do with my life."

The familiar look of skepticism started to overcome her face. "As far as?"

I felt like I was presenting a speech to get accepted into medical school. "As far as what I want to do with my life. I mean, I don't want any sort of business degree that'll guarantee me a seat at a desk for the rest of my life. I want to do something creative. I was looking into trade schools." I offered a small courtesy smile to see if she was still with me.

At this point, the skepticism was joined by one raised eyebrow. "So, what? You're in another school play, and you're going to give up college to what, become an artist? Do you realize how many of them waste money on trade school tuition and end up working at fast-food restaurants?"

"No, of course not. I didn't say that. I was thinking of going to cosmetology school." I didn't want to look at her when I said it, so I decided to focus on the cashier behind the counter, who was staring at her phone instead of ringing people up.

I finally looked back over at her, awaiting her criticism about how I would be wasting my time and money. Instead, that all-too-familiar look had melted off her face, and she appeared interested in hearing what I had to say.

"I think that'd be a wonderful idea."

I could breathe again and offered a legitimate smile. "You do?"

"Of course! You've always been good at hair and makeup. And I honestly didn't want you to get a degree in theater. That would guarantee you a job in any field that included an apron!"

She stood up to give me a hug. I was surprised at her reaction but met her halfway anyway. I was so happy and relieved that she was supportive of my college decision but didn't want to count my chickens by revealing to her that Aaron had contacted me. So I vowed to myself that, good or bad, I would accept the responsibility of the outcome of our meeting and simply enjoy the civility of a short meal with my mother. We spent the rest of the meal catching up on family gossip.

I arrived to rehearsal feeling lethargic from all the chips I had inhaled. The rehearsal schedule had become repetitive and familiar, but I was ripped from my food coma by some somewhat surprising news.

Tracey announced that she would like to have us off-script a week earlier than originally listed. I was ready, but at the same time, I felt like I needed a lot more time. Or was it the fact that I had been dealing with so much useless crap on the side that I wasn't sure I could pack more into my brain. I knew it was time to illuminate another one of my stresses, so I could focus on what mattered.

I texted Aaron while we were all gathered in the seats of the auditorium to get feedback from the night's read. I told him that I got done with rehearsal early and that I could probably swing by afterwards.

He responded that that would be perfect and just to call him when I got to his apartment. It gave me a knowing feeling in my stomach. I didn't want to tell anyone else where I was going, so I snuck out after we concluded everything with our usual good-byes.

I had driven the route to Aaron's apartment at least one hundred times before, but it still seemed strange and uncomfortable making my way over there. It was the last place I wanted to go and pretty much the last person I wanted to see. I was suspicious about what excuse he would be giving me but knew I couldn't turn around now or I'd be just as bad.

I turned into the parking lot and hoped that he wasn't waiting for me and watching out of the patio window. Thinking it was a little coincidental, I found my old parking spot open and decided to take advantage of it. I thought, if nothing else, it was close to the door and I'd be able to make a fast getaway. Reminding myself that I wasn't here to make a drug deal, I tried to laugh off the nerves that had overtaken me when I entered the parking lot.

I turned off the car and looked up to the deck that used to be ours. The curtains were open, and I could see that the light was on. So he was definitely home and waiting for me, just like he had told me. I looked down at my phone, pausing before I called. Regardless of what was or wasn't about to happen, I knew I just wanted to get it over with. I pressed the call button and heard the ring on the other end.

"Hello?" I knew he was going to answer, but it still seemed to surprise me.

"Hey, it's me." I was already mad at myself. Of course, he knew it was me. "I'm here."

"Cool. I'll be right down."

Not wanting to babble again, I simply hung up and got out of my car to head to the front door. Even though I had lived here not that long ago, I still felt like I was in a foreign neighborhood. I felt like I was in the wrong place and essentially had to put myself on autopilot. It was a long walk to the front door, and I seemed to get there just in time to see Aaron rounding the corner from the stairs. He opened the door and smiled at me.

"Hey." He looked at me as if we were on a date.

"What's up?" I remained skeptical that he would have anything of value to share with me.

His body language was a little suspicious to me. He looked like he was about to reach out for a hug but had been shot down. If that was the case, I was perfectly content to be the cause of his disappointment. I had gone out of my way to come over and hear him out, so I stood in the same spot until he directed the next move.

He tried to grab my hand, but I reached up to swipe my hair behind my ear instead. I hated to admit it, but I didn't want him to touch me because I was afraid I would fall for it and the emotions it would stir up.

"Well, let's go upstairs."

The only response I could think to offer was a shrug and a nod. I wasn't sure I wanted to see his apartment again. I didn't know how the smell of his cheap cologne and used furniture was going to affect me. One thing I was sure of, the feeling of the unknown created the effect that I was there to tour the space and see if I was fit to be a new roommate. It was a very odd situation.

We walked in to a muted TV and dim light from the tall lamp in the corner. Aaron left me in the door to head into the kitchen. I assumed it was to grab a couple of beers. I decided to try and take a little control back and walked in to sit on the couch prior to the invitation to do so. I looked around to see that not much had changed. Thinking that he was the one surrounded by memories was a small victory but well worth it.

I had called it, and Aaron came walking out of the kitchen with a beer in each hand and offered me one while he took a drink of the other. I accepted and took a small sip. When he turned around to adjust one of the pillows sitting on his chair, I took an even larger gulp, figuring it would come in handy.

"So how have you been? Surgery went well?" he asked, as if we were long-lost schoolmates.

"Yes, it did. I've been fine. Busy with school and another play." I was offering too much. "And yourself?"

"Fine. Just working a lot." He took another sip.

Tired of circling the airport, I nodded at his response and decided to bring this baby in.

"Apparently too much to go along with me on the day of my surgery like you promised? Apparently too much to even call and check on me, see how it went? You must have pulled in a shit ton of overtime pay because apparently you were way too busy to even respond to any messages."

"Don't do this. I want this to be civil."

All I could do was let out a sarcastic laugh at his attempt to play the innocent mediator. "Right. Your actions have pretty much proven what you want. Do you have any idea how that made me feel?"

"Well, I wasn't on top of the world either," he defended himself.

"News flash, you did this to us. I tried to work things out. I tried to meet you halfway. I've met you more than halfway. I stuck myself in a six-month lease, for God's sake! I have been the only one to make sacrifices, to do things your way. You insisted that you loved me but couldn't even bring yourself to check on me when I needed support." I was on a roll. "Now what the hell could you possibly have to say to me that would make me want to maintain a civil relationship of any kind?"

"I know. I'm sorry. I screwed up."

I waited for something more, but all I got was a silent stare. "You know, the entire time that we've been apart, I thought I wanted to hear you tell me that. But, somehow, it doesn't sound as wonderful as I thought. Do you even know how your whole juvenile, game-playing bullshit made me feel? Do you even know what you're sorry for?"

306

He looked down at his bottle and started pawing at the corner of the label. "Yes, I do. But that's not the whole story. I'm trying to tell you what happened."

Now I was confused. "Tell me what happened?"

"I cheated on you." I had to admire him for the fact that he stopped fidgeting and looked me straight in the eye.

I had to take a deep breath. I couldn't believe what I was hearing. "You what?"

"I slept with someone. After you moved out."

I knew I had to choose my response very carefully and took a moment to down the rest of my beer.

Not giving me a chance, Aaron told me the story I wasn't sure I wanted to hear. "It just happened. It didn't mean a thing. It was some chick that I met at a party. I haven't talk to her since. I just didn't have the heart to tell you when you were about to go through surgery. I couldn't face you."

I tried to think of a response that would cater to his supposed attempt to maintain the humanity. "You selfish prick. You fucked up, and you were too scared to man up and show even the slightest respect for me and tell me? There's nothing more to talk about. Fuck you."

I threw the empty bottle on the couch and headed toward the door, glad I hadn't taken off my shoes or jacket. I didn't watch his next move but could see out of the corner of my eye that Aaron stood up and followed me toward the door. But I kept walking.

"Wait! No! Lisa! Come back!"

I didn't even want to hear him say my name. I could feel my eyes welling up and knew I had to get out before I broke down. I just shook my head and walked toward the stairs, not wanting to get held up in waiting for the elevator. I could hear him behind me. Yelling that he was sorry and begging for me to come back. Now it was my turn to ignore him. I jumped the last few steps and ran out the door to the parking lot, remembering exactly where I had parked my car. I assumed he hadn't taken the time to grab his keys, so he was stuck holding the door to the building open with one hand and his beer with the other.

Feeling safe in my car and the darkness of the late night hour, I knew I couldn't hold it back anymore. I didn't have the urge to scream or yell or make a huge scene. I just needed to get it out of my system, and I could feel the tears running down my cheeks. All I had to wipe them on was my sleeve. I couldn't believe what that piece of shit he had just told me. It just happened? If he had had too much to drink and they had just mopped the floor while his friend was giving away free gynecological exams, that might somehow be a plausible excuse. In reality, it just meant that he was a lying piece of shit. Everything he had ever told me was a lie. He meant none of it.

I got home and headed straight to bed. I wasn't sure if I was more hurt or more pissed about finding out what had really happened, but I knew that it was all over. And for some reason, it gave me a feeling of peace. My tears dried up, and I decided that I didn't have to care about him anymore. I would never go back and try to make things work with him. He wasn't the kind of person I even wanted in my life. It all came down to the consequences listed in the saying about "Fooling me once, or twice," and I knew I had nothing to be ashamed of. So I decided from that point on that Aaron never happened.

The next morning, when I woke up for class, I was amazed at my own tranquility. I wasn't thinking about the past but was excited about the future. I had narrowed down what school I wanted to go to and simply had to work out the financial details. I was feeling better about the concept of not utilizing my script for rehearsals and figured memorizing my lines would be the perfect filler for my spare quiet time, minimal as it may be. And the best part, Mike had sent me a message with a photo of the two of him and Joe next to the California state sign. I was glad they made it safely and quickly and that Mike cared enough to tell me so.

Even though my professors had agendas of their own, including the preparation for midterms, I flowed through my classes in a pretty mellow fashion. True to my intentions, I spent lunch and the time between classes and rehearsal quizzing myself on my own lines and blocking. Emotionally exhausted, I could feel myself leaning toward a positive recovery. That is, until I saw Sara.

While I was usually happy to see her, we went through our usual greetings and then she hit me. "Hey, did you ever get back to Aaron? What did he have to say?"

I wondered what made her remember that and tried to laugh it off. "No. I told you, I don't care about all that. I have better things to worry about."

"Well, suit yourself. But down the road, you might wonder what could've happened."

If she only knew what bliss ignorance would have been in this situation. "Oh well, I'll live."

I must have portrayed an excellent character while convincing her that I didn't care and that it was the end of the conversation because she changed the topic in a positive way. "Are you ready for off-script?"

"I hope so. I've been reading over it and reading over it. It'll happen. Or I'll have to come up with some killer improv!"

We both laughed.

Before we started, the director informed us that while we could still hold our scripts, we should try to look at them as little as possible. It seemed to go very smoothly, with only minor points of self-prompting throughout the performance. It was another step toward sanity for me, until Tracey announced that would add at least one more rehearsal each week until opening night. I still went home with a great feeling of accomplishment, even after seeing multiple missed calls and messages from Aaron. I simply deleted them and went back to my studies.

It kept me busy, and the next few weeks seemed to fly by, overcoming the obstacles of tests and scripts. My schedule got a little busier, but it led to better nights of sleep, and I loved it. Even though it was tedious, the month before opening night seemed to fly by. Rehearsals weren't just filled with reciting lines, but also with wardrobe and makeup sessions. Every aspect of the show was coming together.

My plan for school seemed to be falling into place as well. Sara and I had spent a lot of time together in and out of rehearsal, and I was starting to think that she would be the perfect roommate. She was a lot like me, in that she knew what she wanted and had somewhat of an idea on how to get there. Aside from her dramatic acting side, she was very low maintenance, willing to compromise and find mutually beneficial solutions when needed. Even after my own experiences, I couldn't imagine why her last relationship hadn't worked out when she sounded like she had been very invested. One night, after rehearsal, I decided to ask.

We were packing up our things and putting on our jackets, and I told her we should go get some greasy food to reward our performances. We went to a small restaurant up the road and were seated immediately since it was after the dinner rush. We had been there several times before and almost always ordered the same food and drinks. So we ordered right away and got back to our conversation.

"So can I ask you a weird question." I was trying to tread lightly.

"Yeah, what's up?" she asked, unrolling her silverware.

"Well, I was thinking a lot about why my relationship ended. You know, just the basic crap—what could I have done differently, why did this happen? Blah, blah, blah." I wasn't sure casual applied. "But why do you think yours ended? If you don't mind me asking, of course."

She looked up at me, somewhat surprised, then shrugged. "Well, I can't answer for him, but I feel like it ended because he cheated on me. Why do you ask?"

"Because I wanted to tell you that I did call Aaron back and I did hear him out. And he cheated on me too." It felt good to tell someone, especially someone who could relate.

"It feels like shit." She grabbed her glass. "But here's to leaving it in the past and taking that first step toward the future."

It was exactly what I needed to hear, and I knew I was on the right path. "To the first step."

We each took a sip of our sodas and set our glasses down just in time to receive our plates of food. We finished the meal, discussing timelines for the play, the end of the semester, the end of my lease, and me moving in to her second bedroom. It sounded like a long, tough list to accomplish but very beneficial for both of us.

Between tests and memorized scripts, my feeling of accomplishment was snowballing along with the cold winter weather. Having forgotten to bring another outfit for rehearsal and refusing to bear the scent of beer and greasy fries, I tried to make a quick stop by my apartment, grabbing my mail in the process. I seemed to acquire more and more bills every month.

I figured it wouldn't hurt to open a few and get the bleeding over with. However, I noticed some issues with the bill. My bank account showed that they had cashed last month's check, but for some reason, they hadn't applied it to my account. Most people would be incredibly irritated by this, but seeing as how it was becoming a monthly mistake, I knew almost of the employees of the call center by name and was confident that Julie could help me in the morning.

I just shook my head and walked toward my room to grab another shirt, repeating to myself, "Bills, bills, bills."

I was digging through one of my drawers, hoping that I could find something clean and acceptable to wear in public. It was a tall order at this point. I figured almost anything would be better than what I was wearing. Suddenly, I heard my phone ringing. Thinking that I had to focus on what I was doing so that I wouldn't be late, I decided to ignore it for now and call whoever back while I was driving.

Whoever was trying to get ahold of me didn't feel the same way. Shortly after my phone stopped ringing, it started again. I assumed someone had just butt dialed me or it was simply someone from the play trying to get me to bring a snack for the group. I finally found something decent. It was lying on my bed, so I couldn't guarantee that it was clean but figured I could kill two birds with one stone by hosing myself down with my scented body spray.

I walked out my room, proud of my last-minute accomplishment, and walked toward the kitchen counter to pick up my jacket, keys, and phone. I decided to see who had the bug up his ass and had to talk to me right away. If nothing else, I could simply rule out any kind of emergency. I was a little surprised to see that my lawyer had called. Again. And again. And again. Almost afraid of more bad news, I forced myself to call him back anyway.

"Lisa! Just the one I needed to speak to! How are you?" Frank greeted me, sounding excited.

It seemed odd since he always made me feel like a giant pain in his ass. "I'm good. And you?"

"Great! I'm great! And I have some great news for you!"

I didn't think that confirming the receipt of a few medical bills was enough to brighten someone's day but appreciated his passion and played along with the theme. "Okay. That's great. What's going on?"

"Are you sitting down?"

I had no idea what to expect but lied anyway. "Yeah."

"The insurance company made an offer!"

"Okay. What did they offer?"

"They offered you forty thousand dollars!"

I was shocked, in a good way for once. "Wow. That really is great!"

"It is! But wait, I bet I can get them up at least five grand," he boasted. "Stay by your phone. I'm going to try calling them right now!"

Before I could answer, he had hung up. I wasn't sure what to think. Frank had made it seem like our efforts were for nothing and that the other guy's insurance company would never offer anything. I was so anxious to put the whole thing behind me, I probably would've settled for a fruitcake and a fifty-dollar gift card. But this money would really come in handy. Another step in the right direction. I had barely gotten to my car when my phone rang again. I looked down to see that it was Frank and answered it right away.

"We got it! I wasn't sure what they were going to do! But they agreed on it! Forty-five thousand!" he reminded me, just as excited as me since he wouldn't have been paid if we hadn't won the case.

"That's great!" It was all I could think of to say.

He started dishing out the directions like the old, familiar Frank. "All right, so I just need you to sign a few forms, and then we can work out the financial details on our end after we receive the check. When can you head over?"

"Well, I don't have much time, but if I just need to sign a couple of forms, I could swing by right now?" I offered.

"Sounds great! I'll see you when you get here."

"Okay, bye," I said, realizing that he had hung up already.

As we had planned, I stopped by his office, and we quickly went through the papers I needed to sign. He explained that it was a complete payoff and that the lawsuit was officially settled and that I couldn't come after them ever again for permanent injury ailments. I was more than happy to sign off and not just to receive money. The entire ordeal was something else I wanted to put in my past. Something else I had overcome and didn't want to think about anymore. The settlement would merely help me to keep moving in the right direction. I thanked Frank for all his help and rushed out the door to rehearsal, trying not to be late.

Failing in my attempt, I knew I would find the other girls, including Sara, in the dressing rooms, sitting at the mirrors and putting on their stage makeup. The news I had just received was still a shock, and I was trying to figure out how to hold back my excitement and tap into my inner drama for my character. Figures that Aaron would have been the perfect motivation. He was just the guy to make me feel hurt and angry, but I would have to do it on my own this time.

With the news incredibly fresh in my mind, I was almost shaking as I was trying to put on my own makeup. I should have been concentrating on my performance since the premier was less than a week away, but my mind was soaring with how much that money would help me with school and a huge move.

"Lisa." Sara ripped me from my trance. "Hey, Lisa, can you hand me that brush?"

"Yeah, sorry. Here." I handed her the brush.

"You okay?" she asked, dipping the brush into her eye shadow.

"Oh yeah, I'm great." I couldn't help but smile.

She seemed a little weirded out by my positivity but smiled back. "Okay, great. Did we meet prince charming at a ball last night, or what?"

"Better!"

We only had about five minutes until we had to be on stage. I knew I had already explained to her what had happened with the car accident, so I kept it short and sweet. Not mentioning the amount, I simply revealed to her that the lawsuit was settled and that it was just one more thing I didn't have to worry about. She congratulated me, making a joke about rolling in the dough. I didn't want to focus on that yet, so I just laughed at her. Our conversation was abruptly ended when we were called to the stage. On the short walk out there, I couldn't help thinking that if money wasn't so filthy, I'd actually throw it on my bed and roll around naked in the dough!

This was the first of the final rehearsals in which we would go all the way through, full makeup and wardrobe, without stopping and full set and lighting. We were all excited to see what our time and efforts were going to amount to. And I had to admit, it was exciting to be out on the stage with everything lit up. With the bright lights on us, we couldn't see the chairs in the audience. Regardless of the fact that our audience consisted of the director and her assistant, it was almost like opening night and incredibly motivating.

Being on the stage and running straight through the entire performance, I felt that same rush. That feeling of being able to overcome anything and accomplish whatever I wanted to set my mind to. I couldn't believe the real life drama I had overcome in such a short period of time, and I was thrilled to seal the deal with some positive drama, pouring all my efforts into something I loved.

When we were finished, I was looking even more forward to opening night. Tracey seemed to feel the same way, offering mainly positive critiques and offering all of us the night off the following evening. I was excited to have the free time and decided to share the good news with my family by taking them out to dinner for a girls' night.

With our schedules all over the place, it was almost impossible for Michelle, my mother, and me to get together for anything. I walked in to the restaurant and found them already sitting at a table near the front. We all said our hellos, and I figured that my mother was under the impression that I simply wanted to tell Michelle about going to cosmetology school. The server stopped by, and I ordered my soda.

Trying to get back to the good news, I said, "Well, I wanted us all to get together because I have some really great news."

Michelle looked less than interested. Studying the menu, she interrupted me. "Mom already told me. You're going to go to beauty school. Are we getting appetizers?"

I looked at my mother, who shrugged out of guilt, then back at Michelle. "Well, yes, that's part of it. But I got some other good news today."

I wanted to wait until they were both looking up at me, but they both looked less than amused.

"We won the lawsuit." I waited for their reactions to the news of winning as opposed to their anticipation of free haircuts for life. The announcement I had just made seemed to ignite a bigger reaction.

"That's great!" Mom said, and I couldn't help but laugh at the continuing theme of greatness.

"I know! It's such a relief!"

"Well, how much are you gonna get?" Leave it to Michelle.

"Enough to help with school." Again, I didn't want it to be about money. "And to buy you two a decent meal. Besides, it's not about the amount. It's about the fact that it's over! I don't have to worry about the accident anymore!"

Michelle finally warmed up. "That's awesome too. As long as you got a decent amount."

Hoping she was merely concerned about the fact that I may need the finances down the road due to the effect of having permanent injuries, I shook off her comment and decided to focus on the other positive aspects. I also brought up the play and asked what night they wanted to take advantage of their free tickets. My mother seemed excited, but I wasn't sure about Michelle. She had always been my toughest audience, always willing to point out the flaw of any situation. It was important to have her support, but it certainly wouldn't make or break my performance. I decided to drop the topic and try to enjoy what was left of the dinner.

[?]

Chapter 16

A few more dress rehearsals and a photo shoot provided a great sense of confidence for our first show. I was flattered to discover that they would be using a profile shot of me with the male of my scene in the background facing me. Realistically I knew it wasn't because of our specific characters but because the photographer felt that she had captured an artistic shot.

Opening night fell on a Friday evening, leaving me an open afternoon, which I usually would have spent at work. I decided to take the weekend off to focus on my non-serving performance. Between nerves and last-minute tasks to take care of, it turned out to be a very smart decision.

The set was up in place and ready to go. Costumes were steamed. Makeup was stocked and ready to apply, and the official ticket window was stocked with tickets, ready for purchase. The actors and the crew were incredibly excited, ready to reveal what we had all been working on, but we still had a few hours to kill. We decided to sit back, relax, and order some pizza before the show. Enduring the painful process of sorting out the popular diets of the week to determine what toppings to order, we all sat back to large slices of hot pizza and ice-cold pop.

We had all been working so hard on the last minute details, so it was difficult to slow down and taste the food before devouring it. After satisfying the requirement of a meal, almost everyone scattered back to their individual chores or homework, or even running errands off campus. Sara and I were the only ones left sitting on the edge of the stage with the almost empty pizza boxes and half-full bottles of pop.

"I don't want to jinx anything, but I'm really excited about opening night," I said, studying the seats in the audience, imagining them full.

"Yeah, me too," Sara responded in a cool manner.

"Can you imagine doing this for a living?"

She looked at me, a little surprised at the direction. "Where did that come from?"

"I don't know. I just think, this is what I want to do. Don't you love being on stage?"

"Yeah, of course. It's tough though."

"I get it. It wouldn't be easy. But it seems worth it." I knew it sounded incredibly cheesy, but it was true. "I would love to make a career out of acting. That's it."

"As long as we make a deal. We won't forget the little people." She laughed.

I laughed at her joke but hoped she realized how serious I was. It was one of the first times I had said it out loud because I trusted her, and even though she was laughing it off now, I knew that she wanted the same thing. I was happy to be working with someone who shared the same vision, or at least a glimpse of it. And I was even happier to have her as a friend.

With all the cheese factor aside, it was time to start getting ready for the show. While we were usually critiquing makeup, zipping up costumes, and chatting about our plans for the weekend, tonight we got dressed in silence. Maybe it was nerves, maybe it was excitement, maybe it was just the attempt to see if we could hear how many people were filing into the auditorium.

We filed out of the women's dressing room to find that the guys were also coming out of the men's dressing room at the same time. Tracey had planned for all of us to meet backstage before she went out to make the initial announcements about productions, theater classes, and programs at the college, and introduce the play. It might have just been me, but it seemed that the actors' nerves and anticipation were louder than her pep talk, not assuring that any one of us actually heard the words of encouragement.

Running through the opening scene in my mind, I followed enough of Tracey's speech to see that everyone was smiling and nodding and starting to move toward the assigned sides of the stage. I found my way to my starting mark and watched as the lights of the auditorium were flickered to remind everyone to sit down and settle in as the show was about to start.

Tracey made her way out to the center of the stage and introduced herself to the audience. Her introduction was met with applause. She continued with her speech, never pausing or stuttering, but seeming completely comfortable in the spotlight; and it was reassuring to see her warming up the audience.

I had to admit, I was nervous. But at the same time, I loved every minute of it. I wasn't listening to what Tracey was telling the audience, I simply waited for her to walk off the stage as it was a sign for all of us to assume our positions. The counterpart of my scenes would then take the stage, and I would be soon to follow. I nervously awaited the line that would be my cue to run out onto the stage and present my character. There was no turning back now. I heard the line, and it was time to go.

Everything flowed perfectly, and I had the same amazing, familiar feeling from being on stage. With the spotlights brightening up the stage, I could only see a few feet in the front row. But I figured whoever was sitting there for each show would get the best performance I could provide. The mix of nerves and excitement was priceless and helped to portray each scene in a way that would suck the audience into the plot. Before I knew it, it was time to deliver the last line and I couldn't believe how quickly the first show was over. As we took our bows, it was apparent that all of our hard work had paid off. What made it even more priceless was seeing that my mother and sister were in the second row, giving a standing ovation.

The show was scheduled to play two weekends in a row, including multiple performances on Saturdays. Once opening night broke the ice, each performance seemed to only get better and better. The following weekend, before our final Saturday performance, Tracey asked us all to meet after we were in costume and before the show started. All she told us was that she had a special announcement. Not sure what it was, we all met backstage and waited for her.

"Hey, everyone! Thanks for getting ready a little earlier tonight. I wanted to tell you that we're going to have someone special in the audience tonight." She looked at each one of us to make sure we were paying attention. "I don't want anyone to get nervous, but she's one of the judges for a very prestigious theater scholarship. She'll be selecting three out of the six of you to compete nationally for it. You're all wonderful. I just want you to get out there and do your best!"

Knowing the judge was in the audience didn't make me nervous since I had never heard of the scholarship. The only thoughts the brief announcement left me with was that I wasn't sure if I would want it. After jumping through all the hoops, assuming that I even won the scholarship, would I be bound to pursuing a theater degree? Sure, I loved acting, but I would rather work towards a career on camera. And if I did get a degree in theater, would I have to go to a special school filled with tortured artists where the professors rocked man buns and the students lived with strict vegan diets and wore organic deodorant? It just didn't sound like the right path for me. I told myself the same thing Tracey had told us, to treat the show like any other performance and just do my best. The show ended, and it was time to call it a night once again. It wasn't hard to fall asleep since my schedule had been going nonstop for the past couple of weeks.

We had agreed to meet the next night before the show to find out the reviews from the special guest. We all gathered around and waited for Tracey to reveal the names of the three people that will go on to compete in the next round of auditions for the scholarship. She said two of the names, and I wasn't surprised or disappointed that I didn't hear my name. I started looking through my bag to make sure I had brought the right socks for my costume when I was caught off guard.

"And the third person is Lisa!" She looked right at me.

"What? What did I do?" I was a little embarrassed to be called out.

"You gave an amazing performance! You've been nominated to move on to the second round!"

I smiled. I knew what she was talking about, and I was flattered. But again, I wasn't sure what I would do with it. We all congratulated the actors who had been nominated and headed to the dressing rooms to start getting ready. We started with our hair and makeup and chatted about what we were just told.

"That's really cool. Congrats!" Sara said.

"Thanks." I felt guilty, thinking that Sara could've put this to way better use than I could.

"For the second round, I think you just need to come up with a scene to perform."

Thinking about the pressure of picking out the right scene, I tried to turn things around and get something positive out of it. "Well, if that's the case, will you do a scene with me?"

I figured she would appreciate being asked to participate. And I had to admit, she probably deserved the nomination more than me. Sara was such a natural actress. Her lines flowed very freely, regardless of the genre, and her blocking never appeared forced. She was a great role model for the actors around her and could've helped many more through teaching other students. I knew that I would have to address all of this later and just focus on the show at hand. I had to admit that even if I hadn't planned on the nomination, it was a great confidence booster and really helped my performance that night. However, I kept thinking and thinking about it, and I knew I wasn't the right candidate.

After the show, I explained to Tracey and Sara that although I was incredibly honored to have received the nomination, I had to decline it since I planned on taking another route. They both looked at me as if I had just farted in their direction, revealing what I'd had for dinner, but then said they understood and appreciated my honesty.

The following day, we all arrived to the dressing rooms with heavy hearts since it was the finale. This would be our last performance of this show, and our last appearance with this specific cast and crew. While it was a little emotional, I tried to focus on all the positive things ahead of me. This play was an amazing outlet for the all the drama I had been experiencing over the past few months. I had lost relationships and gained others. One journey was about to end, and another was about to begin. So much had happened in such a short period of time, and it was the show that kept me sane.

Once we were all made up and dressed, we checked each other's costumes to assure we hadn't missed anything, then headed to our starting marks. We must have been the most amazing method actors that evening, so it was probably a good thing that the play wasn't a comedy. The show finished, and with our final bows came a few tears.

We headed back to the dressing rooms to take off our costumes and get ready for the small after party we had planned for closing night. Tracey had asked us to remove all our personal belongings and shut the lights off when we left since we would simply be utilizing the cafeteria for a few snacks and a small cake. I was the last one out of the room, and as I turned around to shut off the light, I expected to feel sad or disappointed that the project was over. But instead, I saw it as being "finished" instead of "over" and felt happy to have been a part of it.

At the after party, we all enjoyed the company and the food. It ended early since we were in the school lunchroom, and everyone left to prepare for his or her Monday. Sara and I went to hang out and have a girls' night and try to figure out a timeline for becoming roomies. Not wanting to repeat the performance of having a slumber party, we loaded up on snacks, soda, and comedic movies.

Staring off with 80s classics, we inhaled the cheesy popcorn. It felt good to think that I would have a little more free time over the next few weeks but at the same time I was a little nervous about how I was going to fill it. Not having to rush from work to rehearsal would preserve my sanity, especially since rush hour traffic only got worse with snow, and winter was around the corner. But what would I do after work? I still had a couple of months before my lease was officially up, and picking up extra shifts at work didn't sound all that wonderful. I decided to get another perspective.

"So what are we gonna do now?" I asked, laughing at my own question.

"What do you mean? You said your lease isn't up for a couple of months. Are you already packing?" Sara and I were talking about two different things.

"No. I mean, the play is over. I like having free time, but I almost feel like I should start auditioning for other shows." I wasn't sure if I was trying to convince her or myself.

"There are other theaters outside of school. Have you ever thought about checking them out?"

"You're right. I haven't looked into it much. I was always more interested in on-camera acting. Theater is hard. There's no 'back to one' when you're on stage. It's a lot of pressure." I sounded like a complete amateur.

"It can be. But if it wasn't, it wouldn't be as much fun. And if we didn't love it, we wouldn't do it," she summed it up perfectly.

We finished a few movies, and I knew I had to break down and go home so I'd be able to wake up in a few hours. I wasn't going to sign up for another semester, but I still wanted to end this one with decent grades. Sara had given me a few websites to check out for local auditions, and I wanted to look them over but knew I had to plan around school first.

I had made an appointment to check out the Cosmetology School of Minnesota on a Monday. I really had no idea what to expect since the last time I was inside a beauty school was when I was eight years old and my mother brought my Girl Scout troop to one to have our hair braided. I walked in to find a very busy environment filled with men and women with multicolored hair, heavy makeup, and random piercings. There was music playing throughout the building, and the air was thick with the aroma of hair products and cigarette breaks.

I went straight to the front desk and, before I could say a word, watched the teenager working as the receptionist set her phone down to greet me with her rehearsed script. "Hi! Welcome to the Cosmetology School of Minnesota! Do you have an appointment?"

I was waiting for her fake smile to give out and make her cheeks and lip ring twitch, but that may have been too long of a pause. "Um, yes. I'm Lisa. I have an appointment to tour the school?"

The girl's cheesy smile, as well as her artificial friendliness, faded. "Okay, great. You can have a seat, and I'll let them know you're here."

"Thanks." I wasn't sure I should thank her yet since she picked up the phone, hit a button, practically whispered a short message to the person on the other end, picked up her phone, and sat back down in her chair.

From my chair, I could see what I thought was the main salon and who I assumed were the students. They were all rushing back and forth between a bar area with random tubes and liter bottles and their chairs. There was a pattern of a couple of people who were walking around and looking at the students' clients. They were wearing name tags, so I was forced to believe that these were the instructors. Regardless of the fact that I was most likely about to be a student, I searched for looks of fear on the clients' faces since they were pretty brave to submit themselves to being school projects.

A few minutes later I was greeted warmly by a woman walking out from one of the hallways over to my chair and extending her hand. "Hello! I'm Alicia, the director of admissions. I think we spoke over the phone when you were making the appointment."

"Yeah, I think that was me." I was pretty sure I couldn't match her volume and passion just yet.

"Great. Okay, well. Let's start with a tour, and then we can head back to my office and discuss start dates, finances, you know, all the specifics." She made it sound so simple.

She guided me through the classrooms, explaining that that is where I would be spending the first couple of months before "graduating" to the floor where I would be allowed to take customers. She was smiling the entire time, but the response from the students was a little less than welcoming. Alicia would introduce the students whose names she could remember, and almost appearing to have been caught, they would look up from their endeavors and give a courtesy smile. Others, whom we would just observe, would make eye contact, not showing a lot of emotion. I chalked it up to the stress of school and the half-inch line of black eye liner caked on their faces. Regardless of their destinations, the students whose paths we accidentally crossed barely looked up to acknowledge us. I wasn't sure if it was because they were studying their notes on the way to the color bar, reciting cutting procedures in their head before greeting their next victim, or had just promoted themselves to the status of diva. I just had to remind myself that I wasn't here to make friends or become involved in extracurricular activities.

After getting my fill of the campus life at the school, Alicia guided me back to her office and offered me a seat. I wasn't sure if talking about the financial aspect of the school would be any better. But I knew it was a bridge I had to cross, so I listened to what she had to tell me. She started out by handing me a folder, one of many from a stack I knew was prepared for potential students. Between the paperwork and her speech, pretty much all my questions were answered about start dates, total overall cost, and payment plans. She finished by explaining that they would also assist in job placement. I secretly hoped not to have to take advantage of this option since I wanted to seek employment out of state.

I left feeling a little better about attending the school and a little more concerned about the cost and having to rearrange my schedule. I wanted to get school done and over with as soon as possible, but I realized that to do this, I would be sacrificing my spring, summer, and even a little of the upcoming fall seasons. I also had to be able to budget for the dehydrated noodles I would be living on for the next eight to ten months. I knew I had to keep calm and concentrate on getting through finals, moving in with my new roommate, and waiting for my settlement check.

Two months later, I had accomplished all my short-term goals. I picked up my settlement check, shook my lawyer's hand, thanked him for all his help, then told him that I hoped to never see him again. It provided a good laugh for both of us and a positive end to our business relationship. I survived finals, passing each of my classes. And I packed up everything in my apartment and tried to fit it into one open bedroom and a small corner of the living room of Sara's apartment.

Before I locked my apartment door for the last time, I took one last look around, remembering why I had moved in to this place. I remembered the great feeling of freedom, knowing the apartment was all mine, that no one could tell me what to put where or when to leave or arrive home. But I also remembered feeling trapped and lonely, angry that it kept me from moving to California with Mike and Joe, and relying on my TV to provide enough proof that there were still other people out there. Through the experiences I had had while living here, I really grew as a person, not to mention as an actress and an adult. I was happy to have been there and thrilled as hell to be moving out.

Sara knew that she had to work on the day I was moving in and had given me a key ahead of time. All the furniture I could neatly pack into the corner of her living room/dining room area was set up, and I tried to stack the rest of my boxes neatly in the bedroom. A little more relaxed about the topic of money since picking up my settlement check and knowing that I would be strictly working weekends at the restaurant once school started, I decided not to pick up any extra shifts at work, instead concentrating on unpacking all the shit I needed.

I wanted to be polite to Sara and have the pizza and beer ready for her when she got home from work. While unpacking, I lost track of my timeline and could at least take solace in the fact that the order had been placed shortly before she got home and the beer was already chilled and waiting. I still had a shit ton of work to do in my room but figured that as long as it was out of the main living areas, it was safe to take a break and practice some personal hygiene.

Sara had gotten home while I was in the shower. Just in case, I had left a Post-it on the fridge handle, telling her to grab a beer and that pizza would be there shortly. Since I didn't hear her come in or any movement once I turned the water off, I figured it was safe to venture out in my towel to grab a beer for myself. It was a twist cap, and I decided to use the corner of my towel to get it off while heading back to my new room to dig out something clean to wear. I was about to the hall, heading into the open door on the left, right across from Sara's room, the closed door on the right.

Suddenly, Sara's door opened, and she was walking out holding her beer. Since I hadn't heard anyone come in and she told me that she always kept her door shut, I didn't know anyone was home. We both screamed from the shock, and with my first instinct being to put my hands up in front of me, I accidentally pulled off my towel and dropped my beer.

"Oh shit!" I tried to cover the important parts and utilize my towel to soak up the liquid at the same time.

"Honey, I'm home!" Sara just laughed at me. "Next time I'll have to give you a warning."

"Bitch." I had to laugh at myself. "You're just lucky I shaved or else that could've been weird."

I would have to get used to having a roommate again. Luckily, it was a welcome task. I found a T-shirt and a pair of jeans that looked safe and headed back out into the living room just in time for the pizza to arrive. Taking a short break and sitting on the couch with my new roomie made me realize how good it was not to be eating dinner alone. Even with our schedules being all over the place and the fact that I would probably be eating a lot of meals solo, it was just cool to know that someone else was there. And the benefit was that that someone had become a very good friend.

The night before I started my new school, I took inventory of all the tasks I had hoped to get done. The paperwork was finished, the planned payments were scheduled, the work schedule was adjusted, a few boxes were unpacked, the dress-code-appropriate clothes were purchased, and the rack in the kitchen was stocked with wine. It was official: I was ready to start my first day of playing with scissors.

I decided to reward myself for all my hard work by getting twacked out on a large, sugary blended coffee drink before heading to school. I was happy to have the caffeine rush when I walked into the school and was led back to a classroom room to locate my name on a seating chart for the large round tables in the room. I saw my name located between two people named Nick and Dana.

I found my seat conveniently marked with handmade name tags and thick packets with the word welcome on the cover. I started to think that I should've gotten two coffees, or at least a canned energy drink. I thought it was funny that most of us came to this trade school to avoid sitting at a desk and that that was exactly how we were going to start off. Picking through the split ends at the bottom of my hair, I started to feel really sorry for the students coming in with ADD. As others were coming in and filling the seats according to the chart, I decided to sit back and observe my new classmates.

People watching at a cosmetology school can be very interesting. I watched a hot guy walk in and sit down, being sure to arch his back, and then checking his face and hair in his compact before looking over his class packet. I watched a very skinny girl with a Mohawk haircut and fishnet stockings walk in and search the name chart. Once she found her spot, she made her way over, face tilted down, barely able to see through her black eyeliner, with one arm protectively crossed over her chest and carrying her purse with the other. She sat down, somewhat hunched over in the chair with her hands and purse in her lap. And finally, I saw a normal-looking girl, whose makeup looked remotely decent and her clothes looked like something I'd be willing to wear out in public too. Trying to be mature in a room full of potential divas might be tougher than I thought, and I was relieved that she was walking over to sit at my table.

Trying not to stare, I tried to watch out of the corner of my eye as she sat down and started reading over the packets in front of us. I tried to focus on looking over the packet myself, but it was pointless, and I assumed the instructors would be going over the information with us anyway.

When the girl sitting at my table decided that she had seen all she wanted to see from the packet, she made a quick glance around the room and looked up at me. I gave a courtesy smile and decided it was a good time to break the ice.

"Hi, I'm Lisa." I said, extending my hand.

"Dana." She gave a short handshake. "Have you been waiting long?"

"Nah, I've only been here about ten minutes." I informed her. "It's been very interesting though. Just getting a feel for what our new classmates will be like."

"Hah! Yeah, I can see that." She looked around again before locating the girl with the thick eyeliner and black fishnets. "I'm willing to bet that that one will have carved the word hair into her arm before we're out of the classroom."

I shouldn't have laughed, but it was cool to meet someone else as blunt as me. "Well, it'd have to be on the right one."

She almost looked confused. "Why the right one?"

"Because she already has 'fear the daylight' carved into her left one."

We both laughed again and tried to focus on the information in front of us before she asked, "Have you looked over this thing to see what we're in for?"

"No, not really. I figured they'd go over every detail of it anyway."

By the end of our conversation, a few more people had filed in but there were still open seats, including a couple at our table. We watched a few people check the list and look over in our direction, then take other seats. Suddenly, a guy walked in. At first glance and from a distance, I would have guessed that he wasn't much older than either one of us. But as he came closer, he looked older than I would have originally thought. His sense of fashion didn't set trends, and we couldn't smell his cologne from over ten feet away, so I was pretty sure we were both assuming that he was straight. Which made me wonder if he was lost, and I could only imagine what Dana was thinking.

"I'm pretty sure I've seen his picture on a WANTED poster before." She leaned in a little to tell me since he appeared to be heading toward our table.

"Oh, special." It almost made sense. "Then what's he doing here?"

"Oh, you know. Those work release programs. You have to pick a trade." She shrugged as she said it.

"Super. Why not move on from a criminal past by getting a license to play with scissors? That won't violate his probation or anything."

We both watched as he sat down, taking a load off and barely acknowledging that we were also sitting at the table. Dana and I looked at each other, wondering what we were in for. His entrance was less than grand, and his introductions were less than inviting. Then again, the social skills you pick up in prison don't necessarily come in handy in school. Before I had a chance to deliberate on what path brought him to cosmetology school, our instructors entered the room and it was time to begin.

"Welcome, everyone! Go ahead and take a seat, and we'll get started." It was the last thing I was really listening to, until it came time for the inevitable introductions.

Instead of standing up in front of the rest of the class of about twenty-five people and presenting our names and announcing our favorite colors, we were told to get to know the person to our right and that we would be introducing them. Super, I would kill two birds with one stone, getting to know my classmate and getting a first-hand glance of what life on the inside was like.

I looked at him and decided to dive right in. "Well, I guess that means that we're partners. I'm Lisa."

I felt like a handshake wasn't appropriate this time since I didn't want to get stuck with any needles.

"Nick." I got the idea that he wasn't very chatty.

"Cool. So what brought you to cosmetology school?" I had no idea what to expect for a response.

"You know, I was just hanging out and got bored. Besides, it's the only trade school that doesn't require a drug test." He waited for a reaction, but all I could do was try to stay focused on what he was saying.

"Huh, I never thought about that. You're probably right." I just nodded.

He laughed. "I'm kidding."

I was a little relieved, so I laughed along with him. "It's true, though, about the tests."

He confirmed what I had originally thought, about being in a class with characters who saw themselves as tortured artists. Souls with plenty of creativity, bitterness against those who couldn't see their talent, and apparently self-medicating tendencies that included legal and illegal substances. It would be quite the shit show once they realized that they would be scraping the dead skin off people's crusty feet.

Once getting over the initial intrigue of starting a new project, the rest of the class, along with the introductions, went pretty smoothly. We were even dismissed early, being informed that we would dive right in to the classroom material the next day and that we should all be on time since those that were tardy would already be in violation of the attendance policy. While I wasn't worried about being on time, between violations and probations, I was wondering just what I had gotten myself into.

Over the next couple of months, we spent forty hours per week studying the anatomy and disorders of hair, skin, and nails. Those who were intimidated by knowledge, bored, or just anxious about being around people were dropping like flies. By the time our final written exams were available, we had lost at least ten students. I decided to take my written exam right out of the classroom, so I could simply focus on putting my skills to work. I passed my test with flying colors but wasn't exactly prepared for the inevitable fun of working with those that would sacrifice quality in order to save a few dollars on their beauty services.

Our clients up until that point had been very easy to work with. The mannequin heads didn't want scalp massages, would never complain about the price or the service, and always had half smiles on their faces. Dana and I were at work stations right across from one another and decided to spend our time racing through the required amount of specified services required for our technical exams.

The first client I helped that wasn't plastic was an absolutely adorable older woman who came in weekly for her roller sets. She was about ninety years old and had gorgeous white hair. She was always wearing a dress with some sort of floral pattern, and her husband would escort her to each appointment, not only because she wasn't able to drive but also so that she had to hold his arm to balance while walking up to the receptionist counter. From there, she would hold on to my arm, and we would walk to my chair, letting her sit for a moment to give her a break before we headed for the sink. Our steps were a little smaller and slower, and I had to talk a little louder, enunciating my words, but she always had a smile on her face. She never complained and would reward me at the end of every service with a crisp one-dollar bill. She was a consistent client, who booked her future appointments weekly and lured me into a false sense of security.

While our appointments were often inconsistent, Dana and I would often run into each other at the color bar, where we could compare formulas and horror stories from the work floor. After my Friday regular left for the day, I walked my cape and towels back to the laundry area, finding her at the bar looking over a few pictures in a trendy magazine.

"Studying the new hairstyles of the season?" I asked her as I threw my laundry into the tall netted bag we used behind the bar.

"Yeah, something like that. I'm just bored. My last client never showed up," Dana informed me. "These models are not cute. They have no eyelids. And look at their noses. They should have to fix this stuff before anyone hires them."

She kept flipping through the pages as we talked. "I have to fix mine."

"Please, you have a nose people would pay for."

"Probably because I did pay for it." I finished shuffling the overfilled laundry and turned to head back to my station.

She looked up from the magazine, thinking that she had offended me and not knowing what to say to remedy it. "Oh. Um, well, you got your money's worth."

I was pretty sure I hadn't seen her speechless since I'd met her and found it very amusing, "Ha! Thanks! It's okay, not a big deal. I just had to have some surgery after a car accident. I don't have a face dysmorphic disorder or anything."

It was hilarious to me that as tough and blunt as Dana came off, she actually seemed to have a conscience. She seemed to help the hours of school fly by when there were no real appointments and all we could do was work on our doll heads. I figured between her confident personality and being one of few students in the school with talent, she would be a really successful stylist.

We had always been warned about the difficult clients and how in an industry where you work with people, not everyone would be that easy to work with. I hadn't had many problems during my first couple of months working on clients and was becoming very confident in my newly acquired skills. That is until the law-of-numbers bitch slapped me. Hard.

One Monday afternoon, I walked to the receptionist's desk to greet my ten o'clock appointment. I was stunned when I saw her. My first impression was that she had a hot date with a hair appointment and borrowed her granddaughter's clothing to attend one. I could only hope that it was because she was legally blind and couldn't see exactly what she had put on. She was wearing a short tank top with her belly hanging out and a tan netted shirt over it, probably thinking that it would be long enough to cover things. However, it certainly wasn't long enough to cover the yoga pants, which were too small, pinching out her muffin top and displaying inappropriate sagginess and dimples. Even though it was still a little cold out, she made sure to wear her wedge shoes to portray her bright orange toenails. I couldn't even focus on her hair since I was trying to convince myself to appreciate the sneak peek of what a few famous pop singers were going to look like, forty years down the road.

I extended my hand and introduced myself. She draped her jacket over her arm long enough to extend her hand as well, handing me her coat as soon as she informed me that her name was Brenda. After volun-telling me to hang up her jacket, she turned to the girl at the desk and made a plea to see if there was a male student available, insisting that she got along better with men. The receptionist just shook her head and shrugged, telling her that Nick was the only male student at the school that day and he wouldn't have any openings for at least two hours. Brenda sighed and decided to settle for me, following me back to my station, where she informed me of her expectations and asked me for my verbal resume.

I explained to her that I had already taken my written test and that I had been working on clients for the past few months. She remained hostile while we went through the usual guest consultation. I tried to ask her questions about what she had done before, what she liked, what she didn't like. She had already pulled out her electronic crossword puzzle, and aside from telling me that she wanted contrast, she was simply giving me yes or no answers. She would barely look up at me when I showed her the colors I wanted to use for her foils and just said that she trusted me, as long as she got contrast.

Dana found it amusing, but I spent the appointment in silence, walking on eggshells and reminding myself to just get through it. I had a few foils left to put in and thought I might actually be in the clear since her short haircut wouldn't take long at all when she decided it was time to chat.

"You know, I haven't had a stylist do my hair the way I like it in about five years. I tell the receptionist that I get along better with male stylists, but she seems to ignore that," Brenda informed me.

Starting to wonder if she had been hired as an employee by the school to give us lessons in customer relations, I asked the only obvious question: "Have you been going to salons or just schools?"

"Salons are too expensive. Besides, someone has to teach you guys how to do things the right way." She looked back down at her game.

It was a relief since telling her what I really thought of her lesson would probably get me sent home for the day. Time was passing at an almost painfully slow pace. I told her that I had to clean up my tools while her hair processed, and when she didn't respond, I took that as permission to do so.

My escape was heaven-sent since I could confide in Dana, who was also laughing at the fact that the woman was wearing this outfit in public. She was incredibly amused by my suffering. Having to set Dana straight, I told her that when the woman sat down, her too small yoga pants stretched out enough to become transparent. I threatened that if Dana kept making fun of my pain, I'd tell her what color thong the woman was wearing.

Once I rinsed her color and styled her hair, I figured it was safe to breathe again since it looked pretty good and I had even incorporated the color contrast she had insisted on. I spun the chair to face the mirror, portraying the biggest smile I could. Her expression was blank, and she started running her fingers through her hair.

"Well? What do you think?" I figured if she wasn't bitching, she might actually like it, but I had no idea what was coming.

"What did you do?" Brenda asked, her eyes welling up with tears. "This is too dark."

I was surprised. "What is, the lowlight? No, it's the same color I showed you."

"No, I told you I wanted to be blonde." She started to wipe her tears away from her eyes.

"You said you wanted contrast, that means two colors. Remember, I tried to show you the color for the lowlight, and you agreed."

Apparently, she had a very selective memory. She was unable to hold back the tears and started crying. "How am I supposed to face people like this?"

"Well, how did you face them before?" I asked.

"What?" Her sadness made a quick change over to anger as she wiped the cheap eyeliner off her cheeks. "What is that supposed to mean?"

"Nothing, I didn't mean anything." I had to take a breath. "Look, this is not the end of the world. We just had a little miscommunication. Let's just take a look, and you tell me specifically what it is you don't like. A first impression."

She sniffled but had that same angry, constipated look on her face as she looked back at the mirror to study her appearance. "Well, my husband is not going to like this."

I was never going to win this one. "Okay, we're role playing. What is it that your husband won't like about your appearance?"

I was pretty sure it would be all the nasty flab being squeezed out from under her teenage wardrobe. Her skin was sinking faster than her sex appeal and any hope of maintaining her youth. That is if you rule out the fact that she smelled like cheap fruity perfume and hot dogs. Even after observing all of this, I still gave her the chance to offer her opinion.

"Well…"

I found it amusing that even she had to narrow down the list.

Then she simply mumbled, "He likes me blonde."

"Gone?" I couldn't believe she was making a joke all of a sudden, portraying yet another personality I wasn't fond of.

"I said blonde! He likes me blonde!"

"Oh. Ooops. I thought you were making a joke." I tried to laugh it off, but I couldn't tell if the look on her face was the lack of amusement or just her jowls.

"I'm not amused." She started running her fingers through her hair again. "This is so dark!"

"It sounds like all we need are a few more highlights. This isn't a bad thing. We'll throw a few more in."

"No! I don't want you to do anything else to my hair. I take my appearance very seriously, and obviously, you have no idea what you're doing!" She stood up out of the chair, looked at me one last time, and walked toward the front door.

The receptionist tried to talk to her about her bill or simply speaking to an instructor, but the woman was on a mission. On her way to the coat rack, she stumbled a little on her right wedge but kept walking. My first reaction was to try and help her but then got freaked out by the ripple effect along her deflated limbs. She never paid her bill and never came back to the school. I'm pretty sure I got extra credit for that.

The next couple of weeks went very smoothly. I figured that I had now seen the craziest client I would ever meet and that no hair experience would match it. I told myself that there was a lesson to be learned from it. That if a client was unhappy, she would usually speak up before I started or at least while I was working on her hair, instead of just waiting until the end to pitch a fit. Dana's advice about the previous experiences is that if they were that particular, they shouldn't be coming into schools or at least be able to tell the stylist what they wanted so that we wouldn't be forced to use our imaginations. My next client, however, taught me that a person didn't have to yell to be a pain in the ass.

I walked up to the front desk to greet my four o'clock appointment. She was a younger girl. I assumed was in her late teens or early twenties. She had longer, dark-brown, curly hair and thick, red-rimmed glasses. She had no expression when I introduced myself with the usual smile. Not sure if she had just gotten dumped by her boy toy, or what, I decided to let her set the mood for the visit.

Part of any good stylist experience is getting to know the client. I started asking general questions about work, school, family, all to which she replied with grunts left to my interpretation. When a person is getting a hair service, the stylist should also discuss hair care and daily regiments, if not future hair goals, or so we were taught.

Courtesy of her short, mumbled answers to my attempts to establish any kind of client relationship, I figured she didn't want to chat about daily life and focused on the topic of hair and skin.

"So, do you wash your hair every day?"

"No."

"That's good. What kind of shampoo are you using?" I asked while I kept coming through her hair to access any issues or concerns.

"Eh, whatever's there."

"Okay, have you had any issues like dandruff or oily scalp or has it been hard to control or style—"

She cut me off. "Look, I didn't come in here to discuss my hairstyle. I just need a haircut."

"Wow. Okay, I'll wing it. Come on back to the shampoo bowl."

I thought it was gutsy of her not to want to discuss the final result, especially when I had met people who acted like they were going to be walking the runway the following week and that one hair out of place would ruin any chance of a long-term career. I continued cutting in silence, and when we were finished, I simply gave her an inquiring look. I took her shrug as a seal of approval and walked her to the desk to pay. I never saw her again either, but I had to appreciate that she kept her crazy somewhat quiet so as not to disturb the sane people around her. Our instructors were right—salons see all kinds, behind the chair, as well as sitting in it.

Before I knew it, it was time to start thinking about state boards, which were the technical exams, basically the finals for getting our licenses. I had been spending the past nine months focusing on going to school six days a week and trying to squeeze in a double shift on Sundays that I hadn't been doing much planning for my impending move. In keeping up on Mike's advice, I had a lot to do and I knew it wouldn't be easy, especially when it came to convincing my mother that it wasn't simply a childish dream but a carefully thought-out goal.

I had randomly mentioned the move to her a few times, and she would blow it off and ask me what I thought of her new nail polish. I wasn't sure if she was in denial or just thought it fell in with the same naïve fantasies I had when I wanted to marry princes from fairy tales so that I could wear tiaras. Sara knew what my goals were since we shared everything. She was very encouraging since her goals were somewhat the same, except she had the love for performing on a live stage instead of in front of a camera. With my technical just around the corner, I had made it a point to talk to Mike more often and get his advice about the move. It came in handy went I needed to spend the last night before my final exam, venting to someone who could understand the pressure.

"So, was it hard for you to get your family to accept the fact that you were moving across the country?" I had finally gotten to talk to Mike on my lunch break, as opposed to our usual game of phone tag.

"Oh, of course not. I think brotherly and mother-son/father-son relationships are a little more relaxed."

I had to admit, I was a little confused since I grew up surrounded by a sister and a mother. "What do you mean, more relaxed?"

"Well, as long as their children don't ask for money or end up in prison, they just don't give a shit."

"That's rough," I said. Although in all honesty, I wasn't sure who had it tougher.

"It can be. But sometimes it can save you the nagging and the guilt trips."

"There really is a silver lining everywhere." I was still nervous about bringing it up with my mother again. "I have a feeling she'll try to talk me out of it."

"You just have to stand your ground and tell her that you'd really like her support but you plan on moving with or without it."

"Hopefully it doesn't come to that. Yuck. Well, I have to try and get some sleep. My final exam is tomorrow!"

"Really? It's early! Why are you taking a written exam?" he asked.

"No. It's the real deal. I'm being tested on my ability to play with scissors. Besides, I took the written exam about laws and rules and terminology. You know, the crap," I informed him. "I'll let you know what happens! Sweet dreams!"

"Oh, you'll do fine! But break a leg!"

And with that, I drifted off to a night of insomnia. My head was spinning, worrying about the test tomorrow and, even more, what I would be doing after that. The next morning I woke up with my usual "important test" attitude. The feeling of knowing what I needed to do, feeling confident in my ability to get it done, but still incredibly nervous about the concept of it.

I treated myself to my usual test-day treat: a large blended iced coffee and a huge piece of cinnamon coffee cake. The sugar rush was incredibly helpful since the buzz of endorphins prevent any inner debates about self-doubt. The only direction to move was forward, and while it was only one of many, it was time to take that step.

There was also a little comfort in the fact that my mother would be my model. I had reminded her that she couldn't complain about anything and only point out what she loved about whatever color, cut, or style I gave her since it would persuade my final "grade." I offered to buy her dinner if she cooperated, to fix anything she didn't like at a later time, and even threatened to move back in and leech off her for the rest of her life. I wasn't sure, but I was hopeful that she might be able to see how important the technical was for me.

I met my mother at the door and figured I'd walk her back to my chair before dropping my coffee off to the fridge in the employee break room. "Did you get me one?"

"No. I wasn't sure what you wanted." I was trying to find my shears and organize my tools.

"How can you not know? I always get the same thing."

"Mother, would you like to have the rest of this one?" I was making a peace offering since one of my classmates would probably finish my drink if I left it in the fridge anyway.

"Maybe. Is it vanilla?"

"Yes, Mother."

"Is it blended?"

"Yes, Mother."

"Is it sugar-free?"

"Really? You always drink sugar free? I have to start setting up. Do you want it or not?"

"Wow, relax. I was just asking. And no. For your information, I prefer hazelnut. But can I have a glass of water or something?"

"Yes, Mother." I was going to walk away but decided to make one final plea. "Please, Mother? Please?"

"Okay, okay. I just wanted a water. No big deal."

I'd never been a deeply religious person, but I did some praying before we all started the exam, not necessarily that I needed the assistance to pass, but that my mother would stop talking until we were done. While she would always be my favorite mother, she did have a social side and loved to chat and make friends, not always at the most convenient times. When the technical began, however, I was proud that she seemed more calm than the other models. She introduced herself to the instructors, seemingly confident that she was about to get a quality service as opposed to the others, who insisted on trying to turn their heads during the cuts to keep an eye on what exactly was being done to them, probably not the best tactic to prevent color bleeding or to promote a straight cut.

Our first task was sectioning. While we were usually encouraged to socialize with our clients, many of the students either kept the conversation quiet or chose not to talk at all. With time to kill while the judges made their rounds, I figured this might be the perfect time to have a chat with Mom, keeping her entertained, even though she may not appreciate my topic of choice.

"So what's going on this weekend?" I asked, getting a feel for her mood.

"Oh, nothing much," she responded, flipping through the magazine she had brought.

"Fun. You know, we should travel more. The clients that come during the week are always telling me what fun they have, traveling on the weekends." It was a cheesy attempt, but I was desperate.

"Really? Just for the weekend? Where are they traveling to?" She still seemed disinterested.

Seeing this as a sign that she was somewhat calm, I kept going. "Oh, here. There. Around the state. Out of the state. The southwest states seem to be really popular."

"With all that desert? I mean, I'd appreciate the heat but it's so dry."

"Or you just go somewhere with an ocean view or access to the water." I tried to make it sound as casual as possible, and since my instructor interrupted us to check my work, I wasn't sure if she was taking it in.

I had to go to the color bar to be observed while mixing color, then headed back to jump into it again. "Yeah, I can't tell you how many people have told me how beautiful California is."

"Oh, that's nice. Isn't Mike still living out there?" she remembered.

"Yeah. He loves it out there. Can you imagine if I were to move out there?"

"You had mentioned it once or twice. But you couldn't do hair out there with a Minnesota license, could you?" She was still reading her articles.

I was grateful that she was bringing up legitimate details that I had already thought of and had the answers to. "I would just have to take a written test to transfer it to another state."

"Oh." She stopped reading and looked up, staring me down in the mirror. "Are you seriously considering moving down there?"

"Mom, hold still!" I was grateful to have an excuse to keep her from freaking out. "I've thought about it. I mean, seriously thought about it."

"Well, wouldn't you miss us?"

"Of course, but I have to try. You know I've always wanted to do the acting stuff. And what better place to learn about the industry?"

"Or get scammed, kidnapped, murdered?"

"Mom, calm down. Mike and Joe are living down there, so I would already know people when I got there." I tried to focus on weaving highlights but couldn't help multitasking. "Besides, I could get murdered walking down the streets of Northeast Minneapolis after bar close."

"Why are you going to bars in Northeast Minneapolis?" Her concern was melting into a scolding.

"Mom, I'm not. What I'm trying to tell you is that once I get my license, I'm planning on moving to LA." Hopefully the best way to break it to her was by coming right out and saying it.

"Have you thought everything through? Where are you going to live? What are you going to do for work? How will you support yourself?"

"Mom, yes, I have thought about all of it. Mike and I have been discussing it a lot lately, and he's been helping me plan and giving me the names of a few complexes he found when he was looking around." I was trying to calm her down. "But let's focus on making you beautiful, and we can talk about all of this over dinner—and hopefully a few rounds of margaritas."

One way or another, it was over and done with. I broke the news to her, and she couldn't freak out on me with all the witnesses around to make statements. She didn't say much for the duration of the technical but would give short answers to any questions asked by the instructors about quality and comfort during the service. I appreciated her acting skills at that point since I knew my mother was dying to either cry or spit on my face.

After the test was over, I approached the head instructor and asked about receiving my results right away. She said she wasn't able to give me the results, that they'd be mailed out, because if or when you passed, the school wanted to enroll you in job placement programs. I reminded her that I had already taken the written exam and decided to break the news of my new gig one more time. I explained that I already had something lined up and that I just needed my paperwork to get my physical license. She hesitated, so I tried to appeal to her sensitive side, utilizing acting skills to flash puppy-dog eyes at her and explaining that if I didn't pass, I would have to know right away. Somehow, I would have to come up with more funds to pay for another technical, as well as try to find time to schedule it as soon as possible so I wouldn't lose out on the pending opportunity. She buckled and handed me a little slip of paper. I unfolded it to see the word pass scribbled with a red marker. I was incredibly relieved. One more mile down, only nine hundred and ninety-nine to go.

Chapter 17

After passing my test, I was happy to hold up my promise to take my newly made-over mother out to dinner. While she was happy with her look, I still felt like something else was bothering her and I was pretty sure I knew what it was.

"All right, we've each had a swig of liquid honesty, let's have it. What's on your mind?" I asked, bracing for impact.

"I think you've got some sort of naïve idea that if you move to Hollywood, all your dreams will come true. That is, assuming, you're not murdered." She had to add it.

"Yes, Mother. I got that when you said it earlier," I reminded her. "Technically, I'm going to die someday, one way or another. Why can't you be happy that I want to go quickly?"

"Oh God, Lisa, that's not funny. Are you listening to anything I'm saying? You don't have a job waiting for you. You don't know anyone out there. Do you realize how much sunscreen you're going to have to buy being under that California sun? And what if you develop asthma from all that smog? That's not a quick death." She really was clutching at straws to talk me out of wanting to go.

"Wow, really? Asthma? You're sure I'm going to get asthma from the smog out there? I mean, you're right, growing up next to an international airport has been a huge breath of clean, fresh air. Wow, you've actually made getting shot sound like a better choice than suffocation," I told her.

"Lisa, that's not funny. Have you thought about how hard it is to just pick up and move to a strange city? Especially one as expensive as LA? Who would do something that stupid?" she asked.

"You did it," I reminded her.

"What? What did I do?"

"When you moved to Minneapolis from your hometown in South Dakota. You didn't know anyone here. You got an education, saved up some money, and decided to just go for it." I tried to point out the silver lining. "And didn't that turn out well?"

"Well, let's just say it wasn't the most horrible decision I ever made." She took another sip of her drink, a very long, drawn-out one.

"Mom, I really want to do this. I need to try. Otherwise, I'll never know." I wanted to be honest. "And that to me sounds worse than developing asthma. So I really need your support on this."

"I shouldn't even say this, but I get it. If you want something, you have to go for it. I'm not happy about it, but I won't stop you from doing it." She raised her glass.

I was relieved that she could at least admit that she knew where I was coming from, and I raised my glass too. "The journey starts with a single step, remember?"

"Ugh, you've got my support. Don't bring up that quack and make me change my mind. He's the one that encouraged you to do all this, and he still owes me, what, fifteen hundred dollars?" She set her drink down and started studying her menu.

"Well, technically, you planted the seed."

"Excuse me?" She looked up at me, trying to figure out how it would be her fault.

"The play in grade school. You got me hooked," I confessed.

"Oh, super. Now when you're murdered, I'll also have to bear the guilt of being the cause of all of it. Thank you for that. I should probably have gotten the large margarita." She looked around for our server.

"Okay, Mom. Calm down. No one's blaming you for anything that can hold up in court," I assured her. "Yet."

We finished our meal in peace, and even had fun planning the trip. She made a few recommendations about which company I should rent the truck from, how I should stack boxes and furniture so that nothing would get broken, and the fact that I should ask my sister to drive down with me. I tried to assure her that I could make it alone, but she told me that that would be stupid. She told me that if I had to go, she was adamant that I had to take someone with me. So there it was, we found a compromise. She wouldn't try to talk me out of going, and I would ask my sister to drive down with me.

I had planned to leave two weeks after finishing school. The first week Sara helped me pack the small stuff when she had time. And it was actually fun since we incorporated wine and movies into the process. With one week to go, I knew it was time to get serious and start packing up the items I could live without until I got to a newfound apartment in Los Angeles since I wasn't sure exactly how long that would be.

I hadn't asked my sister to drive down to LA with me but covered my bases by asking her if she'd be able to get a little extra vacation time to help me pack. We had never been the best of friends, so I knew that what I was about to ask her would be asking a lot of her. While helping me pack, she would fight and argue about why I had to bring certain outfits or electronics with me or that I had something of hers that she didn't know I still had. I started to ponder how bad my mother's nagging could be. If I staggered the energy drinks, there was no reason I couldn't make it all the way there alone with one stop at my aunt's home in Nebraska. It was starting to sound like it'd be worth the risk.

"Really? You've had my rainbow-doll pillow all these years? You knew she was my favorite." The sad part is that she was serious.

"Yes, Michelle, do you want her back?" I offered so we could keep moving forward.

"Don't be ridiculous. I'm an adult. Why would I want a doll?" She squished the pillow into a box full of clothes.

"Okay then." I took a deep breath, trying to drop it since I needed her help. "I knew I should have gotten another bottle of wine."

"You know I don't drink," Michelle reminded me.

"It wasn't for you." I picked up a box to move it to the living room.

"Rude."

I walked back in, ready to cut the crap. "You know, your little nitpicking is getting incredibly old. I would think you'd enjoy packing all of my crap up. It means you're even closer to getting rid of me."

"You mean my crap?" She had to say it. "I never said I wanted to get rid of you."

"There was no need to say it, Michelle. Your attitude speaks volumes."

"You're no picnic either," she fired back.

I turned up the music and did whatever I could to avoid talking to her. It actually made both of us work harder over the course of the next four days. We didn't want to talk, but we also didn't want to die of boredom. So the next option was to work hard and get everything done.

Before she left the apartment for the last time on that fourth day, I decided to try and extend the olive branch one more time. "Thanks for your help. I really appreciate it."

"Well, you know, I'm happy to get you out of here." She stuck her tongue out at me.

"Seriously, I really appreciate it." I decided to go for it, feeling like I was being put into one of the cages at the zoo so I could hand deliver a lion's dinner. "How many days did you take off this week?"

"Oh, I had vacation time I had to use, so I'm actually off until next Thursday," she informed me.

"That's cool. Time to celebrate." I wanted to see her reaction to my attempted humor.

"Yeah, that's it." She rolled her eyes.

"Well, if you're just trying to kill vacation time, you could come with me."

"So that you don't have to pay a mover, or what? You do realize that we'd be stuck in a closed in space for a few days?" She made it sound like a punishment, but I showed her something even worse.

"Well, yes. Not the ideal situation for either one of us. But it was actually Mom's idea. Would you rather be stuck in a car with me for a few days or be the only daughter within shouting distance to suffer her wrath for the next few months? I don't know about you, but I can't afford all the extra minutes on my cell phone bill." I was incredibly thankful for my improv skills, making it sound as if her riding along was all my mother's idea.

"True. Okay. It might be fun to see everyone in Nebraska too. And I haven't been to LA." She was coming around. "But don't expect me to pay for gas."

"Never crossed my mind."

She turned and left for the night, and I went to my room to pile up the blankets I was using for a bed while mine was covered with boxes.

I had planned on spending the second to last night in my room at Sara's apartment and the last night in town at my mom's. It would give me a little time to say good-bye to my friends and one last night with my family. Saying good-bye to Sara wasn't as tough as I had thought. There were a few tears, a few hugs, and a promise to keep things positive and stay in touch at least through social media sites. I was starting to understand what Mike had been talking about, not wanting the situation to take a negative turn.

I headed to my mother's house, not knowing what to expect. I walked in to find that everything was in its usual place. The TV was on, Mom was sitting on the couch, working on her latest craft project, and Michelle was in the kitchen, cooking something that smelled amazing but yelling about where everything was and how she couldn't find any of it. A little normalcy made me feel better about the huge change I was about to make.

Through their individual tasks, they didn't seem to notice that I had walked in so I announced myself. "Hey, everyone, what's going on?"

"Hey, sweetie. Your sister's making dinner, and I'm trying to finish up my little project here for the craft sale on Saturday." She kept looking down and working with her hot glue gun. "Are you hungry? Getting excited?"

I was surprised by how positive she was being. Then my sister swooped in to bring me back to reality. "Yeah, we're both stoked to be stuck in the car with each other for at least eight hours until we get to Aunt Jodie's."

"Glad to know we're in the same boat," I yelled toward the kitchen. "Yeah, I'm excited. A little nervous that I might forget something, but I guess that goes along with any move. I could probably eat."

"Great. It should be done"—we both looked toward the kitchen door as we heard Michelle yelling at the lid to a pot that slammed to the floor— "soon."

Mom smiled at me and went back to gluing. "Sounds great."

I sat next to her on the couch, just wanting to observe what she was doing. It seemed weird to think that once I moved, I wouldn't be able to just come over and hang out with her for a while. I wouldn't be able to just stop over and grab a cup of coffee or get her to cook something for me. The thought was a little scary, but I had to distract myself with something else to keep things moving in a positive direction. So I offered to help her with her crafts. It was something that seemed like a chore as a child, but I was more than happy to help with now.

She seemed surprised that I wanted to get my hands dirty but welcomed the help and showed me how to put everything together. We were incredibly productive until Michelle called us to the kitchen by telling us to come get food if we wanted to eat. We sat at the table and actually enjoyed a very pleasant meal, followed by a dessert my mother used to make for us all the time as children, chocolate lasagna. We spent the evening playing card games we used to save for holidays, and scarfing down at least half of the cake pan. I was very happy that the evening was going to end on such a positive note.

Suddenly, Michelle checked her phone and announced, "Wow, its already midnight. We need to get some sleep if we have to leave at seven in the morning."

"I was having so much fun, I lost track of time and almost forgot how annoying you are when bossing people around." I made a face at her.

"Ha-ha. Keep talking shit, and you'll have to ride in the back of the moving truck."

"I'm pretty sure we did lay out the mattress flat across all the boxes."

"You're hilarious. Gee, how I'm going to miss that sense of humor." Michelle started to gather all the cards off the table and put them back into the box.

"You're both brats. And you both sound like you could use as much sleep as possible. I don't care how old you are, both of you get to bed. I'll clean the rest of this up in the morning." She picked up the dirty dishes and set them in the sink.

Michelle left the room to finish her nightly regiments and go to bed. I stayed behind to help Mom clean up the dishes. It was the perfect opportunity to get a few more minutes with her.

"Thanks, Mom." I wasn't sure of what else to say.

"For what? Dessert? No big deal, takes ten minutes."

"No, I mean, thank you for not making this a sad thing," I told her.

She stopped getting the dishes and sat down next to me. "Well, it is a sad thing. I'm going to miss you so much. But I'd be lying if I said I wasn't happy that I raised such a strong, smart girl who's not afraid to go after what she wants. I'm proud of you, and I know you'll be great."

Both of our eyes started to water. "Thank you. I know you didn't exactly agree with my decision, but thank you for understanding that I have to try. You're my favorite mom."

"By default. Nice try. Now go to bed." She stood up to finish putting the dishes in the sink and stopped to give me a hug. "I love you."

"Love you too." I started to walk toward the door and stopped to get one more look before going to bed. No matter how much she knew how to annoy me, she really was my favorite mom.

I didn't expect to get much sleep that night. But as it turned out, I went to sleep at twelve o'clock and was ripped from it by my alarm going off at six. It was a short night, but I knew I had a very motivating reason to wake up and get moving. I was extremely appreciative that the sun was shining. Considering the state was only a few weeks away from a winter wonderland, the fact that it was fifty-four degrees felt great. With the previous week devoted to sorting my stuff and deciding what was important enough to load into a trailer and drag two-thousand miles across the country and what would simply fit into storage, the thought of an eight-hour drive sounded relaxing.

Not wanting to poke the bear, I didn't strike up a morning chat with Michelle to see if she felt the same way. I started packing up the last of my things, keeping an eye on her slow movements, trying to get a feel for her mood. It was hard to figure out, even when she looked at me with one eye still shut and asked me where her toothpaste was. I was grateful that she was more tired than testy.

We got everything into the truck and even stocked my car with snacks and drinks for the eight-hour trip ahead of us. Finally, we were down to the moment I had been dreading. Even though he didn't want to call it a good-bye scene, it was hard enough when I had to face Mike before his trip, I could only imagine how hard it was going to be to not say good-bye to my mom.

I was a little relieved that she had to leave first so that she could get to work on time. Her usual positive energy was somewhat stifled by her silence while she made her lunch, styled her hair, and packed up her work bag. I pretended not to notice, but it was time to tell her to have a good day and that we would call her when we got to our aunt's house.

"Well, this is it." I smiled at her and wanted to share the excitement.

She had already been crying and grabbed me for one final hug. "This is it."

"Mom, come on. This is a good thing, remember. You said yourself I have to go for what I want. Are you going to cry all day?"

She sniffled and wiped her cheeks but was still crying and could barely get the words out. "Yes. Yes, I am. Now remember, you two don't fight about stupid things during the trip."

Michelle and I looked at each other, rolling our eyes and responding in sync, "Yes, Mother."

Then she focused on me, pointing her finger in my direction. "Don't speed just because you're in a rural area. And be sure to check out a few places before you sign any leases. Don't let just anyone move in with you. And don't get murdered." She hugged me again, this time squeezing much harder and holding on longer.

"I love you, Mom." I was fighting the tears too. "Gotta take that first step."

"I know. The first step." She let go and turned to walk out the front door, then turned around again. "I love you too."

With that, she left for work. Michelle and I looked at each other, both of us obviously affected by what had just happened. But we had to finish up in the house and get moving. Since she had a photographic memory, we agreed that she would be the first driver and I could check out a few of the apartments I had been researching over the past few weeks. With her driving, I knew we wouldn't be listening to music since we had a rule that the driver picks the noise. Once we passed the morning traffic of the Minneapolis area, she started her book on tape. Not what I wanted to hear, but I knew this would rule out any bickering conversation and be the perfect time to try to sleep.

Between the motion of the vehicle and the fact that my sister enjoyed speaking back to the recordings, I didn't think I'd be able to sleep in the car. Before I closed my eyes, I was watching buildings, houses, and apartment complexes zoom by. There were a couple of familiar malls with full parking lots and thick traffic as far as I could see in either direction of the freeway. When I woke up from my accidental nap, we were zooming by cornfields and livestock.

"Wow, how long was I out for?" I asked, rubbing my eyes, trying to wake up.

"Just a few hours," Michelle answered.

I tried to find where I had dropped my energy drink. "Are we in South Dakota yet?"

"No, but probably within the next hour, if there's no construction."

"Cool. Seen anything besides cows yet?" I looked out the window to see if I could answer my own question.

"Nope, nothing yet."

I could tell she wasn't too chatty, and her book wasn't playing. I figured I'd try a little humor to see if I could get the conversation flowing so that the next five-six hours wouldn't be torture. "Do you remember when we were little? What was that game that we used to play when we went on trips to see Grandma? Something about counting horses."

"Zip." She actually cracked a smile. "It was called Zip."

I felt like I was starting to remember. "That's right, and you have to zip every horse you see because whoever has the most by the end of the trip wins."

"And do you remember how you can get rid of the other people's horses?"

"No. How can you get rid of the other players' horses? What, do you see a dead horse and subtract one?"

"No, don't be stupid. When you see a cemetery, you say, 'Zip on the cemetery, bury all your horses'! Then everyone else has to start from zero. You used to get so mad at me when we played that game." She loved to point out moments that made me look bad.

"I didn't get mad at you about the horses. I got mad at you for cheating!" I corrected her.

She shook her head. "No way! How was I cheating, because I could count better than you?"

"Count better than me? How were you even keeping an accurate count when your nose was buried in a book for the whole ride?" It felt good to finally confront her.

"I multitask! Besides, it wouldn't have hurt you entertain yourself with one instead of playing the horse police for twelve-hour car rides." She tried to turn the tables.

I was almost offended. "You know I can't read in cars. I get sick!"

"Well, you could've risked it if it meant you could've gained some common sense and knowledge."

"Excuse me? You were reading books about a group of girls who spent their weekends babysitting and pooling their money for no good reason," I reminded her.

"It taught me the value of sharing and working together." It was cute of her to try.

"It taught you that those who don't work will leech off of those that do! And what did they ever do with it anyway?" I asked.

"Well, I didn't finish the series." She tried to change the subject. "Besides, that game was just some ridiculous thing Mom came up with to keep us from whining about being bored or having to go to the bathroom. She was only trying to keep us busy."

"Yeah, coz the last five minutes of bickering haven't proven that to be a legit scheme." I rolled my eyes at her.

The rest of the trip was devoted to her novels and music we used to listen to when we were kids. It reminded us of yet something else we used to fight over—our cassette tapes. After a short discussion of who used to steal them from who, we decided to get some food. While stopping for the grade-D but still edible fast food, we decided to trade places. I could only hope that sitting in the passenger's seat would afford her the luxury to fall asleep and give me some peace and quiet to drive to.

I couldn't have been more wrong. She stayed awake to point out anything she thought was worth looking at and nagging about the way I drove. I tried to think of a couple of positive reasons for her to stay awake. I figured her bitching would keep me awake and attentive, and with her glued to her phone, she would keep checking online maps so I wouldn't get us lost. Of course, her idea of conversation made me want to stop and get a bottle of vodka, but I tried to tell myself that I would miss her company once she flew back to Minnesota, so I just had to live with it.

After a car ride that seemed like sixteen hours, as opposed to seven and a half, courtesy of my "horrible, fast" driving, we arrived at my aunt Jodie's. At random points during the car ride, we had tried to guess what kind of treat our aunt would have waiting for us. We had narrowed it down, and I bet it would be peanut butter crispy bars and Michelle's guess was lefse. Since we arrived at a decent time, we'd be able to indulge in both if they were available.

Our aunt met us in the driveway to welcome us with hugs. Regardless how old we got, she would always talk to us like we were five years old. She invited us in and insisted that we have a bite to eat. Per the usual, we explained that we had already had dinner so she suggested dessert. It turned out both of our predictions were right. And we utilized the opportunity to show our appreciation of our aunt's efforts by eating a good portion of what she had prepared.

Unfortunately, we had to make it a short visit by going straight to bed after dessert and waking up early to get a head start on the last lap of our trip. There were always hugs and happy tears when we left our aunt's house every year, and this experience would be no different. She packed us up little bags of treats to go. I appreciated it, considering that the sugar rush might help us push through the last few hours without stopping.

I had already worked it out with Mike that I'd be able to stay with him and Joe. I wasn't sure how Joe felt about it and didn't want to make anything uncomfortable or stressful but knew that I didn't have many other options. And I had to admit, I was grateful not to be all alone when I arrived.

I had mixed emotions about arriving in LA. I was incredibly excited since I had been anticipating the move for a while. I had almost idealized LA. I childishly pictured all the old Hollywood actors walking the streets and simply living their blissful daily lives in the gorgeous California weather.

Everyone moving there to pursue any aspect of the entertainment industry dreams of sitting at the table of a corner coffee shop and being approached by a top director who insists that his next film won't be a hit without you playing a lead role. On the other hand, there were so many people with this dream, who knew if the hostess had a waiting list for the lucky table.

There was also that fear of the unknown. How much would I have to push to sell my own image and talent? I wouldn't find out until I pursued auditions and projects and roles. I wouldn't learn anything about the people who lived here until I put myself out there to meet them. Aside from the palm trees and weather that only consisted of gorgeous sunshine, it might be just like home. Then again, there were no orange leaves on the ground or pending snow. Either way, regardless of the lack of seasons, we were definitely in California so it was too late to turn back now.

I couldn't wait to see Mike, and since he and Joe lived in Pasadena, we would see them before we saw Hollywood or any other tourist attractions. I followed the directions my phone was giving me, but I was getting frustrated that it was such a cluster fuck of twists and turns. I tried to focus instead on all the similarities I could see between the town I just arrived in and home. The traffic had picked up, and once again, we were surrounded by buildings and people. The traffic was a little thicker, and the license plates didn't have a blue "Minnesota" on them but instead a red "California."

Finally, after I was sure the directions had forced us to drive in circles for about an hour, we took the final turn onto Mike's street. He lived in a two-bedroom apartment in a huge building, which I was grateful for at that point since I had no idea where I was going. The street parking looked a little tight and intimidating, but we found a spot, and I called Mike to tell him the good news.

The phone rang a few times before I heard his familiar, comforting voice. "Hello! Hello!"

"What's up! We're alive! We made it!" I got more excited just saying it. "We didn't kill each other. And the best part I think I might have found your apartment building!"

"See? I told you it wouldn't be that hard!" He seemed excited that we were there. "Okay, I'll be right down to get you!"

"K. I'm gonna watch for you. If I don't see you in five minutes, I'm calling back!"

"Bye!" He hung up before I had a chance to say it back.

"Are we at the wrong place or something?" Michelle asked, skeptical about our arrival. "I hope not. I have to pee."

I couldn't wait to see Mike. We had been chatting, but it had been so long since we got to hang out. And I wanted to get inside so Michelle could pee, and I could quit hearing about it. I watched both doors, anxiously waiting to see him, when suddenly he came running out and toward the moving trailer. I jumped out to give him a big hug.

"Hello! It's so good to see you! Thank you so much for letting me stay here!"

Michelle slowly got out of the car. "Hey, Mike, how's it going?"

Mike had never been the shy one, so he grabbed her and gave her a hug too. "How are you?"

Seeing him solidified my trip. I had arrived. It was dark out, and Mike invited us in right away. We grabbed the bags we figured we would need to get through the night without convincing onlookers within smelling distance that Minnesotans were against hygiene. Mike had explained that I could move in as a roommate and that the second bedroom would be mine. I assured him it would only be for a little while since I didn't want anything to hurt our friendship. But he opened the door and invited me to stay as long as I wanted and to give him at least thirty days' notice when I wanted to leave.

We walked into the apartment, and right away Michelle asked where the bathroom was. Mike told her which door it was and then gave me a short tour. First was the room I was staying in. There were no noticeable stains on the carpet, and I didn't have to follow my nose to get there. It was a smaller closet than I had hoped for, but I didn't want to be picky. At that point, I probably would have been thrilled with a cardboard box if it was located somewhere near Mike's building. He showed me the furniture he had gotten since moving in and then his room. I took a quick look since I probably wouldn't be in there much, or ever again, since the guys wouldn't exactly want me snuggling with them. But even with a quick look, I noticed something was missing.

"So where's Joe's stuff?" I looked for any sign of his game systems. "Or should I ask, where's Joe?"

"Well, it just wasn't working out." It was confession time. "When we first got here, we lived in a studio. That was pretty much the beginning of the end."

"Why, what happened?" I was waiting for Mike to confirm that I wasn't the final nail in the coffin, that me moving in didn't cause Joe to move out.

"It was just tough. He wasn't motivated to get out of the apartment, just wanted to play video games. He said he wanted to move down here with me, but he acted like this was just a vacation and that I'd give up soon so we could move back home. He wasn't supportive at all. Besides, do you know how hard it is to get away from someone when you're in one tight closed-in space and that person is bugging the shit out of you?"

Just then, we turned to see Michelle come walking out of the bathroom and join us on our tour. I looked back at Mike and said, "Yes. Yes, I do. And I applaud you for making it as long as you did. Just promise me that my moving in here wasn't the final peanut on the shit sundae."

"No, of course not. It ended a long time ago. It's better this way, and he and I are still able to talk like adults." He was always able to find the positive side, and I looked forward to being his roomie.

We decided to leave the boxes in the locked trailer for the night. Since Mike mostly worked weekends, starring in action-packed live hero appearances during the day and bartending at night, he would have the next few days off. Michelle was just as exhausted as I was, and after we all split a pizza, she booked her flight home and decided to pile up a few blankets in the bedroom to try and get some sleep. She and I had both hoped for one later in the day so she could sleep in and help unpack a little before she left, but the only seat available for the next few days was on an early morning flight, so she had to take it.

Since Mike and I didn't have to be up too early, we stayed up and caught up on everything going on over the past year since he had moved to LA. Lucky the story of Joe's exit was a short, sweet one, so the conversation remained on a positive track. I knew there would be time later for the wisdom of getting started, what agencies to check out, which background hotlines to call; so I wanted to know all the fun details.

We sat in the living room, trying to keep our voices down while still trying to hear over the TV. "All right, spill it, who have you run into?"

"Run into? From back home, or what?" He laughed.

"No. You know what I mean, which celebrities autographs have you gotten without having to buy them online. Who have you met face-to-face? Which ones are the scariest without their make up on or their pill fixes? You're a bartender, who do I blame for the shortage of vodka in Los Angeles?" I was ready for the dirt.

"Well, let's see. Where should I start?" He thought for a moment. "Okay, I got one. So about a month ago I was bartending in Hollywood, and there was an actor sitting at one of the bar tables. It was someone I recognized from a few major films." He looked like he was building up to a major climax.

"Who was it!"

"I can't remember his name. He's one of those guys, if you saw him, you'd recognize him. He was really big in the sixties and seventies. Anyway, he had been in a few times, and I had waited on him. So when I saw him again that night, I looked at him and smiled. You know, just acknowledging that I saw him and would be with him in a minute. Plus I wanted to see if he remembered me. And all of a sudden he waved at me! I couldn't believe it. I was so excited that he remembered me. So I waved back and put a few things away behind the bar. I looked up again, and he was waving me over. So I walked over and said hello. And he smiled at me and asked how I was doing."

"That is so cool!"

"Just wait." He kept building. "I told him I was doing well and asked how he was doing. He told me he was also good, but that he really needed some more bread. I thought he recognized me, and I totally waved back! But he was just trying to get someone to refill his bread!"

"Oh, hell no!" I tried to accentuate the positive. "Well, at least he wanted you to bring it to him."

He shook his head. "I was the only one in the bar! His next option was to get it himself!"

We were both laughing hysterically before someone else joined in the conversation.

"You guys aren't being as quiet as you think you are!"

Getting busted by the noise alert just made us laugh even harder. It felt good to be hanging out with Mike again. He was an incredibly strong person but could still have fun. Whispering didn't do us any good, so we came to the conclusion that we were just tired and it might be worth it to try and go to sleep. Mike left to go to his room, and I wandered back to what would be my room once I was unpacked and piled up a few blankets next to Michelle. I felt right at home and passed out almost right away.

The next day we all woke up early to try and empty the moving truck. Only about two hours into the process, it was time to roll my car off the trailer attached to the truck and drive my sister to the airport. We had gotten a lot done, but I was still a little stressed about finishing the unload and saying good-bye to my sister.

Typical to her usual fashion, getting her small bag together for her flight home was nothing but a hassle. I could almost taste the blood from bighting my tongue and holding back the urge to tell her to shut the hell up and throw her shit in her bag already. I knew it would do no good to end on this note; so I ignored my exhaustion, hunger, and severe lack of a shower and tried to drop subtle hints that we needed to get going if she was going to make her flight on time. I even tried humor, enlightening her to the fact that if she missed her flight, she could just stay and live with Mike and me and we could put a bunk bed in our room. In all honesty, though, this was a scary thought since one of us would end up being murdered.

It was hard not to notice the increased traffic on the way to the airport. It seemed like we couldn't catch a break, the line of stop and go seemed to go on forever. While I can usually get myself through annoying traffic with a little loud music and an energy drink, I was treated to Michelle's constant commentary about how annoying it was and how this is what I would deal with from now on. I assured her it would be okay and was relieved when I saw the exit for the airport. I noticed in turning the steering wheel to follow the exit, my hands were a little stiff in letting go since my knuckles were incredibly white.

I was relieved that we didn't have too much time to say everything on our minds before she left. "Well, we made it!"

"Finally." She was still skeptical. "I would've been pissed if I missed my flight."

"I know what you mean." I rushed to hand her the small bag from the backseat.

She didn't say much as she took her bag from me and threw one of the straps over her shoulder while she organized her boarding pass and wallet.

"Well, thanks for helping me out. Have a good flight."

I figured saying any good-byes would just interrupt her flight process and that she'd just wave and leave, but she actually surprised me.

"It was fun. I'm glad I got to see where you're going to be living. And I'm glad it's with Mike."

I gave her a hug. "Me too."

Her eyes started to water. "I'm proud of you for coming out here. For trying."

"You big sap. Thanks. That really means a lot coming from you."

"Seriously. You put a lot of effort into getting down here. Make sure you do your best. Don't sit around and wait for it to happen. Be bitch, go after it." Her advice made sense.

"Okay, I will." I gave her one more hug. "Now get the hell out of here. I can't share a room with you. My headshots will look horrible if I pull all my hair out."

"Oh, good. You're already rehearsing that bitch thing." She rolled her eyes. "And Mom wanted me to remind you not to get murdered, although I'm starting to wonder if we should really challenge fate."

"I learned from the queen." I motioned in her direction. "Call me when you get home."

I watched her walk away. I thought it would be really hard to say good-bye to her since she was my last connection to my family. But I actually felt pretty confident and knew that I had work to do at my new home. I spent the rest of the day just getting the boxes into my room with Mike occasionally helping me with heavier furniture. Dropping the truck off turned out to be less of a hassle than I had imagined and looked forward to just going home, taking a shower, and passing out for the day. But Mike had other plans. He wanted to cook something to celebrate my first night as his roommate, a term that made me nervous since he had always been adamant about not rooming with friends as it could ruin the friendship.

I was happy to participate but felt myself nodding off a few times, watching him cook. I pigged out and told him that I had to get some sleep so I could dive into getting my new life all set up the following day. He laughed and agreed and suggested that we do a little sightseeing the following day and he could show me where the necessities were and where the hot spots were. I was tempted to bring a notebook with me but reminded myself that I had a map program on my phone, something I had never been so grateful for.

We started off in Hollywood. We saw the sign and the extent of views that stretched into elevated hills. Then we moved on to Burbank and the historic studios. It was hard not to feel like a tourist, excited see in real life sites I had only had a glimpse of in film and television. We weren't surrounded by people we had seen in movies either. In fact, there seemed to be people everywhere, wearing fanny packs and taking pictures. I figured these people were the same boat as me, in that they were new in town and wanted to learn more about it, whether they were staying or not. Knowing that I had to find a post office to update my address and a grocery store near his apartment, we also had to tour the necessary places. After my tour, I wasn't as intimidated by the area as I thought I would be and looked forward to getting down to business and pursuing the whole reason I had moved here.

The next morning I woke up a little more refreshed. I was thrilled to have slept on an actual bed, even though I was still surrounded by boxes. Mike had to work, so I had the place to myself. He had made a list of a few hotlines to register with to submit myself for background work. While it wasn't the most glamorous work, it was a very easy way to make money right off the bat. After registering, I waited through a list of current jobs and none of them seemed to require someone of my description. I tried the next one, going through the same process, and still, nothing. So after submitting myself online to casting websites, hotlines, and almost anything else I could find, I drifted back to unpacking or just reorganizing my boxes.

Mike returned to the apartment after his lunch bartending shift and walked in to find me sitting and watching TV. "So how was the first day? Do you already have something lined up for tomorrow?"

"No, I tried those hotlines you showed me. I got registered, but I didn't fit any of the castings." He sounded so excited about the opportunities, I hated to disappoint him.

"Well, how many times did you call?" he asked, setting his things on the table.

"Once. But I tried a few of them and submitted some stuff online. It's all good. I'll try again next week. I mean, there's always something going on around here, right?"

"Yes, there is. Which is why you should be hitting up those numbers multiple times per day until you book something. You have to put yourself out there. Make connections, make friends, make money," he informed me.

I thought it was sweet that he really wanted to help me succeed, so I assured him that I got his point. "Okay, okay. I'll call them again tomorrow. There's nothing wrong with taking a few days off anyway, right?"

"Ah, yes. Yes, there is. You'll miss out on work. And if all you do is sit around here like Joe did, I'll kill you myself.

Anyway, I have to get to the gym." He left the room to change out of his uniform, got his bag, and left for the gym.

Okay, so maybe it wasn't my success that concerned him. I could take a hint. I decided to get out my laptop and take another look at the casting websites, taking his advice and stalking them to see if anything had changed since I'd checked them earlier. It didn't look like anything had changed. I didn't want him to get too annoyed with me, thinking that I was doing nothing but sitting around, so I decided to entertain myself and check out other updates, like what my friends in Minnesota had eaten for breakfast and posted pictures of on social media.

It was pointless. Reading updates from back home took about two minutes since there was nothing much to tell. I reminded myself that acting wasn't the only reason I had moved. I decided to try my luck and see what my competition looked like. So utilizing the same social websites, I started to search for other people my age. Men and women who had profiles that described what they did for a living and where they were originally from. Men and women that could show me what casting directors were looking for.

I saw that the younger women on these sites had the typical selfies posted all over their pages and written updates about their every move during the day. From what they put in their coffee that morning to how many pillows they wanted to sleep on that night. Their looks didn't look that far off from mine. I found a lot of similarities in the clothes we wore, how we styled our hair, and choices in makeup styles. There was a wide range of hair and eye color, as well as physical appearances. I wasn't sure if I should be thrilled about the common ground or intimidated by the cookie cutter availability.

I noticed a bigger difference when I started looking at the men's profiles. I was no expert, but it seemed pretty obvious who would be cast as a leading man and who would be lucky to get a supporting role. I wasn't sure about the skills involved, but it was easy to see who spent more time at the gym since topless shots were expected of the male talent.

One guy in particular had posted a shot of him in a pair of boxer briefs, and he was gorgeous. From the neck down anyway. After counting his ab muscles a few times and thinking of how good it would be for the environment if I just washed my laundry on his washboard stomach, I noticed that his face was just as pretty as the rest of him. He had thick, dark hair, and gorgeous blue eyes. He had plump lips that even when they were stretched into a smile looked soft and inviting. Next to his slightly tan skin, his smile looked brighter than the white backdrop in his picture. I wasn't sure about anyone else, but I knew he could sell me a pair of underwear, or at least get a pair of mine. I was starting to appreciate what Mike meant about getting out there and discovering the city.

I kept searching for others my age, checking out all the competition and seeing what everyone was up to. After spending hours on my laptop, I was ready to shut it down and start thinking about dinner. Before calling it quits, I wanted to look at that scrumptious picture one more time.

Apparently, Mike had the same idea about food, walking in from the gym and heading for the kitchen. "So how did it go? Did you find anything to submit to?"

I bit my lip for a minute and thought beyond the general meaning of his statement. "Yes, I think I did."

"Well, what are you waiting for, send your information!" he instructed me from the kitchen.

It might have been a long shot, but I figured, what the hell. "Done. Now I just have to wait to hear back."

"See, that was easy. Now don't you feel better?"

He was proud of his advice, and so was I since I utilized it to send the guy in the picture a message asking him what he had planned for the weekend. I knew I wouldn't hear anything from him, but it gave me a good laugh, and I joined Mike in the kitchen to help with dinner. After we ate, Mike sat down on the couch and picked up his laptop. I was surprised that he didn't take a second to digest.

"Wow, are you always this busy?" I asked him.

"Well, if you want it, you have to promote yourself," he answered, staring at his screen. "You should be checking yours again too. See if you got any responses."

I figured it wouldn't hurt to try to get in the habit of promoting myself as much as Mike suggested. So I picked up my laptop, yet again making sure to locate my plug in since I felt like I had been on it all day and it would die any minute. I looked at the same casting websites and found that nothing had changed and no one had responded to my submissions. So much for that idea.

He was still checking his e-mail and all his submissions, so I wanted to look like I was just as busy, so I thought I'd check out a few more profiles on social media sites, maybe even see if there were any postings about theaters in the area or other random auditions. That was when I saw it. I had a message waiting for me. I was pretty sure it was one of my friends, checking to see if I had actually made it to California, and I wondered why they wouldn't just text or call me. I opened the message and was even more surprised to find a response to one of my submissions. It was from the hottie I had accidentally discovered. It simply stated, "You tell me."

I wasn't sure what to say next. I wanted to ask Mike but didn't want to admit that I had been a creeper, trying to check out my peers online. I froze for a minute, then decided to be brave and take another random shot, as my first one had apparently paid off. I had to choose my words carefully because even though he made me feel like a little twelve-year-old girl with a random crush, I didn't want to portray that by coming off as desperate. I also didn't want to come off as a total skank, so telling him that I wanted him to show me some efficient cardio might be a little too forward. So I tried to think like Mike and give an answer that would come off as calm, cool, collected, confident, and definitely interested! So I responded by telling him that I would let him buy me dinner on Saturday. I debated actually sending it for a minute, then decided I was being a big baby and to just hit the button. After sending it, I hurried to switch to any other site and thought to log in into my bank account to schedule some bills would keep my mind off everything.

Mike had been performing on the weekends in live action scenes for parties and other events and had a rehearsal that evening. So again I had the place to myself. I decided to force myself to get through the rest of the boxes to maintain some sanity. I was very curious to see if I had received a response to my offer but knew it was silly to get my laptop going just to check it out. So I figured it'd be quicker to check messages on my phone, knowing that I would receive an e-mail notification if he had sent me anything. And there it was. He had replied that he would be happy to. I was shocked at the way this was unfolding. Again, I felt like a teenager who just found out her crush was about to ask her to the prom. There was no turning back now. I decided to give him my phone number since Saturday was only a couple of days away.

The next few days passed a little more slowly since I was waiting to hear about my weekend plans and didn't want to confess what I had done to Mike since they might consist of a movie night and ice cream. By Friday, I had almost given up, assuming that he was just another prick who was playing games. I actually appreciated finding out up front since I hadn't moved across the country to pick up men. I tried to be smooth and check my phone for the twenty-fourth time and noticed I had received a text from a number I didn't recognize.

I was excited to see what it had to say since I didn't recognize the area code either. I opened it to find yet another simple message, straight to the point: "Do you like sushi?" I had never been smooth at dating but promised myself that I wouldn't reply until the next day. So instead I spent the evening deciding what to wear out on my first date in LA.

By the next morning, I had narrowed it down to about three different outfits and needed a second opinion. So I responded to the text, telling him that I loved it and asking if he had a name. I hoped he wouldn't wait too long to respond again and was pleasantly surprised when I received an answer almost immediately, telling me that his name was Jake. I wasn't sure if I had been single too long or if he was just that pretty, but at that moment, I couldn't help thinking that Jake was one of the hottest names I had ever heard.

Jake followed the revelation of his name with an offer to pick me up at seven. I figured it was time to confess what I had done to Mike. Not only to get his opinion about what I should wear, but his overall idea of whether or not I should do it. I was pretty sure Mike would laugh at me and tell me to focus on getting work. But he was surprisingly supportive and to just make sure my phone was fully charged. He may not have been attracted to women, but he helped me choose which outfit to wear, insisting that it was sexy but didn't make me look too easy. Once I showed him a picture of my pending date, he told me that he changed his mind and that I should try to look easy, possibly even draw out a map of easy-access points for my top. I laughed it off and replied to Jake that seven would work well. To top it all off, and just when I thought my day couldn't get any better, I received another response from one of the casting agencies informing me that I had been scheduled for background work on Monday. It was for a popular sitcom that my mother watched religiously, and I knew she'd be excited to hear about it. It seemed like things were already taking off, and it made me feel incredibly optimistic about my future here.

I chatted with my mother for over an hour as she was more excited about the casting than I was, and I had to repeat the story of how I landed it again and again. I thought it was cute that she was acting as if I had been cast in the lead role of an A-list movie when in reality the importance of my "part" was barely rated above the props on the set. The only advantage I had over the table and chairs on the set was that I could move myself. Finally promising her that I would call her afterwards and tell her every detail from the day, she allowed me to get off the phone. It afforded me the necessary two hours to perform my beauty regiment for the natural, low maintenance look I liked to rock.

After wiping off and reapplying my eyeliner three times, I achieved the cat-eye liquid liner look I was going for. My hair was curled, and my lipstick was on, so it was time to put on the outfit Mike had helped me with. Luckily, the party he was performing at had ended a little early, so he got home just in time to judge my efforts. He offered me a glass of wine and teased me to do a runway walk, doing a half-spin so he could get the full view. I appreciated the liquid confidence and made him swear to tell me the truth.

"Are you wearing decent underwear?" he asked, taking a sip of wine.

"Excuse me?" I almost choked on mine. "What do you mean? Decent, as in comfortable?"

"No. You know what I mean. If anything happens, you don't want him to find them on the floor and get the urge to call his mother. But, on the other hand, you don't want to wear the new stuff and risk forgetting it at his place." He gave the advice very casually.

I wasn't sure how I felt about the fact that what he said made sense. "Seriously? That doesn't even matter because nothing like that is going to happen tonight. I don't even know this guy. Oh shit, I should've met him at the restaurant. I'm going to get murdered, aren't I?"

"Shut up. You'll be fine," he assured me. "Besides, you have your phone."

"Great." I thanked him as my phone started ringing, and I saw that it was Jake.

I was a little nervous to actually talk to him but was excited to hear if he sounded as sexy as he looked, so I answered my phone, and he replied, "Hey. What's up? I think I'm here."

I tried to play it cool. "All right. I'll be right down."

?

Chapter 18

I kept my phone handy, just in case, but walked out to find him standing in front of the passenger side of his car. He looked even better in person wearing jeans than he did in the photo of him in his underwear. I smiled and walked toward him. He smiled back and took a few steps in my direction.

Once we were within arm's reach, he extended his hand. "Hello, I'm Jake."

"I'm Lisa." I shook his hand.

Hoping he was as appreciative of his view, we stood there shaking hands for a moment. "Well, should we go get some food?"

He had such a gorgeous smile. "Sounds good."

We walked toward his car, and he made it a point to step in front of me to open the door. I smiled and thanked him, sitting down in the passenger's seat and enjoying the view as he walked around to the driver's side. I noticed that his car smelled just as good as he did, like cologne that was manly but not overpowering.

He sat down in the driver's seat, then looked at me and smiled again. "Hungry?"

I smiled back and nodded.

"Great. Unless you have another idea, I know this great place right up the road," he suggested.

"Sounds like a plan." I hadn't told him that I was new in town.

It was a short ride, catered by the hum of the radio playing hard rock. We parked on the street in front of several different choices of restaurants. Considering it looked like a strip mall, I wasn't sure what to expect of the food. I tried to soak in the sights while he walked around to help me out of the car, closing my door behind me.

"You said you like sushi, so I hope this place is okay." He smiled.

Something about his smile, he could have offered me a shit sandwich and I would have torn it up just to sit and hang out with him. "Yeah, sounds great."

He opened the door of the restaurant for me, and we walked in to be seated. His sense of chivalry was very attractive to me. Very few guys in their twenties and thirties held doors open or pulled out chairs for their dates. I figured he was either very sweet or very smooth. Our server approached us and asked if we wanted to start off with sake. Jake looked at me, eyebrows raised, as if to ask if I'd like some. I nodded, and he ordered a large pitcher for us to share.

When the server left to get us drinks, we looked over the menu to decide what to order. "So what looks good?"

"I've never been here before. Any suggestions?" I asked.

"Is there anything specific you don't like?" he responded to my question with a question.

"No, I'm not very picky," I answered, not sure what I would be signing up for in a sushi restaurant.

When our server returned with two waters and a smaller pitcher of sake, Jake took over and ordered a couple of different options. The server nodded, took the menus, and we were all alone now. Jake reached up, picked up the pitcher, and filled my tiny little glass. Afterwards, he set the pitcher back down on the table without pouring himself any.

"Aren't you having any?" It was an honest question, causing my skepticism to promote thoughts of his intentions for the evening.

He simply looked at me with that melting smile again. "Well, it's bad luck to pour your own sake."

I couldn't help but laugh. For some reason, it was just the icebreaker we needed. I filled his cup, and we shared a little toast. We each took a sip, and I decided I wanted to know more about him. I wasn't sure what to start with. Where was he from? What was he doing here? Did he have siblings? Aside from working out, what were his hobbies?

I decided to start small and go with location. "So, are you originally from California?"

"Nope, actually I'm from East Texas." He took another sip of his drink. "Where are you from?"

"Is it that obvious that I'm not a native?"

"Just a guess. Most people living here now weren't born and raised here," he informed me.

"I'm from Minnesota. But everyone wants to experience life in other places, right? So what brought you here?" I was pretty sure his answer would be the same as mine.

"You grew up on a farm then?"

I just shook my head, hoping he was joking.

"Texas was too humid. What brought you here?"

Once he smiled, I almost forgot my answer. "Minnesota's humid too. So what was that picture from?"

"Just some shoot I did for a men's underwear line."

"I'm sure you made many sales for them."

"Actually they didn't end up using my shots. I just kept the shots for my portfolio."

I couldn't figure out why on earth they wouldn't use his picture to push their product. "Or to pick up random women." I laughed.

"No. I don't show it to random women on the streets." He laughed too, not seeming to understand the connection, even though it was his picture that attracted me.

I figured today must be his pretty day, so I ignored it and changed topics. "So have you done any acting?"

"No, I've been trying to get my stuff out there. Typical actor in Hollywood, taking small roles, hoping for paying work." It was a short answer. "So I do a lot of personal training on the side."

"That's cool. Did you go to school for it, or anything?" I asked.

"Nope. School's not really for me. All those books and studying. It's just not for me." Thank God he had a gorgeous smile.

This cleared a few things up for me, and I was pretty sure at this point that it would be useless to shoot for any of the deeper topics, so it was a good thing our food arrived.

"Wow. This looks great."

"Yeah, it does." He filled up both of our glasses again.

I was glad he reached for the bottle before I did since I was pretty sure we'd have different motivations for the refills. As the evening went on, our conversation focused on where we had worked before and where we wanted to work and what parts of LA we had each seen or wanted to see. All the questions and answers seemed to center around the whats and not the whys.

I even surprised myself in that I didn't mind the lighter conversation. Since there were no awkward silences, we both seemed to be having a great time. We finished our meal and headed out to the corner bar to just sit and chat some more. I wasn't shooting for answering the mysteries of life or even random math problems, so for some reason, things just worked. Before I knew it, the bar was clearing out and it was time for them to close down. We paid our tab and headed outside to walk back to his car. I wasn't sure I wanted the date to end but realized the only place left for us to visit would be some sleazy all-night diner.

We arrived at his car, and he opened the door just like he had when he picked me up, sat down in the driver's seat, and turned and looked at me. "So where to now?"

I assumed he was going to ask me my address, so his question surprised me, and I wasn't sure if it was coming from a point of interest or that whole not flaunting his street-smarts thing, "Well, I'm not sure anything else is open."

"Is it past your bedtime, or do you want to come over?" he asked with a serious look on his face.

Without that shit-eating sexy grin, I started to wonder if he actually had legit intentions. "Sure. Have any good movies to watch?"

"I'm sure I have something. But we should get snacks." It was random.

"Wow, the built ones always have a killer metabolism, don't they?" I wasn't sure I was hungry yet, but could definitely fake it if it involved being in a room with him and a bottle of chocolate syrup.

We stopped and got some ice cream and cookies, another simple fix, and headed to his apartment. I walked in to find dark colors on the walls and posters of crazy rock bands and symbols on his walls. I could tell he had the typical straight guy sense of decorating since his furniture consisted of a collage of a couch, a random chair, and a couple of mismatched shelves that contained his TV, DVD player, and gaming system.

There was very little to be seen in his kitchen, so it almost looked like no one was living there. I got the pleasure of using his bathroom when we arrived and notice the counter was clean, except for his toothbrush and toothpaste, his razor, and a couple of bottles of shaving cream. The toilet on the other hand was either from 1968 or had an extremely hot date with a scrub down. The apartment as a whole had a couple of different aromas.

When we first came in, it smelled like a locker room. A manly locker room, not just one that had slimy floors that made you feel sorry for the people who were stupid enough to walk around barefoot, but a manly one. There was also the smell of good cologne. Not the kind that pricks where to clubs to get everyone's attention and cover the stench of cigarette, but the good stuff that inspires a girl to want to know more about the guy wearing it. It was an interesting mix, but it seemed palatable.

We sat down to watch a movie and broke into the snacks we'd gotten. The food consisted of everything you wouldn't expect someone who spends six hours a day in a gym to be willing to eat. We started with the ice cream, chocolate syrup, and whipped crème, which I insisted on getting but hoped wasn't too suggestive. It was almost impossible to not add the cookies to our sundae bar, and he happened to have some sprinkles in his cupboard that he offered, but I declined after he said he didn't remember buying them. We washed the whole thing down with random shots of whiskey.

We sat on the couch and burned through two movies. I was discovering that there was a lot more to him than his looks. He might not have been the brightest peanut in the turd, but he really was sweet and just fun to be around.

And I was pretty sure it was more than the lethargic liquor buzz and shaky sugar rush battling for my consciousness that inspired me to think so.

He walked over to start a third movie, but I was pretty sure I wasn't going to make it all the way through. I sat on his couch, resting my elbow on the armrest and laying my head on my arm. My eyelids were getting heavy as I enjoyed the view of him switching the DVD and bending over to the put the last one away. It was the perfect scene to pass out to.

We barely made it through the opening scene, when he was nudging me to wake me up. "Are you asleep?"

"Nope." I could tell he was joking but jolted to sit upright and readjust my hair as I fought to open my eyes.

He asked the question a few more times, and I responded with the same reaction before I finally woke up to the end of another movie. "Wasn't that great? And see, you didn't even want to watch it."

Now I knew he was just being a shit since I was curled up in the corner of his couch with a blanket on me. "Well, it's important to expand one's horizons."

Unfortunately, I was officially awake and could tell that I had wrapped myself into the shape of a human pretzel for my short nap. As I was stretching to see if I could wake my foot up too, I noticed that he wasn't saying anything. My eyes were still closed as I moved, but I was somewhat relieved that he had passed out on the couch, so I could go steal his bed without implied pressure. When I opened my eyes to see if it was time to put my mission into play, I saw that he was just sitting there looking at me and smiling. While it was a sexy face to wake up to, it freaked me out a little. I assumed that I had been drooling or had smeared my eyeliner on his couch or had a huge booger in my nose.

"What?" I asked, calmly wiping my eyes and nose.

"Nothing. You're just cute when you sleep." It was a creepy comment, but he said it with that sexy smile.

"Thanks." I could feel myself blush and decided to take it in a comedic fashion. "Because I'm not talking?"

I laughed, but his expression didn't change. "No. I've had fun with you tonight. And you're cute when you sleep."

"Puppies are cute." I never did know how to take a compliment. "You should put in another movie. You'll want to upgrade my status to 'hot'!"

"Nah, let's go to bed." He made it sound like a casual step.

"Go to bed?" I wasn't sure if this was a proposition, yet another example of his eye-candy status, or if he really just wanted to go to sleep.

"Yeah. Unless you have plans for the morning and need to get home?"

I didn't have anywhere to be that morning but wasn't sure about snuggling up to a perfect stranger to pass out. "No, I don't have any plans for the day."

"All right, well, let's get some beauty sleep." He stood up to walk to his room and noticed that I wasn't following him. "Oh, I get it. No worries, I'm too tired to try anything."

I had to give him credit since he was using a statement he probably didn't get to use often. I laughed and got up to follow him. "Well, I had a nap, so who says I won't?"

Crawling into his bed while he went to use the bathroom was the last thing I remembered before passing out. It couldn't have been long, but he woke me up, asking if I needed something else to sleep in and nudging me to pick one side of the bed. Since I was too tired to move, I didn't bother to respond and instead poured all my effort into rolling to one side. He crawled in to his bed, sticking to the opposite side, and I noticed that he was topless and wearing a loose pair of pajama pants and looked damn good. I was wide awake again.

"Sweet dreams," I told him.

"Sweet dreams," he replied.

"I meant for me." I laughed.

"I thought you said you were too tired to try anything." He laughed too with his eyes closed, looking like he was already asleep.

I could resist correcting him. "Actually, you said you were too tired to try anything. I just said I was tired in general."

He rolled over to face me. "Well, you could start with a kiss so I don't feel cheap."

"I figured conversation would make you feel less objectified." I kept laughing.

"A kiss is definitely the way to go." He even looked good when he was sleep talking.

I thought about it for a moment. "Eh, what the hell? Your eyes are already shut."

I leaned in to give him a short kiss. But after finding out that his plump lips were good for more than chugging protein shakes, it turned into a longer kiss. The longer kiss lead to the shedding of clothing and the discovery that lifting weights really had a positive influence on his sense of rhythm. I almost felt like I was in a steamy love scene from a movie of the week with a hot leading actor, and I was hoping for retakes. The rest of the morning turned out to be a pleasurable blur, and it was probably inappropriate, but I couldn't help thinking about Mike. I had to remind myself to thank him for encouraging me to put myself out there.

About five hours later I woke up to the buzzing of my phone. I compromised and opened one eye to locate it and examine just what I had gotten myself into. I saw that it was Mike, and that he had called a few already. I knew he wouldn't stop calling if I didn't answer. I hit Talk and answered to him scolding me for not telling him that I would be staying all night, saying that he was relieved that I wasn't murdered but that if I was being held hostage I should cough twice. I reminded him that if I was being held hostage or had been murdered, I wouldn't have answered my phone. I assured him that I was okay, and he told me that if I needed a ride, I had to let him know soon since her had another party to perform at that day. I told him I just had to figure out what was going on, find my underwear, and that I'd let him know as soon as I could.

Hanging up and looking next to me, I saw that Jake was nowhere to be found. I moved cautiously, making sure to pick all my clothes up off the floor and try to put everything back in place, dressing myself like I had yesterday. I peeked around the corner and didn't hear anything. I had to use the bathroom, and after tiptoeing in there, I was relieved that he wasn't there either.

Before I shut the door, I figured it was best to cover all the bases. "Hello?"

When I got no response, I went into the bathroom and closed the door. I stopped to look in the mirror to fix what was left of my makeup and saw the Post-it in the middle of the mirror. He had written me a note telling me that he had gone to the gym and would be back by ten, which was about an hour away. I had no idea when he left but knew that he would be back soon. I didn't have any time to waste. I multitasked, texting Mike to hurry and pick me up and I would buy him lunch and tell him the whole story— or at least, what I remembered before getting into the good stuff.

While waiting for Mike to find me, I took advantage of a few more cookies before my stomach reminded me of the other fun I had had last night. I decided that food wasn't the best idea and focused on rehydrating instead. While chugging the first three glasses of water, I kept checking my phone to check the time and see if Mike had called to texted me to let me know that he was there.

Luckily, I got his message before time expired. I felt bad leaving Jake's apartment while he was gone, sort of bailing out and leaving the door unlocked behind me. But I'd had a good time, and I'm sure he was just after the same, so why ruin everything with small talk and a glimpse at what I look like in the morning? Dipping out before talking to him was the lesser of the evils, and I couldn't wait to do it. I rushed out the front door to the parking lot and saw Mike's car parked by the curb. I jumped in and told him to go.

"What is this? A spy movie? Has the enemy found you?" he joked.

"Yes, that's totally it." I didn't want to get into details just yet. "I'm hungry. I want food."

"Oh, burned that many calories, huh?" He winked.

"Yes. Running for my life because he tried to lock me up so he could murder me," I dished back.

"Stop it. You had a good time, right?"

"Yes."

"That's a good thing." I appreciated his optimism. "Admit it, you slept with him. Was he good?"

I gave him the death glare, then had to look away. I was busted. "Yes."

"Not the route I would have gone. But as long as you were safe. I didn't want to have to tell you, but you needed to get laid."

"Thanks a lot. And, yes, we were responsible adults."

"Okay, good. Then I can cancel your appointment at the morning-after clinic. And you didn't get murdered! Now, if the cheap bastards at this party tip me, it'll be a great weekend!"

He dropped me off at the apartment and took off for his party. I was thrilled to take a shower and pass out for the day. I had my first day of acting ahead of me, and Mike warned me that it would probably be a thirteen-hour day, so I wanted to bring my A-game. Assuming Jake had only been looking for a quick piece of ass, I wouldn't have to worry about him calling me so I put my phone on silent. I woke up once during the evening to choke down a sandwich and a glass of water and then slept through the night until my alarm went off at seven in the morning.

I was happy to turn off my alarm and jump out of bed. I had to get ready for my first day on set. I was pretty excited, though not as excited as my mother was when I told her what show I'd be working on. She was convinced that as soon as I walked into the lot at the studio that I'd be discovered. Luckily, I wasn't that naïve, but I was glad that I already had something to report back home to justify my move.

The casting hotline had sent me instructions to bring a few simple outfits for wardrobe to choose from. The pants were the easy part since jeans were on the list of acceptable clothing. The shirts, however, were a little tougher to choose from since I wanted it to look like I was familiar with the process. Since I had slept pretty much all day the day before, I didn't get to bug Mike for his advice when picking out an outfit for the camera. But I chose a couple of flattering solid-color V-neck T-shirts and one that had stripes but they were cooler colored and flattered my skin tone. So I was pretty sure I had this one down. They didn't seem too concerned with my hair and makeup since I would be styling it pretty similarly to the picture I had sent them. It was a very old one that a friend had accidentally taken when we were at some party, but it had to work until I got new headshots.

I had everything packed up that I was sure I would need, including the instructions, which I had written down on a piece of paper so I wouldn't have to worry about losing my signal. After finding Mike's apartment, this would be my first time maneuvering the streets of my neighborhood, searching for the studio, then finding my way back home. I had a feeling it would be a very exciting day, working with the stars.

After making a few wrong turns, I finally got back on track and found the entrance we were instructed to utilize. I confirmed my name with the security guard, and he opened the gate for me, telling me where to drive to, to park. He seemed a little less than excited to see me, and scoping out the buildings around the gate I had just entered, I noticed that there was no one around. It seemed like I was parking behind them and that I was using the same back entrance as the cleaning crew.

I brushed the feeling off and grabbed my bag to walk into the building I was directed to. As I made my way to the front door, I noticed a long tent along the outside of the building housing a long line of folding chairs. Only a few of them, the ones closest to the door, were occupied. I opened the door to walk in and find out who to talk to and found myself holding it open to allow a few people with clipboards and headsets to exit. They were busy talking to each other, so no one stopped to thank me. There were even more people inside, running back and forth in front of a huge black wall. I figured the set was on the other side of that wall and these were the workers getting everything together. I knew it was a long shot, but I was hoping to see one of the familiar actors from the show. After looking over the behind the scenes scene, I found a stand with a big sign that said check-in.

I smiled at the guy behind the stand, who was also wearing a headset and studying the papers in front of him, "Hi, I'm—"

"Background?" He didn't bother looking up.

"Yup. I figured—"

"Outside. You can take a seat in one of the chairs." He pointed back to the door and then walked away from the stand, chatting into his headset.

"Okay." I was talking to myself as I turned around and walked back out to find a chair.

My glamorous day on set turned out to be just like a quiet day at the beach, sitting under an umbrella. Only there was no beach, and it certainly wasn't quiet. Watching everyone run around almost made me sleepy. It was written in our instructions, as well as posted on every wall within a twenty-foot distance, that cell phones weren't allowed on sets. However, I watched as others were taking out their phones to keep themselves awake, as people watching was only fun for about the first two hours.

I checked the time on my phone and noticed that there were still a few hours to kill before we would even get a lunch break. Figuring I could utilize the time to submit for more work and answer e-mails, I started shuffling through my phone, looking for ways for the entertainment to be entertained. Mike had warned me that it was a game of hurry up and wait, but I thought he was just being dramatic, until now. I opened my texts to tell him that he had been right, seeing if he had time to respond to me between customers at work.

I had never been so excited to get a response. Maybe he could give me a heads up of what to do for fun on set. I opened the message to find that it wasn't from Mike. It was from Jake. I was nervous and excited at the same time. We hadn't chatted since I skipped out the previous morning. His message simply said, "What's up?"

Why did men always use that statement as an automatic "go to"? It could mean so many different things, but I was determined not to let things go down a shitty path. After all, as sweet as he came off, he was most likely just after a piece of ass. Fortunately, or unfortunately, he'd gotten it; so I wasn't sure why he was texting me or what I had to lose by being honest. I responded by telling him about my morning on set and apologizing for sneaking out, explaining that I passed out as soon as I got home and didn't get a chance to tell him. It was a long message, but for some reason it was easier to type.

A few minutes after I sent the message, my phone rang and I answered without checking who it was. "Hello?"

"Hey, it's Jake. I figured it was easier the talk than type," he informed me.

"Yeah, I suppose so." I really didn't know what to say.

"So what are you up to?" I couldn't believe he was making conversation.

"Actually, I'm at work. I'm not really supposed to be on my phone. Can I call you back when I leave?" I was glad to have the easy out.

"Sure, just don't punk out again.' He laughed, but I figured there was probably some truth to it.

"Whoa, tiger, I didn't punk out of anything. You dipped out to go to the gym," I reminded him.

"But I left you a note to tell you I was coming back. You didn't even say good-bye."

"Well, I wasn't shipping off to Europe or anything. I just had things to do before coming to work today." I had no idea what to tell him.

"I had fun with you. It'd be fun to see you again."

I was screwed. He really was sweet—and looked damn good topless.

"I think it'd be fun to see me again too." I cringed that I caught my mistake too late. "You! I think it'd be fun to see you again too. Okay, well, I guess I'll talk to you later."

"Sounds good. Have a good day." Even his voice was sexy.

I hung up and laid my phone in my lap, pretty sure that no one important had seen me using it. We killed another few hours before an eccentric stagehand with another headset and clipboard walked down the line of background actors. In the time that I had been sitting and waiting, a larger group had come to utilize the chairs. He walked down the aisle, looking us over like cattle and confirming the names of those he chose to be in the scene.

Half unconscious from boredom, I snapped back to reality when he pointed at me, simply stating, "Her."

Another person, who I assumed was his assistant told the ten of us that were selected to bring out bags with our clothing choices with us and follow her to wardrobe so they could pick out what they wanted us to wear. From there, it was about a half hour process of picking and choosing what to drape each actor in so that he or she could take a place ten feet behind the main actors. All of this was managed by a woman with half of her head shaved and the other side stained green. Her arms were covered in tattoos and her eyes in thick liner, which carefully tucked behind her blue cat-eye-shaped glasses. She smelled like cigarettes and looked like she hadn't eaten in about six months. Not the chatty type, she picked clothing by pointing at it and walking away, leaving in her wake the insinuation that we were to change and make out way to the set.

After changing twice, it was determined that what I had on was the best choice. It was made clear to me that horizontal stripes were not the most flattering choice for me and made me look too fat. I never got the chance to tell her how much I appreciated her professional opinion but thought it might be appropriate to get her a piece of acidic fruit for when she catered to her bulimia later.

We were paired up with actors of the opposite sex and hoarded to the tables, being seated two by two. The main actors were not scheduled to show up until the scene was ready to shoot. They wanted us to stay quiet, but I thought it appropriate to introduce myself to my pseudo date. My first impression was that he seemed about ten years older than me. He had dark-blond hair and a receding hairline. He was wearing a sweater comparable to one I had a hand in giving my grandfather in 1986. He wasn't exactly my type, but I suppose that's why they call it acting.

We were informed that there were other background actors selected to play the servers and that they would be bringing us plates of food. We weren't supposed to eat the food and were to focus more on engaging the other person in a conversation without making any noise. This would be very interesting since you had to utilize indications from the other person's expression to tell when he would be done talking. I suppose this was where the expression "acting is reacting" had come from.

We rehearsed the scene once, practicing our sitting and not actually talking or eating skills. The food smelled horrible. I was pretty sure it had been sitting out since prop and craft services workers had arrived at work that morning. The plates looked like chicken, pasta, and vegetables, almost something a person would order at a nice restaurant. But they smelled like tuna in urine sauce with a side of diaper. So when they were dropped off at the table, my partner and I amused ourselves by spinning them and mouthing to one another to try a bite of the "shit surprise." We could only hope to convince audiences at home that we were satisfied customers, enjoying our meals as well as the company.

We watched as they prepared a sort-of red carpet path for one of the main characters to make his way to the bar to speak to a bartender. We figured the rest of the characters that we recognized from the show would be sitting at one of the open tables between us and the camera. After an hour of staging everything, we discovered that we would only be seeing one of the actors, as he literally walks into the restaurant and up to the bar and the tables were left open for more background that wouldn't be "served" with plates during the scene.

While watching him walk by was super, though not as exciting for me to watch as it would be for someone who appreciated the tight jeans he was wearing. It sucked that with all the work, it wasn't a longer scene involving more characters. It was a little disappointing to think that I wouldn't have any fun celebrity stories for my mother about one of her favorite shows. But I figured she'd be amused by the fact that my lips were moving and I was almost making shadow puppets in the background.

Another ten hours and two meal breaks later, we were finished. I discovered that we as the background actors were practically bottom-feeders, almost having to rely the leftovers and crumbs that fell off the main actors' and stage crews' plates. The main cast and crew got shrimp scampi, but by the time it came to feeding us, there was nothing left but bags of chips and plates with leftover cheese and crackers from the morning to be washed down by bottles of pop that were left in the sun and lost their brisk temperatures. I knew we weren't supposed to take any pictures with our phones, but I also thought I was going to get decent food on set and get to sit close enough to a popular sitcom star to smell the cologne he used to cover the scent of his whiskey mouthwash. I guess both sides were doomed to be disappointed. And to top it off, I didn't get any shrimp scampi.

So before we were dismissed, I utilized one of the paper napkins, a guaranteed supply available to anyone on set, and wrote "will act for shrimp" on it. Then I took a sad-faced selfie and sent it to my mother, insisting that I would explain the whole thing to her tomorrow. The whole experience was definitely interesting, and it got even better since I was able to collect my money on my way off the set.

I arrived home around nine, just in time to see Mike before he went to sleep. I tried to flaunt my cash and offer to buy him dinner, but he insisted that he was exhausted and had eaten earlier so that he could crash and be up early for work. The whole day, as boring and slow as it may have seemed when I was there, was actually a lot of fun. It was easy to see that if nothing else, a person could make a living doing this. It made me feel better to have multiple options to fall back on. The whole thing actually motivated me to really apply myself, checking hotlines and websites, and submitting to everything I could.

Over the next couple of weeks, I became quite the expert at booking background work. I had gotten a few more jobs on other popular shows that I had to admit I didn't watch but was still excited to work on. I got to meet a few of the main actors, who seemed to be friendly enough to sit with everyone during meals. They offered advice and answers to questions about getting started. And regardless of their specific answers, I found the general consensus to be the concept of "who you knew." The actors who weren't willing to lower themselves to dining with the help usually spent meals and breaks in their dressing rooms, employing stereotypes and disappointing fans. At this point, I knew my connection was Mike. But little did I know what this would do to me.

I had made sure to reply to Jakes messages when I received them but had to admit that I didn't go out of my way to talk to him. I really did want to, but it seemed like something always came up. And the following day would be no different. Mike had gotten cast for background on a comedic sitcom. He told me that they were going to cover the wardrobe since the scene was set at a costume party with a superhero theme. He said they still had it posted and invited me to go along with him, the only disclaimer being that I had to be willing to wear spandex in public, having the experience taped for all to see. I didn't want to overthink the costumes since I was pretty sure it would give me a complex but knew it would be fun to work with Mike and get a paycheck at the end of the day.

We arrived to the set to see the usual set up, shuffling the background to a space just in front of the bathrooms, usually a space that no other department wanted to claim. However, we could see the food table from where we were sitting, so things could work. We spent the first few hours joking and entertaining ourselves about what type of costumes they would have us wearing. We watched as other backgrounders filed in and found spots on the cattle farm. Finally, wardrobe came to check out the meat. We were picked a few at a time to follow the assistant to be dressed by the usual tortured artist/designer. That day our designer was either chosen for his vision of bold costuming or had dressed himself in preparation for the rain that falls once every two years in LA. He squeaked over in his rain boots and plastic pants and started to assign costumes. He assigned me an orange spandex costume with a short yellow skirt. I felt like a huge cough drop. I was pretty sure I hadn't slept with his boyfriend, so the only source left for this apparent revenge was that of his plastic pants chafing his sweaty ass. I knew I had seen him wriggling when he walked back to the rack. I was told to go back to the holding pen and wait for further instruction. I could only hope that Mike would look as ridiculous as I did. But once he walked out, I saw that he had been assigned a sweet-looking black costume that flattered his build and even had padded abs added to it.

"You flirted, didn't you?" I asked with skepticism.

He could barely catch his breath from laughing at me. "I had to. Look what they did to you!"

"Thank you. Just what I wanted to hear."

"Holy shit! And they're going to film this! Remind me to get the link so I can find the uncut takes online!" He kept laughing at me, reminding me how unflattering a color orange was on me.

"And how sweet of them to put something on me that would help me blend into the background." I couldn't help but laugh at myself. "And now, if you need me, I'll be in the bathroom, crying."

Before I had a chance to hide behind others who might possibly look more ridiculous than me, thereby not being selected to stand by main characters, a member of the crew was already herding us toward the stage. While it's an actor's job to be able to laugh at himself, I didn't necessarily have a good feeling about this. I mean, I wasn't vain enough to think that the camera would be focused on me the whole time, but I knew I'd certainly stand out from the crowd in this outfit.

We endured the usual hour of staging. And it would be pretty simple, considering that our only directions were to look like we were partying but to stay completely silent. Before they brought the main actors out to be placed among the party, wardrobe took one last shot at perfecting his creations. He was almost done checking everyone out and then went to chat with a few people standing around the main camera. After that, he walked up and selected a few people, including those whose costumes didn't seem that obnoxious, and they left the stage with him. I figured there would a few of us left on stage that he would want to talk to and was bracing for impact, assuming one of them would be me. But I had to remind myself, the costume I was going to put on instead had to look better than this one. I'd always heard it said that a person can't fall off the floor. But there really is always something new to learn.

I simply watched as the wardrobe manager sent an assistant to select a few more people, who then walked over to be looked over by the people behind the camera and the manager himself. I looked at Mike, who had been left on set, and he shrugged, not sure of what they were doing either.

Suddenly, I was selected to find out. "You. Come with me."

"Oh, okay." I followed the assistant to the group by the camera.

I stood there for a moment, being looked over like a pig at a county fair, before the wardrobe manager shifted his plastic pants and revealed the purpose of my selection. "No. This won't work. We need something else. Don't you think?"

He didn't look up, so I assumed he was contemplating my costume, as well as trying to wriggle his testicles free from the cheap plastic sweat box. No one responded for a moment, just whispered into their headsets. Randomly, one of the people behind the camera approached me and started brushing my blond hair off my shoulder. I thought it was odd since my hair wasn't long enough to cover that much, but she insisted on twisting my hair a few different ways, almost testing different looks.

"No, you're right. We can't use this one," she agreed. "What do you want to do?"

I thought she was looking me in the eye when she asked, so I suggested something else. "Yeah, orange has never been a good color for me. With my ivory skin, I've always found cooler tones to be a little more flattering. You should see what I can do with blues or purp—"

"No. I was talking to him," she cut me off, seemingly annoyed that I was talking, and pointed at another member of the crew.

"She's too white," he said randomly.

I looked back at him, nodding and mouthing the word purple, then got brave and said quietly, "I told you, I'm pasty."

The woman looked back at me, annoyed again that I dared to respond. "No, he means you're too white."

"Yeah, I heard him. But I'm from the Midwest, if I try to get a tan, I'll just burn and peel. Does anyone in makeup have one of those spray machine things." I started making the spray pen motion to show her what I was talking about.

"No." She started scribbling on her clipboard, and I was afraid they were about to fire me for talking. "He means you're too Caucasian. We need more ethnic actors for this shot."

"Whoa, wait. You're taking me out of this shot because I'm Caucasian?" Now I was annoyed. "I can't control that. Why is it a bad thing?"

"No one said it was a bad thing. It's just that the industry isn't looking for blond hair and blue eyes anymore. It doesn't sell. Don't worry, though, you'll still get paid. Just change at checkout before you go. Your money will be waiting." She just kept writing.

"Wow, that's bullshit. You couldn't have attacked me for something I can actually control, like my weight?" I offered.

The wardrobe manager finally came out of his creative coma. "The costume really isn't that flattering. She could stand to lose like forty pounds."

I turned to look at him. "Well, thank you very much. Something I can work on. By the way, you're giving your pants stretch marks."

He gasped and started trying to examine his own ass. When he felt like a dog chasing his own tail, he made a few of the other crew members check his pants for marks. I walked back to the wardrobe area and changed back into my street clothes. It was one thing if they didn't like my look but telling me that my ethnicity wouldn't be welcomed anywhere in Hollywood was pretty messed up. The peanut on the shit sundae of the day, I collected my money and got the pleasure of sitting and waiting for Mike to be finished on set. I was hoping, at least for the day, that the face value of men having it easier in this industry would work out in his favor.

I had nothing but time to kill, so I grabbed some chocolate from the food table and decided to put Jake's offer into effect. I couldn't help it. I needed someone to bitch to. He made the mistake of answering his phone, and I regurgitated the entire story to him, barely giving him a chance to say anything. After I had poured it all out, I figured, if nothing else, it would be the final nail in the coffin of pursuing any type of relationship with him. Apparently, I was on some sort of subconscious suicide mission. When I finally finished bitching about everything I thought I needed to, I took another bite of chocolate and awaited his response.

"Calm down. It's just the industry. You can't take it personally, remember?" He was so gentle and consoling me even though we both knew I was acting like I had just lost prom queen.

"I know, but it's frustrating. I can't change my ethnicity. They're not talking about the color of my hair. Am I going to be turned down all the time because I'm white?"

"Why don't you color your hair?" Jake asked.

"What, why would I color my hair?" I was seriously confused.

"Well, you said that they made a comment about blond hair and blue eyes not working. You can't change your eye color unless you get contacts, so why don't you change your hair color?" he repeated.

I was a little surprised that he picked up on that. "You might be right."

"I may not be the smartest guy around, but I've been criticized by this industry too."

I felt guilty for thinking he was all about the good looks and had nothing else to offer. Sometimes it just takes a simple person to find a simple solution, and this was one of those times. I was starting to picture what I would look like as a brunette with blue eyes.

"You're right. And I'm sorry if I gave you that impression." It felt good to fess up. "What are you up to this weekend?"

He came back with what I was to find would be his classic answer. "You tell me."

We followed my drama with a conversation about what I had been up to over the past couple of weeks and stories of clients he was training at the gym. Not the most interesting of topics, but I liked the fact that he had managed to talk me off the ledge. I hung up feeling a lot better about what had happened and focusing instead on people watching and entertaining myself until Mike was dismissed. I walked out with him and stopping to pick up his check saw the wardrobe manager organizing a heap of costumes, squeaking as he leaned to pick them up one after another. Still holding on to a little bitterness about his words earlier, I waited until I thought I had gotten his attention and mouthed the words muffin top to him. I was pretty sure he saw me since he threw the clothes he was holding over the bar of a nearby rack and started feeling the waistline of his pants for bulges.

The car ride home was spent listening to Mike's stories from the set—who he had met, what they ended up shooting, and how he had heard the whole story about who they were picking to take out of the shot. I told him about calling Jake, and Jake reminding me that criticism was just the nature of the industry. I also told him about Jake's idea that I would try coloring my hair since I had to get new headshots anyway. Too my surprise, he agreed, telling me that it was definitely worth a try.

That ride home helped me to do a little wriggling myself, the therapy helping the stick of the whole situation to fall out of my ass. I decided to be proactive and pick up hair color on the way home. I had scheduled a shoot with the photographer Mike suggested since he was really happy with his shots, and I wanted to be ready for it, in case the dark hair wasn't as flattering as I hoped.

We got home, and I locked myself in the bathroom for an hour, reading the instructions and spending the processing time cleaning all my spills off the counter as best I could so that Mike wouldn't kill me. I decided that I wanted my first impression of my new look to be clean styled, so I dried it and curled it before I showed Mike. Getting his opinion was a mix of getting feedback from a diva stylist and a male cousin in that I wasn't trying to turn him on with my exotic brown hair, but I did want him to tell me if I looked good enough to book.

"Yeah, it looks good." He smiled as I stood in front of him.

"That's it, it looks good?" I was disappointed in his response. "Good, like I should start submitting right away?"

"You should always be submitting," he reminded me. "What's wrong with saying it looks good?"

"Well, I'm not joining the witness protection program. I want to look hot! Does this help or should I just start shooting for movies of the week about young mothers with estranged toddlers?"

"It would add to your resume," he told me. "Now move, I'm watching my shows."

"Bitch." I sat down on the couch and threw a pillow at him. "So I think I want you to meet Jake."

"Really? Instead of him meeting your mother?" He gave me a side glare. "Do I need to post something for a new roommate?"

"Shut up. No, it's nothing like that. I learned not to rush into things. Fooled me once, right?" I laughed off his comment. "I just think he's cool. And he might be around a little more often."

"Oh, and you want me to see if he's gay?"

"No, of course not."

"Okay, because he is good looking and I'm willing to do the undercover work." He smiled.

"No. You can't have all the hot guys." I went back to my point. "It's just that, you're important to me. And I want him to meet you too."

"Cool. I'm down." He went back to watching his show. "Now, shush."

We planned for Jake to come over for dinner a few nights later. It was perfect timing in that it gave me the opportunity to clean up the rest of my boxes and the paint by number line of color across my forehead had time to fade and look more natural. Not having been blessed with skills in the kitchen, I planned a simple menu, knowing that pasta was one food that I could rarely screw up. Mike had been extremely supportive and helped me throw everything together, which probably added a lot more quality and class to the appearance and flavor of our meal.

It was stupid to feel nervous, but I wanted everything to come together and for Mike and Jake to get along, regardless what was or wasn't going to happen in the future. I knew that Mike wouldn't embarrass me or Jake. At least not on purpose. So I just had to stay calm, cool, and collected and hope that no one said anything stupid.

Jake had no trouble finding the apartment again, and after he texted me to tell me that he had parked, I told Mike to come to the window and get a sneak peek. "Check that out."

"Where?" It was a little darker outside, so it took him a minute to find him, but once he did, there was no doubt. "Oh yeah, he looks good!"

We were talking quietly, covering the bases so no one would hear us. "I know, right?"

"I hate to have to tell you this, but he's gay." He thought for a second. "Wait, I'm glad to have to tell you that."

"What makes you say that?" I asked.

He looked at me and broke the news. "No one can look that good in a pair of name brand jeans and be straight."

I turned to him. "Plenty of straight men look hot in trendy jeans."

We laughed and debated the point for another minute or two, when our conversation was interrupted unexpectedly.

"Hey, guys. I'm here." Jake looked up at us, smiling.

"Shit." I hadn't really wanted him to hear that part of the conversation and tried to wave and recover quickly. "Um, be right down."

I wasn't completely nervous about anything but Mike's opinion until I was caught with my foot in my mouth. I simply hoped he wasn't really paying attention and missed it all together. When he greeted me with a huge kiss, I was hoping that that had been the case. We walked back up to the apartment as I tried to gain back my composure enough to introduce them.

We walked in to Mike setting the table, and I knew it was now or never. "Hey. So, Mike, this is Jake. Jake, Mike."

Mike walked over to him, extending his hand. "Hey, how you doin'?"

"Cool. What's up?" There was that generic statement again.

"Well, we made dinner. Grab a seat." I motioned toward a chair as Mike walked into the kitchen to get a bottle of wine.

Aside from the fact that I was noticing that Jake was setting the trend of eating like a starving farm animal, dinner went well with minimum awkward silences. I felt relieved that things were going so well, especially since watching him eat had probably killed any inkling that he might be gay. I told the two of them to move to the living room and threw the dirty dishes on the kitchen counter so I could join them.

I could hear them talking, and for some reason, the conversation had taken a turn toward football. "I think Green Bay's gonna kick ass next season. They're making some smart trades."

"Nah, I don't think Iowa's that good," Jake responded.

Mike knew better than to say anything, and I decided to leave the rest of the dishes to rush in and interrupt, "Hey, guys! Anyone for more wine?"

Mike rolled his eyes at me and declined the offer. Jake said he would take a refill. I made a face at Mike, communicating that he had to be nice and not push anything. After refilling our glasses, I set the bottle on the table and walked back toward the couch. Just then, focused on the TV in the background, Jake decided to stretch out his legs after being at the gym all day. He got me at just the right moment, and I tumbled forward, spilling my glass of wine all over one of the seat cushions of Mike's couch.

I had never seen two guys move so fast. Jake jumped up to see if I was okay, and Mike tried to rescue his cushion. Jake kept apologizing, and I kept assuring both of them that I was fine. I just felt bad about the spill. I could tell that Mike was pissed. But on the positive side, I was pretty sure that Jake's clumsy manner had proven to him that he was into me and not him. I offered to help Mike try and rinse the stain, hoping to get out whatever he could, but he declined, and I knew it was best just to leave him alone.

We sat and tried to rekindle what was left of the evening. Luckily, Jake had an early client and had to get home. I was grateful for the chance to perform some damage control and decided just to clean up and scrub everything else down, letting Mike break the ice when he was ready to speak to me again.

He was in his bathroom, still working on the cushion, and I wanted to know if he truly hated me at this point. "Well, he's gone. I hated to see him go but loved to watch him leave!"

Mike gave me a death glare while I tried to laugh at my own joke, and I figured it was best to just walk away, but he stopped me. "He's not good for arousing conversation. But he can certainly arouse other senses."

He said it with an angry tone, but I knew it was a confirmation of his approval. "Yes. Yes, he certainly can. Can I do anything to help?"

"No, I'm using this special stain remover shit. Hopefully it works. Of course, we won't find out until it dries. And if it doesn't work by then, it's fucked anyway." He was still rubbing at the spot.

"Guilt? Really?" He didn't have to try to make me feel guilty, I already did. "If it makes you feel better, I landed on my wrist. And it hurts. Did you want to massage the bruise or anything?"

"I'll wait until tomorrow. It'll be even more painful then. Besides, I'm not trying to make you feel guilty, even though the couch was incredibly expensive and it was your boy toy that tripped you and your wine that spilled all over. But that's it. That's all I wanted to say, no guilt." He looked back down at the task at hand.

"Does this mean you won't help me out with outfits for my shoot?" Again, I was trying to shift the conversation.

He kept looking down. "The same 'neutral' outfits you bring to sets."

"Gee, that's it? Why did I wait to get pictures?" I knew he could sense my sarcasm, but there wasn't much else I could say.

He seemed pretty pissed at the situation, and I knew it was best just to leave him alone. So instead, I started focusing on getting everything ready for my photo shoot the following day.

Chapter 19

Trying to sleep that night was incredibly tricky. I had planned on dropping off a few applications for part-time jobs in the area. I figured if I looked good enough to take a picture, I was going to distribute to half the people in Los Angeles. Though the majority would probably use them as coasters, I would look confident enough to nail a part-time job interview. I set out that morning, a little nervous about what to expect.

I went over the list of makeup, hair products, and all the clothes I was supposed to bring. I may have gone a little overboard, but I was okay with that. I arrived at the small studio early, proud of myself for sparing enough time to find it, not being completely familiar with the area. I was told to just come in the front door, which felt a little odd carrying all my luggage and having no one to greet or direct me once I walked in.

I walked slowly down a long hall. The black-and-white photos decorating the walls told me I was headed in the right direction. Finally, getting to the end of one hall, there were two opposite directions I could go. Luckily someone decided it might be wise to put up some kind of directory to help those of us who weren't familiar with the building.

I turned to walk down the hallway to the right, as directed by the arrow or the handmade sign. It was a short walk to a doorway that had no window to peek inside. I stopped to listen for a moment to try and make sure that I wouldn't be walking in and interrupting anyone else's session. I could hear some music playing, I was guessing from a radio, but no one was speaking. Getting closer to the time of my appointment, I decided to just walk in.

I opened the door to discover a huge white backdrop surrounded by lights to the right and a trendy studio space with a tall table and vanity mirror on the left. I also found the source of the music, which was actually a laptop located on the desk. Someone must have heard the door shut, and suddenly two women were walking toward me, looking serious and ready to discover my purpose for being there.

One of the women was dressed very conservatively, her hair back in a low ponytail, glasses serving as a headband, and casually wearing jeans and tennis shoes. I figured she was the photographer since the other had very bright, extreme makeup painted all over her face, also with her hair in a ponytail, but hers was perched on top of her head. She was wearing leggings and an apron with at least twenty brushes filling pockets and loops.

"Hi, do you have an appointment?" the photographer asked me, taking her glasses off her hair and putting them on her face.

"Yes. I'm Lisa?" I said, somewhat questioning that I was in the right place.

"Lisa. Yes, I'm Alicia. I'll be taking the pictures. And this is Jade, she'll be doing your hair and makeup," she announced.

I had guessed right. "Okay, I brought some outfits." I could only push my large suitcase on wheels out in front of me.

"All right," Alicia said, looking down at the luggage I had brought with me. "Jade will help you pick something out."

Before I could respond, Alicia walked over to the lights and camera and Jade was motioning me over to the desk. I must have had a very naïve idea of how everything would go. I could only picture my shoot for senior photos. It had been a long time, but I could still picture the wardrobe focused on memorabilia from my high school, including a jacket, T-shirts, and my cheerleading costume. Apparently, this would be nothing like that.

I had started a little of the base work to help the makeup artist out and had curled some beach waves into my hair. Nothing too extreme, but she obviously didn't like what I had done. Which she made clear when she wiped everything off with a few disposable cleansing cloths and started over. She didn't say much to be throughout the process, aside from asking if I was there to get my headshots, so it seemed to take a good while. Wondering if I really needed that much work, I checked my phone when she walked away to get more products and it had only been about a half hour.

Alicia gave a five-minute countdown to begin shooting, and Jade worked a little faster to finish and have me lay out the outfits I had brought. I saw myself in the mirror before heading to change and was afraid I looked a little too simple. I wasn't sure what the plain look was going to accomplish but starting to wonder if I hadn't paid enough since apparently, she charged by the amount of product used. I told myself to trust the experts and hope that the pictures turned out well.

After studying the options, they both agreed on a solid light-blue shirt with jeans. Again, my horizontal striped shirt had been ruled out since it would "accentuate" my midsection, which was apparently unacceptable. I changed clothes and headed back toward the backdrop. Alicia had rearranged a lot of the lights and turned the white sheet so that I would be facing the window. She insisted that natural light would be the best way to go. I thought the wall of windows was beautiful, but since it was incredibly bright out and approaching the early afternoon, I could only hope that I'd still be able to see when it was time to drive home.

Courtesy of Alicia barking the orders to move left, turn right, and back again, we worked out the perfect point of interest for the pictures. Jade silently made a few last-minute adjustments to my hair and makeup, and we were ready to begin. I loved acting, but I was never going to be a model. And I was perfectly fine with that. The only reference I had to "striking a pose" was positioning myself around my pom-poms while making sure my skirt was covering my vital areas.

Sensing my rookie status, Alicia started with the orders again. "Okay, stand and face the wall, now turn and look at me. Okay, good. Good. Wait, okay, smile. Not too much, you're not laughing. Wait, we need to move the camera a little to try and work with your chin."

I was glad that she was taking into account all my unique aspects but had never been told that anyone had to rearrange to accommodate my chin. "Okay."

Five minutes later, we were right back at it. By this time, I was looking right into the afternoon sun. I didn't think squinting would help my wrinkly smirk but figured I shouldn't question the expert.

"All right, let's go again," Alicia warned me. "Okay, tilt your chin down and look up, a little to the left and turn back. More, more, more. Okay, back to the right. Try and look sexy."

I had no idea that looking sexy was so complicated. This probably explained why I was single since looking sexy meant being a contortionist and that meant a trip to the chiropractor. The orders went on and on. Finally, we took a five-minute break to switch outfits, touch up hair and makeup, and check out a few of the photos. I had no idea what I was in for.

The photos were awful. Squinting and trying to tilt down and force a sexy smile, which turned into a grunt, wasn't flattering at all. Minus a couple of pulsating veins in my forehead, I looked like I was trying to give birth. Alicia smiled at me, scrolling down the page and seeing if there was anything that jumped out at me. But I had to be honest. If I ever had an audition for a hemorrhoid commercial, these would be my go-to shots.

She seemed a little irritated by my amateur opinion, but we moved on. This time, they selected a darker green shirt, and all the equipment had been turned away from the focused beams of sunlight. I felt a lot better with this round since there was nowhere to go but up from the last one. For some reason, seeing the unflattering photos and knowing that everything had been rearranged gave me a sense of confidence in that we were heading for improvement. Oddly enough, seeing the horrible photos had showed me that the makeup artist was right in her style choices. She gave me a flattering, non-trendy look, as she had explained, that would allow me to utilize these shots for as long as I stayed brunette. I learned that if I hated it when I looked in the mirror, the camera would love it.

The second half went a lot more quickly since we had broken the ice. Alicia was giving fewer orders, so we were able to enjoy the music. I felt more confident, and it showed after we wound down and looked over the pictures. I found a few that Alicia and I agreed had potential and might even graduate me from suppository ads to those of feminine products. Alicia told me that she would look over the group that we picked out, pick out which ones she thought were the best for headshots, edit them, and send me the bunch to make the final choice. We said good-bye on a much lighter note, and I left feeling positive, confident that my headshots would far surpass my graduation announcements. I was proud at how far I had come, even if they were only small steps.

When I got to my car and recaptured my breath from lifting my suitcase into the trunk, I decided to check my phone, seeing who was available to hang out and not let my good look go to waste. I noticed a message from Jake, seeing if I could hang out, but before I answered, I decided to listen to the voicemail from the phone call I had missed that morning. To my surprise, it was a message from the popular electronics store I had filled out an application at for part-time work when I was utilizing my time to practice my submission skills as Mike had insisted.

Apparently, the store had reviewed my application and wanted me to come in for an interview as soon as possible. I returned the call and set up the interview for that afternoon. I figured that looking this good, I'd be guaranteed a position. Unfortunately, that meant that I had to tell Jake that I'd have to let him know when I got my schedule. I figured it wasn't a big deal since he simply replied to my message with an okay.

I arrived at the store, excited to get in and meet my future boss. It was only a part-time job to help between acting gigs, but I had a feeling it would come in very handy. I walked into the store and went straight over to customer service as I was instructed to do. This was a much more structured meeting than my photo shoot, and I hoped it was a good sign. The employee I greeted said that he'd go get the manager and would be back in a minute. Five minutes later I was still "patiently" waiting, and someone had come to join the line to get some customer service.

The man behind me only had a small pack in his hand that I assumed were batteries. I figured it wasn't too heavy, so I didn't move away from the open spot at the register, where I had been left to wait. After another two minutes, the man behind me got a little impatient and started inching forward toward the counter. I wasn't sure I wanted him to come to the counter and snuggle with me. He was wearing a simple pair of jeans, an older looking T-shirt, and a baseball cap that was obviously smothering long curly hair that appeared to be eligible for a significant cut. Not my idea of attractive, but he was tall and fit. I gave him a simple smile, which apparently fell on ignorant observations as the courtesy was not returned.

I figured there was nothing else I could do to get the attention of available employees, so I turned back toward the counter to wait for my turn as well. After another minute passed, the man became incredibly impatient and stormed up next to me and, in a patronizing tone, asked if I was actually doing anything at the counter.

Surprised, I turned to look at him. "Yes. Actually, I'm waiting for the manager."

"Well, I actually have places to be, and I need to check out, so would you mind?" he asked, helping himself to counter space to set down his heavy pack of AAs.

"Wow, by all means." I took a small step to the side and swept my hand over the space to present him with open counter.

I couldn't believe how rude he was to me, but I was about to find out that that was his polite side. "Hello? Can someone actually help me?" he hollered.

A riled teenage employee came rushing around the corner, looking behind him to see if he had reinforcements. "Um, yes, sir. I'm sorry. How can I help you?"

"I hope so. I just want to buy this," he said, tossing the battery pack on the counter. "If that's not too much trouble."

"No, sir. Of course not." The employee picked up the pack and scanned it, giving the disgruntled customer the total.

He took out his card to pay, and the employee had to give him the bad news. "Oh, I can take that for you, our machine is down. And I'll just have to see your ID."

"Really?" The man looked at the employee with a surprised and annoyed look. "You don't know who I am?"

I felt bad for the employee and interrupted, "There's a sign right there that says they need to see it."

He shook his head, reaching into his wallet. He flipped through a few cards, pulled one out, and threw it at the counter. It bounced, and luckily, the cashier caught it before it hit the floor. Who knows what kind of hell that would have unleashed. The transaction was finished, and he started to put the cards back in his wallet.

"Wait, weren't you that guy from that movie with the computer animation, something about machines and anarchy?" I asked him.

"Yeah, that was probably me." He suddenly seemed interested in talking about himself.

"Fun. Well, tell that blue machine thing that he's hot." I smiled.

"He's not even real." His smile faded.

"Well, every movie has to have a hot leading man." I stared at him.

"Whatever." He waved me off and walked out.

Just then another employee came walking around the corner but was wearing a suit and tie instead of a uniform. He walked up to the counter and introduced himself as the assistant manager in charge of hiring and invited me to the back room to discuss my application. We walked to an area with a couple of tables and a wall lined with pop and snack machines, and he motioned to me to have a seat.

We went over a few details of scheduling and availability, positions available, and then he brought up the uniforms. "Okay, so we prefer our employees to wear natural hair colors, not too heavy with makeup and jewelry. It looks like you'd be a pretty good fit. You've got a plain, simple look."

I was glad he looked back down at his paper to move onto the next topic because I was pretty sure that my forced smile faded to a look of annoyance. I had just paid a makeup artist to provide me with a flattering look to highlight my good looks, to set me apart from other women in my category, and to get me noticed. I didn't remember asking her to give me a plain, simple look. That manager sure knew how to make a girl feel pretty.

We finished our interview on a better note, and he said he would call once they had completed the callbacks of all the desirable candidates. I was pretty sure I nailed it with my "simple" look and everything. I drove home, relieved to have completed my shoot and my interview. I knew I had to call Jake but put if off for a while so I could hang out with Mike for a while and catch up on current events. Between the two of us, we had such opposite schedules that it almost seemed like we were each living alone.

I walked in to find him relaxing on the couch with his laptop. "What's u? You're looking at a possibly employed woman with a sweet new headshot."

"That's cool. Show me one," he said, still pushing buttons on his computer.

"Well, okay, just promise not to fall in love!" I pulled up my e-mail to show him the pics she had sent me.

"Oh, those are good. A nice plain look. Versatile," he approved.

Again, I didn't appreciate the "plain" critique. "Okay, so is 'plain' like saying I'm ugly so I should be in a tower ringing a bell or something?"

"No! Of course not. You don't have a hump," he joked. "It's just saying that you're showing your assets and showing casting directors that they can take your look in any direction that they want."

"Fair enough." I felt a little better about it. "This schedule is crazy. How do you keep up?"

"Welcome to LA. You've only been here for a couple of months. Imagine doing this for years on end."

He was absolutely right.

"I barely have the energy for a social life. Maybe I should tell Jake that I won't be able to see him after I start my new job."

"Well, you wouldn't have to work as much overtime to replace your furniture." He smiled.

"Shut up. He's so hot," I reminded him.

"Then just tell him that you want to take things slow," he suggested. "Or that you just want to use him for sex."

"Most men would be so happy about that, but I don't know. He's different. He's sweet. He had emotions, or something. It's weird," I confessed.

"You like him."

"No, I just met him. He just looks good naked." I got up to leave. "Who knows if we can even build on that."

"Well, if you do decide to build on that, you better figure out how to divide up your time between work and play. That was the issue for me and Joe." He was still looking at his laptop but loved to accentuate the obvious for me.

I figured it would all work itself out, and I needed to just relax and not overthink everything, so I went in my room to call and see if he could hang out. "Hey, what are you up to?"

"Nothing. What are you up to?" He displayed his flair for conversation.

"I was just hoping you were available to hang out tonight." I made it sound as cheerful as I could.

He seemed to lighten up. "Yeah, I just have to finish up at the gym. Want to head over to my place in about an hour?"

"Sounds like a plan."

An hour later I had enough time to turn my "plain" look into something a little more sexy and desirable and was driving over to his apartment. I still wasn't sure if I should bring up the topic of seeing even less of each other or to just assume that he wasn't after anything more than a physical relationship.

I called after I parked, and he met me at the door to let me in. We walked into his bachelor pad, and as I turned around to ask him how the gym was, he gave me a long, passionate kiss, like something you'd see in a cheesy romantic film. I thought it was sexy that he was trying to jump right to the point, and once I caught my breath, I commended his direct manner.

"Wow, how was your day?" I tried to kiss him again.

He pulled away with his arms still around my waist. "It was cool. But it's better now."

"Glad I could help." I leaned in again, refusing to be turned down.

He gave me a quick peck, then pulled away to walk over to the couch, leaving me mid-smooch. "So, are you hungry, wanting to get dinner?"

I adjusted my hair and shirt, trying to regain my composure. "No, actually I ate a little something after I talked to you. Sorry, I didn't think you'd want to eat this late."

After I walked over to the couch to sit close to him, he stopped putting on his shoes and looked at me. "Oh, ok, well, I can grab something when we're out. Were you wanting to catch a movie?"

I moved in to kiss his neck. "That's a good idea. But wouldn't it be more fun to stay in and watch one."

He seemed to be fighting the urge to give in and tried to turn away from me nibbling on his ear. "That's what we did last time."

"Did we not have a good time?" I started moving my hand up his leg.

He stopped my hand and held it down, completely pulling away from my grasp so that he could face me. "We did. But don't you want to do something more than just hang around here and spend twelve hours having sex?"

I had to stop and think for a moment, but unfortunately, I didn't have an answer. "Well, you know."

"You seriously think that I'm only after sex?" he asked.

"No, I didn't say that." Somehow, the roles had been reversed, and I now had a new sense of empathy for men who felt that they couldn't win.

"Look, I may not be the sharpest peanut in the turd, but I know what I don't want." He gave me another chance to guess.

Not knowing how exactly to make things better, I tried humor. "That sharp peanut thing? That...that is a very good trait. I prefer dull peanuts in my turds. The other ones are just, you know, painful."

I quit talking when I saw from his expression that my humor was falling on deaf ears. "You know what I'm saying. I want more than sex. I want to see what can happen. If you don't want that, then you should at least have the courtesy to tell me."

I was shocked how had he kept his ovaries hidden from me this long. "I want more than sex too. I just don't know what my schedule's going to be like. I mean, I just moved here. I'm trying to start a career. I have to market myself. I have to get a part-time job. I know, like two people. Trying to navigate this town, I have a comfort range of about two blocks. I'm trying to adjust to a ridiculously fast-paced schedule, but I've rushed into relationships before, and they just didn't work out. I wasn't sure I'd have the emotional capacity to pursue someone else this quickly. I didn't plan on meeting someone so awesome. You're awesome. I just don't have five days a week to hang out. And if that's not okay, then should at least have the courtesy to tell me."

He smiled, gave me a kiss, and looked me in the eye. "That's okay. I get it. I'm trying to break into everything here too, remember?"

"You're a sexy bitch." Damn his sweetness, it made his shortcomings obsolete. "How about a movie?"

We snuggled up on the couch and watched a few movies. We never did have sex that night, but instead sat up talking about our experiences on sets. I obviously had a shorter list, so I spent most of that time listening to his. I told him about my shoot, and he gave me a few pointers there too. I had no idea what was going to happen down the road, but for some reason I was excited that he wanted to be more than a pretty piece of ass. He had to be up early in the morning and invited me to spend the night. As much as I wanted to, I warned him that he probably wouldn't get much sleep if I did, so instead, I went back home to find Mike awake and still on his laptop.

He heard me come in and looked up. "Oh, good. You can still walk. And you look surprisingly put together. Quickie?"

"Ha-ha. You're hilarious," I told him. "Have you been on your computer all night? I'm surprised the keys aren't sticking."

"Oh, you're good. The S seems to get stuck sometimes, but you know, I work with it. So? How'd things go with your himbo?" he asked.

"Everything seems to be such a shit show. I have no idea if I can keep up with all of this." I plopped down on the couch. "I'm pretty sure I've done more to promote any kind of a career in the last two months than I have in the last ten years!"

He looked right at me. "Welcome to LA. Did things go that badly? What'd he freak out on you?"

"Actually? Things went well. He said he didn't want a sex-only relationship. And I told him that I agreed, but that I wouldn't be able to guarantee that I'd always have time to hang out. So, we agreed to be patient, keep seeing each other, and take baby steps."

"Another step in the journey. Good for you. You may still have a shit load of obstacles to go, but you should be proud of every step you've taken to put yourself right here, right now." His words were incredibly encouraging.

"True. And, by my calculations, I should only have about nine hundred and ninety-nine and a half to go? I better get some sleep, so I can get to steppin'!"

He gave me the "shut up" look.

"I'm kidding. You're right. Thanks, I couldn't do it without you."

"It really is about who you know." He winked.

He was right though. I was incredibly proud of myself. Though they may have seemed like a childish dream or a huge waste of time to others, my efforts spoke volumes to me. Regardless of the things that had happened and regardless of the things that were going to happen in the future, I had worked hard to put myself in a position in which I could try and pursue my goals. I had taken the first step, and I was on my journey with a thousand miles to go, and I wouldn't have had it any other way.

⍰

Chapter 20

So that's it. That's how I wound up here. And as crazy as it sounds, I think I'm in the right place. Looking around the room, I realize that there's nothing that my competition has that I don't, except for breast implants and an emergency stash of condoms. I have just as much, if not more, to offer the part as anyone sitting in this room. I'm here because I want to be. I love my pets, but I have no desire to have to give them treats to take their temperatures.

Just as I start to think of all the goals that have changed in my life, my name is called and I snap back to reality to stand up to adjust my appearance. By calling my name and inviting be back, the man at the sign-up sheet has reminded me of the reason I'm here. Good or bad, up or down, cast or denied, it's my turn to discover what's on the other side of the mysterious black door. I get to take one last look at the girls sitting around me. I'm pretty sure they're giving me the same unsure once-over as I had given them when they walked in, or they're turning their heads to check their hair and makeup. Either way, it's time to take a step and hope that it leads me on my journey— or at least from making a fool out of myself by tripping over one of the shoes of my competition conveniently resting in my path. All I can do is my best, then wait and see what the next lap brings.